In his long fictional career (1929–68) at the hands of his creator Margery Allingham, Mr Albert Campion was never a policeman, simply a very gifted amateur detective. He did, however, work closely with a triptych of notable policemen: Superintendent Stanislaus Oates, Detective Chief Inspector P. 'Freddie' Yeo and Detective Inspector Charles Luke. All three rose to the very top of their profession over the years and remained, remarkably, on very good terms with Mr Campion.

Readers familiar with Margery Allingham's backlist and keen to explore that of Evadne Childe may notice that *The Robbers Are Coming to Town* was the provisional title of Allingham's classic, *The Tiger in the Smoke*, and *Pearls Before Swine* was the title adopted in 1945 for the American edition of *Coroner's Pidgin*. For the uninitiated, the Allingham novels are well worth seeking out. Evadne Childe's much less accomplished work is rather more difficult to find.

Also by Evadne Childe

A Richer Dust (1933)
Death in the Diplomatic Bag (1934)
Murder on Air (1935)
Here Be Dragons (1936)
Tears of a Clown (1936)
Right Body, Wrong Grave (1937)
The Beauregard Inheritance (1938)
The Murders at Six Mile Bottom (1939)
With Smoke and Mirrors (1941)
The Body in the Blitz (1943)
Dark Moon Over Soho (1945)
The Bottle Party Murders (1946)
Old Bones, New Bones (1947)
The Coffin Comes Free (1948)
Burial Mound (1949)
The Moving Mosaic (1950)
The Robbers Are Coming to Town (1951)
Camera Obscuring (1952)
Murder Imperial (1955)
The Collector of Skulls (1958)
Terrifying Angel (1960)
Pearls Before Swine (1963)
Cozenage (1966)*

*Published posthumously

MR CAMPION'S SÉANCE

Mike Ripley

This first world edition published 2020
in Great Britain and the USA by
SEVERN HOUSE PUBLISHERS LTD of
Eardley House, 4 Uxbridge Street, London W8 7SY.
Trade paperback edition first published
in Great Britain and the USA 2021 by
SEVERN HOUSE PUBLISHERS LTD.

British Library Cataloguing in Publication Data
A CIP catalogue record for this title is available from the British Library.

ISBN-13: 978-0-7278-8961-4 (cased)
ISBN-13: 978-1-78029-710-1 (trade paper)
ISBN-13: 978-1-4483-0431-8 (e-book)

All Severn House titles are printed on acid-free paper.

Severn House Publishers support the Forest Stewardship Council™ [FSC™],
the leading international forest certification organisation.
All our titles that are printed on FSC certified paper carry the FSC logo.

Typeset by Palimpsest Book Production Ltd.,
Falkirk, Stirlingshire, Scotland.
Printed and bound in Great Britain by
TJ Books Limited, Padstow, Cornwall.

CONTENTS

Part Five: Albert Campion, 1965

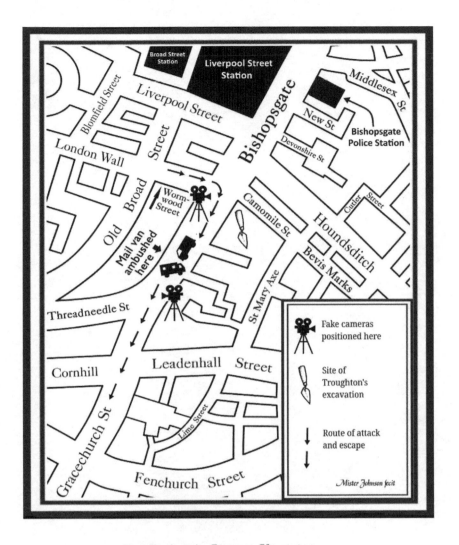

Frontispiece to *Camera Obscuring*
(a Rex Troughton adventure)
by Evadne Childe
J. Gilpin & Co., London and New York
1952

PART ONE
Evadne Child, 1940

Extract from the journals (unpublished) of Evadne Walker-Pyne (née Childe).

We are alone. The capitulation of the French was accepted with a strange calm. There was more fear (and a touch of panic) at the news of the surrender of poor little Belgium in May, but now the inevitability of it all spreads across the country like a blanket of autumn fog barging aside what looks like being a summer of glorious weather.

For the last nine months we have been in a sinister trance. This 'Bore War' has put us all to sleep, although as children have been conceived and born in the time we have been at war, clearly not everyone was bored. And then, whilst we were rubbing the crust from our eyes, our friends and allies disappeared one by one: Denmark, Norway, Holland, Belgium, now France.

With Edmund gone, I am more alone than most and, if I cannot have my husband at my side, I will not stay in London. I don't care what the authorities say about whether my journey is necessary or not. I deem it is. I have a mother to care for, after all, so I will de-camp to wildest Essex even if I end up having to walk there.

Note to Self: Things to do

     (i) Deposit leases, jewellery, Will, so forth, at bank.

    (ii) Warn House Manager about empty flat – see to gas, electric, etc.

    (iii) Dispose of house plants and put out rubbish, cancel milk.

    (iv) Give forwarding address to postman.

    (v) Stop newspapers. Tip newspaper lad.

    (vi) Leave cash for cleaner with doorman. £5 or £10?

(vii) *Write to Reuben telling him to have car meet me. Ask if Miss Kitto is still in business.*

(viii) *Collect laundry. Buy coffee to take to Essex as Mother will not have any. (Also whisky and gin just in case!)*

(ix) *Have lunch with Veronica to deliver (final?) manuscript.*

(x) *Buy gun oil and clean Daddy's service revolver. Ask at police station where to buy ammunition.*

ONE
Shooting Gallery

'But that must have been an absolute hoot, my dear! I mean to say, Evadne Childe, positively the *queen* of detective-story writers, having to ask the bumbling British policeman for advice on a murder weapon! Surely, it ought to be the other way round, shouldn't it?'

'If you can't behave yourself, Veronica, at least keep your voice down. It's too early to be decently drunk and I have a lot to say to you, so pay attention.'

'Yes, miss.'

'And don't give me *that* look, young lady. You know it doesn't work on me, and anyway, you have shreds of tobacco in your lipstick, which make you look quite common. No, bottom lip. Oh, come here, I'll do it. Spit.'

Had anyone been observing them closely (though no one was), they would have assumed they were witnessing a simple domestic scene and could have been forgiven for thinking this was standard mother-hen behaviour as the older woman held up her napkin for the younger one to wet, daintily, with spittle for a minor, but necessary, cleaning operation.

The two women were lunching together at a table dangerously close (had they considered it) to the cross-taped glass window bearing the legend *Café Bucci* which looked out on to Charlotte Street. They were not, however, mother and daughter, but author and 'publisher's representative' respectively and, even though the latter, and younger, of the two was the one having to have her face wiped in public, it would be she who would pay the bill.

'What do you mean by *that look*?' asked Veronica huskily, fluttering her eyelashes at the older woman. 'If you mean my own patented "petulant schoolgirl" look – well, it might not work on you, but it has never failed me when I needed it to persuade a well-filled uniform to buy me a drink or get me into a nightclub. Oh, I'm sorry, Evie, have I shocked you?'

Evadne Walker-Pyne, better known to the reading public by
her maiden name of Evadne Childe, smoothed her napkin back
across the lap of her skirt and tried to suppress a smile.

'My dear Veronica, I am, I believe, a highly valued asset to
the publishing house which, out of charity I presume, sees fit
to employ you. Your duties today consist of buying me lunch
and flattering me ceaselessly; if, that is, you want to take possession of your firm's next bestselling detective story. Do not attempt
to shock me with outrageous tales of the sordid goings-on in
those dim and dusty clubs you frequent down Dean Street. I am
a respectable, middle-aged English woman who earns her own
living by writing modestly successful stories of murder and
mayhem, and I have visited Egypt on more than one occasion.
I am, therefore, unshockable. Though as a writer, of course, I
am – purely professionally, you understand – always interested
in the less respectable establishments you frequent. I rely on you
for my research into the twilight world of the capital's
clubland.'

Veronica Hatherall crushed out her cigarette into a small metal
ashtray and sighed loudly; the sort of sigh practised to perfection
by young women with very little to actually sigh about.

'I could shock you if I wanted to,' she said, producing a small
lacquered mirror and lipstick from her purse, 'with tales of the
clubs I visited last year in New York. There were some, off
Forty-Second Street, which shocked even me. They're so much
more *strict* than the ones down Dean Street, if I can put it that
way. Really quite aggressively strict, if you know what I mean.'

Veronica concentrated on repairing her lipstick, airily ignoring
her guest, but when the older woman failed to rise to the bait
she snapped shut her compact.

'Oh, don't look at me like that! This Bore War is, well, boring.
A girl has to find her thrills somewhere.'

'The war is no longer boring, you foolish little thing! You
might think the real shooting war has only just started, but for
those on our ships out there on the sea, it began months ago and
it was far from boring.'

Evadne Childe spoke quietly and deliberately, but each word
carried a weight and force of a pile-driving hammer and Veronica
Hatherall recoiled under the impact.

'Oh my God, Evie, I am so sorry. I simply wasn't thinking.

Please forgive me, say you forgive me. You won't tell Gilpin's, will you?'

The girl was contrite and her embarrassment genuine and Evadne Childe had no intention of tormenting her; the fact that she was concerned about her faux pas being reported to her employers, who she knew valued Evadne's services more than hers, merely emphasized her youth. Outwardly worldly and confident, mentally she was an innocent in the school playground. What could she know about widowhood?

'No, I will not tell Gilpin's.' Evadne hoped the girl did not notice the twinkle in her eye. 'My dear child, it would surely be pointless for a mere vicar's daughter to try and tell a publisher anything about being rude and tactless to an author?'

Seven years and seven successful novels had left Evadne Childe in a position of armed neutrality with her publishing house, the firm of J.P. Gilpin and Company of New York and London; a position in which many an author who has tasted early success find themselves.

It had been Gilpin's, or JP's, as they were sometimes known, who had picked up Evadne's first detective novel, *A Richer Dust*, for publication initially in America and then in Britain, in 1933. The book had enjoyed more than modest sales and immoderately generous reviews, with Charles Williams, writing in the *Westminster Gazette*, calling it 'a singularly agreeable book' and no less than Dorothy Sayers hailing it as a 'bloodthirsty yet highly moral debut' in the *Sunday Times*. Seven more novels had followed, all with increasing sales and all featuring her detective hero, the resourceful and breathtakingly handsome Rex Troughton, and many who knew her had said it was fate, though Evadne favoured mere chance, that having created a dashing hero on the page who was an amateur sleuth but professional archaeologist, she should then fall in love in life (as well as on the page) with a real archaeologist, Edmund Walker-Pyne.

In those pages of the popular press which tottered on the knife edge between 'arts and culture' and 'society gossip', the marriage of a successful female writer of detective stories at the age of forty-seven to a penniless archaeologist, albeit a Cambridge one, some twenty-two years her junior, filled many column inches in that brief period of calm between the Abdication Crisis in England and the rather more significant crisis looming in Europe.

Undoubtedly his position as the consort of one of England's 'queens of crime' made Edmund Walker-Pyne's archaeological excavations in Egypt more newsworthy than usual, especially as it was hinted loudly that they were being funded by the British and American reading public and were no more than an expensive hobby for the dashing Edmund – a hobby which kept him well out of range of the army of young female (pointedly younger than his wife) fans who had come to swoon over the adventures of his fictional alter ego Rex Troughton.

All thinly veiled sniping ceased abruptly on the outbreak of war when it became publicly known that Edmund, a keen sailor in his youth and a member of the Royal Navy Volunteer Reserve, had abandoned the desert to serve his country on the high seas. Archaeology's loss was likely to become popular fiction's gain, as Rex Troughton, it was assumed, would now put his considerable skills as an amateur sleuth to fighting the biggest villain he had yet encountered within a dust jacket.

There was genuine sympathy for Evadne Childe when the news was released that she had lost both her husband and her muse, as Edmund achieved the unenviable distinction of being among the first British fatalities with the war not yet six weeks old. Given the rank of sub-lieutenant, Edmund had been assigned as a signals and communications officer on the passenger steamer SS *West Riding*, bound for Rangoon, which was a hundred miles off Cape Finisterre when it was shelled and sunk by a surfaced U-boat with the loss of more than sixty passengers and crew. It was little consolation to his widow to learn that Edmund had done his duty and his radio distress calls had been heard by an American steamship which was quickly able to pick up survivors, but not quickly enough to prevent Sub-Lieutenant Walker-Pyne from dying of his injuries in a leaky lifeboat. His body, and the survivors, were unloaded at Bordeaux, and a British consulate official (and avid reader of detective fiction) arranged for interment in the Protestant cemetery there, writing personally to express his sympathies to Evadne Childe, care of her publisher, and offering to assist in arranging a visit to her husband's grave. It was an offer Evadne politely refused, pointing out that there was a war on, and her journey would not, technically, be necessary as long as the consulate could supply her with a plan of the cemetery and the exact geographical co-ordinates of Edmund's resting place. A somewhat confused consulate official complied with her wishes to the letter while harbouring the thought that, however intelligent, a bereaved woman was still a woman, and thus unpredictable if not downright inexplicable.

'But it was unthinking of me,' Veronica said gently. 'How could I forget Edmund's heroic sacrifice? You must be very proud of him.'

Evadne carefully rearranged the cutlery on the table in front of her before replying.

'There may be something tragic in being the last to be killed in a war just as an armistice is being signed, but there is very little noble about being one of the first. You are right, though, that Edmund is a hero to me.'

'Just as Rex Troughton is to millions of readers.' Veronica's face brightened then immediately dulled, as if a footlight had been switched off. 'Oh dear, I didn't mean . . .'

'I'm sure you didn't, my dear,' said Evadne, wielding her maturity like a rapier. 'Your generation does not lack sympathy, merely the ability to express it. Do not confuse my fictional hero with my late husband. Both still clearly exist in my world, but the one you are most interested in is alive and well and in a perfectly typed, double-spaced manuscript, wrapped up in brown paper and string and currently nestling under my chair.'

The footlights aimed at Veronica's face came on again, putting a sparkle into her eyes and pulling her pout into a smile.

'You've finished it? The new book?'

The older woman nodded. 'Unless you have an ulterior motive for buying me lunch.'

'*Dahling,*' drawled Veronica, her smile now impish, 'who needs an excuse to have lunch with mystery maven Evadne Childe? Especially if Gilpin's are paying. They were terribly upset not to have a book out in 1940, though for perfectly understandable reasons, and they'll be delighted to be able to announce a new Rex Troughton for their spring 1941 list. What's the title?'

'*With Smoke and Mirrors.*'

'Brilliant! Gilpin's will get behind it and it will positively fly off the shelves! The Americans will love it too.'

'Do you think someone at JP's should read it first? They might reject it.'

Veronica flapped a hand over the table, wafting away the very idea as if extinguishing a candle or dispersing a bad smell.

'Are you happy with it, *dahling*?'

'I am as happy as a writer can be. It is always difficult to know when to stop dabbing paint on to one's canvas, but I am happy with what I have concocted this time. The clues are good, or at least fair, I think, and the characters all stand up and can be counted as vital to the plot. Yes, I'm happy with it, and I am certain Edmund would be. In fact, I know he is.'

'Then Gilpin's have another bestseller on their hands!' said a gleeful Veronica, clapping her hands to illustrate the point. 'And that calls for champagne.'

'Don't be ridiculous, Veronica, you know I don't drink alcohol during the day, and these are hardly the times for splashy celebrations. There is a war on.'

'Then how about ice cream? Bucci's is famous for it; the owners are Italian, after all, and they know a thing or two about ice cream.'

'That sounds perfect,' said Evadne. 'Let us have something more substantial first, then treat ourselves to as many flavours as they can offer.'

Veronica waved a leather-covered menu above her head to attract a waiter.

'Let's have *every* flavour! Let's eat ice cream until we're sick! We might as well, the owners are being interned next week. It might be our last chance.'

'Really?'

'*Dahling*, there is a war on.' Veronica allowed herself a thin victory smile, which was quickly erased by Evadne's quietly cutting response.

'I must remember to tell Edmund that, next time I speak to him.'

The two pistols boomed in unison again; three rounds of indistinguishable rapid fire, the reverberations bouncing off the damp-stained concrete walls of the cellar and penetrating the earplugs of the two shooters and the third person present; an observer who had, turtle-like, pulled his neck as far into the protective shell of his overcoat as he could, so that his bowler hat, jammed on to salt-and-pepper hair, seemed to act as a lid.

Lowering his pistol, the tall thin man adjusted his large round spectacles and then removed his earplugs with his left hand, coughing slightly as the floating wisps of cordite caught the back of his throat.

'Have you not thought about air-conditioning, Stanislaus? Even the Romans had it in a crude form, and I hear the Americans have perfected the idea. A desk fan at a pinch, or perhaps a spare constable could act as a punkah-wallah?'

The older man tipped back his bowler with the stab of a fore-finger, allowing his disapproving stare the widest possible scope, but when he spoke there was genuine, almost fatherly, warmth in his voice.

'Good to see you've got your spirits up again after the Coachingford business, Albert. The old brainbox back to normal now, is it?'

The bespectacled man grinned inanely and touched the side of his head with the barrel of his pistol, having carefully removed his index finger from the trigger guard.

'Ticking over nicely, thank you. All the natural wool padding in there comes in very useful as protection against unwarranted blows to the head.'

'Come in handy that, now you're a married man.'

'Yes, I understand congratulations are in order,' said the third person in that dank, windowless space, a smartly dressed woman of a certain age who could have been in the queue for one of Myra Hess's lunchtime concerts at the National Gallery, were it not for the Webley Mark 5 short-barrelled service revolver she hefted in her right hand, as though trying to guess its weight.

'Thank you, they are indeed,' said Albert Campion politely, 'but do be careful with that gun. Unless my eyes deceive me, that model does not possess a safety catch.'

'Neither does yours, Mr Campion. It is a Webley Mark 4, isn't it? Takes a .38 cartridge, whereas mine takes a .455?'

Mr Campion was suitably impressed.

'You have an impressive knowledge of firearms, Mrs Walker-Pyne, I suspect on a level with Superintendent Oates here; but then, you are both in the business of dealing with dangerous criminals, are you not?'

Campion laid his pistol on the flat surface in front of them, next to an open box of cartridges and a stack of square paper targets. It was a curious piece of furniture in any context, but a particularly unusual item to be found in the basement of a police station, having its origins in a five-foot section of mahogany-topped bar counter from a Victorian public house; but, with innards of multiple layers of cardboard sheets, it served as a firing platform for the makeshift shooting range while hopefully offering a modicum of protection from ricochets. When installed there had been many a ribald comment from the serving officers at Bottle Street that it would have been more use than ornament if only the beer pumps had been left attached.

'Fortunately the criminals I deal with are fictional,' said Evadne. 'The real ones I gladly leave to Mr Oates and his admirable force of detectives, to whom I often turn for advice.'

'Allow me,' said Oates, taking the pistol from the woman's hand and unloading the spent shells as he talked. 'Mrs Walker-Pyne, or Miss Childe as we call her, does a lot of research for her stories, Albert. Very thorough she is and, unlike many a writer of penny dreadfuls, she gets her facts right; well, most of the time.'

'Come, come, Stanislaus, "penny dreadfuls"? You're showing your age now, aren't you?' Campion grinned. 'The dear Baron Tweedsmuir, who died this year far too young, called his John Buchan books "shilling shockers", which would have been a bit more up to date, even though they don't cost a shilling any more.'

'All I'm saying,' said Oates slowly, a faint but unthreatening rural accent creeping into his speech, 'is that Miss Childe here takes her backgrounds seriously when writing her stories, but at the end of the day, that's just what they are: stories. They may not be as bad as the current crop of gunmen, gals and gangsters rubbish, with their lurid covers plastered all over the railway kiosks these days but, with all due respect, they're as far removed from proper police work as the man in the moon.'

'I'll have you a small wager, Stanislaus, that when your young constables are allowed a tea break, or when they get home to their lodgings after a hard day pounding the beat, they'll put their size twelve feet up and their noses into *No Orchids For Miss Blandish*.' Campion's idiotic expression became instantaneously more human as he turned to Evadne. 'Not that for a moment I am making comparisons . . .'

'Do not distress yourself, Mr Campion, I am flattered to be

mentioned in the same breath as John Buchan, though, as you say, my books would be at least seven-shillings-and-sixpenny shockers these days. I am unacquainted with the adventures of Miss Blandish or her author, perhaps mercifully so, and therefore unable to judge a comparison, if one had been intended.' She held up a finger to forestall an apology; it stopped Campion as effectively as a bullet. 'But Superintendent Oates is quite correct. The policemen in my stories always have to be helped out by a complete amateur whose only expertise is in archaeology. In reality, only if the police were investigating a murder from two thousand years ago would Rex Troughton be more useful to them than the man in the moon, but though my trade is in entertainment and not reality, I do pride myself on the accuracy of the research I do for my backgrounds. In that, Mr Oates has been very helpful.'

Campion indicated the two pistols now side by side on the bar counter, as though posed for the final frames of one of Mr Ford's elegiac Westerns.

'And this is your latest research project? Am I helping to inspire a dramatic gunfight in one of your books? Perhaps we should call ourselves the Piccadilly Cowboys. I wouldn't mind being in your stories at all, though you'd have to change my name. I've found Tootles Ash and Mornington Dodd to be useful aliases in the past. You're welcome to either. Has a thinly disguised Stanislaus appeared in one of your novels? If he has, I will buy up every copy and distribute them to the residents of all His Majesty's Prisons in London and the Home Counties.'

Campion mugged a double-take and put the palms of his hands up to both cheeks, as if something appalling had just occurred to him.

'But of course I can't do *that*, it might give the old lags some new ideas, perhaps give away some tricks of the trade; the detective trade, that is.'

'That new wife of yours hasn't crimped the edges of your clown suit, Albert,' observed Mr Oates, adding with some force, 'yet, but give her time and she could do us all a favour.'

'I read about your marriage in *The Times*, Mr Campion,' said Evadne. 'Rather sudden, wasn't it? Not that I'm implying anything untoward by that.'

'Nothing *un*toward implied or involved. In fact, you might say it was an event that had been hurtling *towards* its logical conclusion for some time. Amanda decided it was going to happen eight years ago, and when she makes up her mind, it usually stays made. It was just circumstances and the chaos of wartime that meant it was a last-minute thing at the end. Still, that avoided the need to break bread with tiresome relations.'

'And you are happy together?'

'It's a perfect fit.'

'Despite the age difference?'

If Campion was surprised, shocked or offended by the question, he hid it well, but Evadne sensed discomfort and possibly a little guilt. That was, after all, one of her skills as a writer of detective stories.

'I am not being rude,' she said, 'but genuinely curious. You see, I was some years older than my late husband and there was gossip. Well, if not gossip, then definite murmurings in certain quarters, though it was a subject never once discussed between us. Therefore, I do not know if it played on my husband's mind. I was curious if it was a concern for a man in a similar situation.'

Campion answered carefully. 'I cannot, of course, speak from the female perspective, but from a purely personal point of view, I can say that the age difference between Amanda and me has never been seen as just impediment to our happiness or, for that matter, a subject of concern for society, either high or low.'

'And he'd know about the lower division,' Oates confided theatrically. 'Albert knows more shady characters, highwaymen and cut-pursers than I do, and is on pints of mild-and-bitter terms with most of them. If you need to research the grubby underworld, Miss Childe, Albert here is better than an AA Touring Guide when it comes to finding your way around.'

'You are being far too modest, Stanislaus,' said Campion. 'Now be a good chap and retrieve our targets so we can see who won the last round. You'd better do it, as you know I'll try and cheat.'

Superintendent Oates snorted, shook his head and began to clump down the length of the cellar, his boots ringing on the damp concrete floor, towards the pair of iron candle stands which had been artfully adapted with a lump hammer in order to hold the square paper targets. Behind the candlesticks, a full-size horsehair mattress was propped against the end wall to cushion the bullets passing through – or around – the roundel bullseye targets.

'And this is research for your latest book?' Campion asked Evadne. 'I'm not prying, by the way. I have no intention of stealing your plot.'

Mrs Walker-Pyne fixed him with a curious eye. She knew of Campion by reputation, despite the fact, it was rumoured, that his name had been kept out of the press coverage of some recent rather sensational criminal cases. One executive at Gilpin's, her publisher, had even asked her opinion as to whether Mr Campion's adventures might be turned into commercial fiction – an opinion, if she had one, she had kept to herself. But now, as he stood disarmingly in front of her, what did she make of him? How would she shoehorn him into one of her novels, alongside her established cast of characters? He could not be the heroic amateur detective; she already had one of those and her readers would not tolerate a rival, even if her publisher might be tempted to add a second string to her bow.

He could, at best, be a secondary character, perhaps a comic foil for Rex Troughton who would, naturally, handle the rough stuff and meet the villains with a square jaw and unflinching defiance. Used to working alone, Rex did not suffer fools gladly, if at all, and Campion could certainly come across as a fool, something which belied the rumours of his exploits and his obvious friendship with senior CID officers.

'No, I'm not here for research, Mr Campion, but for self-preservation. I intend to move out of London to East Anglia to look after my ageing mother and, if an invasion comes, I intend to be prepared. My father was given that pistol after the first war.'

'After?'

'He was a chaplain during the war on the Western Front and naturally went unarmed, but he was always demanding a pistol from fellow officers to put wounded horses out of their misery, something he felt most strongly about. His regiment gave him that pistol after the war in case he came across animals in distress in peacetime. I think it was an attempt at black humour and, although he never used it, he would clean it regularly until the day he died. Despite what Superintendent Oates may say, I am blissfully ignorant of firearms, and so when necessity demanded it, I reported to Seymour Street police station and asked where I could buy ammunition. The nice sergeant there gave me the name of a Bond Street gunsmith but suggested I might benefit from a few shooting lessons. My fame as a writer of detective stories preceded me and I found myself invited here to Bottle Street for some target practice. I had no idea they had a shooting gallery in the basement.'

'Neither had I,' said Campion innocently, 'and I live here. Well, not here, these used to be the cells, you know, but a bad case of rising damp made conditions a bit Dickensian and so His Majesty's bed-and-breakfast facility was moved upstairs. I have a flat above, with a secluded private side entrance so I don't have to mix with the convicts prior to transportation.'

'Then this must be convenient for regular target practice.'

'Oh no, I only keep my eye in at the funfair with the air rifles. You'd be amazed how many goldfish I win that way.'

Mrs Walker-Pyne kept a straight face, even though she was beginning to find Campion's tomfoolery rather endearing.

'I hope the Germans, when they invade, are suitably impressed with your skill.'

'I'm thinking of taking out advertisements in some of their papers,' Campion said lazily, 'that should deter them from coming at all. If I could say that Evadne Childe was also a dead shot, it might seal the deal. Your books are published in Germany, are they not?'

'They were,' said the authoress sternly, 'up until '37 when the Nazis decided that my Berlin publisher, being Jewish, was not a fit and proper person to be in such a dangerous business as the production of books. Or any business, it seems. The new Nazi owners offered to publish me if I signed a contract which specified publicly that I was not of the Jewish race. I refused.'

'Good for you,' said Campion with enthusiasm. 'But hang on, did you say you were heading out to East Anglia? That could be the front line if they come by parachute or glider, as they did in Belgium. There have already been big air raids there, with nine people killed in Cambridge last month. The whole place is a big military area, with restricted access.'

'Which is exactly why I am going there. My mother is too old and frail to be evacuated, and where is safe these days?

I have the required permission to return to my family home and have offered the War Office the use of my London flat.'

'I'm sure they'll take good care of it.'

Evadne raised an eyebrow.

'I believe that about as much as I believed the story that the Luftwaffe would never bomb Essex because Ribbentrop had a mistress who lived in Dunmow when he was ambassador.'

'Yes,' Campion agreed, 'I never put much faith in that one either. O-ho, stand by your beds, he comes the sergeant major.'

Oates materialized in front of them, the other side of the requisitioned bar counter, holding a tattered paper target in each hand, almost as if presenting two foaming tankards.

'Two rounds of three shots,' he announced with grim formality. 'Like I said, Miss Childe, unless you're in a proper battle, don't load more than three cartridges and make sure the hammer's on an empty chamber, that way you avoid accidents. Anyway, six shots each in all. Four bulls and an inner on one card, two inners and three outers on the other.'

Oates exhaled slowly through his nose. 'You seem to be a natural, Miss Childe, whereas you, Albert – you sure you have the right specs on?'

TWO

The Godsiblings

Before she decamped from London, Evadne Childe was called upon to perform a small patriotic duty. As a best-selling author and also one of the first widows of the war, she had agreed to accept an invitation to a preview at the War Office of the new public information film *Miss Grant Goes to the Door*, the story of two sisters isolated in the country-side having to defend themselves against Nazi parachutists. While having reservations about the rather undramatic title, she had to admit that the short propaganda piece would scare its intended audiences silly, as it did her. It did not, however, dent her resolve to move from the city to the country and to an isolated house in an area designated as a likely landing zone for airborne invaders.

Her journey to Essex was every bit as uncomfortable as she had feared. From the pavement outside the Great Eastern Hotel to the ticket barriers on Liverpool Street station itself, she was greeted with a rippling sea of uniformed humanity. Almost everyone in the crowd was in a uniform of one sort or another, the blues, browns and drab greens bleeding into a murky tide which ebbed and slapped into the station concourse.

Evadne congratulated herself on the foresight to be travelling with only one suitcase and one capacious satchel slung around her neck, along with her gas-mask box, for amid all those uniforms, there was no sign of a porter.

Well, she said to herself, *there is a war on*, and she took a firm grip on the handle of her suitcase and began to shoulder her way through the crowd. It was a physical experience, to say the least, to push her way through what she decided to describe in her fiction as a 'very polite rugby scrum smelling of fresh tobacco and stale sweat'. Although the cap badges and shoulder flashes which swam before her eyes meant little to her, the accents and languages she heard as she squeezed through that thicket of wool-covered shoulders and rough canvas haversacks told her that she was in the middle of a truly cosmopolitan force, if it could be called a force at all, for there seemed little order or purpose to this milling throng. Apart from English and French, which she spoke well (as she did German), she heard and recognized Dutch and Polish, and at least two languages she did not know but guessed could be Norwegian or Swedish and Czech. As for the English, she heard it spoken in dialects originating from Cornwall to Scotland, and everywhere in between, and even, though only once, the gentle lilt of a genuine Essex accent.

It was the same on the train when she managed to struggle on board, pushing her suitcase in front of her as she threaded her way along the narrow corridors, where every inch seemed to have been claimed by a soldier, as if they were standing on guard duty. She was aware that her stockings were being snagged and that her coat (not her best, but a good one nonetheless) was suffering from a bombardment of burning flecks from the cigarettes of the men she pushed by.

Eventually she found a seat in a first-class carriage occupied by two colonels, a travelling salesman, and a bitter old woman who complained incessantly about her son being left on the beach at Dunkirk until she got off at Stratford. Evadne guessed that the woman would cross the station and travel back to Liverpool Street in order to continue her diatribe on the next Colchester train, unless a brave ticket inspector finally caught up with her.

Colchester had been a garrison town since Claudius's XXth Legion had built a fort there, but could rarely have seen such a concentrated swarm of confused soldiery as that which confronted Evadne on Colchester station as her train wheezed to a halt. The platforms overflowed with uniforms, hobnailed boots scraped on concrete, and angry sergeants shouted impenetrable commands in a vain attempt to bring order to the chaos. Above the bobbing sea of tin-helmeted heads hung a low cloud of cigarette smoke, but through it and the wire fence surrounding the station entrance, Evadne caught sight of a familiar figure, or rather two.

Despite the crush and the buffeting, Evadne could not help but smile at the sight of Reuben Stopes, dressed in his Sunday best, standing protectively and proudly over a maroon-coloured Austin Ascot.

When Evadne's father, the Revd. Henry Childe, had been made vicar of Eight Ash, he had inherited Reuben as a sidesman for his church and quickly recognized, and appropriated, his talents for the care and nurturing of anything mechanical. A farm labourer born and bred in the village, Reuben Stopes was a confirmed teetotaller and devout Christian who, like the Reverend Childe, had experienced the horrors of the Western Front, though he had never been known to talk about them.

The death of Henry Childe in 1928 meant that his widow Alice had to vacate the Eight Ash vicarage to make way for a new incumbent. She was fortunate in that, being the last in her own family line, she had inherited Mill House, an almost derelict structure which had fallen into disrepair since the village water mill had gone out of business in 1913. The widow Childe was even more fortunate to be able to inherit the services of Reuben Stopes who, dedicated and loyal to the memory of the vicar, spent most of his spare hours helping to make Mill House habitable for his widow, from resurrecting ancient plumbing and securing the roof, to installing a new stove and unblocking chimneys.

Now thought to be well over sixty – it had always seemed inappropriate to ask his actual age – Reuben's duties were limited to light maintenance, grass-cutting and the cossetting and driving of the Austin Ascot which Evadne had bought for her mother.

That little car had been Evadne's passport to freedom – and sanity.

Alice Childe had taken widowhood seriously and had been determined to enjoy it, despite her reduced social and economic status within the village. For that she needed help, a housekeeper at least, and after years of dispensing charity to others, surely she deserved a maid and staff to service Mill House. Yet the Revd. Childe had left little in the way of worldly wealth or pension, only the devotion of Reuben Stopes, and so Alice called upon her sole asset, her daughter.

Bowing to the pressure a widowed mother could exert on an only child, Evadne abandoned the independent life she had carved out for herself in London as a secretary in a small travel agency by day while learning French and German at evening classes run by the Regent Street Polytechnic and spending her spare hours reading fiction of all shades in the Marylebone public library.

Even at her father's graveside, her mother was whispering that she really ought to come home to Eight Ash and 'make herself useful' and, before the funeral meats had been cleared away, Evadne knew in her heart that she would have to abandon her independence and her professional income – she might as well never have got the vote! – and accept whatever roles – nurse, cook and housekeeper among them – her widowed mother thought fit.

Spinsterhood beckoned, and she saw little hope of escaping from an isolated Mill House, until on a rare trip into Colchester to hear a lecture on the excavations at the city's Balkerne Gate and the findings of an inspirational archaeologist called Mortimer Wheeler. She returned to Eight Ash and began to write the first chapter of what would become *A Richer Dust*, featuring her archaeologist detective Rex Troughton solving the murder of a domineering widow living in an isolated watermill in a remote East Anglian village.

Its success, and that of Troughton's three following adventures, brought Evadne invitations to speak at numerous literary gatherings in bookshops and libraries; at one she was approached by a penniless young archaeology graduate who said he saw much of himself in Rex Troughton. After one further meeting and a dinner together, Evadne could only agree. They were married within a year, but it was not the speed of the wedding but the fact that Evadne was twenty years older than Edmund Pyne-Walker which raised the more prurient of eyebrows.

Married life meant a return to London and freedom from Mill House, leaving the widow Alice alone in an isolation she resented, and made sure Evadne knew she resented. As a salve to her conscience, Evadne bought her mother the Austin Ascot, even though the idea of a woman driving was an anathema to Alice, and arranged to pay a stipend to Reuben Stopes to act as mechanic and chauffeur. The prospect of being driven around the village in what locally counted as imperial splendour, soothed Alice's resentment somewhat, as did a selection of ladies from the Eight Ash Mothers' Union, suitably bribed by Evadne, who agreed to work on a rota system as her housekeeper.

Now Evadne was returning to Eight Ash herself a widow and the country was at war. The only bright thought she had, as she pushed through the sea of khaki and out of the station, was that Reuben Stopes looked as solid and undemanding as he always had, and the little maroon Austin had been polished to within an inch of its life to receive her.

'Home again, are we, Miss Evadne?' said Reuben as he opened the car door for her.

'I suppose so,' said the prodigal daughter reluctantly.

The village of Eight Ash lay some five miles to the northwest of Colchester in farmland and water meadows abutting the River Colne. As Reuben Stope steered the Austin carefully along narrow lanes, mindful of meeting 'one o' them big army lorries' coming the other way, he pointed out the recent crop of stubby grey concrete pillboxes which had been planted by the army at every crossroads and seemingly at random in fields sloping down to the river.

'Harvest will be well guarded this year,' observed Reuben.

Evadne did not reply but she knew the pillboxes were not there on agricultural duty. Having researched moving into a sensitive military zone as carefully as she researched her murder plots, Evadne was well aware that the pillboxes had been strategically placed to provide crossfire over the water meadows and fields in the river valley, as they had been identified as prime landing grounds for silent, glider-borne invaders from across the North Sea and the airfields of Holland, which were now in enemy hands.

There was even a pillbox at the top of the single-track lane which led down to Mill House and the river. As no other properties were served by that lane, Evadne mused that she would at least have her own personal sentries in these dangerous times, though her mother probably felt it more of an imposition than a privilege. (She did.)

Throughout that hot, blue-skied Spitfire Summer, Evadne threw herself into the running of Mill House and the Eight Ash war effort, insisting that everyone she dealt with referred to her as Mrs Walker-Pyne rather than her maiden name, and though there were many in the village who automatically called her Childe, it was because they recognized her as the daughter of the old vicar, rather than as a bestselling author, a career her mother had never recognized as suitable or approved of.

Alice Childe would also not have approved of her daughter volunteering Mill House as a billet to the military authorities in Colchester, had she known about it. With her daughter home, however, she saw no reason to answer the telephone or deal with tradesmen, salesmen, soldiers or officials of any hue. Indeed, most days she rarely saw the need to leave her bedroom, preferring to have Evadne serve her meals on a tray. Thus, when the army noisily arrived at Mill House on a glorious September afternoon, the first Alice Childe knew of it was from behind a twitching upstairs net curtain.

The car came across the bridge over the mill stream far too fast; as it screeched to a halt its wheels sent gravel scuttering across the driveway frontage of Mill House. It was followed by two motorcycles travelling at a more sedate pace, whose riders parked in parallel behind the car and dismounted in unison.

The car was a stylish left-hand drive Ford V8 coupé, which had recently been painted olive green. Evadne prided herself on noticing such things for future reference and made a mental note to ask after the provenance of the motorbikes, which might come in useful at some point. She had, after all, many male readers who appreciated such details and who were quick to point out any errors made by a mere woman.

But such thoughts of dutiful research slipped to the back of her mind as she stepped out of the front door of Mill House to greet her visitors and realized that she recognized the long, thin figure unwinding himself from behind the steering wheel of the Ford.

'Good afternoon, Miss Childe. Up for a bit more target practice?'

'Why, Mr Campion, what an unexpected pleasure. What are you doing here?'

Campion place a hand across his heart and bowed. 'I have the pleasure of delivering your two temporary, I hope, house guests.'

He swept his arm to indicate the two motorcyclists struggling with comic haste to divest themselves of greatcoats, leather helmets and goggles.

'Simon, Peter, this is the famous writer Evadne Childe. Oh, I'm sorry, that does sound slightly biblical. Miss Childe, allow me to present Lieutenants Simon Moorgat and Peter Verloet, formerly of the Ardennes Rifle Corps of the Belgian army. They are polite, entirely house-trained, and come complete with their own ration books and, as you can see, transport.'

'I am delighted to have them,' said Evadne, offering a hand to the two motorcyclists in turn, 'and of course to see you again, Mr Campion, but I prefer my married name these days.'

'That doesn't mean you've given up writing, does it?' Campion asked, deflated. 'My wife will be most upset as she's a great fan of yours. Mind you, she'll be furious when she hears I've met you without her. It was she who told me we were related.'

'We are?'

'Well, sort of. We are godsiblings, or perhaps I've just made that up. It was my wife who reminded me that we share a godmother, the Countess of Costigan and Dorn.'

'I suspect the countess has a considerable number of godchildren, though she always sends me a wonderful note on lavender notepaper when a new book comes out.'

Campion turned to the two motorcyclists, now stripped down to the drab uniforms of privates in the Essex Yeomanry. They had revealed themselves to be fresh-faced, frighteningly young and utterly confused.

'I should explain,' Campion said to them, 'that the Countess of Costigan and Dorn is possibly the last great political hostess in the country, who once scuppered the career of a potential prime minister by describing his only saving grace as a politician being that he had a lack of opinion on just about everything. A clever woman, as is your hostess. She writes jolly exciting detective stories, don't you know, or at least she did.'

'I have not abandoned writing fiction, Mr Campion,' said Evadne, keen to steer the conversation away from further diversions. 'I have merely set it to one side during the current period of national uncertainty. If we survive an invasion, I will pick up my pen once more.'

'Glad to hear it. Your books are good for morale – and my wife will be mightily relieved.'

'They are very good books,' said the slightly taller of the young Belgians. 'I have read one, in French of course.'

'Thank you,' said Evadne politely, as all authors do when complimented. 'It's Simon, isn't it?'

The curly-haired young man nodded enthusiastically. 'Yes, I am Simon. My friend Peter does not speak English so well and does not read books at all, I think.'

Peter, who clearly spoke enough English, gave his compatriot a friendly punch on the arm.

'No matter.' Evadne smiled. 'While you are here you can help me improve my French.'

'An excellent arrangement,' said Campion. 'I just know you'll get on like a house on fire and, while they are abusing your hospitality, I am sure my brave Belgian boys will help out around the place.'

He looked over Evadne's shoulder at the front of Mill House and noted the twitching curtain in the central first-floor window. Given the summer heat, all the upstairs sash windows were open to some degree, and it was clear that they were being heard as well as seen.

'My mother and I manage well enough,' said Evadne, 'but help with some of the more physical tasks is always welcome. Chopping firewood for the winter, for instance, should we still be here when winter comes.'

'Oh, I have no fears on that score; I've seen you on the shooting range. I have no idea how long Simon and Peter will be with you, but I am sure they will be perfectly safe under your protection.'

'I am flattered, Mr Campion, but still rather vague on exactly why you are here in Eight Ash today.'

Campion spread his hands in a *mea culpa* gesture. 'I simply couldn't resist. I was sent out to Wivenhoe House to talk to these two chaps to see what they could tell us about the situation in Belgium after they made their rather dramatic escape.'

'So you are in Intelligence,' Evadne said. It was not a question.

'I'm afraid so. Incredible, isn't it?' Campion grinned inanely. 'They're letting just anyone in these days. So we had a good long chat and these boys told me all they could. Then I discovered that they were to be billeted in the home of my godsibling and I just had to escort them out here personally and hand them over to you.'

Campion had been sent to Wivenhoe House, a country manor on the other side of Colchester made famous by a John Constable painting, but now pressed into service as a debriefing centre for military flotsam washed up on English shores in the aftermath of Dunkirk by an enthusiastic colonel in a tank regiment desperately in need of battlefield intelligence. He had been convinced that two Belgian officers, however young and wet behind the ears, who had experienced action around Dinant and the assault on the River Meuse by the Seventh Panzer Division in May, would surely be able to provide an insight into the methods and tactics of a German general called Rommel, a figure of much interest to the War Office.

Campion had doubted very much that two green recruits in an army which only had forty-two tanks of its own could offer much insight into a *blitzkrieg* from which they were fleeing for their lives, especially after hearing the story of their escape.

Verloet and Moorgat had survived their first, and only, encounter with the German army but then, finding themselves separated from their unit, had made their way across Belgium, being passed on by their retreating French and then British allies until they found their way to the coast north of Ostend at a place called Bredene aan Zee. Hungry, exhausted, and unwilling to trust anyone, they stumbled across two schoolboys only half a dozen years younger than themselves, earnestly preparing a small sailing dinghy for an escape to England. Impressed by the fact that the two men carried pistols, which would surely come in useful against air attack, the boys were happy to allow their elders to guard the boat overnight until they could, together, catch the morning tide. They had already provisioned the dinghy with fresh water, biscuits, sausage, cheese and chocolate, and it was the loss of those supplies, carefully purloined from their parents' closely guarded larders, which hurt the boys almost as much as when the dawn came to show that their dinghy had sailed without them.

Verloet and Moorgat had little experience of small boats or the sea but were blessed with phenomenal luck. They heard the sound of heavy guns from around Dunkirk and Calais and saw pillars of smoke rising high into the air. Though they escaped the attention of enemy aircraft, they were almost run down by a British destroyer with soldiers clinging to every surface like bees on a honeycomb. Waving their tunics in a clear signal of distress at the destroyer resulted only in an officer with a megaphone shouting 'That way' and pointing an outstretched arm vaguely to the northwest.

After a day and a night of sailing, rowing and drifting, the dinghy was spotted by an aircraft of Coastal Command just off Foulness Island.

'I'm sure Peter and Simon will fill you in on their adventures,' said Campion. 'They may even give you material for your next book.'

Evadne looked at the two young men in turn and then back to Campion. 'I would be delighted to hear their stories, but I have to say that whenever I am approached, as I often am, by someone saying "I've got a great idea for your next book", I always reply, "So do I!".'

'Quite right, too.' Campion laughed. 'But whatever your next book is about, be assured that you will have made a sale in the Campion household.'

It was not her next, but it was an Evadne Childe novel which was to cause the problem.

PART TWO
Oates, 1946

THREE
Victory Parade

'As a child, did you ever have a knitted cosy, like a little hat, to pull over the top of your boiled egg at breakfast to keep it warm?'

Amanda was balancing on tiptoe, two hands on her husband's left shoulder, weighing it down so that his ear was lowered closer to her mouth in order to make sure she was heard above the noise of the cheering crowds, the marching feet and the strident whine of massed bagpipes.

'I still do,' shouted Mr Campion, 'but whatever made you ask that, my dear?'

Amanda jabbed a pointing finger through the mêlée of squashed bodies, bobbing hats, waving flags and cardboard periscope contraptions, swaying like marram grass in an onshore breeze, which lined The Mall.

Campion knew exactly where to look, for that particular piece of London, not more than ten feet from his outstretched arm, but unreachable due to the press of humanity, had been under his constant surveillance for over two hours. There, in a prime position from which to view the Victory Parade – in fact, but for the thin blue line of policemen and St John's ambulancemen they would form part of the parade – were his young son Rupert and the one man he would trust implicitly with his son's safety, Mr Magersfontein Lugg, whom Campion often described as 'a family retainer with ambitions to be a henchman'. Mr Lugg, when asked to define his position and status – which was rare, as few dared

to do so – might admit to being 'a gent's gent', but any suggestion that he was a mere butler, servant, lackey, scullion, hireling
or flunkey would almost certainly result in a burst of sarcastic
vitriol, possibly outright violence. Campion had once suggested
that, with a better education, Lugg might have fancied the title
of seneschal or perhaps housecarl, but he had done so without
cruelty and in genuine admiration and gratitude for the fat man's
loyalty.

And it was Mr Lugg's considerable bulk which had enabled
him to push his way through to the front of the crowd, even
though wartime restrictions – 'the government's idea of an 'ealthy
diet' – and exertions had reduced his fighting weight to a mere
eighteen stone. It was still an impressively solid eighteen stone
and, when it swivelled left or right in order to take in more of
the military procession snaking by, the crowd had to breathe in
to allow him room to move in comfort.

Not that it was Lugg's view of proceedings that was important.
He himself would have been the first to admit that he had seen
enough highly polished boots and swirling kilts, and certainly
heard enough military bands and more than enough bagpipes, to
last a lifetime. But for the excited not-yet-four-year-old in his
charge, the experience was as if his toy cupboard had come to
life and he was determined not to miss an inch of the two-mile-
long snake of men and machines as it slithered noisily by. Rupert
Campion had never seen anything like the spectacle of that June
Victory Parade and, though his adult escorts hoped he would
never have the opportunity to see another, they were determined
to allow him a good view of this one.

Which was where Lugg came in, or rather Lugg's shoulders,
by providing for Rupert the best seat in the house, short of sitting
on the King's knee on the saluting platform. With his bare legs
looped around Lugg's neck and his feet crossed under the chin
like a badly tied bowtie, Rupert had made himself comfortable
and rested his chest and folded arms over the large bald dome
that was Lugg's head.

Campion found himself agreeing with his wife that, from that
angle, behind and slightly to the left, Rupert's short-trousered
legs formed the rim of an egg cup, Lugg's shining head was the
egg, and Rupert's relaxed form – so relaxed it was as if he had
melted into position – was the 'cosy' keeping it warm, a living

one rather than one knitted by an industrious but unimaginative aunt, though an imaginative one would have added a small orange bobble of wool to represent Rupert's bright red hair.

Amanda pushed herself up on her toes again and shouted into her husband's ear at full volume though, thanks to the surrounding cacophony, he could only just make out the words, 'He'll sleep well tonight.'

Slowly and deliberately, Campion mouthed the silent reply: 'So will Rupert.'

Their only child had already had an exhausting day, taking in the sights of a shredded and dusty London landscape from his elevated observation post around Lugg's shoulders. As a beast of burden Lugg had proved exemplary, having the patience of a biblical donkey in a Renaissance painting, the sturdiness of a Suffolk Punch, and the gait of a camel treading a secure path through a minefield.

Rupert had been treated to a panoramic view of the Saluting Platform as it filled with dignitaries and assorted crowned heads, taking particular interest, or at least making cooing noises, at the Duchess of Kent in her WRENs uniform and actually applauding the Boy-King Faisal of Iraq, though the arrival together of Mr Atlee and Mr Churchill passed without comment. When royalty was settled, the serious business of the day began, and the lad became mesmerized by the steady rhythm of marching men and women from all services and almost all countries, the often harsh clamour of military music, down to the last deep rumble of tank, truck, fire engine and ambulance.

He was, surprisingly, still awake as the crowd began to disperse and the Campions, Lugg and his passenger made their way across Green Park to Piccadilly, where the Bottle Street flat provided a somewhat cramped refuge for the party to rest and be restored by tea and bacon sandwiches (Lugg having a seemingly unlimited supply of bacon from an unspecified source) before the festivities continued into the evening with a searchlight and fireworks display.

As Amanda, on her knees, buttoned him into his best overcoat, however, Rupert's eyelids began to droop.

'Oh darling, do try and stay awake for the fireworks. You'll love them,' she chided, popping a forefinger on to the child's button nose, 'and Uncle Magers will look after you.'

'Your trusty steed awaits, young Trooper Rooper,' said Lugg, bending down on one knee, 'but mind yer 'ead when I stands up. If you grow any more, we're going to have to get the ceiling lifted.'

As Rupert scrambled to mount the bulk now bending before him, the doorbell rang.

'I'll get it,' said Mr Campion, striding past the kneeling tableau, 'though I wasn't expecting any callers. Hardly anyone knew we'd be in London tonight.'

'I might have mentioned we'd be in the royal box, if only the invitation hadn't got lost in the post; but only to a select few,' said Lugg, giving Amanda a grotesque stage wink.

'The select few in the snug down the Platelayers' Arms, I suppose,' said Campion over his shoulder as he opened the flat door to reveal a uniformed police constable. 'Well, just remember what we used to say, until very recently, about loose tongues. Good evening, Constable, do you have a warrant for treason about your person?'

The young policeman removed his helmet and held it under his right arm as he would an unwieldy sporting trophy.

'No, sir,' he replied smartly, 'but if you are Mr Albert Campion, I have a message for you, from Superintendent Oates at the Central Department of the CID, who would like to ask you a question, in the morning, at your convenience.'

Mr Campion turned to his nearest and dearest, who were now his devoted audience.

'Well, that's the politest summons I've ever been served. Of course I will see my mentor and sometime guardian angel Stanislaus. Delighted to do so. I don't suppose you know what question he has in mind to ask me?'

'Oh yes, sir,' said the constable proudly, 'because he said you'd ask. He wants to know if you've read any good books lately?'

It had been a fine night for fireworks but, after six years of bombing, Londoners would have stood naked in a hailstorm to enjoy a pyrotechnic display which did not end in the destruction of life and property. It also lightened Campion's heart that hundreds of people, many in family groups, were sleeping out in the open in the capital's public spaces, with every park bench occupied by a tired reveller, and doing so out of choice rather than cruel necessity. Most of them would be out-of-towners who had been drawn to the metropolis for the grand show that had been the Victory Parade, which they saw as a celebration of and a reward for their stoicism. Londoners moving about their own Sunday morning business eyed the impromptu campsites with bemusement at their country-bumpkin cousins who clearly did not know the value of a solid roof over their heads.

Like a certain theatre on Great Windmill Street, the Central Office of the Criminal Investigation Department of the Metropolitan Police boasted that it never closed. Similarities between the two establishments ended there, but even with church bells ringing and the capital replete with good cheer at the previous day's long-awaited celebrations, it was business as usual for the city's detective force.

'All things considered,' pronounced Superintendent Stanislaus Oates, stirring a meagre ration of sugar into a mug of tea with symphonic violence, 'we can ask "went the day well?" and answer "yes it did" with a straight face. The night passed peaceful too, considering the number of visitors that were up for the cup without a bed for the night, and that a fair number of pubs made sure their clocks were running slow as they knew most of the beat bobbies were otherwise occupied getting all the troops back to their billeting areas.'

Albert Campion, who had known Oates for more than twenty years, balanced his teacup and saucer on his crossed knee and waited for the superintendent to get to the nub and crux of the meeting to which he had reported without hesitation.

'I copped for duty on the other Victory Parade, you know, back in 1919 after the last big show. I remember it well; the most trouble we had was with half the Belgian army camping in Kensington Gardens. The Belgians put on a good show again this time, along with the Czechs, the Frenchies, the Canucks and the Kiwis, even a few Chinese, all very smartly turned out – not to mention the noisy Yanks. We had a few problems with some of them down Soho after dark, I can tell you, and the bandsmen were the worst. Off-duty musicians in Soho? Do me a favour.'

'There were no Poles.'

'Pardon?'

'There were no Polish forces marching in the parade,' said Campion. 'I was very sad not to see them there.'

'Yes, well.' Oates cleared his throat to give him time to pick his words. 'That's politics for you. Can't be seen to be snubbing our nose at dear old Uncle Joe Stalin. Poland belongs to 'im now, not the Poles – and the Ruskies were our allies, after all.'

'So were the Poles, and for longer, and the Battle of Britain might have turned out a bit differently without Poles flying a few Spitfires.'

'I can't say you're wrong, Albert, and it's a crying shame, like most things political, but it's funny you should mention 1940, as that's why I wanted to pick your brains.'

'As I always say, if you can find 'em, you can pick 'em, old chum.'

Superintendent Oates slurped his tea loudly in comradely acceptance of the challenge.

'You remember having a few shooting lessons down in the cellars of Bottle Street with that nice lady writer of whodunits?'

'Mrs Walker-Pyne, though she goes by her maiden name of Evadne Childe when she's spreading murder and mayhem.'

'That's the one.'

'She's a charming lady,' said Campion, 'and I'm not just saying that because we share a godmother, or because my wife is one of her biggest fans.'

Oates narrowed his eyes over the rim of his large white china mug.

'Has Amanda read her latest?'

'I don't think so. She doesn't get all that much time for reading these days, unless it's a bedtime story or the odd nursery rhyme.'

The policeman nodded wisely, as if encouraged that Campion had remembered he was now a father.

'I saw the nipper yesterday getting an eyeful of the parade. Lugg was doing his St Christopher act, carrying his burden like a good 'un.'

'Rupert has certainly taken to old Lugg,' Campion said, smiling softly. 'They seem to have a calming effect on each other, though I've never thought of Lugg as St Christopher before. Still, the origin of the St Christopher legend was supposed to be a character called Reprobus, a Canaanite who was over seven feet tall and fearsomely ugly, so I suppose there could be a family resemblance.'

'Can't say I keep up with my Bible studies, but the description could fit. Good to hear they're keeping each other out of trouble. Amanda bearing up all right?'

'Busy as a bee doing about ten jobs simultaneously, sorting out the problems of peacetime aviation, dealing with our new socialist government who want to nationalize everything that moves, finding us a family home, being a mother to Rupert – and to Lugg – and a strict aunt to me. She's even got ideas for a major redevelopment of the Bottle Street flat.'

Oates raised a suspicious eyebrow.

'So, no more bachelor hideaway for you, eh?'

Mr Campion shrugged his shoulders. 'I am no longer a bachelor and so must put away foolish things, or at least make sure they are suitable for family life.'

'You've never considered a family life abroad?'

Mr Campion, not for the first time in their acquaintance, was thankful that Oates was asking questions to a friend rather than a suspect.

'What do you mean, Stanislaus?'

'Just a rumour I heard; that you were being offered a colonial post. Governor-general of somewhere hot and lazy perhaps, with palm trees and coconuts, all pith helmets with feathers and cere-monial swords.'

Mr Campion shook his head. 'Doesn't sound like my sort of thing at all. Would you put me in charge of a colony you wanted to keep? Margrave of the Eastern Marches would be about my limit, chum, but I don't think that post's vacant, or if it even exists, so banish that from your thoughts and tell me why you want my considered opinion on the detective stories of Evadne Childe.'

'Have you read any of them?'

'Of course I have. Well, one of them, out of politeness. Amanda is the real fan.'

'But not the latest?' Oates put down his mug and reached down to pull open a desk drawer from which he produced a book with a colourful dust jacket. He consulted the spine before pointing it towards his visitor. '*The Bottle Party Murders*. Came out last month.'

'Can't say I've heard of it, but it looks jolly exciting if, that is, one really can judge a book by its cover.'

The book's dust jacket featured Evadne Childe's name in suit-able bold and blood-curdling red type, and then a painting of a seedy Soho club, possibly inspired by a bad copy of Manet's *Bar at the Folies-Bergère*, down to the bottle of Bass on the counter, but instead of Manet's expressionless barmaid, a cigarette girl with her tray of wares ('Players, Please') slung from her neck and dressed in a very short French maid's costume, took centre stage. This girl was anything but expressionless, her long, flame-red hair flying and her hands reaching up to stifle a scream at some unspeakable horror only she had seen and which the reader was going to have to wait for.

'You know what a bottle party is?' asked Oates, as if enquiring if Campion was sitting comfortably.

'I've heard things,' said Campion carefully. 'They were a very inventive way of circumventing our draconian licensing laws. From the look on your face, they probably still are.'

'The idea is that you order your booze before you get to your club – and I'm talking dodgy drinking den here, not one of your gentlemen's clubs. The club flogs a mug temporary membership and passes his order to a wine and spirits merchant; again, the dodgy sort who operates out of a lock-up off-licence, not the sort of bespoke firm that decants your port for you.'

Mr Campion wafted his empty teacup dismissively. 'Do I detect a whiff of socialism around here? It is quite fashionable, I suppose.'

The superintendent ignored him. 'The idea being that the club never actually owns the booze, the member does, so they can't get prosecuted for selling after hours 'cos they're not *selling* it, just serving it, often alongside certain other goods and services. Until the law's changed, there's very little we can do about it.'

'But you've tried, haven't you?'

'Too right we have, but do you know how many clubs there are in the West End? Hundreds. Even now – and at the start of the war there were probably thousands. The Piccadilly, Mother Hubbard, Blue Lagoon, Kit-Kat Club, The Panama, The Silver Ring, Calves Club . . . they've all been visited more than once, and you'd be surprised how many peers of the realm we've found in there.'

'No, I wouldn't.'

'All the raids used to be organized out of the old Vine Street station, but the clubs had touts on look-out at the end of the street, and when they saw movement out of the station, they would leg it for the nearest phone box and ring through an early warning. 'Course Vine Street's now closed and operations were moved to the Savile Row station, not that that helped.'

'Wasn't Vine Street supposed to be haunted?' Campion asked.

'If you believe in that sort of thing.' Oates cleared his throat. 'There was an officer, whose name I cannot bring myself to speak, before the war this is, who was on the fiddle. No other way to put it. He took backhanders from the clubs for years, ended up with £17,000 in the bank. Seventeen thousand! Can you imagine that much cash in a copper's savings account? When he was rumbled, he topped himself, though frankly, nobody mourned his passing. It's his ghost that's supposed to haunt Vine Street, and in my opinion he's welcome to do that for all eternity, or until Hell lets him in.'

'That's all very interesting, Stanislaus, but what's it got to do with Evadne Childe's latest whodunit?'

'Far too much for my liking,' said the superintendent in his most official policeman's voice, holding up the book in question as if deterring a demon with a Bible. 'Have you ever come across the Grafton Club?'

'I can't say it's a regular haunt of mine, but I've been rather busy in the last few years. My clubland excursions have been extremely limited due to my commitments to serve King and Country and, more importantly, not frequenting places of which my wife would disapprove. I take it this Grafton Club is that sort of establishment.'

'I can't see Lady Amanda being a member,' said Oates, as if he had given the matter serious thought, 'but if she's a fan of Evadne Childe, she might be interested in a visit, as a tourist, say, to view the scene of the crime.'

'That sounds a bit ghoulish, old chum. We are talking a *fictional* crime, aren't we?'

''Fraid not. The Grafton Club had a very real murder last year, just before Christmas. Gangland stuff, robbery gone wrong, one of the club owners dispatched with a bullet to the back of the head.'

Campion shuddered in his seat.

'I thought the traditional method was to put a neat hole between the eyes with hardly any blood visible.'

'This is non-fiction, Albert, real-world stuff; it's as nasty and messy as it comes.'

'Then you'd better tell me all about it, because I have absolutely no idea what it could have to do with Evadne Childe.'

'This,' Oates brandished the book again, 'is not just a detective story, it's virtually a blueprint for the murder at the Grafton, which she calls Reynard's Club.'

Mr Campion seemed nonplussed. 'Good writers do their research thoroughly. And you know Evadne Childe often consulted with the police. Think back to the shooting practice we had in Bottle Street years ago; she was perfectly comfortable consulting with the police.'

'Fair point, but *The Bottle Party Murders* doesn't so much report the Grafton shooting as predict it, and very accurately. What niggles me is that she wrote the flamin' book *before* the murder happened. Now that means she's either psychic or there's something very fishy going on.'

'Was the killer caught?'

Oates shook his head and, as he did so, he turned the book to look at the illustration on the dust jacket.

'No arrests were ever made,' he said mournfully, 'but I can tell you one thing: it wasn't the cigarette girl who did it. She had a watertight alibi, sharing a very expensive bottle of fizzy cordial masquerading as champagne with a Yorkshire MP who should have known better. That's one thing Evadne Childe got wrong in the book.'

'Well, that proves she's not psychic,' said Campion lightly. 'Pity really, she could have saved you chaps a lot of time and trouble. I must try and remember not to spoil the ending for Amanda, but now you've got me interested, you'd better give me the full facts. Or do I have to read the book and sit an exam on it?'

It was not Mr Campion, but rather Amanda who was given the new Rex Troughton mystery to study that evening, once Rupert – who demanded to know if there would be another firework show that night – was tucked up, disappointed, in his temporary bed at the Bottle Street flat. It was homework which Amanda accepted with a squeal of delight. She made her husband pour her a weak whisky and water 'to aid concentration' and retired to the master bedroom, insisting that she not be disturbed as she began to turn the pages.

Once his son and wife were settled, Mr Campion armed himself with his reading material, a police file on the Grafton Club shooting of Monday 17 December 1945. He had got no further than page one of the initial incident report by the beat constable first to the scene, when he felt the presence of Lugg, who had approached Campion's winged armchair with incredible stealth, reading over his shoulder.

'Bit racy that, ain't it? Give yer nightmares, that sort of thing.'

'I forgot you were endowed with the power to read a police report upside down from a distance of several yards,' said Campion without looking up. 'But as you're here and palely loitering with nothing to do, you might be able to help. Do we have any beer on the premises?'

'There's half a crate of stout under the kitchen sink.'

'Of course there is. Fish out a couple of bottles and pour us both a glass, then pull up a chair and give me the benefit of your vast experience on matters criminous.'

'Having trouble with the long words, are we?' Lugg said over his shoulder as he organized glasses and a bottle opener.

'Do the words "shooting" and "Grafton Club" ring any bells, perchance?'

'Ding-dong, they certainly do,' said Lugg, pouring beer. 'It was the talk of Mayfair last Christmas.'

'I'm sure it was, but I wasn't in Mayfair moving in the exalted circles you do at the time.'

'Missed a treat, then, you did. Mind you, there weren't many that shed a tear over Tony Valetta getting his comeuppance like that, robbed and shot in one evening. Nobody saw that coming.'

'Apparently somebody did,' said Mr Campion.

FOUR
Dark Moon Over Soho

The police report might have been technically and legally more accurate, but Lugg's version of events was far more colourful, once Campion had worked out that when Lugg spoke of 'Epsom Salts' he was using rhyming slang for 'Malts',

itself a form of shorthand for 'Maltese', a nationality automatically associated by him with organized prostitution, gambling and
the operation of clubs in Mayfair and Soho.

The clubs in question, little more than drinking dens for people
who don't know their way around a decent pub, in Lugg's not-
so-humble opinion, were not of course to be confused with the
'gentlemen's clubs' of St James's, where the behaviour might
not be better but at least people knew their place. Often it was
only the width of Piccadilly which separated a traditionally exclu-
sive and, frankly, stuffy institution from its unruly and often
lawless twentieth-century incarnation.

The Grafton Club was a third-floor hideaway entered via an
unremarkable door between two perfectly ordinary mews garages
in Bruton Place, a thin canyon of a street always in shade thanks
to the height of the buildings, between Berkeley Square and New
Bond Street. Visitors would have to climb three flights of dingy
stairs until confronted by a far from unremarkable door, one
reinforced with metal sheets and bearing three deadlocks. A
sliding panel at eye level served to identify customers who would
then be admitted – few, except policemen, were ever turned away
– through a heavy blackout curtain hanging from a semi-circular
rail. Once the curtain was negotiated, the brightly lit reception
area – with smiling hat-check and cigarette girls in skimpy, shiny
satin uniforms – disorientated the unwary and, before their
eyesight had adjusted, they were ushered into a dimly lit bar
where the serious taking of pleasure could commence, their pre-
ordered refreshments – and much more – eagerly awaiting them
and available into the wee small hours, well beyond legal closing
time.

Clubs such as the Grafton were not born out of wartime, but
the war had certainly nourished them; according to police esti-
mates, up to three hundred 'bottle party' clubs were operating
in the West End alone.

How Tony Valetta had come to own the Grafton was not clear,
though Lugg's theory that he'd won it in a card game was as
plausible as any, and although it sounded suspiciously like a
character in a Peter Cheyney novel, Anthony Valetta was in fact
the victim's real name.

On the reputation of the deceased there was that rare alignment
of the stars when Lugg and the Metropolitan Police appeared to

be in total agreement. Tony Valetta had conformed alarmingly well to the popular stereotype of the Maltese businessman in a particular business in central London, in that he was a criminal, albeit one never convicted of anything other than minor breaches of the peace. Numerous police raids on and undercover operations in the Grafton Club had failed to find enough solid evidence for a court case of any substance, and although one raid had discovered two very senior naval officers in compromising positions with the club's 'hostesses', no further action was thought appropriate despite the fist fight which ensued.

Valetta's criminal record may have been suspiciously short, but it had at least justified a police mugshot, for which he had adopted a Chicago gangster's scowl to go with his heavy jowls, swarthy complexion and eyebrows shaved into diabolic acute-accent shapes. Peter Cheyney may not have come up with the name, but he would have used the word 'tough' every time Tony Valetta had entered a scene.

Mr Campion had been entrusted with the police file on two conditions: that he returned it to the desk sergeant downstairs at Bottle Street first thing Monday morning, and that he did not show the explicit crime-scene photographs to anyone of a nervous disposition. Campion was in no doubt that Lugg did not fall into that category.

'Tony'd put on a bit of weight since I last 'ad the pleasure,' said Lugg, looming over Campion's shoulder. 'Won't be puttin' on any more, will he?'

'Is that your considered medical opinion, Doctor? Have you considered a career as a police surgeon?'

'Only saying what I sees,' sulked Lugg. 'Don't expect any flowers at the funeral from me for the likes of Tony Valetta. He never shed a single tear for the people he done over, which were legion from what I hear.'

Campion held up the black-and-white photograph at arm's length to give Lugg a clearer view. 'Without the moralizing, if you don't mind, tell me what you think happened.'

Lugg, jaw jutted, lips pursed and eyes narrowed in concentration, advanced his globe of a head towards the print, which showed the body of an overweight man collapsed like a deflating barrage balloon in front of an open and mostly empty iron office safe. Whatever colour of carpet the corpse and the safe had rested on had been stained by a dark liquid pool. Within inches of the corpse's pudgy right hand, a large revolver lay as an island in the dark sea.

'Obvious, innit,' Lugg snorted. 'Tony had the safe open and was probably putting the night's takings away, it being three thirty in the morning by the face of that wall clock you've got your thumb over.'

'Why not three thirty in the afternoon?'

'If the Grafton was open at that time, business would only just have got going and there'd be nothing worth stashing in the safe. Anyway, there's a glass of something, probably American rye whiskey, knowing Tony, on the safe. He was said to be partial to a nightcap when he cashed up, though this time he cashed in, didn't 'e?'

'Could he have disturbed somebody cracking the safe?'

'Doubtful, that's a good safe; a Milners Patent Fire-Resisting model, maybe fifty years old but still solid. Supposed to be gunpowder proof, drill proof and unpickable. Key and drop handle locking. Milners of Liverpool made safes for the Duke of Wellington and the old War Office. They had five on board the *Titanic* and I'll bet they're still waterproof.'

'I'm sure that's a comfort to somebody,' said Campion, pulling the print closer to his spectacles, 'and I'm glad to find you haven't lost your skills as a Peterman.'

'Peterman?' Lugg was indignant. 'I've never blown a safe in my life. Noisy, dangerous business, blowing safes – and you knows why a Peterman is no good at arithmetic?'

'You're going to tell me, aren't you?'

''Cos he ain't got enough fingers left to count above six!'

'Very droll, and don't take this the wrong way, but I value your professional criminal opinion far more than your frustrated ambition to grace the music halls. So what do you think happened?'

'Like I said previous, Tony was putting away the night's takings. If he'd been running a card game or two, there might be a couple of thousand quid's worth, especially if the Grafton was playing Faro. That seems to be the current craze, as the punters think they've got a good chance of beating the house. But you know the old saying, don't yer?'

'The house always wins,' said Campion, 'which is why I stick to Happy Families. I always had a soft spot for Mr Bung the

Brewer and then there was Mr Carriage the Undertaker.' He waved the photograph to emphasize his point. 'And poor Mr Valetta here is certainly more work for Mr Carriage. Shot and robbed by persons unknown who disturbed him, or were waiting for him to open the safe?'

'Hard to tell, but it was somebody who knew his routine. Tony wouldn't have let that safe key out of his sight. He would have 'ad it on a chain round 'is neck or 'anging from his rosary. You'd have had to kill him to get it off him, but this looked easier. Wait until Tony opens it, then jump him. Only trouble was, Tony had a gun in there, so the uninvited guest shoots first, then cleans out the safe.'

'Not quite, there are still a few things in there.'

Lugg peered even closer.

'No cash I can see, just some papers, some clothing coupons and a book.'

'Now that's interesting. Let's see what Mr Valetta was reading. Do you have such a thing as a magnifying glass about your ample person?'

'Oi, cheek! Less of the ample, and no I don't. Who do you think I am, Sherlock Bleedin' Holmes? Look in the file, there'll be a list of property recovered somewhere, and if I know Mr Oates, it'll be in great detail as *he* don't miss much.'

Campion flipped the typed pages of the file.

'By Jove, you're right, Watson. Here we are. According to the staff of the club interviewed the next day, Mr Valetta was in the habit of keeping a one-thousand-pound cash float in the safe at all times and would have secured the previous week's takings in there, along with that night's receipts. Perhaps something around three thousand pounds, none of which was recovered. So, if it was a robbery, the thief got away with four thousand pounds, which is not a bad night's work.'

'If yer don't mind risking the hangman,' muttered Lugg.

'Quite, but tempting nevertheless, and Mr Valetta appreciated that as he was known to keep a gun in there. That's the one in the photograph. The police think he was kneeling to open the safe when he heard something or someone behind him and immediately pulled the gun, but was shot before he could pull the trigger.'

'Not quick enough on the draw,' said Lugg, 'or he come up against somebody quicker.'

'It is a sad fact, old fruit, that there are, thanks to the war, far

too many guns around and far too many people who know how
to use them. Now let's see what the thief left behind.'

'Apart from a dead Epsom Salt.'

Campion turned his head to give the fat man a withering
look, but Lugg did not flinch let alone wither, and Campion
returned to the police report.

'There were a couple of account books which probably record
the legitimate business of the club and are therefore of no
interest to anyone except the Revenue. Much more interesting,
at least to some of the popular Sunday newspapers, would have
been the bundle of IOUs held together with a bulldog clip.
They've been listed by the police and, my, they *are* interesting,
all for amounts of at least one hundred pounds and signed by
some rather well-known names.'

'Maybe Tony was collecting autographs.'

'Well, he seems to have acquired some valuable ones. There
are several society names on the list, an actor who is in the matinee
idol stakes, a French diplomat and two – no, three – Members of
Parliament.'

'Know 'em all, do yer?' Lugg asked but was ignored.

'And there was one other thing in Tony's safe, a book. Well,
would you credit it?'

'What? That Tony could read?'

'Oh, I'm sure he could read a summons, or a blackmail note,
but I never had him down as a lover of murder stories.'

'Too close to home for him?'

'You could say that, in the light of what happened, but this
book was obviously a cherished possession, hence he kept it in
his safe.'

'Is it valuable?'

'Not especially. Published last year, according to the file note.
It's a thriller called *Dark Moon Over Soho* and this particular
copy had an inscription "To Tony" from the author, that well-
known queen of crime, Evadne Childe.'

'What time did you come to bed, darling?

'It was after two o'clock. I'm afraid I got lost in a good book,'
said Amanda. 'You should have woken me. Rupert needs his
breakfast.'

'Don't worry about Rupert,' said Mr Campion, pouring tea

into his wife's proffered cup. 'Lugg was up with the lark, which was just as well as Rupert was up *before* the lark, demanding another parade and more fireworks. Lugg had him washed, dressed and breakfasted before I could raise a sleepy eyebrow. He's now taken him for a walk in search of a newspaper and some off-ration sweets.'

'I don't think we should encourage that,' said his wife in a tone which brooked little argument.

'Come, come, my dear, you know as well as I do that if Lugg gets his hands on an illicit Mars Bar or a tube of Rolos, Rupert would only get half at best. Lugg's sweet tooth may well get the better of him one day, but the lad has only known rationing and shortage, so let him enjoy a treat now and then. What about you? Can I get you some breakfast? There's a crust of bread which I could probably convert into toast without burning the flat down and, thanks to Lugg, we have plenty of bacon. No eggs, though, I'm afraid.'

'Tea will be fine,' said Amanda, sitting down opposite her husband at the small kitchen table. 'You can take us somewhere nice for lunch before we go back to the country.'

'Ah, now, about that,' Campion said hesitantly, 'we may have to stay in town another night.'

Amanda turned her heart-shaped face to one side to study her husband and opened her eyes wide. Campion recognized it as her *I'm making a polite enquiry, but I know something's going on* expression.

'Is it to do with the offer from the Colonial Office?' she asked delicately.

'Oh, the Caribbean thing,' said Campion, mildly surprised. 'No, it's not, though it was hardly a job offer, more a suggestion, and I'm not sure we should consider it seriously. I mean, you would be torn away from your career, Rupert would grow up without knowing what a decent smog looked like, and Lugg would spend his days like a stranded whale lying on a beach under a palm tree drinking rum.'

Amanda considered these options. 'Probably for the best if you turn it down,' she said at last. 'Lugg would only attract sand flies. He'd hate it, especially when the rum ran out.'

'They make quite a lot in the Caribbean,' observed Mr Campion.

'Not enough for Lugg. So what is to keep us in London?'
Even as she asked, her expression changed. 'It's about that book
you told me to read last night, isn't it?'

'Have you finished it?'

'Not quite, I'm about three-quarters of the way through, so
don't you dare tell me who did it.'

'Not having read it myself, I cannot, but I assumed from the
cover that the cigarette girl was a prime suspect,' Campion teased.

'Now that's what's called an apprentice error. In detective
stories, it's *never* the most obvious person, in this case, the cigarette girl at the Reynard Club, even though she had the means,
motive and opportunity.'

'I am sure your conclusion is perfectly sound, darling, and
you are a loss to Scotland Yard. Would you mind telling me
about it?'

'Telling you what?'

'The plot, the setting, those sort of things.'

'Why?'

'Humour me, please. Naturally I'm interested in the latest
creation of my godsibling.'

'Are you sure there really is such a thing as a godsibling? I
think you made that up and, anyway, why not read it
yourself?'

'You know I'm of a delicate constitution and reading such
racy material would no doubt give me heart palpitations and
cruelly fray my nerves. Besides, I value your opinion above all
others. I presume it has something to do with a murder at one
of those rather dubious clubs which host bottle parties.'

'Well, that's fairly obvious from the title, and I suppose it
might cause a rise in blood pressure among members of the club
you belong to.'

'Puffins? I should say so! Apart from *The Times* and *Wisden*'s,
reading is positively discouraged at the Junior Greys. Can't have
anything inflaming the members.'

'*The Bottle Party Murders* certainly would. Evadne Childe
doesn't pull her punches about the goings-on in these places.'

'Does she write from personal experience?' Campion asked
with a raised eyebrow.

'If you mean, does she go around murdering people, of course
not, but she is noted for her immaculate and detailed research.

She would have visited one or more of these shady clubs as background for her setting. The club in her book is called Reynard's, which is the fox in some medieval fable.'

'Reynard the Trickster, some called him. The stories come from the Low Countries I think,' said Campion. 'It's quite a well-known cycle of tales which have been plundered by many a writer down the centuries. Apart from Reynard the fox, there was Bruin the bear, Chanticleer the cockerel and Tybalt the cat, who pops up in Shakespeare, if memory serves. The Dutch Nazi Party made an atrocious anti-Semitic cartoon film of the fables back in '42. Horrible, quite horrible, but so bad hardly anyone saw it, thank goodness.'

'Stop showing off, Albert.'

'I'm sorry, darling, don't let me interrupt your flow.'

'So, Reynard's is a hotbed of vice, not only drinking out of licensing hours, but running card games and roulette for select customers – some of whom are socially very well-connected – and then there are the girls who encourage customers to buy them champagne, which is usually coloured soda water at two-and-six the glass. Sometimes the girls act as dance hostesses when there's music and the dancing often leads to other things, and more money changes hands. Needless to say, the customers are invariably men, though females are attracted to some of the card games – a certain type of female, that is. Most of the working girls in these places seem to be very young and Belgian, pretending to be French.'

'That's certainly accurate,' said Campion, who was immediately fixed by his wife's chilling stare.

'And you know that how?'

'The Public Morality Council, which has been combatting vice and indecency in London since 1899, according to its own publicity material, issued reports throughout the war saying exactly that. I do try to keep up with the PMC's reports as they make riveting reading, and my godmother, who is also godmother to Evadne Childe, sits on their board – or at least she used to and probably still thinks she does.'

'Hmmm.' Amanda left a pregnant pause before continuing. 'Well, you get the idea. The club generates a large amount of cash for the owner, an all-round sleazy character called Jake Muscat.'

'I make it a rule of life never to trust anyone called Jake,' said Campion. 'Would he, by any chance, be Maltese?'

'How did you know?'

'Shot in the dark, my dear. One hates to generalize, but the Maltese have got themselves a bit of a reputation when it comes to organizing crime in Soho. I take it your Reynard's Club is in Soho?'

'I think technically it's supposed to be in Mayfair, just off Grafton Street, but she keeps it pretty vague. After all, it's fiction. Reynard's doesn't have to exist, merely be convincingly enough described so that it might be a real place. I was certainly convinced.'

'So who gets murdered?'

'Jake Muscat, the club owner, of course. He's found – by the startled cigarette girl on the dust jacket – shot dead in the course of a robbery.'

'Really? How dramatic.'

'Oh, it was. Evadne doesn't hold back on the gruesome details like some do. Muscat takes a bullet to the back of the head and there's blood and bits everywhere. No wonder Sapphire screams the house down.'

'Sapphire?'

'The cigarette girl who finds the body. Do try and keep up.'

'Where does she find it?'

'In Muscat's office. He'd been putting the nightly takings away and had the office safe open when the thief appears to rob him.'

'Shoots him and then robs him?'

'That's what it looks like. There was a pistol in the safe. Muscat called it his insurance policy, but it didn't pay out that night. He must have heard the intruder and reached for it.'

'But wasn't quite quick enough on the draw,' said Campion quietly. 'How did the killer get into the office? I'm assuming this is late at night or early in the morning if the owner's cashing up.'

'I haven't got to that bit yet,' admitted Amanda, 'but I'm sure Evadne's got a credible explanation. She's very good that way, even with her red herrings. One thing would amuse you.'

'Only one?'

'Early on in the story, there's a minor character – a very minor character – wearing big round glasses and a fedora who turns up driving a left-hand-drive, olive-green Ford V8 coupé. Ring any bells?'

'Good heavens! That's the car I had at the start of the war. It was an American roadster donated to the War Office by a friendly official at the American Embassy, and we had few of those back then. Good little car; in fact, I drove it when I visited Evadne Childe at her home in Essex back in 1940.'

'And she remembered it, both you and the car. I told you she was good at her research.'

'Do you mind if I test that?'

'What do you mean?'

'Does she go into detail about the pistol in Jake Muscat's safe?'

'You don't think women know anything about guns, is that it?'

'I was merely interested in how much research she did on the subject.'

'I'll have to get the book.'

As Amanda disappeared into the bedroom, Campion hurried to the police file he had hidden under the cushion of his armchair, consulted it and replaced it, returning to the breakfast table just as his wife came back, flicking through the pages of *The Bottle Party Murders*.

'The gun in the safe was a Smith & Wesson .38 calibre revolver,' Amanda read aloud, 'sometimes referred to as the 200 British Service version because it could take the 200-grain British service round – whatever that is – as manufactured for us by the Americans in 1940.'

'That's very impressive,' said Mr Campion, while thinking: *And absolutely correct.*

The London office of J.P. Gilpin & Co, a converted four-storey mews house off Bedford Place, smelled as a traditional publisher's should – of old leather, beeswax polish and bookbinder's glue. Or perhaps, thought Mr Campion, that was just his imagination working overtime. The dominant colour scheme was of light oak brown, which extended to wallpaper, paint and carpets, and visitors to the firm were confronted – rather than greeted – by an impressive Victorian stand-up desk, at which one just knew that the chairman, or a designated relative, would ceremonially open the post each morning and afternoon. It was not beyond the bounds of fancy that a ceremonial sword or a bayonet last used at Corunna would be employed to slice open the larger envelopes or parcels of books, but as Albert and Amanda's arrival followed well in the wake of the morning postman, they were greeted by the slightly less daunting figure of a diminutive lady of a certain age bristling behind steel-rimmed spectacles and brandishing a notebook as a shield and a pencil sharpened to a lethal point as a sword.

'My name is Miss Prim,' she said in a rolling Scots accent.

'I'll bet it is,' said Mr Campion *sotto voce*, and received a swift wifely kick on the ankle for his impudence.

The Campions had walked from the Bottle Street flat via Oxford Street, having left Rupert once more in the care of his guardian angel (if angels came in the size and with the temperament of hungry brown bears), Lugg, who suggested that he distract the lad with a stroll down through Green Park. Now that the Victory Parade crowds had dispersed – '*Some* must 'ave 'omes to go to' – it would be a chance to show Rupert Buckingham Palace and some red-coated guardsmen behaving like proper soldiers. That way the youngster would not have to see the bomb damage which still scarred much of the West End.

Mr Campion agreed with the plan immediately, on condition that Lugg did not fill Rupert's head with seditious, and completely fanciful, notions that 'One day all this will be yours'. He knew full well that Lugg had an ulterior motive for avoiding the Bedford Square area: during the Blitz of 1941 he had, as part of a Heavy Rescue squad, been involved in clearing the site of the Jewish Girls' Club on Alfred Place, which had been destroyed in a bombing raid with considerable loss of life. It had been an experience the big man longed to forget.

Amanda, a wartime bride and mother, had been forcibly re-located out of London by her husband, but remembered the early air raids which had hit the length of Oxford Street from Marble Arch to Tottenham Court Road, damaging some landmark retail emporia. Selfridges, hit on several occasions, had lost its famous roof garden and Palm Court restaurant but, though disrupted, continued to trade throughout the war; she had read that its impressive internal lifts had been restored to working order the previous year. As she reminisced about peacetime afternoon teas and the delights of the famous Food Hall, her husband smiled but remained silent as he was still, by official decree, forbidden to tell even his wife of his regular dealings during the war with the Selfridge Annex, which had served as a hub for joint activities by British and American intelligence services.

Further along Oxford Street, the devastated John Lewis store remained a bomb site, its jagged remains reminding one journalist of 'the ruins of a Greek temple'. Even the lightest of breezes would result in a film of brick and concrete dust covering the street until rain washed it away as a grey slurry, but Amanda found the most heart-wrenching sight to be the children, mostly rough boys aged around nine or ten, who scoured the ruins and the gutters for 'dumpers' – discarded cigarette butts, which they collected in old tobacco tins. If questioned by a policeman – or indeed any adult – about this activity, they would respond pugnaciously that they were doing it for a father or an elder brother, but Campion knew a good proportion of them would already be hardened smokers, carrying boxes of matches containing wads of cotton wool so the matches did not rattle and give away their habit.

This was Mayfair, thought Amanda, and yet she was seeing scenes which Pathé News could have brought her fresh from a German city on which the Blitz had been repaid with interest, and the dust, dirt and cracked, uneven pavements would have played havoc with a pair of decent shoes. Bomb craters had been colonized by brambles, which at least offered the prospect of a blackberry harvest, a much-prized treat for a population of foragers. Suddenly the spoils of victory seemed rather thin.

But that was churlish, she chided herself. We are at peace, and life will return to normal. Her husband, her son and their closest friends had survived and, though Britain may be changing, it was still Britain, perhaps no longer the ruler of the high seas or even the great imperial powerhouse it had once been, but still British through and through. Which meant that normality would soon be restored.

And for her husband, Albert Campion, clambering over building rubble to get to a publisher's office to investigate the connection between a detective story written by a woman with whom he shared a godmother, and a real-life clubland murder; well, that was fairly normal, wasn't it?

Cheered by the thought, Amanda took command when her

husband was confronted by Miss Prim. She had never once
thought of Mr Campion as ox-like or at all bullish, but she knew
a red rag when she saw one.

'I am Lady Amanda Fitton,' she said with crystal clarity, 'and
I would like to speak to a person of consequence about one of
your recent novels, *The Bottle Party Murders*. I think you call
them editors. Is one available?'

FIVE

Editorial

Amanda may have been unsure of the operational hierarchy
of publishing, but Veronica Hatherall, being a devotee of
the society columns (one never knew who had a bestselling scandalous autobiography in them), was well aware of
Lady Amanda, one of the sisters of the Earl of Pontisbright, and,
like herself, an independently minded woman with a career rather
than just a husband.

Admittedly, Veronica's chosen path diverged somewhat from
Amanda's foray into aeronautical engineering, as it was not
uncommon to find women in key positions – though rarely on
the board – in publishing firms. For the general run of tasks
involved in producing a piece of fiction, the mothering and
cosseting of outrageously sensitive authors was seen as essential
and the female touch vital, as well as cost-effective. Female
employees were loyal, many of them clinging to the belief that
publishing was a respectable occupation, especially when their
mothers (with whom they lived) thought so too. They were obviously cheaper to run than men and their lunches with authors
rarely lasted more than three hours.

During the war years, Veronica had progressed from publisher's
representative (itself an advancement on her first position as copy
typist) to proof-reader, to copy editor to commissioning editor.
It was, she realized, perhaps as high as she could hope to rise
within the Gilpin empire, for all above her who were resplendent
with titles such as Publisher or Editorial Director (Fiction,

Non-Fiction and Educational), were, to a man, men. But her advantage – her trump card in the game of inter-office jockeying – was her long working relationship with Evadne Childe, an author whom the American office classed as 'a banker', and the London end of the firm referred to formally as 'a major asset' and, informally, in the safety of the cocktail bars of Bloomsbury, as their 'cash cow'.

Gilpin's bestselling author had insisted on dealing with Veronica Hatherall, and only Veronica Hatherall, throughout the war, her demand underscored by the threat that the alternative might be that Evadne would seek representation by a *literary agent*, who would take control of the translation, film and subsidiary rights to her work out of the hands of Gilpin's. Given that such a situation was the subject of the worst nightmares of the board members of J.P. Gilpin, Veronica's position, while probably static, was certainly secure.

By default of being female, one of Veronica's duties was to be the second line of the firm's defence should an unwanted visitor arrive without an appointment and somehow succeed in overrunning Gilpin's first line of defence, the steely Miss Prim. Almost invariably, such intruders into the inner sanctum were would-be authors, charmingly nervous young spinsters or boisterous, overconfident young men, demanding to know if the manuscript they had submitted several weeks before had been read yet, or indeed opened. Veronica had especially vivid memories, and the occasional nightmare, of a demure, sweetly spoken Froebel nanny, who had carried a brown paper parcel tied up with string into Gilpin's and, once she was seated in Veronica's shoebox of an office, claimed that it contained, 'Seventy-five thousand words of deathless prose, but *nobody* will publish it!' While this was hardly the most encouraging sales pitch, it was the nanny's subsequent behaviour which lingered in Veronica's mind, and in the mythology of the company.

Before Veronica could say anything either polite or sensible, the nanny had produced a cigarette lighter, set fire to the parcel and pushed the burning bundle across Veronica's desk, all the time emitting a continuous scream at such a pitch it threatened the glassware in the directors' dining room two floors above.

The fact that Veronica managed to extinguish the blaze on her desk without the need to call the fire brigade, and calm and then escort the hysterical nanny from the building without the aid of a policeman (or, heaven forfend, bothering one of the directors) – securing her in a taxi and even paying the fare, from her own purse, to a very respectable Knightsbridge address – only cemented her reputation as a safe pair of hands. More than one of Gilpin's directors remarked that he had expected nothing less as, after all, she could handle Evadne Childe, so a clearly disturbed nanny with literary aspirations should not have posed much of a problem, but the incident showed once more that publishing would be a much more pleasant business to be in if only it did not involve authors.

Veronica knew that Lady Amanda was unlikely to announce that she had seventy-five thousand words of deathless prose demanding to be appreciated by a wider audience, though, if she did, it might be a manuscript worth reading rather than igniting. Just to make sure, she sneaked a look into the entrance hall from around a corner in the staircase to assure herself that no brown paper parcels were in evidence, before descending, putting on her best smile and greeting the visitors, who were apparently rooted to the spot under the Gorgon stare of Miss Prim.

'Lady Amanda?' she said, offering a hand. 'My name is Veronica Hatherall. Please follow me. I do apologize for keeping you standing around.'

Her apology was accompanied by a chastening glare in the direction of Miss Prim. Lady Amanda did not seem to notice; Miss Prim did not seem to care.

'It's good of you to see us without an appointment,' said Amanda. 'This is my husband, by the way, but it's me who is the true fan.'

As Veronica led them up the stairs to her office, she flicked her eyes over the well-dressed man following Lady Amanda like a shadow. Initially she had concentrated only on Amanda, taking in and admiring her fashion sense, which was pure Katharine Hepburn: high-waisted grey flannel slacks with razor-sharp front creases, a checked shirt and a powder blue, very masculine blazer.

Veronica then turned her full attention to the tall, thin, bespectacled older man who hovered at Amanda's shoulder, but in a protective rather than threatening manner. So this was Albert Campion. She had heard of him, and often wondered why no one had ever written a book about him, although his hatred of public notoriety was as well known as his real identity was secret.

As they climbed the stairs, she spoke to Amanda, but constantly flicked her eyes over Campion. She knew he must be older than his wife, but not by how much, and what had she seen in this stick of a man in those ridiculously big round tortoiseshell spectacles which made him look like a bemused country parson in a second-rate amateur-dramatic production? And yet she knew, or had at least heard it said, that Albert Campion was nobody's fool, and a far wiser choice as a friend than an enemy. Had not Evadne Childe claimed that they were related in some obscure way? She had certainly mentioned his name.

'This is me,' said Veronica, indicating a door bearing the stencilled word Editorial. 'Do come in and please ignore the mess.'

The office, which had no windows, was just big enough to contain a desk piled high with unbound manuscripts and two plain chairs for visitors. There was one long shelf of books along the length of one wall at head height. Their spines invariably proclaimed the words 'Death' or 'Murder', and the majority, in various editions, were by Evadne Childe.

'You do not know the meaning of the word "mess" until you have a toddler tearing up the place,' said Amanda. 'Do you have children?'

'Between fifteen and twenty in a good year, but they're my authors. No actual children. It's Miss Hatherall, I'm not married.'

'I suppose with writers you have more than your fair share of infants "mewling and puking in the nurse's arms", as somebody once said. A writer probably,' offered Mr Campion.

'It was Shakespeare, as I'm sure you know full well,' Veronica smiled, 'and sadly, he is not one of my authors.'

'But Evadne Childe is,' said Amanda, not wanting Miss Hatherall to be distracted by her husband. 'At least I hope so, otherwise we may be wasting your time.'

'Oh, indeed she is. Evadne is at the top of my author list and, I like to think, a personal friend. Is she some relative of yours, Mr Campion?'

'They share a godmother,' Amanda answered, 'so the relationship is rather tenuous.'

'I would say spiritual,' said Mr Campion, 'but not close. I met her twice early on in the war. It would have been 1940.'

'And now you want to make contact again? I'm afraid I cannot reveal her address. That's the firm's policy. If we did she'd have flocks of readers mooching round her front door wanting her to sign copies of her books or even worse, offering their detective stories to her in the hope she could get them published.'

Mr Campion glanced slyly at his wife when he said, 'Yes, I'm sure fans can be an irritant, though I'm glad to hear they come in flocks rather than stampeding herds. Does Evadne still have that place out in Essex? She used to live in a village called Eight Ash near Colchester, under her married name of Walker-Pyne.'

'If you know that already, what is the purpose of your visit here?'

Amanda, as the better-qualified member of the Childe fan flock, re-established her authority.

'We wanted to talk to somebody about Miss Childe's plots,' she began, then swerved so smoothly that Mr Campion struggled to contain a gasp of admiration, 'but before we do, can I say how much that dress suits you. It's one of the Berketex models designed by Norman Hartnell, isn't it?'

Miss Hatherall, surprised, looked down her chin as if seeing the red, short-sleeved belted dress with shallow pleats for the first time.

'It's only Utility.'

'Needs must,' conceded Amanda, 'but you make it look good.'

Veronica acknowledged the compliment with a thin smile before returning it.

'I was admiring your slacks earlier. Very stylish, very Hollywood.'

'We all got used to wearing trousers in the war, didn't we? And I was always something of a tomboy as a child. But these are nothing special. A friend in America sent them over. Got them from catalogue called Sears or something for a few dollars. Of course, they haven't had the strict rationing we have.'

'I wore trousers quite enough during the war, thank you,' Veronica raised her eyebrows, 'and the directors of Gilpin's would certainly not approve of them as office wear.'

'Were you in the forces?'

'I was a proud member of the Women's Timber Corps, part of the Women's Land Army but without the awful early starts and the constant whiff of manure. We were sort of lumberjacks – lumberjills, I suppose – but they called us pole cats because much of our work was cutting down trees suitable for telegraph poles. Two years of fresh air and fun, mostly in the woodlands around Bury St Edmunds in Suffolk.' She paused to allow the Campions to make the connection. 'Which is how I know all about the Fittons of Pontisbright, as well as being close enough to Evadne to work with her on her books.'

The latter being something which had ensured her return, with advancement, to the Gilpin fold when hostilities – the international ones if not the internal publishing ones – had ceased.

'My wife's family is indeed well known in Suffolk,' said Mr Campion. 'Her ancestors went there in the 1920s, direct from the fifteenth century.'

'Please feel free to ignore my husband; it's about Evadne's recent books that we wanted to ask.'

'Ask where she gets her plots? *Everyone* wants to know that, Lady Amanda. If I could bottle her imagination and sell it to a rival publishing house, I would make a pretty penny.'

'That's the secret of her success? A vivid imagination?'

'Coupled with painstaking research. Evadne is very thorough. You will not find ridiculous methods of murder in her books, no exotic Amazonian poisons for her or alibis established to the second on a clock which then turns out to have run ten minutes fast since the Russian Revolution. She's particularly good at low-life as well. Her crimes rarely take place in country houses or vicarages or on luxury liners.'

'It's the low-life in her books we were interested in, particularly in her new book, *The Bottle Party Murders*.'

'You've read it?'

'And enjoyed it immensely, but I'm dying to know where she got the idea for the Reynard Club. The background is so convincing and yet—'

'How could a middle-aged widow, and a vicar's daughter at that, living out in wilds of Essex, get the atmosphere of a seedy Mayfair club down so pat? You are not the first to ask that, Lady Amanda. Several of the board directors here have, but as long as Evadne's sales continue to grow, they are not going to ask too persistently. May I ask, though, *why* you are asking?'

Amanda clasped her hands in her lap and leaned forward,

resisting the urge to make eye contact with her husband as she gave the answer they had rehearsed.

'I will be frank, Miss Hatherall. We have acquaintances – I will not call them friends – who have, shall we say, been involved in some dubious dealings in such clubs, or rather one specific one which bears an uncanny resemblance to the Reynard Club in Evadne's book.'

'You mean the Grafton Club.'

Miss Hatherall had not said it as a question, but the effect on both Campions was as if she had asked them to describe a spiral staircase in Mandarin Chinese and without using their hands.

'Why, yes,' said Amanda, recovering quickly.

'I told her she was so good at those scenes that someone was bound to recognize that the Reynard was actually the Grafton, but she just laughed and said none of her respectable readers would own up to it even if they did.'

'But she wasn't a member of the Grafton, was she? Surely not.'

'Technically, she was a temporary member, but you won't find her name on any list.' Veronica's face lit up in a huge smile. 'She used to sign in as Mrs Agatha Leigh Sayers.'

Amanda stifled a giggle. 'But she went to the club, actually visited it?'

'Oh yes, several times. Never alone, of course, she was always escorted. It was all quite proper, and she got on really well with the owner, who knew exactly why she was there and took her under his wing.'

'The owner?'

'A charming man, she said, even if a little bit villainous, if you know what I mean. Evadne got on really well with him, even signed her latest book for him; a chap called Tony Valetta.'

'*Dark Moon Over Soho*,' said Mr Campion.

'Why yes, it would have been that one, but how did you know?'

'It was found among Mr Valetta's possessions. The late Mr Valetta.'

'Oh goodness, how sad. I suppose you want to know how much it's worth.'

'Why would I want to know that?' Mr Campion was genuinely taken aback.

'We get asked it all the time. How much is a signed Evadne

Childe first edition worth? Well, I'm afraid in the case of *Dark Moon Over Soho*, my advice would be to look at the price on the dust jacket. The book was only published last year and the print run was substantial, so it hasn't had time to acquire rarity value.'

Campion decided it was time to rattle Miss Hatherall's professional cage.

'What about novelty value? If, say, the book was found in the possession of a murdered man, wouldn't that add to the value of a detective story?'

'Murder?'

'That is your business, isn't it?' said Campion, pointing a finger to the line of books standing to attention along the wall shelf.

'On the printed page; in fiction, and only in fiction,' said a flustered Miss Hatherall. 'Are you really saying that this man Valetta has been murdered?'

'I'm afraid so,' said Campion. 'Just before Christmas. It made all the London papers.'

'I see far too many fanciful stories and wild inaccuracies in the manuscripts I have to read to seek out more in the newspapers. Anyway, I never met the man, it was Evadne who knew him, so even if I did see a news item, it probably didn't connect with me.'

'Would Miss Childe know about his demise?' Amanda asked quietly.

'I have no idea; I shouldn't think so, though she does have some peculiar sources of information. She cuts herself off out in Essex when she's writing, and she certainly never mentioned it while we worked together on the new book.'

'That would be *The Bottle Party Murders*,' said Campion, 'the current bestseller.'

'That's right. We did the final copy-edit on it in December. I remember it being the last job I had to put to bed before the firm closed for the Christmas holidays. We shut up shop until the second of January,' she explained limply. 'It saves on the heating and lighting.'

'And nobody noticed the similarities in the new book?' Campion asked her.

'Similarities?' Veronica treated the word with suspicion, as in publishing it was a word which came with the same diabolic implications as 'plagiarism' or 'copyright infringement'.

'Tony Valetta ran a bottle party club called the Grafton, where Evadne Childe did her research, you say. He is murdered by an unknown gunman. In her new novel, the owner of the Reynard Club . . .' Campion looked to his wife for guidance.

'Jake Muscat.'

'Thank you. Jake Muscat is murdered in almost identical circumstances, while opening the safe in his office.'

'One may be real, but the other is pure fiction, and in Evadne's novel the murderer is not unknown. He's revealed by her detective Rex Troughton to be . . .'

'Please!' Amanda wailed, putting her hands over her ears, 'I haven't finished it yet!'

Veronica smiled at that, for it was the reaction every publisher sought from a reader.

'I am not suggesting for a moment,' Campion soldiered on, 'that the real live murderer of Tony Valetta is the fictional murderer of Jake Muscat. That would be highly suspicious, possibly supernatural, and would open a can of legal worms wiggly enough to keep the best minds of the Old Bailey, not to mention your company lawyers, squirming for years. I could foresee legal arguments on the scale of Jarndyce versus Jarndyce in *Bleak House*, with a similar Pyrrhic outcome. But there are worrying similarities between the real and the fictional crimes.'

'Authors often draw inspiration from real events,' Veronica offered.

'Certainly,' agreed Campion, 'but you have told us that Evadne Childe was unlikely to have read of the Valetta murder and, in any case, the timing cannot be right, can it? When did Evadne deliver her manuscript of *The Bottle Party Murders*?'

'I can tell you that exactly, because it was my birthday,' Veronica's face brightened at the memory, 'and it was the best present I could have had. It was the twenty-third of November, a Friday, which meant I could take it home for the weekend and be the first to read the latest Rex Troughton adventure. Evadne brought it up on the train and stayed in town overnight so we could go and see *The Wicked Lady*, which had just come out.'

'That must have been exciting,' said Amanda, 'being the first to see the book I mean, not the film.'

'So am I right in thinking that you had the manuscript into December and no one else saw it?' Campion asked.

'Basically that is correct. Evadne is a tried and trusted author and so there was no need to send it to an outside reader, and she and I worked together on the copy-editing up until Christmas. It was the first script we sent to the typesetters in the new year. The directors would have read the galley proofs in January, but up to that point, the only other person to have seen the manuscript would be my opposite number in the firm's New York office.'

'I think we may discount a trans-Atlantic connection as unlikely if not improbable,' said Campion, 'but just out of interest, when does the book come out in America?'

'Last week, actually. That's where Evadne is at the moment, on a promotional tour doing talks and signings.'

'So we can't get to see her?' Amanda made little attempt to keep the disappointment out of her voice.

'Not for another three weeks at least, though our New York office could get her to a telephone if it was important.'

'I don't think that will be necessary,' said Campion, 'but I would like to know how she got the idea for a seedy clubland murder in the first place.'

'Who knows where writers get their ideas from?' Veronica shrugged her Utility dress shoulders. 'Perhaps Peter showed her too much of the low-life and she saw the possibilities.'

'Peter?'

'Evadne's friend Peter. He was her guide when she researched her last book.'

'*Dark Moon Over Soho*,' volunteered Amanda, then turned to answer her husband's unasked question. 'It's about black marketeering in Soho. Rex Troughton uncovers a criminal gang while doodlebugs are landing all around. It's jolly exciting.'

'And this Peter showed Evadne around the fleshpots of Soho?'

'Well, she couldn't very well go there alone, could she?' Veronica was indignant in defence of her author. 'And anyway, she wasn't interested in what happened after dark, but the spivs and the hawkers who sold things from impromptu street markets or out of the cellars of bombed-out houses in broad daylight. Peter went along to show her the ropes and make sure she didn't get into trouble.'

'Or arrested,' said Campion. 'That would have been embarrassing.'

'Or very good publicity,' said Veronica, to whom the thought was clearly not new. 'The truth is I don't really know how or why she moved from Soho to Mayfair and the clubs, but it's not a big leap when you think about it. From what she told me, Peter seemed to know his way around the dark half of London and it's more than likely he took her to the Grafton Club. Evadne's imagination did the rest. Perhaps you should ask Sapphire.'

'Who is Sapphire?'

Amanda patted her husband's knee and treated Veronica to a weak smile asking forgiveness for her husband's ignorance.

'I've told you. She's the girl on the jacket of the book,' she said patiently, 'the cigarette girl from the Reynard Club, one of the main characters and very well drawn, very sympathetic.'

'Thank you,' said Veronica, 'I will pass that on to Evadne on her return. Have you ever thought about reviewing detective stories for the magazines?'

Mr Campion jumped in before the suggestion could take root.

'But this "Sapphire" is a fictional character, is she not?'

'Yes, of course, but based on a real person Evadne met at the Grafton, a cigarette girl there who goes by the wonderful name of Rags. That's a super name for such a character, but we had to change it and so we went for something just as exotic.'

'Perhaps we should have a word with Rags, but it might also be useful to talk to Evadne's right-hand man, Peter. Just who is Peter?'

'I only met him once or twice, and then briefly,' said Veronica, 'but from how she described their research trips, Evadne was clearly taken with him. "Smitten" might be going too far, but she was on the way there. I think she said he was French, and he came over here at the time of Dunkirk. She said her husband Edmund thought very highly of him.'

Mr Campion uncrossed his long legs and stretched himself upright.

'Miss Hatherall, you have been most helpful, and it was kind of you to put up with our inane questions. You have, single-handed, dispelled all my previous reservations about publishers which, admittedly, I have only held based on the colourful, not to say violent, opinions of unpublished or rejected authors.'

'Yes,' said Miss Hatherall wistfully, 'we do have to have rather thick skins.'

Albert and Amanda were no more than fifty paces from the Gilpin office before Amanda tugged on her husband's arm, then hugged it to her cheek.

'I thought that was a very interesting meeting.'

'You got some free books out of it.' Campion observed the trio of Evadne Childe titles tucked under her other arm.

'Which I will read and enjoy. They would be wasted on you.'

'Very possibly, but I agree, it was a very interesting meeting.'

'Because? Go on, you're itching to tell me.'

'Evadne's friend and mentor Peter.'

'What about him?'

'She said her husband, Edmund Walker-Pyne, held him in high regard, and that he'd come over to England at the time of Dunkirk.'

'So?'

'Edmund died more than six months before Dunkirk.'

SIX

Riches to Rags

'Believe it or not,' said Superintendent Oates, 'that's her real name. Rags Donovan. Story is that her father hopped it the day she was born, and her mother told her that meant it would be "a life clothed in rags for you my girl". Trouble was she made a habit of taking off her clothes, rags or not, rather than putting them on. She got collared twice during the war working as a fan dancer in one of the clubs. Second time she got fined five pounds, which was more money than she would have ever seen in one place at one time, and rumour has it that a high-born gentleman admirer paid it for her.'

'How wonderfully Victorian, Stanislaus! In the telling if not the substance – quite worthy of Dickens,' said Mr Campion, easing his stride to allow the older man to keep pace. 'The long and the short and possibly the tall of it being that Miss Donovan is known to the police, and not just as Sapphire in one of Evadne Childe's entertainments.'

'Known, but not being sought. At least, not today.'

The pair were strolling along Victoria Embankment, away from New Scotland Yard towards Charing Cross and the Hungerford Bridge. It was a dull evening, though there was still enough light for Campion's wandering eye to be caught by multicoloured slicks of petrol twinkling on the grey surface of a sluggish Thames as two tugs, *Hurricane* and *George Salt*, shimmered sedately downriver. Over the muddy tang of the water, Campion was sure he could still detect the perfume of spent fireworks.

Oates had suggested the walk in order to escape his office and a day of 'wall-to-wall meetings' and had looked forward to receiving Campion's report on his unofficial enquiries, which he was confident had been conducted discreetly.

'You interviewed Rags Donovan, I presume?' Campion asked.

'One of the investigating officers did. She was the last person to see Tony Valetta alive, apart from whoever shot him. Can't say she was ever seriously in the frame; not her sort of crime. She sounded to be the sort who might help herself to the petty cash or a few packets of fags from her tray, but she's an East End girl at heart. She had looks once, but the war bashed her about a bit, like it did to most things, but she's not blessed in the brain department. At least that's the impression from the files.'

'So you haven't spoken to her yourself?'

Oates heaved a sigh. 'I'm loathe to say a crime – any crime – is unworthy of my attention, Albert, but we had to spread our resources thin during the war.'

'And you have been called to higher things at the Yard, I understand. Such a position of responsibility means you have to direct operations from on high, Stanislaus, and forgo the satisfaction of being the thief-taker on the beat. Anyway, the war is over, or so I'm reliably informed. Indeed, I was at a parade this very weekend celebrating the fact, unless you are going to tell me it was all an elaborate hoax put on simply to confuse and befuddle me.'

'War's over, crime isn't,' said the older man. 'A war like the one we've come through meant there are a lot more laws to break. Things you took for granted in peacetime become valuable and, if it's got value, it's worth pinching, or trading, or forging like currency. Did you know that clothing coupons are now more valuable on the black market than petrol coupons or ration books?'

'Ah yes, rationing,' said Campion, 'a government-inspired perpetual Lent. Surely it cannot go on much longer.'

'Don't hold your breath. There's bread rationing coming in next month and we didn't get that desperate during the hostilities. That won't be popular.'

'You're not predicting bread riots, are you? Or a thriving black market in decent flour?'

Superintendent Oates dismissed the suggestion with a snort loud enough to echo under the arches of Hungerford Bridge, a feature of the structure much appreciated by buskers whenever they could perform in between the trains rattling and wheezing overhead.

'When did you last see any decent flour? I've almost got used to my bread and dripping coming with seeds and sweepings. The wife says it makes my teeth work for a living.'

Campion, who appreciated little of Oates's off-duty domestic life, despite the fact that he had known him for the better part of twenty years, refrained from comment and tried to lighten the mood of the policeman. 'Cheer up, old sport, at least we've got bananas now, and penicillin went on sale at the chemist's only last week.'

'I wouldn't say that was a rosy future. Penicillin might cure all the things men don't talk about now they're out of the army, and it might be available over the counter, but that means there'll be stocks of the stuff providing a tempting target for them that knows they can make a fortune out of selling it over in Germany or Austria.'

'Please tell me there's no black market in bananas.'

'Not yet.'

'Thank goodness; I do love a banana, and I try to leave the skins wherever Lugg is likely to step out so I can remind him that there's many a slip, though between and betwixt what exactly I was never quite sure.'

Oates shook his bowler-hatted head wearily. 'How did we end up with me and you doing cross-talk about bananas? I was trying to make a serious point about police manpower.'

'But I thought recruitment was up,' said Campion. 'Lots of

demobbed sergeant majors – or should that be sergeants major?
– lining up to swap khaki for blue.'

'We had a couple of thousand, right enough, but most of 'em
are still learning the ropes and not yet fit to direct traffic, let
alone put their hobnails on a murder scene.'

'What are you trying to say, Stanislaus? I get the distinct
feeling you're trying to put me off something.'

'I'm feeling guilty about putting you *on* to something,' growled
Oates. 'Shouldn't have wasted your time with the Tony Valetta
business and the Childe woman and her whodunits.'

Campion stopped in his tracks and faced Oates, then waited
for a train to clank its way over the bridge and into Charing
Cross before he spoke.

'Time spent reading, even a detective novel, is rarely wasted.
Amanda was thrilled at the prospect and I was happy to increase
my word power as well as being quite proud of my
godsibling.'

'Your what?'

'I told you I was increasing my vocabulary, though I may have
made that word up; but please don't feel you need to apologize.
I'm not charging you by the hour, or the mile. In fact, I'm not
charging you anything, which is probably just as well as I haven't
discovered much. I'm happy to sniff around a bit more. I quite
like being your gundog.'

'I'm not apologizing to you, Albert, I am saying sorry to
myself. As you know, I'm moving up at the Yard, and it has been
made abundantly clear to me that my time at the coalface is
going to be severely curtailed in future. I asked you to look into
this woman's book writing because I thought it would amuse
you and because we never made a collar on the Valetta murder.'

'And I've turned up nothing of value so far.'

'Neither did we and it's been on our books for more than six
months. Well, it will still remain as an open case – we don't
forget murder – but not for me, that's been made clear. I hate to
let a killer get away with it, even if it was a killer who was doing
society a favour by getting rid of scum like Valetta.'

'Sticks in the craw, doesn't it,' Campion agreed.

'Too right, but it's a question of priorities.' Oates clenched his
fists and his upper body went rigid. 'Priorities, dammit! All I'm
saying is don't waste any more time on this, Albert; get your

wife and your son back to the country and grow vegetables. Better still, plant a field of wheat if you can and make your own bread. I reckon there'll be a good black market for a decent loaf this time next year.'

'Thanks for the tip, old chap, but I think I'll waste a few more hours, just to satisfy my curiosity. I'm planning on seeing Rags Donovan, if she's on duty, at the Grafton Club tonight. After all, she did make the cover of Evadne Childe's latest bestseller, so she must be a celebrity.'

'You're not taking Lady Amanda with you?' asked Oates, clearly alarmed at the prospect.

'Good Lord, no; I will have Lugg at my side.'

'Then heaven help Miss Donovan.'

Lugg's stentorian roar split the night, frightening at least three cats and several nocturnal creatures best left unidentified, as it filled the narrow canyon formed by the four-storey buildings in the dank mews.

'Open Sesame!' he bellowed, as a fist the size of a Shire's hoof battered the solid wood door.

To Lugg's amazement, his magical intonation produced a result, as something did open on his command. Not the whole door, but a small portion of it in the form of a sliding panel at a height slightly above where a letter box might have been placed had the door, and the address it guarded, run to such luxuries.

'Yus?' came the challenge from the dark rectangle.

Campion leaned in to speak into the void. 'We are two gentlemen new in town, footloose and fancy-free. We have placed our order with Miss Donovan, who has promised us rest and recuperation to accompany our libations.'

Even as Lugg was mouthing the word 'libations' with a look of astonishment, the voice guarding the door spoke again.

'You'll be needing temporary membership then.'

''Ow d'you know we ain't members?' Lugg asked the open portal, showing it his most threatening aspect – his face – in extreme close-up.

'Think I'd forget a fizzog as distinctive as that?' asked the darkness. 'That'll be thirty bob.' The voice allowed his announcement of the tariff to sink in before adding: 'Each.'

Mr Campion's wallet was already out. 'Let us not argue with Charon. If we wish to cross the threshold, if not the Styx, we must pay the ferryman.'

Lugg expelled a long sigh through pursed lips and shook his head slowly in dismay as he watched Campion post three one-pound notes into the slot, but he did deign to raise an approving eyebrow when he heard the distinctive sound of a bolt being slid back and the door swung inwards.

If anything the darkness inside was more complete than outside in the mews, and it took a moment for Campion's senses to identify that he was standing inside a large thick blackout curtain, heavy with dust and ripe with the smell of tobacco, hanging from a curved rail. During the war it had provided a security cordon against air raids and air-raid wardens; now it was a useful prop to delay and disorientate unwanted visitors.

The curtain was drawn back by a small, gnarled hand, and the sudden burst of light from beyond showed that it belonged to a small, gnarled man. There was only one direction of travel, up the bare wooden staircase revealed before them, but the old gnarled hand helpfully pointed the way in case of doubt.

'Three flights up and you'll see the sign. Don't try any of the other doors on the way up. Gawd 'elp yer if yer does. And if yer passes anyone coming down, don't make idle chit-chat, just avert yer gaze and keep moving, our members appreciate a bit o' discretion. Is that crystal?'

'Message received and with the utmost clarity,' said Mr Campion, leading the way, but the diminutive doorman had a further instruction for Lugg, on whom his head barely reach a meaty elbow.

'You go careful on that first landing,' he advised as Lugg squeezed by. 'The floorboards there ain't what they were and won't take kindly to weight such as you're carrying.'

Breathing heavily, Lugg kept his peace until he had navigated that treacherous first-floor landing without causing structural collapse.

'Cheek!' he said over his shoulder, but the dwarfish guardian had disappeared behind the blackout curtain. 'Who do 'e think he is? Bet 'e was never more than a lance corporal, and a jumped-up one at that.'

'Oh, definitely ex-military,' Campion agreed, 'but I'm not sure

from which war. From the look of him, I suspect any battledress
he wore was bright red.'

'Yeah, well, you know what they say about really old soldiers.'

'That they fade away?'

'Nah, that they tend to smell.'

'Don't be coarse. Here we are. Best behaviour, if that's at all
possible.'

They had reached the third floor and the door, as promised,
which bore a small brass plaque engraved in copperplate script
worthy of a country solicitor's office, announcing the Grafton
Club. It was, Campion thought, the most valuable thing they had
seen since entering the building, which had the distinct odour of
damp and mouse droppings.

This door had no guardian and opened smoothly at the slightest
pressure from Mr Campion's fingertips, and the bright lights
which greeted him proved that the building ran to more than the
three light bulbs he had counted on the staircase.

What had once been a spacious two-bedroomed apartment had
been converted into the Grafton Club by the liberal use of plywood
panels painted in dark, muted colours shaded from red to violet,
to separate an entertainment area from a business area, although
from what Campion had heard of such establishments, 'business'
of all sorts was conducted in every nook and cranny. To Campion's
left a narrow corridor ended in a tall sash window where the
panes had been blacked out with paint, and he remembered from
the floor plan on the police file that the four doors in the corridor
led to male and female toilets, a kitchen (unused) which doubled
as a storeroom, and the office where the body of Tony Valetta
had been found. To Campion's right was the open floor of the
club proper, a bar running along the far wall, ceiling-to-floor
burgundy drapes masking the windows, which he guessed overlooked the mews, and – in the gap between the drapes – an
upright piano tinkled a mournful tune, a tall, thin black man
wearing a US army GI's blouson with sergeant's stripes hunched
over the keyboard. At the bar, a frizzy-haired redhead was pouring
from a bottle, presumably bought in advance, for two middle-
aged men in dark shiny suits sitting on bar stools. Three other
men, this group dressed in country tweeds, were squashed on to
a sagging sofa and were being attended to by two blondes in
short black froufrou dresses and dangerously high heels, holding

cigarette trays slung from their necks, but probably explaining that there was more on offer than a packet of ten Gold Flake.

'Not h'exactly an 'otbed of vice, is it?' hissed Lugg in Campion's ear.

'The night is yet young,' Campion whispered, 'in fact the evening is hardly middle-aged. I suspect things will liven up later when the roulette wheels and the dancing girls are wheeled out.'

'What time does the show start?'

'Long after your bedtime, old son. We're not here to enjoy ourselves. Now wait here and refuse anything that's offered to you. Back in a mo'.'

Campion strode towards the bar, removed his fedora with a flourish and presented himself to the redhead, who was dispensing semi-sparkling liquid from a bottle without a label. 'Excuse me, miss.'

'She's with us,' said one of the shiny suits without turning his head. He was, sensibly, concentrating on getting his money's worth of the drink he'd already paid for.

'I'm sure she is,' said Campion cheerfully, 'and I have no desire to distract the charming lady. I am merely seeking the whereabouts of Miss Donovan, should she be on the premises. Could madam possibly help me?'

'You talk real nice,' said the redhead with a smile and an accent more Midlands than Mayfair. 'Rags'll like that. She's in the office. First door round the corner before you get to the lavatories. Just knock and go in.'

'Thank you kindly, madam,' Campion said, bowing gracefully, much to the annoyance of the shiny suit she was pouring wine for.

''Ere, come on, doll, we're paying for your company as well as the fizz.'

'But clearly not enough,' said Campion as he turned away, noting the broad grin which lit up the redhead's face.

An immobile Lugg, standing blocking the doorway like the colossus of Rhodes, jerked his head towards the two girls bending over the three customers on the sofa, who were taking an inordinate amount of time choosing smoking materials.

'We here to see one of them?' said Lugg out of the corner of his mouth.

'No,' said Campion. 'I think Miss Donovan has been promoted.'

*   *   *

Whatever her position on the career ladder, Rags Donovan no longer had a dress sense to match her name; far from it. She wore a sharply cut two-piece grey suit with a fox-fur collar to the jacket, and her shoes and sheer stockings were of a quality beyond the means of a working cigarette girl. Her light brown hair was cut short and neat, her make-up perfectly applied, her lipstick bright red but not strikingly so, and as she sat perched on the edge of a desk regarding her visitors calmly with an air of cool curiosity, she could not have looked less like the 'Sapphire' depicted on the cover of *The Bottle Party Murders*.

'So youse is the new temporary members. Samson told me you wus on yer way up.'

'Samson?' Campion was confused by both the name and the mangled accent.

'Doorman. He piped you up.'

Miss Donovan pointed a well-manicured forefinger nail to an ancient voice pipe contraption, possibly of nautical heritage, nailed to the wall.

'Your man Samson,' said Lugg politely, 'was he by any chance a military man?'

'A chief petty officer Royal Navy, long retired. D'you know 'im?'

'Not personally, just the type.'

Campion's eye had strayed to the other item of interest behind the desk, a Milners fire-resistant iron safe, familiar from police photographs, but he returned his gaze to the young woman who was settling into the chair behind the desk and arranging a large diary in front of her. She removed the cap from a slim black pen.

'I 'as to make a note of your names, dearies, I'm afraid. The coppers insist on it these days.'

'Since the murder, I presume?' Campion asked gently, with a smile.

The woman looked up sharply. 'Matter of fact, yes, but they don't 'ave to be yer real monikers. The rozzers don't bother to check any more.'

'In that case, I am J. Mornington Dodd and my companion is Theophilus Shepstone Junior.'

With the air of someone who had heard far worse, Miss Donovan began writing in neat, flowing script.

'I say, is that one of those new Biro pens? Are they any good?'

Campion felt it was just the sort of question a Mornington Dodd would ask.

'A bit pricey,' said the woman, concentrating on her penmanship, 'but very useful and there's no need for ink bottles and blotting paper.'

She stabbed a final full stop and closed the diary with a snap, then replaced the cap on the Biro before looking up into Campion's eyes.

'So why're you here? You ain't regulars at this game, that's for sure.'

'Were our names a little too exotic?'

'Not really, we get our fair share of Neville Chamberlains and Clark Gables, but you told Samson down below that you'd ordered your refreshments in advance, as is required.' She ignored Lugg's snigger at the word refreshments. 'Yet I have no record of any order.'

Campion raised his hands in surrender. 'It is, to coin a phrase, a fair cop, Rags. May I call you Rags? It's such an unusual name it seems a shame not to use it.'

'Depends if you're here to waste my time or not. If you're here to cause me aggravation, I'll have you ejected toot-sweet.'

Her eyes, shining like emeralds, flashed towards Lugg and calculated his bulk.

'Oh, I know what you're thinking. Mr Samson down below would bounce off an outhouse wall like him, but Thaddeus could 'andle the both of youse with one hand tied behind 'is back, and there's a lot of stairs to fall down before you hit the street.'

'I take it Thaddeus is the American gentleman playing the piano in the bar. He's rather good and I would hate to disturb his performance.'

'He's not a deserter, if that's what you're thinking. He chose to stay here with his English wife rather than go home to where they don't allow such mixes.'

'I was thinking nothing of the sort, and I wish him and his wife the very best.'

Campion saw the girl relax slightly and felt that he had passed some form of test.

'You are correct in assuming we are not legitimate customers and we may well be wasting your time. If we do, it should not be without recompense.'

'Wot?' Rags's voice went up in pitch. 'You think you can hire me for an hour by buyin' a bottle of the club's champagne? You've got a nerve. I ain't in that game any more.'

'Please forgive me,' Campion said quickly, 'I meant no disrespect. Clearly you are now in a position of some responsibility and in exchange for a little information we may be able to offer you something in return.'

Miss Donovan screwed up her face, the cool professional businesswoman giving way to something coarser, more aggressive.

'You ain't police, are yer?'

'No, we are not, nor are we members of the press, so any information will remain confidential.'

'It'll be about Tony's murder, won't it? That's all anybody comes sniffing around here for.'

'Actually, it is.'

'Well *hactually*,' said Rags, impersonating Campion's diction, 'it always bloody is and I can't tell you anything I didn't tell the flatfoots six months ago.'

'We were rather more interested in what happened perhaps twelve months ago.'

Miss Donovan's facial hostility melted slowly, replaced by an expression of puzzlement behind which a brain was working overtime.

'*Twelve* months back? What are you suggesting? Oh, I get it,' she drawled, as anger flared to replace confusion. 'You think there was something going on between me an' Tony, don't yer? Well, let me tell you, Mister Whatever-your-name-is, there wasn't. Tony was a good Catholic, like what I am, and he 'ad a wife and kids back in Malta. That's who I'm looking after the club for, now he's gone. It's his widow's name on the lease, not mine. Tony trusted me with most of his paperwork as he wasn't strong on the reading and writing.'

'I am not suggesting anything inappropriate, Miss Donovan. As far as I am aware, and I believe the police share my opinion, Mr Valetta was killed during the course of a robbery by persons unknown.' As he spoke, Campion's eyes wandered automatically towards the floor safe. 'I am not aware you are a suspect.'

'I wasn't even on the premises.'

So, Campion mused, the cover of *The Bottle Party Murders* was even more misleading than he had first thought.

'I was on my way home,' she continued. 'I 'ave rooms round in Shepherd Market. Samson was doing the rounds locking up when he heard a shot. By the time he got up the stairs' – Lugg sniffed loudly at that – 'the killer had done a runner, down the corridor and out the window at the end. Used the drainpipe to shimmy down three flights to the mews.'

'Any ideas how he got in?'

'Must have been a customer, we were busy that night. The police reckon he hid in the Gents' toilets until we stopped serving about three o'clock and started chucking out.'

'So it must have been somebody who knew the workings of the club.'

'Doesn't take a genius to work that out.'

This time Miss Donovan's observation received a quiet chuckle of approval from Lugg.

'A regular club member, perhaps?'

'Who knows? We didn't keep a list of names back then and, like I said, it was a busy night. Anyways, that was then. You said you wanted to talk about stuff a year ago.'

'Quite so. I am interested in a visitor to the club at some point in 1945, I'm not exactly sure when – a woman called Evadne Childe.'

'The book writer? I remember her; nice lady. I called her Evie, but she didn't like that, I could tell. Bit stuck up, I thought, but at least she took an interest in what I did. I was one of the cigarette girls back then and the women who come here never notice us usually, only the men.'

'She didn't just wander in here, like we did, did she though?'

Rags Donovan chuckled at a remembered image and Campion thought the girl had a very attractive, gentle laugh when she allowed it to escape.

'A woman of her class? Not likely, and with the best will in the world, a woman of her age ain't lookin' for a job as an 'ostess. I mean, she must have been pushing seventy.'

Mentally, Campion revised his opinion of Rags's sense of humour.

'Being of the same generation, I was brought up never to question a lady's age, but I happen to know your estimate is wildly wrong. However, my point, which you seem to be confirming, is that she was introduced to the club by someone – a male escort, perhaps?'

Miss Donovan's brow creased in concentration.

'I suppose that would have been Pierre Le Frog; he came with her and he was mates with Tony.'

'Pierre . . . *Le Frog*?' asked Campion, cutting off an expected guffaw from Lugg.

'Tony called him that and he didn't seem to mind. Nice-looking lad he was. Gawd knows how he got to team up with the writer lady, but he'd shown her around the black-market scene in Soho. She called it research for one of her books. I remember that, b'cos she gave Tony a copy.'

'*Dark Moon Over Soho*,' said Campion. 'Tony kept it in the safe, didn't he?'

'Tony weren't much of a reader.' The girl's eyes sharpened. 'How did you know that?'

'I have a friend in the police who mentioned it.'

'I thought the police had given up on catching Tony's killer.'

'They never give up on murder, but I think it fair to say the trail has gone cool if not cold.'

'And you suspect the old lady writer?'

'Not suspect,' said Campion carefully, 'but I am concerned about her connection to the case.'

'What connection?'

'Have you read any of her novels?'

'My idea of a good book these days is *Teach Yourself Book-Keeping*, not one of Evie's whodunits, but I know a lot of people like them.'

'She is rather well known,' Campion agreed. 'A well-enough-known figure to be of interest to the newspapers if they smell a connection between her and this club.'

'What you trying to say? Come on, spit it out.'

'Evadne Childe's new novel, *The Bottle Party Murders*, features a murder in a club called Reynard's. A murder during a robbery, where the owner, Jake Muscat, is shot while opening the office safe – a safe just like that one.'

'I ain't never heard of any Jake Muscat, and there's no club called Reynard's.'

'I'm sure all that is true, but there are strange coincidences between story and fact. In the book, the body is found by a cigarette girl called Sapphire.'

'Nobody by that name worked here.'

'Think back, Miss Donovan. When Evadne Childe came here with her amphibian friend, you were working as a cigarette girl.' Rags nodded slowly. 'And by any chance were you a redhead back then?'

Rags Donovan pursed her lips, but the silence was broken by Lugg.

'Penny's starting to drop.'

'You mean I'm supposed to be this Sapphire?'

'There we go,' said Lugg with satisfaction.

'That is the inference the press will draw,' said Campion, 'though the illustration on the dust jacket doesn't do you justice.'

'I'm on the cover of a book?'

'They'll be queuing up for your autograph,' said Lugg helpfully. 'Good as being a film star.'

'I wouldn't worry too much,' said Campion at his most concerned. 'Most people take the dust jackets off and throw them away, especially rather gaudy ones like that. They don't want to be seen reading such a thing on the train or in front of the neighbours, but I think some of the gossip columnists will make hay when they realize that *The Bottle Party Murders* is based on a real murder case.'

'Could be very good for business,' added Lugg.

Miss Donovan clearly did not think so. Indeed, she seemed rather alarmed at the prospect.

'The last thing our clientele wants is to find themselves on the society pages. This is a discreet establishment. We do not court publicity.'

'That's where I may be able to help,' said Campion, reaching for his wallet, but producing a visiting card rather than currency. 'This is me. My name is Albert Campion and you can always reach me at that address and telephone number.'

Miss Donovan studied the square of white card carefully. 'Isn't this near the Bottle Street police station?'

'Reasonably adjacent, but independent in sovereignty,' Campion said primly.

'And you can keep me – the club – out of the papers?'

'I will do my best, that is a promise. I happen to know the publisher of the book and I am related to the author. Hopefully no one will make the connection . . . unless prompted, of course.'

'Why would you do that?'

'I said I would reimburse you for your time if you answered a few questions.'

'And have I done that?'

'Not quite. Could you be more specific on *when* Evadne Childe and Pierre Le Frog visited the club?'

'It must have been five or six months before the robbery in December, but it was definitely after VE Day, so I'd say late May.'

'And how many times did she visit?'

'Just the once that I saw.'

'What about Pierre Le Frog? I'm guessing that's not his real name.'

'That would be a good guess. Tony had dealings with him in Soho and always said he was in the Free French.'

'Was he a regular at the Grafton?'

'Not really. I'd never seen him before that time with the old woman and only once after that.'

'Which was when?'

'November time? I can't be sure.'

'Did you tell the police about him?'

'No, why should I? They never asked.'

'No, of course they wouldn't have. Look, Miss Donovan, unless you can think of anything useful about the mysterious Monsieur Le Frog, we'll leave you in peace.'

'You should ask the writer lady. She seemed rather taken with him.'

'Perhaps I will. Please hang on to my card, just in case you think of anything which might be useful.'

Rags Donovan shrugged her shoulders, her fox-fur collar rising and falling around her neck. 'Can't imagine how I could do anything useful.'

'You could lose the fake accent, love,' said Lugg at his menacing best, ''cos you're not fooling nobody. You're trying to come across as dead common, but I reckon you've got more education than you like to let on. Don't do yourself down, girl, you're better than that.'

The two men left the office without another word being said. From the bar they could hear Thaddeus at the piano playing 'Don't Fence Me In'. It seemed somehow appropriate.

* * *

As they made their way down the staircase, Mr Campion gave his companion a sideways glance.

'That was quite a sermon back there and, like the best sermons, blissfully short.'

'She was beginning to grate on me, putting on a fake act like that. Did you notice her clothes?'

'Hard to miss,' said Campion. 'Amanda would call her stylish.'

'Don't know about that, but I can spot quality when I see it. That girl's doing well for herself, or maybe she came into some money last December.'

'I would guess that some of the clothing coupons the late Mr Valetta kept in his safe might have gone missing, but if she made off with three or four thousand pounds, why would she still be hanging around six months on? No, I think Rags Donovan is genuinely trying to improve herself, but is wary of showing that to strangers, hence the rather pathetic attempts to sound like a costermonger's apprentice.'

'You feeling sorry for the poor little girlie?'

Campion paused one step below Lugg and turned to face his old friend, idly estimating that very little thicker than a sheet of paper would get past Lugg's bulk on that staircase.

'Can you really see Miss Donovan shooting her boss and then shinning down three floors of drainpipe?'

'Not in them shoes,' sniffed Lugg.

'Well then, let's give her the benefit of the doubt. She's trying to run a business – it might not be a very nice business – but she's running it for Tony Valetta's widow by the sound of things, and she's keeping it on the straight and narrow. Note the fact that she pulled us up on not buying a bottle in advance. She's trying to keep her nose clean.'

'Which is why she was keen to stay out of the papers, like you offered?'

'I suspect she didn't want a hungry newshound digging up her fan-dancer past as much as anything.'

The big man raised an eyebrow; slowly, as if it weighed a ton. 'Fan-dancer, eh? How did you spot that?'

'I should claim magical powers or X-ray eyes, but in fact Stanislaus Oates told me.'

Lugg's eyebrow collapsed in disappointment. 'And what are you going to tell Mr Oates?'

'Not much, I'm afraid. I'm tempted to mention the mysterious Monsieur Pierre Le Frog, or Peter as Evadne's publisher called him, although the only person who knows who he was seems to be Evadne herself. I can't ask her just at the moment and nobody else seems to have hide nor hair of him for eight months, so he may well be long gone.'

'Maybe with four thousand quid in his pocket.'

'You might have a point, old fruit. I will certainly ask my godsibling about him the minute she gets back from America.'

But other people had other plans for Mr Campion.

There was a car waiting on the corner of Bottle Street, a big black Railton Straight Eight, which sprang into fearsome life as its four headlamps flashed on then off, briefly blinding the approaching pair of pedestrians.

'Go on ahead,' said Campion, 'and tell Amanda I'll be along in a few minutes.'

'You expecting visitors?' asked Lugg, automatically clenching his fists.

'No,' said Campion wistfully, 'and I could have sworn the war was over.'

The rear passenger door clicked and swung open as Campion approached the car; the interior vanity light revealed a figure in full army uniform hunched in the far corner.

'Good evening, Brigadier, or may I call you Elsie now I no longer take the King's shilling?'

'I always thought you were overpaid,' said L.C. Corkran, who until recently had been Mr Campion's commanding officer in a department of the Foreign Office which did not advertise its services. 'Climb in, but don't get too comfortable, this won't take long.'

'Are we going for a moonlight drive? How romantic. Your driver, I am sure, can be trusted to be discreet.'

'*We* are not going anywhere, but you are. I telephoned your friend Oates at the Yard tonight, just to check up on you. He said you were footloose and fancy-free and not doing anything which couldn't wait. I, on the other hand, have a little job for you which can't wait. It's not dangerous and you might even find it interesting. Probably won't take more than a couple of weeks, three months at the most.'

'Three months? What will I be doing; trekking across the Sahara?'

'You'll be observing a trial, picking through evidence and chatting to some witnesses.'

'A trial? At the Old Bailey?'

'No. In Nuremberg.'

PART THREE
Yeo, 1952

SEVEN
Whistles in the Dark

'Darling, you've done it again!'

Veronica Hatherall could hardly contain her excitement and certainly could not control the bottle of champagne she had just opened with more of the foam splashing on to the table rather than into the glasses expecting it.

'And you're making a mess of Simpson's table linen,' Evadne Childe retorted but without any real anger. 'You should have let the waiter do that. Now the staff are giving us dirty looks.'

'Let them. Serves them right for making us sit upstairs, even though Gilpin's directors spend a fortune in here.'

'They have their rules,' said Evadne, mopping a damp patch on the tablecloth with her linen napkin.

Miss Hatherall may have bridled at the restaurant's ruling that at lunchtime ladies were directed to the upstairs dining room, with its more feminine pastel shades of decoration, rather than share the oak-panelled atmosphere of the ground-floor restaurant with the gentlemen, but she was not going to be denied the pleasure of launching a new Evadne Childe novel with a glass or two of champagne, charged, naturally, to her J.P. Gilpin expense account.

'And I simply *love* the title, *Camera Obscuring* – deliciously clever – and it's back in London for the setting after all those trips out to archaeological sites in the back of nowhere.'

'I should not have to remind you, my dear editor, that Rex Troughton is an archaeologist first, detective second, and so it is perfectly natural for him to visit fascinating sites of antiquity such as Pompeii, Rome, Nîmes, Tintagel and Colchester.'

'Hmm,' mused Veronica into her glass. 'I would not have called Colchester fascinating.'

'Which is why I threw more murders than usual into that one, but I thought Rex should visit London again; he'd been away too long.'

'As have you. Unless you're delivering a manuscript, we never see you at Gilpin's these days. Are you hiding out there in Essex? Isn't it lonely since your mother died?'

'I am perfectly happy and you keep me quite busy enough,' said Evadne, determined to remind this young woman that she was a valuable asset to her firm. 'You've had a book a year since 1945 out of me, and I think they have all sold well, plus there are paperback editions coming out and you have hinted of interest from a film company, though your hints have been rather vague.'

'It's a vague business to have to deal with.'

'Perhaps an agent might be better equipped to handle such vagaries,' said the bestselling author with relish.

'Oh, darling, you don't need an agent taking all that commission. Haven't Gilpin's looked after you well enough?'

'I will tell you at the end of this lunch when we get to the coffee and the inevitable point when you put on your trademark Little Girl Lost expression and ask me "What about the next one?" And don't look at me like that, Veronica, you are very predictable.'

The younger woman laughed nervously. 'It's an editor's job to keep a good writer's nose to the grindstone.'

'That's as may be, but it is also a writer's duty not to be ground away to dust. You do realize that it was twenty years ago this year that I wrote my first Rex Troughton adventure and I am now sixty-two years old. I think both he and I are due a change.'

Miss Hatherall's glass suddenly stopped in mid-air, well short of her mouth. 'Good God, Evadne, you're not going to kill him off, are you?'

'Of course not!' snapped Evadne. 'Who was it said that one should never kill off a good character because they are so difficult to create? Nor do I intend to marry him off. He was created as a very eligible bachelor and he remains one, totally unscathed by the ravages of time.'

'That's a relief, darling, you mustn't kill the golden goose. What you need is a holiday, that's all. You never take a holiday, do you? All those trips to places with old ruins are research for you, and that's work, not pleasure.'

'I pop across to the Continent quite often for short breaks.'

'Yes, I know, thanks to your postcards, but they always seem to be from the same place, Bruges, wasn't it? You should spread your wings, go for a cruise somewhere.'

'It was Brussels, not Bruges,' said Evadne, 'but I have been thinking of a long sea voyage, perhaps South Africa or India. See some of the Empire before it all disappears.'

'Excellent! And you'll certainly get a book out of it. Rex Troughton can solve some crimes even in places where there's no archaeology.'

Evadne Childe set her face in what she liked to call her cat visage. She had long observed the way cats could, with no physical change, simultaneously appear to be smiling or chastising, or simply exasperated at the stupidity of humans. They were wonderfully expressive animals that could win an argument with a raised eyebrow, even though they did not possess eyebrows.

'There is archaeology everywhere, Veronica, with the possible exception of Antarctica – and I have no intention of going there. I think I deserve some sunshine.'

'Of course you do, darling. Get away from the frightful London smog and find a tropical beach somewhere so you can lie in the sand and the surf. Agatha Christie went to South Africa and took up surf-boarding. Supposedly got quite good at it.'

Evadne picked up a menu and fitted the spectacles hanging from a gold chain around her neck.

'I've been accused of taking too much inspiration from Mrs Mallowan already,' she said, concentrating on the menu. 'There are those who think I got the idea for Rex because she went and married an archaeologist. And I do not have the slightest urge to take up surf-boarding, not at my age. Not at any age.'

'Well, you deserve a holiday; you could even go round the world,' said Veronica, resisting the urge to add that her star author could well afford it, 'and be back in time for the Coronation next year. Or sooner, if you'd like to do some publicity or book signings. We're looking at a November publication date both here and in America for *Camera Obscuring* to catch the Christmas present market.'

Miss Hatherall refreshed herself with a slurp of champagne as she also consulted a menu, but the wine acted as a nudge to her memory.

'Oh, I almost forgot. As next year will mark twenty years writing exclusively for the same publisher – something dear Agatha cannot claim – Gilpin's want to celebrate the event, certainly here in London but perhaps also in New York. The directors want a full publicity push, wining and dining the reviewers and especially the magazine editors, and there will be a banquet when they make their presentation.'

Evadne looked at Veronica over the tops of her spectacles, a trick she was sure a cat could do without the aid of the National Health glasses which everyone seemed to be wearing these days.

'Presentation of what?'

'There's the thing.' Veronica went into conspiratorial mode. 'I'm supposed to sound you out on that. One of the directors thinks that a gold trowel, or possibly a silver one depending on . . . er . . . availability, would be a suitable reward for twenty years' service as an archaeologist detective.'

Evadne considered this for a moment, then said decisively: 'I think that's awfully kind of Gilpin's. I, and Rex Troughton, would be happy to be so honoured and I am sure Edmund, and even my mother, will approve.'

That the Campions were in London in September when the letter arrived was fortuitous and mostly predicated on the need for Master Rupert Campion to be fitted out with a new school uniform. Their residency at the Bottle Street flat, even for a 'quick shopping trip' up from the country, would only be possible, Lady Amanda had decided, if *something was done* about the flat, which was uncomfortable, outdated and, frankly, embarrassing. Mr Campion, with over a decade of marital experience behind him, realized that here was an opportunity to strike a deal. He would have no objection at all to a complete modernization and redecoration of the flat, on condition that Amanda agreed to the purchase of a new family car.

The Campions had inherited a Daimler landau from Albert's

sister Val, a vehicle whose coachwork had been designed jointly by Val and Amanda in a fit of high spirits. The result had been more a tribute to *haute couture* than to anything to do with streamlined automotive engineering or passenger comfort. The two girls had called the rather stately result 'The Running Footman' while Lugg always referred to it as 'that flamin' hatbox' and had squirmed with embarrassment whenever he was called upon for chauffeuring duties.

Amanda agreed to the deal without admitting to the fact that the coachwork of The Running Footman was perhaps a joke wearing thin, and that even Rupert, entering his tenth year, was beginning to make disparaging remarks about how ridiculous the Daimler looked compared to the sleek vehicles he had admired in *The Eagle* and his *Champion Annual for Boys*.

To ensure that the menfolk did not have too much fun touring the car showrooms, Amanda had insisted they both take an active role in preparing the flat for its transformation and in supervising the plumbers, electricians and decorators she had hand-picked to carry out her very detailed instructions. Alternatively she offered them the option of accompanying Rupert around a variety of school outfitters in order to purchase an entire wardrobe from socks upwards and underpants outwards. They would also, she advised them, have to explain to Rupert why his favourite elasticated belt of green and red stripes with its metal snake clip did not conform to the strict definition of approved school uniform.

Consequently Mr Campion and 'Magers', as Amanda insisted on calling him, resigned themselves to wearing boiler suits, packing tea chests, taking down bookshelves, rolling up carpets for disposal to deserving homes and arranging for furniture to be taken into temporary storage. To make such a punishing schedule bearable, Lugg had insisted on regular tea breaks, claiming that, as he was closer to the working classes than Campion ever would be, their working conditions should show solidarity with the proletariat. Mr Campion had agreed with a sigh and the reminder, totally unacknowledged, that tea was still being rationed.

With a steaming porcelain pot holding a pint of brown liquid, Lugg settled himself on, appropriately enough, an empty upturned tea chest, and began to flick through the previous evening's newspaper.

'Here's one for you,' he said, as if discovering a life truth which had so far eluded him. 'It says here that Bile Beans are recommended to young ladies for "inner health and graceful charm" and will keep 'em youthful and attractive, then on the next page there's an advertisement which says: "When a bright lad looks dull, give him California Syrup of Figs." You tried any of them on Lady A. or Rupert?'

'I will not dignify that with an answer,' said Campion after lighting a cigarette. 'Amanda is, remains and always will be youthful and attractive, and Rupert is never dull. You should not be swayed by advertising.'

'Isn't that one of them fashionable Bachelor ciggies with the newfangled filter tip?' observed Lugg without looking up from his newspaper.

'I have not been seduced by fashion, I just prefer a milder taste and I am not afraid to try something new. Just remember that when your contract of employment comes up for renewal.'

'Wot contract?'

Mr Campion was relieved to hear the clatter of a letter box echoing through the empty flat which was now stripped down to wallpaper and light bulbs.

'That may be the new draft in the second post,' said the tall, thin man striding towards the narrow staircase which led down to the street door. 'I asked the United Nations to make this one watertight.'

When he returned he was holding a small ivory-coloured envelope and whistling a melody which hardly deserved the name. He stopped dead in the middle of what had been the living room but was now an empty shell save for Lugg, sitting like Rodin's *Thinker* on the upturned tea-chest.

'I have received a personal *billet-doux* from a female admirer, I deduce,' he announced, wafting the envelope.

'No kidding, Sherlock,' muttered Lugg from behind the sporting pages.

'And yet I have no desk, no quills nor ink to enable me to reply. Worse, if it is a declaration of undying love, my trusty *chaise longue,* or fainting couch as Amanda calls it, is somewhere near Stepney in the back of a removal van.'

'Oh, cut out the dramatics,' said Lugg, 'and open the flamin' thing. And don't whinge that you haven't got your posh Black

Dudley letter-opener either. Use your trigger finger like us common folk have to. I bet it's a final demand from the Revenue when all's said and done.'

'Handwritten on matching stationery? My God, but the tax man's getting clever,' said Campion, opening the envelope.

After a full two minutes, Lugg broke the silence. 'Well? Come on, cough it.'

'It's rather extraordinary,' said Campion, holding up a single sheet of notepaper. 'It must be five years since . . . no, more . . . but you'll remember this. Listen.'

And he began to read aloud.

> *Dear Mr Albert Campion,*
> *I know that is not your given name, but neither is J. Mornington Dodd, which is how you introduced yourself when we met in the Grafton Club. You had a bodyguard with you the size of a Sherman tank and were asking questions about the shooting of Tony Valetta, or rather the visit to the club of the Childe woman who writes all those books.*
>
> *I have nothing to report on her, other than to say I have tried a couple of her books and found them not to my taste. I have, however, recently seen the man she came to the club with, the one we called Pierre Le Frog. He is here, now, in London.*
>
> *You treated me decently and I kept your card. If you are still at Bottle Street and interested in the matter, then I am prepared to meet and tell you what I know. I have not included a return address because I have moved on, and hopefully upwards, in life and I no longer work at the Grafton.*
>
> *I will make a point of being in the Fitzroy Tavern in Charlotte Street, at 8 o'clock for the next three evenings, should you wish to meet.*
> *Yours sincerely,*
> *Rags Donovan*
> *(not my current name).*

'My goodness,' said Campion, 'Rags Donovan. Remember her?'

'Yus, I do,' said Lugg, 'a bright popsy who always did herself down quite deliberately. We saw her just before you disappeared

off to Germany in '46 on one of your top-secret missions. Three
months you were gone, and you've never let on what you were
up to.'

'I was reminded that once you sign the Official Secrets Act,
it is more binding than a wedding service and there is absolutely
no option of a divorce. All I will say in my defence is that what
I learned over in Nuremberg put almost everything else out of
my mind. I honestly forgot all about Rags Donovan and Tony
Valetta and Evadne Childe's rather prescient thrillers, though I
think Amanda still reads them. No one seemed really bothered
about who killed Valetta. I take it no one has been charged.'

'Not that I know of,' said Lugg. 'Most people thought it was
good riddance to bad rubbish.'

'So you don't think there's much point in meeting Miss
Donovan in the Fitzroy Tavern tonight then?'

'What time do they open?' asked Lugg, as if he didn't know.

During the renovation, though 're-creation' might have been more
accurate, of 17a Bottle Street, the Campions had taken a small
suite at the York Hotel on Berners Street, conveniently only a street
and a half away from the Fitzroy Tavern. This allowed Mr Campion
to take dinner with his family before his rendezvous, first with
Lugg, who had lodged himself with some distant, and unsuspecting,
relatives in Camden Town, and then later with Rags Donovan.

Before he could wash and change for dinner, he was regaled
with flattery by his wife, who claimed that the dusty brown boiler
suit he was wearing made him look like the strong and silent
type who was not afraid of hard physical labour. But then she
punctured the balloon by saying that they should really face facts
and admit that she would fill the boiler suit far more attractively,
which her husband could not deny.

Then he entered into an unsatisfactory debate with his son
Rupert who had, resourceful chap that he was, discovered that
the York Hotel possessed a television which was freely available
for the entertainment of residents. Campion argued that the word
'entertainment' was often misused, but if Rupert insisted, he
would allow him to join 'the babies and toddlers' watching *Andy
Pandy*, which he was sure was the only programme being broadcast that evening. To assuage the disappointment on his son's
face, Mr Campion indicated the Bakelite Bush radio, commonly

nicknamed 'the toaster', which had been supplied with the suite, and urged Rupert to find the Light programme as there was a jolly fine *Book at Bedtime* on at the moment, C.S. Forester's *Brown on Resolution*, which was a terrific ripping yarn. Amanda told her husband not to put ideas into their son's head, as there was no possible chance of him being allowed to stay up until eleven o'clock. That was, she said emphatically, way past bedtime.

'He knows that,' said Mr Campion.

'I was talking to you,' said his wife.

Bathed, changed, and replete with a family dinner in the hotel restaurant, Campion assured his wife that he would not be late and, to pique her interest, that the purpose of his evening's excursion was to do with her favourite author.

Amanda could not miss the opportunity to brief Campion on recent episodes in the exciting life of Rex Troughton in such titles as *Burial Mound* ('murder on an archaeological dig near Colchester'), *The Moving Mosaic* ('how to steal twenty square feet of mosaic flooring from a Roman villa near Dorchester') and *The Robbers Are Coming to Town* ('grave robbers, that is, from a royal Anglo-Saxon site in Suffolk').

'My goodness,' Mr Campion had said, 'who knew archaeology could be so exciting?'

'Is it about her new book? There's a new one due in November,' Amanda had said with anticipation.

'No, I think it might be about an old book, the one about the bottle parties in a seedy club. We visited the publisher, remember?'

'That was ages ago; did anything ever come of it?'

'Not that I'm aware of. Perhaps nothing will tonight, but I feel I ought to investigate as somebody has come forward who may have some information.'

'Is it . . . *dubious*?' She chose the word carefully as Rupert was still at the table.

'Not at all, I'm sure it will be far safer than archaeology and I'll have Lugg with me.'

'With Lugg, out on the town for an evening in a public house? Sounds dubious to me.'

Fortunately for Mr Campion, he had not revealed that more than one public house was involved in his evening out 'on the town', as Lugg was waiting for him, a pint glass in each fist, in the Blue Posts, directly across the road from the York Hotel.

'Got 'ouse leave, 'ave yer?' he said with a grin, handing
Campion a glass.

'Of course, and a late pass as long as we're on best behaviour,
and by "we" I mean you.'

'Don't blame me if you get the wrong side of Lady A.'

'Why not? I usually do.'

They drank half their beer in silence, observing the evening
crowd which filtered in and then out of the pub, and then Lugg
asked the question that had been hovering somewhere at the back
of Campion's mind, just out of reach, just out of sight.

'You reckon this bird is on the level? Is she trying to shake
us down?'

Mr Campion assumed what he liked to call his 'Injured Aunt'
expression.

'Have you been reading Hank Janson? You'll be called her a
"frail" or a "skirt" next. As I recall, Miss Donovan was an intelligent young woman seeking to improve her station in life. You
took exception to her because she was deliberately punching
below her weight, putting on the common so we would naturally
underestimate her.'

'That stuck in my craw, I'll admit,' said Lugg, draining his
glass. 'If yer common and there's nothing you can do about it,
yer stays common. If yer bettering yerself, then you behaves
proper. She 'ad the brains, and the clothes, and the looks, and
all mod cons like that Biro she used. That was the first one I'd
ever seen. Thort I might put it on my Christmas List 'til I saw
how much they were. Fifty-five shillings! Strewth, that was nearly
seven gallons of bitter back then.'

Mr Campion's empty glass joined Lugg's on the bar counter.
'On such matters, I trust your grasp of liquid arithmetic implicitly;
now let's wander round to the Fitzroy and see what Rags has to
tell us.'

As they strolled along an Oxford Street that was rapidly
emptying for the night, Lugg assumed the role of the tourist
guide one normally found oneself with in Rome, especially near
the Vatican, whether one needed or wanted one.

'The Fitzroy was a coffee house to start with, then was turned
into a pub called the Hundred Marks because it was run by
German immigrants. One of the famous landlords was Judah
Kleinfeld, but everyone called him "Pop". Smashing fellow, and

though he couldn't read a word of English, he encouraged all the arty types as regulars. Augustus John was one, Dylan Thomas was another.'

'And Malcolm Lowry,' added Campion.

'Who?'

'Young chap who liked his beer. Wrote his first novel when he was up at Cambridge. Was a regular before the war and great things were expected of him, but I think he's decamped to America. Still, we must be at our sharpest in there as we could be rubbing shoulders with the literary elite. Let's keep the conversation on a high intellectual level so we fit in with the clientele. No arguing about the price of pickled herrings or the Arsenal's chances this year.'

'Gonna be a quiet night, then,' muttered Lugg.

And it was; at least to begin with.

While Lugg murmured about the quality of the beer, Campion quietly scanned the bar looking to identify the next genius likely to emerge from the Bohemian hotbed that was the Fitzrovia area.

Eight o'clock came and went, with Lugg still muttering and Campion no nearer to spotting the next big thing when it came to literary or artistic achievement. The Fitzroy had filled quickly with bodies, overloud conversation and acrid smoke from cigarettes and pipe smoke, which Campion was sure he could actually see staining the Anaglypta ceiling paper the colour of pale toast. There was an upright piano against one wall, but blissfully without a pianist, not that one might have been heard above the background swell of a hundred conversations and shouted greetings, the clatter of bottles and glasses, and the scraping of chairs and tables as the raucous clientele jostled for elbow room. As always, there was one voice of a particular timbre which could be heard across the bar above the hubbub whatever the volume and, as always, that voice was speaking rubbish. It never failed to fascinate Campion how a London pub, or at least one in the West End or the City, would quickly fill to capacity early in the evening and then go quiet, as if in the eye of a storm, for perhaps an hour until it refilled, often with even louder customers, for a final, legal, hour of revelry.

It was after nine and the Fitzroy was enjoying that breath of calm before the final storm of the evening when Campion decided to call it a night.

'I think we've been stood up, old chum; it doesn't look as if she's coming,' he said as Lugg placed two more pints of beer on the wobbly table they had commandeered, 'so let's make these our last orders.'

'Is it worth popping round the Grafton, just for a snoop?' Lugg suggested and then, more in hope than expectation, 'And a nightcap, mebbe?'

'These days, a nightcap is something I wear when the nights start drawing in, and I honestly don't see much point in trooping round the Grafton. Our Miss Donovan has moved on from such seedy premises, or so she said in her letter.'

'You believe her as far as I could throw her?'

'I am much more trusting in human nature than you are, you old grump. I have no reason not to believe Rags Donovan, or whatever she calls herself now.'

'The Duchess of Shepherd Market probably.'

'Well good luck to her, that's all I can say.'

Campion reached for his glass and Lugg, like a distorted funfair mirror reflection, matched him. Their drinks were halfway to their lips when, from outside in the street, the shrill sound of a whistle blowing short sharp blasts reduced the pub to silence.

'That's a police whistle,' said Campion.

'They're playing our tune,' said Lugg.

EIGHT
Loose Ends

A small crowd of what Lugg called 'gawkers' had gathered in front of a shop doorway on the other side of Charlotte Street, closely observing in shocked silence two uniformed police constables armed with torches and whistles. The policemen were gathered around the folded body of a woman lying in the gutter and were far from silent, issuing orders seemingly at random to call for an ambulance, stay back, give us some room, and all the time trying to assure the gawkers that there was nothing to see here and they might as well move along.

Campion had assessed the situation from the doorway of the Fitzroy and whispered instructions to Lugg. When Lugg had retreated back into the pub, Campion strode across Charlotte Street towards the policemen and the body, noting with a catch in his breath that one of the woman's shoes was lying in the gutter a yard from a stockinged foot. A brief sweep of one of the policeman's torches showed a length of stockinged leg protruding from a ridden-up skirt, the upturned palm of a hand sleeved in a pale blue suit jacket and finally a face, half turned away, resting on the pavement next to a leather handbag.

'My name is Campion,' he told the constables, 'and I know this lady. I was due to meet her in the Fitzroy earlier this evening. My friend has asked the pub to telephone for an ambulance. I am more than happy to make a statement.'

One of the policemen took his standard-issue whistle from his lips, clearly deciding that a shrill blast a few inches from the face of a potentially helpful witness was probably not best police procedure.

'That'll be for the CID, sir,' he said politely. 'They'll be here soon, so if you don't mind waiting down the pavement a bit, I'm sure the superintendent will be grateful for a chat.'

'Do you know which superintendent that would be?' Campion asked equally politely, but the constable bristled.

'It's Detective Superintendent Yeo who's on duty tonight, if that's of any interest to you.'

'Yeo? Good fellow, solid chap. Still in Office 49 down at headquarters, is he?'

The constable looked into Campion's unblinking eyes, pushed his face to within an inch or two of that blank, bespectacled expression and brought the whistle to his lips again; but then thought the better of it.

Detective Superintendent Yeo had been the Senior Investigating Officer on the 'Jack Havoc' case the year before, although the younger and supremely energetic Divisional Detective Inspector Charles Luke had done what Lugg liked to call 'most of the heavy lifting'. Yeo was a square, bullet-headed figure with a snub nose and round, brown eyes. A man of infinite patience, what he lacked in flair he more than made up for in efficiency. The most remarkable thing about him was that few people

knew his Christian name; in fact some believed he did not
possess one. Within the police force, he was naturally addressed
only by his rank, or simply as Yeo by officers of equivalent
or superior status. A few – a very few – who were closest to
him, and that included his wife, referred to him as 'Freddie',
though as it was clearly ludicrous to have a senior policeman
known only by a surname given the amount of paperwork
involved in fighting crime, he did, when required, sign himself
as 'P. Yeo' on official documents. Campion was one of only
a handful of people outside the Home Office who knew that
Yeo's baptismal name was Pellinore, but he was happy to have
been sworn to secrecy and had taken great pleasure in
convincing Lugg that his name was Frederick, but spelled the
Greek way with a 'Ph'.

'Thanks for dropping by, Albert,' Yeo greeted him the next
morning as Campion reported to the fabled Room 49.

'A pleasure as always. Anything I can do to help, Freddie?'

'You can stop misleading the Metropolitan Police for a start,'
said Yeo, sniffing loudly. He looked exhausted and Campion
realized the man could not have had much sleep.

'Misleading you? How? I am shocked you should think that;
nay, aggrieved and possibly cut to the quick, though I was never
sure where my quick was.'

'I'll put it down to overexcitement in the heat of the moment.'
Yeo granted Campion a thin smile. 'I suppose you were only
trying to help when you identified our lady corpse on Charlotte
Street last night as Rags Donovan.'

'But it was,' said Campion. 'I saw her face quite clearly, plus
the fact that I was expecting her. She had asked to meet me in the
Fitzroy earlier. That was my story last night and I'm sticking to
it. Where have I gone wrong?'

'Probably you meant well. You usually do, but my lads were
a bit confused when they opened her handbag and found docu-
mentary proof that she was now Mrs Rachel Daubney.'

'Well, I admit she had hinted that she didn't go by Rags
Donovan any more,' Campion admitted. 'Had she held on to her
old ID card?'

'No, she'd got herself a driving licence last year and it gave
us her address out in Mortlake. We sent a car round there first
thing to confirm it and we had to break the news to a husband

who was climbing the walls, wondering why she hadn't come home.'

'The husband is in the clear?'

'Almost certainly. Sounds like a decent enough chap, a book-keeper and accountant with the brewery down there; steady job, nice little terraced house. Bit older than her, but grateful, I reckon. Doesn't sound the murdering type, leastways not that way.'

'What way?'

'Strangled with a length of clothes line from behind, the doctor says.'

'Clothes line? They haven't hung out the washing in Charlotte Street since the war.'

'Funny you should say that, because the doc said he'd seen the same technique during the war when he was in the RAMC. Commandos used to carry a yard of line which they'd wrap around each hand then flip the loop over the head of a sentry or similar. Knee in the back, pull, cross the line, and Bob's your uncle – or, in this case, aunt. I suppose you'd call that garrotting.'

'I'd rather not.' Campion sighed. 'The poor girl. I don't suppose there's anything in the fact that Rags Donovan and Rachel Daubney have the same initials, is there?'

Yeo shook his head. 'Coincidence, that's all. My lads checked the marriage certificate. She was Miss Donovan before she became Mrs Daubney, and if she wanted to be called Rachel rather than Rags, then that's her business. It sounds more digni-fied in a church service and it saves on any engraving she already had, if you want to be practical about such things.'

'Oh, I think she was a very practical young lady,' said Campion, 'and not the sort who would knowingly put herself in danger.'

'What are you saying?'

'She sent me a message asking to meet. She had spotted a man I was interested in, or rather I was curious about six years ago in connection with the murder of a chap called Tony Valetta.'

'The Grafton Club robbery?'

Campion raised an appreciative eyebrow. 'You remember the case?'

'Unsolved murders are never forgotten, Albert, but sometimes they fade to the back of the mind. What's the connection between the late and unlamented Tony Valetta and the tragic Mrs Daubney?'

'May I?' Campion indicated the straight-backed chair on the visitor's side of Yeo's desk; when he received the nodded permission, he sat down and exhaled long and hard before he began.

'The connection between them is one of our most popular writers of detective stories, Evadne Childe, who just happens to have a part share with me in a godmother. I know, I know, that's a bit of a tenuous link, but I felt a twinge of responsibility when I heard of her involvement in the Grafton case and now I have deep regrets that I did not take things more seriously back in '46.'

'Mmmm,' Yeo murmured thoughtfully. 'You're not the only one with regrets about the Valetta murder. No arrests, nobody charged, too many loose ends and we don't like loose ends. Stanislaus Oates told me about this writer woman, how she'd described a similar killing in one of her books before the real murder happened, but it must just have been coincidence. I mean, it's not like she gave somebody a blueprint for robbing the Grafton, is it?'

'Not in the book, no,' said Campion. 'By the time that was in the bookshops and libraries, Tony Valetta had been robbed, shot and buried; only Evadne's editor or somebody at the publishing house or a typesetter or a printer reading her plot when the book was in manuscript form, might have been tempted to try it out for real. I know publishers have a rotten reputation, at least among writers, but I can't really see them resorting to robbery-with-violence.'

'So where does the late Mrs Daubney come into all this?'

'Rags, I knew her as Rags and can't think of her in any other context, worked for Valetta, and she was in the Grafton when Evadne Childe visited doing research for her book. Rags is actually in the book, as a cigarette girl called Sapphire, though she wasn't aware of that. Evadne went to the club with a man nicknamed Pierre Le Frog, who sounds to have known his way around Soho, but no one seems to know anything about him.'

'Presumably,' said the slow-but-sure Yeo, 'the writer lady did.'

'Yes, of course, she must have,' Campion averted his eyes, 'and I know I should have followed that up and gone and asked her outright, but I was distracted by other things.'

'You were in Germany – at the trials.'

'I was; but unofficially, and you are remarkably well informed, Freddie.'

'We try our best, Albert, we try. So Rags contacts you out of the blue six years on. Is that the way of it?'

'That's exactly it. When I met her I gave her my card and she must have kept it.'

'She did. We found it in her purse, so we would have been in touch sooner or later if you hadn't actually been on the spot, so to speak.'

'She wrote to me, asking for a meeting. I have the letter here.' Campion reached into his inside jacket pocket. 'You might as well have it as it might be of interest to the coroner. It seems she had seen the mysterious Monsieur Pierre Le Frog recently in London and was willing to tell me about him if I was still interested.'

Yeo shrugged his sharp, thin shoulders. 'Unfortunately,' he began slowly, 'he saw her first.'

Mr Campion appeared to defer to Detective Superintendent Yeo's assurance that he was in no way to blame for the death of Rags Donovan, and listened politely to his pep-talk, which insisted that the nebulous Le Frog was now the subject of a major police manhunt that would surely bring him to justice without, he emphasized, the need for Campion to be involved.

Mr Campion had never considered himself to be an actor of any competence, not even at the most basic village hall 'am-dram' level, for his range, he told himself, was limited by his natural honesty and sincerity. He realized, however, that acting was mostly *re-acting* and so he reacted to Yeo's entreaties, he hoped, honestly and sincerely.

Within ten strides of leaving CID headquarters, he was planning his campaign and, after confirming that he was carrying his chequebook, he hailed a taxi and put it into action.

'You go out on the tiles with Magers and get involved in a murder,' Amanda began as if summing up for the prosecution, 'then you do your civic duty and go to help the police with their enquiries and waltz back in here to casually announce you've bought a Bentley.'

'Without consulting your mechanical expert,' Lugg interjected.

'Is that another name for a plumber?' asked an innocent Rupert. 'Them that never turn up when they's supposed to,' he added in an ominously good impersonation of Mr Lugg.

Campion reached out and ruffled his son's curls. 'Promise me you will never use that voice at school, Rupert, except perhaps during Maths lessons. I found that the more unintelligible you are there, the more they think you are a genius.'

'What does "unintelligible" mean?' the boy asked sharply.

'It's Latin for Uncle Lugg, who is rightly miffed that I didn't take him with me to play in the car showrooms, but needs must. I have to drive out to Essex, and we needed a new car anyway.'

'You could have taken the 'atbox,' said Lugg with a malicious grin. 'She still goes, after a fashion.'

'I won't have a word said against The Running Footman,' said Amanda, turning on the fat man. 'He was designed and built with love and imagination.'

'Aye, 'e was,' muttered Lugg, 'with coachwork by Dr Frankenstein. Did you get much for 'im in part-exchange?'

Campion looked convincingly horrified. Perhaps he wasn't such a bad actor, after all.

'Perish the thought that I would part with the Daimler after all the work the girls put into its . . . upholstery. We will get it back home and put it on display as a work of art somewhere. Charge the public sixpence a go to have their pictures taken in it.'

He pressed his forefinger gently to Amanda's cherubic lips to forestall further objections. 'From this afternoon we will be transported swiftly and with style in a new Bentley Mark VII saloon. It can do nought to sixty in fifteen seconds and has a huge boot, big enough to hide a Lugg in. An automobile fit for a prince or a king, should we ever spot one thumbing a lift by the side of the road.'

They were in the Bottle Street flat which was now quite naked save for boxes and packing cases awaiting removal into storage and an invasion of builders and decorators. Lugg and Amanda, hot and dusty in overalls, their hands ink-stained from newspapers used as wrappings, had completed the packing in a frantic two hours without tea breaks. Mr Campion looked around the empty space as if taking a cue.

'And as there is little more we can do here until the workmen arrive at crack of dawn tomorrow, I've come up with a way to pass the time.'

'By taking us for a drive out to Essex in our new car,' said Amanda.

'Not quite.'

'But you said . . .'

'I said *I* had to go to Essex. You, my dear, will pop round to Gilpin's the publisher, and because you are Evadne Childe's number one fan, you will demand to see her editor, that nice Veronica lady.'

'You want me to snoop for you?'

'Don't call it snooping,' said Lugg, 'it makes it sound common.'

'I want you charm Miss Hatherall, and I know you can, into telling you what the next Evadne Childe book is likely to be about. Not "whodunit", I know that's sacrosanct, just a rough outline of the plot and setting. I'm especially interested in whether my godsibling—'

'Or for goodness' sake, stop saying that, it's not a real thing.'

'I rather like it, and I think Evadne could use it in one of her titles, but as I was saying, I want to know if the old dear has been researching the dark underbelly of Soho or clubland again, and especially if she did so in the company of her French friend Pierre or Peter, who supposedly introduced her to the Grafton Club which became the Reynard Club in *The Bottle Party Murders*. If she's revisiting that sort of territory in her new book, I would be most interested.'

'Why don't I just ask for an advance copy?' said Amanda drily.

'Would they give you one if you said pretty please?'

'I doubt it; a new Evadne Childe is a big event and they don't want to spoil the surprise. Of course, we could pretend to be normal people and wait until November and buy one.'

'Oh, I don't want to read it, though I'm sure you are chomping at the bit, darling. All I need is a feel for what it's about, the gubbins of the plot or whatever writers call it. Go and charm Miss Hatherall and see what you, as a die-hard fan, can find out. Take Rupert with you. Even a publisher's stony heart will melt if he puts on his lost orphan look. As a bribe to ensure good behaviour, tell the lad you'll take him to Davenport's magic shop to buy a few tricks. It's round on New Oxford Street, not far from Gilpin's.'

'You've got this all worked out, haven't you?' said Amanda, tiny fists clenched at her hips. 'And don't tell me I look good in dungarees; I know I do.'

'So we're off for a jaunt in the new motor, are we?' sniffed Lugg, delicately brushing dust from the bulging folds of his overalls.

'Not you, my faithful bloodhound, you are going on another pub crawl, or rather a club crawl to tie up another loose end. You suggested last night that we should pop round to the Grafton and I rather poo-pooed the idea, but I've come around to your way of thinking. Remember that diminutive doorman they had called Samson?'

'Cheeky little sod.'

It was one of Lugg's most endearing traits that he never forgot an insult about his weight.

'Well, if he's still there, it might be worth finding out if he's seen anything of Rags or Pierre Le Frog recently.'

Lugg put his ham-hocks of hands together, cracked his knuckles and grinned a quite evil grin. 'You want me to ask him a few questions – delicately, of course?'

'Be your usual subtle self,' said Campion.

Before he took his new car on a test run on the old Roman road out to Essex, Mr Campion made a telephone call, quoting an authority he had not used since the war and claiming a military rank he had never held.

In doing so, he ascertained the whereabouts of certain twelve-year-old military files and the name of the officer in charge of the dusty archive which held them in the secure confines of Hyderabad Barracks inside the garrison at Colchester. He then made a second call to book a room for the night at the George Hotel there.

'Of course I remember you, Lady Amanda.'

'Your Miss Prim downstairs made it quite clear she did not.'

'You must forgive her – she is rather set in her ways and you can't teach an old guard dog new tricks. Please do come in and take a seat. Is this charming young gentleman your son?'

'I have that distinction,' said Rupert, his back to Veronica

Hatherall as he admired the spines of the books lining her office shelves, which now extended from floor to ceiling.

'Rupert!' snapped his mother. 'Manners! I'm sorry, Miss Hatherall, I don't know where he picked that up. Actually, I do, but never mind. I see you've been promoted. Your door now says Editorial Director. Might I ask if the position comes with shares in the business?'

'Well, no; those are reserved for members of the Gilpin family, but I am very proud of my new title. It shows the directors' faith in me.'

'Keep pushing them, Miss Hatherall, we need more women at the top of their professions. Indeed, it is a woman who has achieved such heights that I wish to talk about.'

'Evadne Childe,' said Miss Hatherall firmly. 'I take it you are still a fan?'

A small voice from the bookshelf confirmed this.

'Mummy's got that one, and that one, and that one . . .'

'I hope your hands are clean, Rupert,' warned Amanda as her son ran his fingers over the regimented spines.

So did Veronica Hatherall, or at least not sticky, but she could not suppress a smile when Rupert lighted on one novel by a rather precious cleric popular in academic circles.

'And Daddy's read that one and called it ridiculous!'

'He's a bright lad,' said Veronica.

'Unfortunately so, at times,' said Amanda, but with pride rather than concern. 'You don't have a Biggles book to keep him occupied, do you? Or one of those new ones . . . Rupert, what's the name of those schoolboy stories you like?'

'Jennings,' said Rupert, still distracted by the bloodthirsty genre on display.

'I'm afraid we don't publish either Biggles or Jennings,' said Veronica, 'much to our regret. I could ring down to Children's Fiction to see what they've got on the stocks.'

'Please don't go to any trouble; I won't take up too much of your time. Rupert will just have to sit quietly for five minutes.' She raised her voice a half-tone: her mummy-means-business voice. '*If that's at all possible.*'

'So what exactly can I do for you, Lady Amanda?'

'Answer some rather impertinent questions, if you would, without asking too closely why I want the answers.'

'For a distinguished fan such as yourself, Lady Amanda, anything short of breaching the sanctity of the royalty statement or agreeing to accept an unsolicited manuscript.'

'Yes, well,' Amanda began uncertainly, 'it's to do with Evadne Childe's new book.'

'*Camera Obscuring* comes out in November and it's a cracking thriller, though you'll understand that I cannot give too much away.'

'I understand perfectly, but if you remember when my husband and I dropped in on you some years ago and we talked about *The Bottle Party Murders*?'

'Of course. You asked about Evadne's researches into the seamier side of life.'

'So we did. Well, we were wondering if Evadne was still – how can I put this? – using the same sources.'

'I'm not sure I follow, Lady Amanda, but the new book, apart from being set in London, has nothing to do with seedy clubs in Mayfair or Soho. Evadne's last four or five books have all been set outside London and she rarely visits these days. Quite where she gets her ideas, I really don't know.'

'You mentioned, last time we pestered you, that Miss Childe had a sort of guide or mentor when it came to seedy old Soho; someone called Peter . . .' Amanda left it as a hanging question and stared hopefully into Veronica's slightly bemused face.

'Did I? Good heavens, you have a better memory than I have. Let me think . . . yes, Peter, I'm sure he was called Peter, though he spoke with a rather sexy accent, so I assumed he was French. I only met him the once, when Evadne was writing *Dark Moon Over Soho* and coming up to London quite a lot, even though it was pretty scary back then, what with the buzz bombs and rockets dropping everywhere. That would be back in '44 and I told her she was safer out in the country, but her mother had died and she was clearly lonely, so her friendship with Peter probably did her good. It did me good just to look at him; he was a handsome young buck with all that dark curly hair. Evie called him her Heathcliff because there was a bit of the gypsy about him.'

Amanda expressed no emotion at all at that point, and certainly neither shock nor outrage, but Miss Hatherall automatically assumed she had.

'Oh, I know what you're thinking,' Veronica said, although

Amanda doubted it, 'but there was nothing . . . untoward, if I may use a word from romantic fiction . . . going on between them. I mean, she was old enough to be his grandmother! She might have paid him for his time when he was showing her around, and she would have bought him drinks and meals and perhaps a present or two, but there was nothing sordid about it. She was doing research and Peter was helping her. It was a purely professional arrangement.'

Mr Lugg, as was his wont, preferred to schedule his business appointments after dark, but not too late to interfere with his beauty sleep.

It was shortly after nine when he knocked on the door of the Grafton Club. Although the club was said to have achieved respectability since its wartime incarnation, it was the same inconspicuous door in the same dimly lit alley and the same letter box opening at eye level which slid open.

'Chief Petty Officer Samson?' Lugg, standing to one side, spoke quietly so that the guardian of the door had to lean closer to the open slot to hear.

'Yus?'

Lugg thrust his hand through the slot and, though it was a tight fit, his fingers quickly made contact with identifiable human elements of flesh and bristle. There was a nose, a moustache under it and cheeks either side, for the hand's span was wide, and his fingers may have been as thick as sausages, but they gripped like G-clamps.

A satisfactory squeal of shock and discomfort came from behind the door.

'Now be a good little petty officer, Mr Samson,' said Lugg, 'and slip the bolt and let me in so we can have us a conversation where I hope to hear something to my advantage.'

Over a muffled grunt of pain there was the sound of a bolt being slipped and the door opened enough for Lugg's booted foot to act as a doorstop. Only then did he withdraw his arm from the rectangular slit, step over the threshold and grab the diminutive figure cowering in the folds of the heavy blackout curtain. Lugg registered surprise that the curtain was still there so long after the last air raid, but then his ears caught the tinkling of a piano coming from the club above and realized that the curtain had been pressed into service in the cause of sound-, rather than light-proofing.

Within those black, sticky and, frankly, pungent drapes, the unfortunate Mr Samson was wriggling like a sprat on a fish-hook. Lugg plunged both hands into the dark swirl, took a firm grip on the lapels of his victim's jacket and lifted him a good six inches off the floor, pinning him against the door jamb.

'Now, Mr Chief Petty Officer,' he said slowly, 'tell me something I want to know, and we can both be about our business. Rags Donovan. Used to work here, was a cigarette girl when Tony Valetta got bumped off. You seen her lately? Think carefully, because you're hardly any weight at all an' I could probably 'old you up wiv one hand all night.'

To prove his point, the big man adjusted his feet and grabbed a handful of shirt-front with his right paw and straightened his arm, producing a satisfying whimper from the suspended Samson. Lugg then used the forefinger of his left hand to poke his prisoner's nose, jabbing gently to emphasize his points.

'Rags . . . Donovan . . . Nice girl determined to get on in life . . . Only she ain't going to now, is she? . . . Heard about that?'

'I 'eard,' rasped Samson. 'Nothin' to do wiv me. Ain't seen her for six months.'

'Come now, Mr Samson, I said I wanted to hear something to my advantage and I haven't done that yet. You'll have to do better. I reckon you hide here behind your door and your curtain, but you keep your eyes and ears open at all the comings and goings. You must 'ave somethin' for me.'

'Thaddeus,' croaked the little man, his eyes flicking upwards. 'Oo?'

'The darkie upstairs tinkling the ivories.'

Lugg's massive head rolled back on his tree trunk of a neck, as if following the music floating down the staircase.

'The pianist? What about 'im?'

'He's married to Rags's sister.'

Lugg relaxed his grip and the doorman dropped to ground level, then flinched as Lugg patted him on the head before starting up the staircase.

He felt rather proud of himself and made a mental note to tell Campion how he had defeated a Samson one-handed.

Surely that would count as being subtle.

NINE
Miss Kitto's Front Room

M r Campion was looking not quite down the barrel of a Lee Enfield No.5 carbine, but near enough to the business end to make him very uneasy. He took little comfort in knowing that particular model of army-issue rifle, developed for jungle warfare, had not proved popular and had been discontinued in 1947. He was also certain that the weapon was not loaded; well, almost certain.

'So you don't actually have a pass, then, sir?' asked the corporal holding the rifle.

'Better than that, I have an *appointment* with a Captain Johnson,' said Campion through the open window of his new Bentley. 'I'm sure he informed the duty officer. He said he would, and he sounded jolly reliable on the phone.'

'Nobody is supposed to get into Hyderabad without a pass, them's standing orders. But you wait here and I'll see if I can get hold of this Captain . . . Johnson, did you say?'

'Thank you, Corporal. Yes, Captain Johnson, Roger Johnson.'

'Never 'eard of 'im,' muttered the corporal, making a show of ignoring the driver but concentrating hard on the car's number plate. 'Better turn your engine off while you're waiting.'

Having had some experience of just how fast the mills of military procedure did grind, and 'exceeding slow' was being generous, Campion was glad to switch off the ignition and preserve the Bentley's petrol consumption.

On the run out to Colchester, his new car had performed almost as well as the salesman had suggested, which really was all a purchaser could ask for, and had certainly drawn far fewer looks of astonishment from pedestrians and passing motorists than the Daimler as it had been customized by Amanda and his sister. There again, far fewer motorists passed the Bentley.

He was thankful too that he was not now sitting in The Running Footman at this precise moment, at the white-painted barrier

strung with suitably dramatic commands telling him to 'Halt!'
and that 'All Passes Must Be Shown', which blocked his entry
into Hyderabad Barracks, as behind him several large army trucks
revved their engines loudly in impatience. It was almost as if
there was a war on, which of course there was, far away in Korea,
and though it involved British and Commonwealth troops as well
as American, it seemed almost a conflict too far and too foreign
to be real and was in danger of being forgotten while it was still
going on.

The corporal disappeared into the guardhouse, and through a
window Campion could see him leaning over a desk to use a
telephone. When the corporal straightened up at attention, and
so smartly that Campion imagined he heard boot heels clicking
together, it was clear that a higher authority was being consulted
and orders, or at least permissions, were being dispensed.

When he emerged, he raised the barrier, pointed to his left
with his rifle and barked instructions to the Bentley.

'Park up over there on the parade ground and follow the first
path round to the tennis courts. Captain Johnson will be waiting
for you at the pavilion. Now come on, get that crate moving.
You're blocking important military vehicles, who haven't got all
day.'

The corporal looked at the drivers of the lorries waiting in line
and shrugged his shoulders in a gesture of exasperation as if to
say 'Civilians!'

Campion flapped a hand in a mock salute and followed orders,
idly wondering if Captain Johnson would be wearing white shorts,
carrying a racquet and asking if anyone was for tennis.

To his relief, Captain Johnson wore a smart, pressed uniform
and was all business rather than sport or exercise as he marched
briskly across the net-less clay-court surface towards him.

'Mr Campion? Excellent, Roger Johnson. Happy to put
myself at your disposal. Your clearance came from really quite
high up.'

'Not embarrassingly high, I hope.'

'I would say impressively high, certainly high enough to brook
no argument from a mere captain, not that captains ever question
orders, of course.'

'Of course,' Campion agreed with a grin, instantly warming
to his host. 'Though I must say I am slightly surprised at our

surroundings. I never thought to bring shorts and pumps. I'm afraid I won't give you much of a game.'

The officer glanced around as if noticing their location for the first time.

'Oh, the famous officers-only tennis courts, which nobody's used for twenty years. It turns out they were laid down over a load of surplus munitions from the 14–18 show. You know the army. If you can't get rid of it and don't have to account for it, you get a platoon to dig a dirty great hole and you bury it so it's out of sight, out of mind. When the Officers' Mess discovered that they'd put their shiny new tennis court on top of an ammo dump, suddenly there wasn't a queue to walk out here and start bouncing balls on the ground, so it became a bit of a white elephant. Lucky for me, though.'

'How so?' Campion asked, following the captain's lead towards the wooden pavilion which still housed a forlorn, weather-beaten scoreboard showing no sets and no games played and no points scored.

'They let me work there with my files. As a clubhouse and changing rooms it may be pretty flimsy, but they built a pretty solid, and capacious, air-raid shelter underneath it. Electric light, running water, most mod cons, and ideal for storing all those files from the war which we haven't got around to sorting yet, even though it's been seven years now.'

'And that's what you do?'

'For my sins. I was a librarian and trainee archivist when I was called up right at the last knockings of hostilities and the army, bless them, recognized that my natural talents did not lie on a front line anywhere, but I did have a flair for organizing records and paperwork. Got lucky and was seconded to a general writing his memoirs. Helped two more tell the story of how *they* won the war and worked on a few regimental histories. Decided to stay in uniform and somehow ended up a captain. I'm more or less left to my own devices because I shuffle old papers no one else wants to handle. This is my lair.'

Johnson held a creaking wooden door open for Campion to enter into what had been some sort of bar area where officers could shelter if rain stopped play. It was now an empty, musty space, devoid of furniture and decoration, apart from two crossed tennis racquets on a door bearing a faded sign saying Changing Rooms.

It took a moment for Campion to realize that a dark shape in the far corner was in fact an open trapdoor.

'Let me go first and get the lights,' said Johnson, who rapidly started to shrink before Campion's eyes, his boots clumping down concrete steps as he descended into the cellar. His disappearing act complete, a rectangle of light appeared, and he called for Campion to join him.

Captain Johnson's private sanctum – Campion could not think of it as an office – was a folding card table and a chair surrounded by stacks of metal ammunition boxes, each with a label tied on with string, reminding Campion of the luggage of evacuee children on London's railway stations in 1939. The concrete walls of the shelter, where visible between the piles of boxes, were grey and glisteningly damp under the metal-caged bulkhead lights.

'Snug,' said Mr Campion.

'Hardly,' replied the captain, 'more a breeding ground for pneumonia. I'm not allowed an oil heater down here, not because I might gas myself with the fumes, but because of the fire risk to the documents.'

'Which you seem to have in abundance.'

'My dear chap, this is but the tip of the army's iceberg. Everything here relates to this garrison and Wivenhoe House during the war, which is the bit I'm told you are interested in.' He paused and frowned. 'I take it you have signed the Act?'

'Official Secrets? They are my middle names, but I don't think I'm after anything particularly secret.'

'You'd be amazed at what the army would like to keep secret; or perhaps not. As it happens, the files kept on members of foreign armed forces who were assessed at Wivenhoe House were classed as no higher than "Sensitive", and that includes the file on you.'

'Me?' Campion gave a passable impersonation of an outraged Victorian governess and clutched at his heart with both hands.

'September 1940, wasn't it? Your one and only visit, to interview two Belgian officers who had escaped around the time of Dunkirk.'

'I am so impressed, Captain,' said Campion with genuine admiration, 'considering you've only had a few hours to find that particular needle in this awesome haystack.'

Captain Johnson was a picture of flustered modesty. If the

light had been better, Campion could swear he was actually blushing.

'Oh, I found the file months ago while indexing the Wivenhoe House material and the name Albert Campion jumped out at me, plus the fact that your authority was not, shall we say, from one of the uniformed services, but rather the hush-hush brigade. I had a feeling it might be worth remembering it, just in case someone in the future were to write your biography, for example.'

'I think that highly unlikely, but should the need arise I will insist you have first refusal on the job, once you've finished the memoirs of all your generals. Is it possible to see my file?'

'It's pretty thin,' said Johnson, opening an ammunition box and plucking out a cardboard folder.

'Story of my life,' said Campion.

'And I can't let it out of my sight, so you'll have to read it here. Please, have a seat. Have *the* seat. I don't get many visitors down here.'

'Would you know if anyone else has consulted this file?'

'I doubt it very much. Wivenhoe House ceased to be a Reception Centre, as they called it then, round about 1942, and suspect foreign nationals were interrogated by MI5 somewhere in London.'

'Wormwood Scrubs,' said Campion, adding quickly, 'I think I read somewhere.'

'Once the house was turned over to a tank regiment and then some special forces unit for training, all the files were sealed and shipped here for the duration. I'm pretty sure no one has looked at that file since then, until I did.'

'Thank you, Captain.' Campion took the file from him and placed it on the square card table, pulled out the chair and sat down. He removed his large round spectacles and polished the lenses on a handkerchief before opening the file and starting to read the few flimsy pages inside.

'Please, it's Roger, and if there's anything you require . . .'

'No, I'm fine. I just need to refresh my memory then I'll be out of your hair.'

Captain Johnson's face fell at the prospect of losing such a distinguished visitor, for as a professional student of official documents, he had a very good idea who Albert Campion really was.

'You would be more than welcome to join us for dinner in the Officers' Mess,' he pleaded. 'In fact, we'd be honoured.'

'I'm afraid I'm booked into the George in Colchester,' said Campion.

'Oh, do go there,' said Captain Johnson with enthusiasm, 'the food is so much better.'

Mr Campion feared for Captain Johnson's career prospects as a keeper of the army's secret history and, he suspected, as a ghost-writer of military memoirs. He was far too intelligent, far too helpful and, worst of all, far too honest to be ever allowed to escape from his bunker.

The next morning, Mr Campion followed, in the Bentley, the Cambridge road he had taken twelve years before in a borrowed Ford V8, out to the village of Eight Ash. The hedgerows were thick with blackberries and he comforted himself that it was not yet St Michael's Day, for it was a well-known piece of folklore in that part of Essex that one shouldn't pick blackberries after Saint Michael's Day on 29 September, for that marked the date the Devil walked abroad and cursed the berries by touching them with his dark, satanic fingernails. It was, Campion knew, simply a colourful country way of marking a natural season, the Satanic embellishment being understandably popular in an area with a dark history of witches and witch-finding.

In the fields which had already been harvested, he could see the ugly pimples of concrete pillboxes, and vaguely recalled that the junction of the lane leading to Mill House was guarded with one. Having served its function and successfully defended the village of Eight Ash with its single street, sole pub and flint-encrusted church, against a mighty invader, that pillbox had been removed except for its thick concrete base, which could only have been shifted with dynamite. On it was a circle of tubs planted with flowers to soften the scar and, helpfully, a fingerpost sign pointing down the lane to the right, directing travellers to Mill House.

Campion guided the Bentley slowly across the bridge over the old mill stream on to the gravel forecourt, parking directly outside the front door. He turned off the engine and surveyed the house, which remained silent, windows and doors firmly shut, curtains closed. The only sign of habitation was provided by the open doors of the garage to the side, which showed a shiny, recently polished, maroon-coloured Austin of pre-war vintage.

Cursing himself for not telephoning ahead, Campion clambered out of the Bentley and was startled by a crunching of gravel which he was sure had not been made by his own feet.

'Can h'oi 'elp youse?'

The Essex accent belonged to an elderly figure wearing brown overalls with dark stains and gumboots, with a flat tweed cap pulled down over much of a weather-beaten face. The figure gave off a scent of metal polish and his ruddy complexion suggested that he might have used it on himself.

'Oh, hello. My name's Campion. I was hoping to find Mrs Walker-Pyne at home.'

'Well, she ain't.'

Campion had come across most sorts of faithful family retainers, gamekeepers, poachers and gardeners, and knew to choose his words carefully. He followed the smell of polish in his nose and guessed the stains of the old man's overalls were motor oil.

'You must be her driver,' he said after considering the word 'chauffeur' on the grounds that he could keep it in reserve.

'Among other things,' said the man, who must, Campion thought, already have overspent his three score years and ten, and who seemed reluctant to volunteer anything further.

'Would you happen to know when she is likely to return? You see I was in the area and thought I'd drop by and pay my respects. Spur-of-the-moment thing.'

'You one of them fanatics?'

'I beg your pardon?'

'One of them fanatics who likes her stories, reads all her books.'

'Oh, a *fan*. Well, yes, of course I like her novels, but I'm not some stage-door Johnny looking for an autograph. I met Evadne during the war, when we discovered that we have the same godmother.'

The old man tilted his head quizzically. 'Is that like being related?'

'As good as. I was hoping to show dear Evie my new car.' Campion smiled inanely.

'Nice motor,' the old man agreed, suggesting a driver-to-driver bond might be formed, 'but you'd never get Mrs Pyne to agree to chopping in the Austin, not even in part-exchange.'

'A bad case of sentimental attachment, is it? My wife had strong feelings about our old car, but I just had to get something with a bit more zip, you know.'

'Women, eh?' Mr Campion was unsure what sort of a question that was, so merely nodded. 'They won't be told. Still, the Austin will see me out, and whoever looks after it after me; it'll probably see Mrs Pyne out too.'

'Evadne never struck me as a dedicated motorist,' Campion said innocently.

'She ain't. Leaves all that to me. Got the car for her late mother. She didn't drive either, so I 'ad to. Made me wear a chauffer's 'at, the late Mrs Childe did. I arsk you, a chauffeur's 'at in an Austin Ascot! Wouldn't have minded if I'd had this 'ere Bentley. Bet it goes like a dream.'

'Still running her in,' Campion said with man-to-man confidentiality, 'but she really does. Pity Evie's not here so I could show her off. You wouldn't happen to know when she's likely to be back, do you, Mr . . .?'

'Stopes. Reuben Stopes. I won't shake hands, I've been doin' the car. Always give it a spruce-up after a run to Harwich.'

'Harwich?'

'Aye, Harwich,' Reuben Stopes said slowly, as if Campion was himself 'a bit slow'. 'Parkeston Quay in Harwich for the boat.'

'The boat?'

'The ferry, to Antwerp. Goes regular, does Mrs P. Caught the six o'clock boat last night.'

'On her holidays, is she? Any idea when she'll be back?'

The old man pushed up the peak of his cap and scratched the side of his temple with a grubby finger.

'Usually she spends five or six days over there when she goes.'

'In Antwerp?'

'That's where the boat takes her, but she don't stay there, she goes on to Brussels. Brought me some chocolate back from there once, though I told her it should have been sprouts.'

Campion allowed himself a polite chuckle; just enough, he felt, not to encourage the old man.

'And she makes this trip regularly, you say?'

'Oh aye, once a year, reg'lar as clockwork, but not always the same time of year. Depends how her book-writing's going.'

'Really? Does she pop over to Brussels for her research, or just a break, to recharge her imaginative batteries?'

'Oi wouldn't know anything about that,' said Stopes, shaking his head. 'All I knows is she usually comes back more cheerful than when she went.'

'As her driver, I suppose you take Evie to the station when she goes up to London?' Campion asked.

'Right oi do. Takes her to Colchester North station for the Lunnun train and picks her up when she comes back.'

'Do you take her anywhere else?'

'Can't say oi do.' Reuben Stopes pondered the question for half a minute. 'She don't go anywhere much else. 'Course I takes her shopping in Colchester an' I used to run her up the village to see Miss Kitto if the weather was bad or in the winter when it's too dark to walk across the fields.'

'Miss Kitto? Is she a friend of Evie's?'

'Nearest thing to it in Eight Ash, I reckon. Since her mother died, she don't mix much.'

'And this Miss Kitto lives in the village?'

'Holt Cottage; last place on the right past the Brick & Tile. Been in need of a thatching as long as I can remember. You can't miss it, but if you're thinking of paying a call there, you'd better watch yourself.'

'Really?' Campion's eyes widened behind his glasses. 'Why would that be?'

Stopes stroked his stubbly chin, then leaned forward into Campion.

'She's an odd one is our Miss Kitto,' he said with relish. 'She calls herself a medium, but my old dad called her a spiritualist; and *his* dad would have called her a witch.'

If Miss Kitto was a witch, then she advertised her profession in the name of her cottage on a poker-burned sign on the garden gate. While 'Holt' was a place in Norfolk which Campion knew well, in addition to being a common name for an animal's den or lair, particularly an otter, it also brought to mind the ravings of the seventeenth-century 'Witchfinder General' Matthew Hopkins, who claimed that a devilish imp had appeared to one of his victims in the form of a white kitten called 'Holt'.

At first sight, Miss Kitto would almost certainly have attracted the attentions of Matthew Hopkins. She wore a long-sleeved, high-throated black dress with frills of black lace, Victorian in style but not that dissimilar to traditional Puritan garb, and she was an elderly woman who lived alone in a cottage, situated as far away from the church as it could be and still be within the village – a sure sign of guilt as far as Mr Hopkins was concerned, for he had been a man who had required only the minimum of circumstantial evidence before pronouncing guilt.

Miss Kitto also had cats, a herd of them, if three constituted a herd, though none was white and none was called Holt as far as Campion could tell, though he had not been formally introduced to any of them.

'I do hope I am not intruding, turning up unannounced like this.'

'You're very welcome,' said Miss Kitto, in a voice which bore traces of Cockney but had been smoothed by exposure to the local dialect. 'I don't get many visitors. What can I do for you? Would you like tea? It's herbal. I make it myself from nature's bounty.'

Nature's droppings and off-cuts, thought Campion, pine needles for body, tree bark for colour and rosemary or thyme for flavour. If you were lucky, the pine needles would act as an anaesthetic.

'Please do not go to any trouble on my account,' he said politely. 'Reuben Stopes said you might be able to help me.'

Miss Kitto made a dismissive 'Pah!' sound, making Campion feel as if he had led with the wrong card.

'Reuben is an ignorant, but then he was never too bright. He's snared more than one hare to my knowledge, and you should never harm hares. Rabbits is good eating but hares is magical.'

'Forgive me, but I'm afraid I too was ignorant of that fact,' Campion said respectfully.

Miss Kitto wrinkled her nose, a distinctly simian nose, and pursed her thin lips, then shook her head slowly. 'No, I don't think so. You may not appreciate the supernatural powers of the hare, but you're not an ignorant. Ignorants is them that don't believe in the world beyond apart from what they're spoon-fed in church. You don't strike me as one of them.'

Campion's immediate thought was that Miss Kitto would indeed have been a prime candidate for the attentions of Matthew Hopkins and his usual operational directive: if she floats, she burns. Fortunately for Miss Kitto there did not seem to be a village pond and ducking stool in Eight Ash. At least not yet.

'I try and keep an open mind on things I do not understand,' he said, 'which is most things, but I will say I have no faith whatsoever in astrology. I think it is bunkum, but then that's just what a Taurean would say, isn't it?'

'Good job you don't want your fortune told, then, because it would be a wasted journey coming here. Mediums don't try and predict the future. You'd have more luck with old Mrs Price at the post office who throws on a gypsy shawl for the annual fete and has a tent where she tells your fortune for sixpence. I says to them that queues up for her to offer a threepenny bit *and* ask for change!'

Miss Kitto chuckled at the thought. It was a singsong, gentle laugh, not at all a witch's cackle.

'Then I will not insult you by offering to cross your palm with silver,' said Campion with a broad grin.

'I'm perfectly happy to take a cheque,' said Miss Kitto, no longer chuckling.

'And I am more than happy to recompense you for your time and forbearance if the information I seek is in any way delicate or distressing. You see I'm not terribly clear on the confidentiality arrangements between mediums and their clients; is it similar to doctors and their patients?'

'We don't call them clients, or patients.'

'Visitors?'

'Certainly not. They come to *meet* the visitors who speak to them across the void. I regard them as guests at my table.'

Campion resisted the foolish urge to ask if this meant Miss Kitto provided catering if not clairvoyance.

'There are no strange rituals, no incantations, no blood sacrifices,' she added with relish. 'My guests and I sit around a table in my front room and communicate calmly and reasonably with the dead. Come through and I'll show you. There might be someone trying to contact you.'

'Oh, I do hope not,' said Mr Campion. 'I have no wish to disturb the peacefully dead.'

Campion's abiding impression of Miss Kitto's front room was the ticking of clocks, an unusually large number of clocks. There were four on the mantlepiece above the black iron fireplace, three on a wall shelf interspersed between a collection of china ornaments, three more on a small square table covered with an embroidered cloth and a mismatched brace of slim, long-cased 'grandmother' clocks. Normally one did not notice a single timepiece in a room, but this was a positive orchestra of clockwork mechanisms which, Campion thought, could provide something akin to the *1812 Overture* if they chimed simultaneously on the hour.

'I know what you're thinking,' said Miss Kitto, and Campion bit his tongue to stop the quip 'Of course you do.'

'The clocks don't chime, but the sound of time passing regularly provides a calming rhythm to my sessions. Please sit.'

She indicated the centrepiece of the room, a round table covered by a plush red cloth with dangling tassels. A small pine box with a hinged lid lay in the centre of the table and four chairs nestled under it. Campion and Miss Kitto sat opposite each other and automatically rested their forearms on it, like card players waiting to cut to see who would deal.

'This is where I do what I can to put lost souls in touch with each other,' said Miss Kitto. 'No wires, no hidden bells, no assistants hiding under the table. You are welcome to check. But you are not here to investigate my methods, are you? You are here to ask me about Mrs Walker-Pyne.'

'You are very perceptive.'

'You made it very easy for me by mentioning Reuben Stopes, who is Evadne's handyman down at Mill House. Plus that fine car outside. We don't see many like that in Eight Ash, unless it's something to do with our local celebrity.'

'I am afraid you are correct. If I may, I would like to ask you about Mrs Walker-Pyne's visits here, assuming you would not be breaking any confidences.'

'Have you asked her?' Miss Kitto narrowed her eyes.

'I would if she were at home. It appears that she is on holiday on the Continent.'

Miss Kitto gave a delicate but very audible sniff of disapproval, but Campion could not tell whether it was aimed at the concept of holidays or the foolishness of foreign travel. Whichever it was, it seemed to spur Miss Kitto into action.

'I've known her since she was a child. Her father was the vicar here, and he was a good vicar. Her mother was not a good vicar's wife and she was unbearable as a vicar's widow, far too stuck up and above herself, and she certainly didn't approve of me.'

Campion silently agreed that a country vicar's wife would, in a place like Eight Ash, have had to have, at least in public, a fairly disparaging view of mediums, spiritualists and even witches.

'Did Evadne come and consult you when her mother died?'

Another delicate chuckle. 'Oh no, before then, when she moved back here in 1940 to act as her mother's skivvy. She was anxious to contact her husband, and knew the exact location of his grave, which helped immensely.'

'Ah yes, Edmund, an early casualty of the war. His death must have hit her hard.'

'It did; she loved him very much and had consulted the London Spiritualist Alliance before she moved here and knew what she wanted. They had many interesting talks did Evadne and Edmund, through me, of course, and the cards.'

'The cards?'

Miss Kitto nodded towards the box in the middle of the table and Campion reached out and flipped the lid. Inside were squares of card, bigger than playing cards, each one marked with a large capital letter of the alphabet.

'Automatic writing on the Ouija board principle?' enquired Campion.

'You are familiar with this method of communication?'

'Vaguely,' said Campion. 'I think it is probably quicker and more accurate than my typing. You arrange the letters in a circle and then the medium points to them in turn to spell out an answer when a question is asked of the . . . the person being contacted.'

'If contact can be made, and that is not always guaranteed.' Campion noticed that Miss Kitto, now in professional mode, had lost her mixture of accents. 'In my case, I am blindfolded during the visit and I use an object belonging to the one who has passed over to point out the letters. In the case of Evadne's husband, it was a fountain pen he had owned since his schooldays.'

'I will not impose or intrude by asking what messages passed between husband and wife.'

'Nor would I tell you if you did ask. Suffice it to say, Evadne took great comfort from the sessions.'

'And her mother died . . . during the war?'

'Yes, it would have been 1942. Most of the village turned out for the funeral just to make sure she was gone.'

'Did Evadne try to contact her mother – through you, that is?'

Miss Kitto shook her head. 'No, not once. Never suggested it. She just wanted to talk to Edmund . . . until . . .'

'Until what, Miss Kitto?' Campion prompted, but when the woman remained stubbornly silent, he added, 'Or should that be when?'

'Towards the end of the war, that last winter, she asked me to contact somebody called Peter. Wouldn't say anything much about him and didn't have anything that belonged to him which could have helped.'

'And was contact established?'

'No, there was nothing. I felt nothing. We tried three times then Evadne stormed out in a huff saying she would find another medium, a good one! My services were no longer required!'

Campion contained his surprise. 'Mrs Walker-Pyne was sure that this Peter had . . . passed over to the other side?'

'Well, of course, otherwise she'd have written him a letter!'

'And you say this was 1944?'

'January '45 more likely. Evie ain't been in this house or at this table since.'

'And had she tried to contact any other . . . spirits?'

'No, just her husband Edmund and this Peter chap. She wouldn't tell me his proper name, but I got the impression he was a foreigner.'

Campion got to his feet, his left hand straying to the wallet pocket in his jacket.

'You've been most helpful, Miss Kitto. May I offer you some compensation for your time?'

'Put yer money away.' The Cockney accent was returning. Perhaps money was the trigger. 'I tried to 'elp Evie, but I failed her, and I don't take payment for not giving satisfaction.'

'Well, rest assured, I'm looking out for Mrs Walker-Pyne's best interests, so anything you've told me will not be used to hurt her in any way.'

'I knows that,' said Miss Kitto smugly. 'I could tell you were trustworthy when I saw you coming.'

This time Campion could not restrain the surprise on his face.

'I got the impression – from you yourself – that mediums were not in the clairvoyance business.'

'We ain't. I said I saw you coming. I was in the village earlier and I saw that nice car of yours turning down the lane to Mill House. A car like that belongs to a real gent, not a scallywag.'

Campion absorbed this wisdom in silence, and for the first time in a quarter of an hour, he was conscious of the persistent throbbing of ticking clocks.

'I must remember to tell my wife that,' he said at last.

TEN

Remembrancer

At the first telephone box he spotted, Mr Campion pulled off the road and sifted enough coins from various pockets in order to make two telephone calls to London, the first to Superintendent Yeo to give him a name and an invitation to dinner that evening, the second to his wife at the York Hotel asking her to call 'all his troops together for a debriefing' and book a table for dinner.

To the casual observer, and there were many of those among the resident guests of the hotel, it was no more than a family get-together, albeit perhaps with more kindly uncles than was usual. Murder seemed the least likely of topics to be on the conversational agenda, and for the early courses the table talk revolved around motor cars (new), Amanda's designs for the Bottle Street flat renovation (universally praised), the chances of another winter of pea-souper fogs and smog as bad as in 1951 (with Campion quoting Carlyle's description of 'liquid ink'), the introduction of the shilling charge for prescriptions from the doctor (a thorn in the sciatic side of Lugg's sister) and how the taxman now seemed to have more power than the policeman (a particular bugbear of Yeo's, but one which found a very sympathetic audience). The conversational honours, however, went to young Rupert who, between main course and dessert suddenly announced, rather loudly: 'What does *un-expunge-ugated* mean?'

To break the ensuing silence, where cutlery remained frozen to hands and glasses hovered halfway between table and open mouths, Campion turned to his son with admiration and affection.

'Are you sure that's a word, Rupert? And if so, where did you learn it?'

'I think he means "unexpurgated",' said Rupert's mother. 'He picked it up when riffling through some books at Gilpin's yesterday.'

'It usually means that the book is not for young, innocent minds below the age of twenty-one,' said his father. 'They are the favourite type of books read by Uncle Lugg, but he can only read in short sharp bursts because his lips get tired.'

Lugg grunted so loudly a waiter on the other side of the dining room started in surprise and the crockery on the tray he was carrying rattled violently, like a windowpane in a hailstorm.

'You be careful, talking like that in front of the lad,' growled Lugg, pointing a fork at Rupert. 'If 'e picks up on your vocabulary, he'll develop a nice line in snark which could get him in trouble at his new school.'

'You could be right, old fruit,' Campion admitted, 'so we'd better choose our words carefully while we report our respective findings. *Pas devant les enfants*, as they say.'

'*Pas devant l'enfant, mon père*,' said Rupert with concentrated seriousness. 'There's only one of me.'

'Quite right,' said his mother proudly.

'Bright lad, he'll go far,' said Yeo.

'To the end of the pier, like his dad,' muttered Lugg.

Campion pinged the edge of his knife against a glass to call for order.

'Can we get down to business, please? Let us pool our accumulated knowledge.

'Amanda, darling, you first; beauty before age and all that.'

Amanda reported briefly and succinctly on her visit to Gilpin's and her meeting with Veronica Hatherall, confirming that she had only met the mysterious "Peter" once, back in 1944, and that Evadne Childe's forthcoming novel had no connection with Soho or London clubland.

'And she hasn't seen him since?' Campion asked.

'She didn't say she had.'

'But do you think she would recognize him after six years?'

'Oh yes,' said Amanda in the knowing way that is distinctly female. 'She waxed quite lyrical about his dark curls and gypsy good looks. Evadne called him her Heathcliff, she said, though I can't remember my *Wuthering Heights* too well, but I'm sure Veronica could pick him out of an identity parade. I think she'd be quite keen to.'

'And one other thing, my dear; did Miss Hatherall say anything about Evadne consulting a spiritualist?'

'No, should I have asked about that?'

'What's a spirits-alist?' chirped Rupert, reminding the table of his presence.

'Somebody who does horoscopes,' Amanda said quickly. 'You know what horoscopes are, don't you?'

'I know they can't be trusted when you're doing the football pools,' Rupert declaimed solemnly.

Superintendent Yeo laughed and said, 'I wonder where he picked that up?' The way Mr and Mrs Campion were glaring at Lugg gave him his answer.

'I'm a sheep,' Rupert continued, 'that's my horror-scope.'

'Your *Chinese* horoscope,' said Campion, 'where everyone gets an animal depending on the year they were born, and there's nothing wrong with being a sheep. Pity me, because I was born in the Year of the Rat, which means I am a clever, quick thinker, but content with living a quiet life, whereas your mother is a tiger, so we should both be very careful not to upset her. Now if you keep quiet – as quiet as a sheep – and let the adults talk, I'll see if the hotel can rustle up some ice cream.'

'Albert, you shouldn't spoil him,' whispered Amanda.

'I'm not spoiling him, I'm bribing him,' replied her husband under his breath.

'What's Uncle Lugg?' Rupert persisted. 'If I'm a sheep, what's he?'

'Oh, he was born in the Year of the Brontosaurus, one of the larger and clumsier dinosaurs, noted for getting very irritable if they're interrupted. So you sit quietly thinking of how big an ice cream you can manage, and let Uncle Lugg regale us with the fruits of his investigations.'

Lugg began his report with a statement which stunned the adults around the table into silence.

'Well, I've made a new friend,' said the fat man, leaning back in his chair, which creaked ominously.

'One cannot have too many,' observed Rupert, in a passable imitation of his father, without looking up from the spoon he was polishing with his napkin in anticipation of the treat to come.

Mr Lugg, unperturbed, ignored the interruption and informed a rapt audience of how he had, at great personal inconvenience (unspecified) infiltrated the Grafton Club and interviewed the doorman there. By means of subtle questioning and his natural powers of persuasion (at which Superintendent Yeo's eyebrows jumped upwards), he had discovered that the club's resident pianist was in fact the brother-in-law of Rags Donovan, the lady they were interested in.

'Thaddeus P. Honeycutt,' he announced proudly, as if introducing the top-of-the-bill act. 'Lovely fella, and no mean tinkler of the old ivories. Came over with the GIs in the war and drove supply trucks all over Normandy in '44. Couldn't believe how friendly we Londoners were; very friendly in the case of Rags Donovan's sister, and they fell for each other hook, line and sinker. But Thad, as I call him, couldn't go back to Alabama with a white wife; they're very funny about things like that over there. So they stayed and now have two kiddies and a house in Brixton, one of the bomb-damaged ones they bought for a song and they're doing up. Rags got Thad to play at the Grafton when he was off-duty and then a regular job there after his demob, though he does jam sessions and recording sessions on the side.'

'You're not his agent by any chance, are you?' asked Campion. 'Never mind, do carry on.'

Lugg took a breath deep enough to strain his shirt buttons. 'Well, even though Rags had left the Grafton for pastures new, she kept in touch with Thaddeus and occasionally popped into the Grafton to make sure they were treating him right, buy him a Guinness or two – he likes his Guinness does Thad. Anyways, last week she got a message to him, wanting a meet before he went to work and after she'd finished work, so they went for a drink early evening in the Fitzroy. That would have been a couple of days before . . .' Lugg glanced at Rupert who was fortunately concentrating on polishing cutlery, '. . . she wrote that letter to you.'

Lugg drained his wine glass and smacked his lips, as if such an incantation would magically refill it. 'According to Thaddeus, Rags wanted to know if he remembered the foreign chap who had brought your writer-lady friend to the Grafton that time. You know, the year Tony . . . the year of the Valetta incident. Well, Thad wasn't sure he could; in fact, he was pretty sure he couldn't, but he played along with his sister-in-law, knowing that he'd get grief at home if he didn't. Rags was in a bit of a state because she was sure she'd seen the guy that very morning in Wardour Street.'

'That would make sense,' said Yeo, and when confronted by three inquisitive stares, he added: 'Mrs Daubney worked there, for a company that hires out film equipment.'

Lugg waited politely for any further contribution, as he was always polite to policemen over the rank of chief inspector, but when Yeo offered nothing more, he continued, 'Rags was shaken up because even though they didn't speak, she was pretty sure that the bloke she recognized as Pierre Le Frog *had recognized her* and was convinced he was following her. Thaddeus poured a couple of gins down her throat and walked her to Goodge Street to put her on the tube. It was 'im who suggested she get in touch with 'is nibs here, as we'd been to the Grafton sniffing around the very same frog six years ago. As it's a well-known fact that women only clear out their handbags once every ten years, Rags still had the card you gave her back in 1946, so she dropped you a line and suggested the Fitzroy because she felt safe there.'

'Sadly, she was mistaken,' Campion began quietly, and Lugg could only purse his thick lips and nod agreement. 'Did Thaddeus actually see this Peter or Pierre for himself? Could he identify him?'

'No, and I did ask, and he was still in the army when Le Frog brought the writer woman to the Grafton in '45. Said he remembered *me* though, when we met Rags that time.'

'You're difficult to miss, and once glimpsed, ne'er forgotten.'

'I'll take that as a compliment,' said Lugg, dabbing his lips delicately with his napkin.

'I wouldn't,' said Amanda. 'Now can we get on, please?'

She jerked her head towards Rupert, who was yawning quite spectacularly, and tapped her wristwatch with a fingernail.

'My turn then,' said Campion. 'I had a very interesting trip out to Colchester in our new motor which, though you haven't asked, goes like a dream.' He caught the flash in Amanda's eyes. 'But that's not important. At Colchester garrison I saw a very helpful captain who had exactly what I'd asked for; it was like having one's own personal remembrancer.'

'What's one of them when they're at home?' snapped Lugg.

'Search me,' added Yeo.

'It's an ancient office from the good old feudal days. The remembrancer worked for the King's Exchequer, kept records and reminded forgetful barons of pending business. Captain Johnson had found just the file to remind me of the business I had out near Colchester back in 1940 when, I am possibly afraid to admit, it was little old me who introduced Evadne Childe to Pierre Le Frog.'

Mr Campion peered warily over the tops of his large round tortoiseshell glasses to check the mood of his audience.

'For reasons I won't bore you with, I was sent to Wivenhoe House, which was a sort of staging post for the lost and found after Dunkirk, to interview a couple of Belgian officers; lads really, hardly out of their teens. By pure coincidence, they were going to be billeted locally until the Belgian powers-that-be-in-exile could find them useful employment.'

'Once you'd decided they weren't spies, I suppose?' said Amanda.

Lugg's face twisted into a devilish grin. 'Give them the third degree, did yer? Chinese burns all round?'

'Don't be ridiculous,' said Campion. 'Anyone could see they weren't spies; they were lost boys far from home, a home that didn't exist any more. When I learned the pair of them were going to be housed with Evadne Walker-Pyne, better known as Evadne Childe and a godsibling of mine . . .'

Both Amanda and Lugg groaned at Campion's use of the spurious relationship he claimed with the writer, but it failed to deter him.

'. . . I just had to be on hand to do the formal introductions, and I left the two of them in the very capable hands of the nation's favourite writer of detective stories. Their names, thanks to my remembrancer Captain Johnson, were Simon Moorgat and' – he paused dramatically – 'Peter Verloet. So now, I thought, we had a name for Pierre Le Frog, and I telephoned it through to Freddie here this morning.'

'But this Peter, or Pierre, can't still be living with Evadne Childe, can he?' asked Amanda.

'Of course not. According to the army's records, the two Belgians stayed with Evadne until January 1941, when they were posted to the Free Belgian Forces camp at Tenby in Wales. There my Colchester remembrancer loses track of them, and so I thought I would tootle out to Evadne's house to see if I could pick up their trail there.

'With immaculate timing, I arrived a day too late, having just missed Evadne who had nipped over to the Continent for a short holiday, something she does quite regularly I believe, and of course by Continent, I mean Belgium.'

Lugg expelled a snort of displeasure.

'You don't approve of Belgium as a holiday destination?' Campion asked him.

'Went once and they started shooting at me. No inclination to go back there.'

'Don't take it too personally, everybody was shooting at everybody back then, but I doubt Evadne's visits were anything to do with that particular conflict. Still, we'll have to wait a few days to ask her on her return. What I did discover, however, was that she had been a regular visitor to a local spiritualist – hence my earlier question, my dear, about your interview with her editor.'

Amanda acknowledged her husband with a curt nod and a thin smile. 'She lost her husband very early in the war and even highly educated people turned to mediums to try and contact lost loved ones,' she said.

'Quite right, darling, it was a boom industry during the war, with séances and Ouija boards replacing dinner parties and bridge nights. Indeed, I remember the case of a senior naval officer involved in quite advanced scientific research, who had to be warned off holding séances at his house down in Hampshire in case one of the spirits from beyond was a curious German spy.

'Not that I'm suggesting Evadne Childe was up to anything like that. As Amanda says, she was trying to contact her late husband, and perhaps she did, or thought she did, and it probably brought her some comfort. But then, in early 1945 she switched tack and asked her medium, a formidable local lady called Miss Kitto, to try and contact someone called Peter.'

'That would make sense too,' said Yeo, who suddenly found himself the centre of attention.

'How's that then?' Lugg shot at him.

'When Albert rang me with the name Peter Verloet this morning, I got straight on to the liaison officer at the Belgian Embassy, who got on to their military records people. They came back quick as a flash, no slouches those Belgians, because the name was familiar to them. It turns out Peter Verloet was a bit of a hero among the Free Belgians. Went for commando training and did special courses in sabotage, then got his wings as a paratrooper. Ended up as an acting major in the Belgian squadron of the SAS. Bit of a hero, Peter Verloet was.'

'*Was?*' asked Campion.

'Yes, past tense. That's why contacting him through a medium would have been the only way. He was killed on patrol in the Ardennes on Christmas Day 1944.'

It was Amanda who broke the silence. 'So this Rags Donovan couldn't have seen him on Wardour Street last week, could she?'

'Nor could he have been involved in the . . .' Campion checked to see if Rupert was listening, '. . . the . . . incident with Tony Valetta at the Grafton, or at least it seems unlikely.'

'Highly unlikely,' said Yeo, in the droning voice he usually reserved for reading from notes in court. 'I would call it very unlikely that Verloet was anywhere near London in 1944. His unit landed in Normandy on D-Day plus two and fought across France and Belgium. Before D-Day he would have been on lockdown for several months for security reasons.'

'So Rags,' said Amanda slowly, 'and presumably Veronica Hatherall, couldn't have seen him when he was taking Evadne round the clubs of Soho back then?'

'As Freddie says, that's unlikely, but they both saw someone they thought was Peter or Pierre,' said Campion. 'The only person who knows for sure is Evadne Childe, so you should have a man waiting for her at Harwich and as soon as she steps off the boat, whip her in for questioning.'

Not even Yeo's most vicious critics would accuse him of being excitable or emotional, but at that moment his patience was wearing transparently thin.

'On what grounds? That she might have been seen in the Grafton Club back in 1945 with somebody who might have been seen in Wardour Street last week, but who is actually . . .' a glance towards Rupert again, '. . . no longer with us? What crime has she committed?'

'Herself? None that I'm aware of,' said Campion, 'but she is involved, if only on the periphery, with two crimes. Two *capital* crimes, involving Tony Valetta and Rags Donovan.'

'That's mighty thin, Albert. Stanislaus Oates and you got it into your heads that the mur . . . that the Valetta case was down to this Pierre Le Frog due to his connection with Evadne Childe, but we didn't even have a proper name back then and now we have no witnesses who could identify him.'

'We have one, but she's currently in Belgium,' Campion observed, 'and only one. So might it not be worth keeping an eye on her?'

Yeo wrinkled his snub nose. 'If she returns via Harwich, I can pull a few strings and get advance warning of which ferry she'll be on, but I can't put any men on it. I've got enough on my plate as it is and we'll find who . . . who helped Mrs Daubney shuffle off this mortal coil without recourse to mediums and spiritualists, or detective story writers!'

'But you have no objection if I continue to poke around?'

Yeo shook his head wearily. 'Even if I wanted to, could I stop you?

'He's got your measure, no mistake,' said Lugg with a gigantic belly-laugh which he stopped abruptly. 'As long as I don't have to go to 'arwich.'

'Then I think we are concluded,' said Campion, 'apart from coffee and a brandy.'

'No, we're not,' said Rupert loudly, drawing all eyes to him. 'I have a question.'

'Yes, darling?' prompted his mother.

'It's about the re-mem-ber-encer. Was it his job to remember the ice cream I was promised ages ago?'

'You are determined to get involved in this business, aren't you?' declared Amanda, as she began to remove her make-up in front of the dressing-table mirror with the concentration of a Renaissance painter.

Albert, buttoning his pyjama jacket, watched the process, as he always did, with a mixture of adoration and fascination.

'I would feel a lot happier if I knew what this business actually was,' he said to the nape of his wife's neck.

'You can't seriously think that Evadne Childe is involved in two murders six years apart, can you?'

Amanda watched for her husband's reaction in the mirror.

'Not in the dirty deed themselves, no, but there is a link.'

'The link is the Grafton Club, surely?'

'Well, yes, but Evadne uncannily prophesied the murder of Tony Valetta in her novel after visiting the place in the company of the mysterious Peter Verloet, who was spotted in London by the late Rags Donovan.'

'The mysterious and also himself late Peter Verloet.'

'Quite.'

'So Rags Donovan was murdered by a ghost?'

'Perhaps we should hold a séance and ask him directly.'

'Don't be an idiot.'

'Evadne Childe appears to have thought that possible and I don't think you would call her an idiot.'

Amanda picked up her hairbrush and began to slowly brush her hair, something usually guaranteed to distract her husband. In the mirror, however, she saw Albert's face struggling with confusion and indecision.

'I am sure Evadne is not an idiot and I know you are not, but you can be idiotic at times and perhaps this is one of them. Just what is it you feel you can do that the police cannot?'

'I have been asked that on many occasions,' said Campion, 'and my answer is always the same: very little. Yet I feel I must do something.'

'Why? You didn't lure Rags Donovan to her death.'

'No, I did not, but it was I who planted the seed of doubt about Pierre Le Frog in her mind six years ago. If I hadn't suggested that he was a person of interest, she might have thought no more about him and perhaps not recognized him last week in Wardour Street, or remembered who he was.'

'But Albert, she couldn't have recognized your Peter Verloet if he died in 1944!'

'He's not my Peter Verloet, he's Evadne's, and Rags recognized *somebody*. Somebody who didn't want to be recognized. The only connection we have is Evadne, and I have a responsibility to find out what she knows – if anything.'

'Why is it your responsibility, darling? This isn't some fanciful loyalty to a woman you hardly know but feel obliged to because you share the same godmother? Why can't you leave it to the police?'

'It's not a police matter, as Evadne is not suspected of anything other than writing a novel with a plot which mirrored a real crime, and I promised Stanislaus Oates I would look into that back in 1946 but I was distracted.'

Amanda smacked down her hairbrush on the dressing table.

'With good reason!' she said angrily. 'It wasn't your idea to go to those horrible trials in Nuremberg.'

'I was only on the periphery, merely an observer . . .'

'You still saw and heard things no normal person should have to. You were in a terrible state when you got home. I'm sure Stanis understood perfectly well why you never followed up on the Grafton case.'

'Nonetheless, I feel guilty about it,' said Campion, 'and now it's come back to haunt me. Oh dear, I could have chosen my words better, couldn't I?'

Amanda had completely forgotten that she had told Veronica Hatherall she was staying at the York, and when the hotel exchange put through her telephone call just after 7 a.m., she sounded dazed and confused, even though she had actually been awake and supervising Rupert's ablutions for a good twenty minutes.

'Lady Amanda?'

'Yes.'

'It's Veronica, from Gilpin's, the publisher – Evadne Childe's publisher.'

'Of course, what is it, Veronica?'

'Have you seen a newspaper this morning?'
'No, not yet. Why?'
'It's Evadne. She's done it again!'

ELEVEN
The Honest Job

The press had, in the idiom of Fleet Street, had a field day. Even the usually sedate newspapers had been tempted to employ the largest possible typeface, use grainy images which would not normally have passed the picture editor's scrutiny, and had resisted, but only just, the urge to sprinkle their breathless prose with exclamation marks.

'Audacious Robbery', 'Daylight Robbery', 'Film Drama Was Real', 'Lights, Action, Robbery', 'No Ealing Comedy' and, more parochially, 'Highway Robbery in Somers Town' were just some of the headlines. For their three halfpennies, readers of the *Daily Mail* and the *Daily Mirror* received the additional scandalous information that the heinous event had been witnessed by at least thirty members of the public who had each been paid ten shillings to act as 'extras' in what they thought was a film, only to discover they were aiding and abetting a crime. Readers of the *News Chronicle* and the *Daily Sketch* were reassured that the prime minister, Mr Churchill, was already taking a personal interest in the case. Those fortunate enough to have the 4 a.m. edition of the *Daily Telegraph* at their breakfast table were no doubt encouraged to learn that the police had already reported 'an early lead' in the case.

What the combined forces of the Fourth Estate were trying to tell their audience, often with poorly concealed glee, was the story of what became known as the Great Somers Town Hold-Up.

A post office consignment of high-value packets, mostly containing soiled or old bank notes to the estimated value of £109,000, had arrived by mail train at Euston station and was being transferred by unmarked van to the Eastern Central Delivery

Office. Within less than a quarter of a mile, before it had even reached the Euston Road, the van almost collided with another van, a dark blue Bedford, careering out of Euston Square and blocking the route. If that was not enough to disconcert the driver and his fellow guardian, the post office van found itself surrounded by a crowd of seemingly angry pedestrians, jeering loudly and banging fists and umbrellas against the panels of the vehicle for no apparent reason. Added to which, the whole spectacle was being filmed by two cameras on tripods on either side of the street.

No one seemed surprised in all that confusion when two masked men jumped out of the blue Bedford and began to drag the post office driver and his mate from their seats, and hardly anyone noticed that the two men previously working the cameras had deserted their posts and were now levering open the rear doors of the post office van with crowbars.

The transfer of numerous anonymous, but bulging, mail sacks from one van to the other was not, technically, aided by the dozens of law-abiding Londoners at the scene, but nor was it hindered. The first suspicions that something was terribly wrong was when the blue Bedford, now fully loaded, sped off and disappeared to the left down Euston Road, leaving two cameras on tripods but no cameramen and two post office employees battered and unconscious, their bodies rolled under the axle of their van. More than one of the crowd-scene extras, for which they had each received ten shillings for ten minute's shouting and rioting, remarked that the make-up department had done a top-notch job on the bruises and didn't that fake blood look realistic.

The police, rapidly on the scene, discovered two film cameras, neither of which contained actual film, and no fewer than twenty-five eyewitnesses to a robbery they had unwittingly aided and abetted, although their statements were uniformly vague. They had been going about their lawful business when they had noticed the film cameras being set up on Eversholt Street and stopped to take a closer look – well, who wouldn't? – just in case a film star could be spotted. A film director – he must have been because he carried one of those clapperboard things and he was dressed like one, in an astrakhan coat, a wide-brimmed fedora and a long silk scarf flamboyantly wrapped around his neck and lower face – told them no stars were going to arrive, but they could be film stars themselves, as extras. And they could earn ten bob doing it.

The extras did not need to understand the plot of the film, but the title was *The Honest Job* and they should look out for it at the pictures next year. All they needed to know was that two villains posing as post office guards had stolen a vanload of mail at Euston station and would be along at any moment. The real post office men, disguised as robbers, were out to steal the mail back and clear their names, though of exactly what was never made clear. The extras were all supposed to be neighbours or friends of the real heroes and therefore their job was to hamper the (fake) post office guards and their van and allow the 'robbery' to take place and the 'good guys' to escape.

Strangely, none of the extras could give a good facial description of the 'film director', having been distracted by the wallet stuffed with ten-shilling notes which he wafted under their noses. As to the cameramen, well, no one notices the man *behind* the camera, do they? And the fake 'robbers' – or perhaps the real ones – in the blue Bedford; they wore masks as they were supposed to and they were probably stuntmen rather than proper film stars, so it is hardly surprising they were not recognized. Thankfully, the ad-hoc crowd of extras contained two young men who had yet to discover the distractions of the female of the species and still retained their youthful enthusiasm for spotting and memorizing car number plates. Hence, in fairly short order, the police were looking for a blue Bedford van with the plate LKL 238 and, to their surprise and also disappointment, they found it within half an hour, still in Somers Town, abandoned in the goods yards of St Pancras station on Ossulston Street, 'just rahnd the bleedin' corner' as one detective constable groaned wearily, examining the abandoned, and very empty, vehicle.

Of the vehicle or vehicles to which the robbers had transferred, the five men themselves, and £109,000-worth of high-value packets, there was no sign. The only glimmer of light afforded to Detective Superintendent Yeo's hard-pressed men (coming just in time for the 4 a.m. edition of the *Telegraph*) was the fact that the 'inside man' (for there always was one), a disgruntled railway employee at Euston, who had tipped off the robbers about the

consignment of high value packets, had been identified, appre-
hended and was being interrogated.

The robbers' 'inside man' was a fifty-year-old luggage porter
with a reputation for a quick temper, a fondness for gambling
on greyhound races and an over-fondness for alcohol, named
John Janes. His apprehension was a ridiculously simple affair,
almost clichéd, as within a few hours of the robbery, Janes had
reported for his evening shift in a state of intoxication greater
than usual, and with £95 in bank notes about his person which
no one believed for a minute were his winnings from a night
down the dogs.

Interviewed by Superintendent Yeo himself, Janes became
more talkative as he sobered up, which is usually the reverse
behaviour of men of his nature and temperament. What tipped
Janes from hostile to friendly witness was the information,
imparted by Yeo with a certain amount of sadistic glee, that while
he might have made one hundred pounds, five of which had
already been drunk, the robbers had made off with over £100,000,
which hardly seemed fair, did it? Once he had been convinced
that he had somehow been swindled out of an equitable share of
the robbery, or at least sold short, John Janes may have become
more friendly to the police, but he did not prove especially helpful.

He had been approached one evening while patronizing his
favourite alehouse – and here Yeo felt the nineteenth-century
designation totally appropriate – near his lodgings just west of
the old Camden Town cattle market, in the area still quaintly
known as Low Holloway. The 'gent' who stood him several
rounds of light-and-bitter was a well-heeled foreigner, probably
a Frog, though John Janes was not good on accents and firmly
believed that foreigners started at Stoke Newington. And no, he
could not describe him, for he wore a wide-brimmed hat and a
scarf, masking most of his face. His wallet, however, he could
describe in detail, for all those five-pound notes in exchange
for a little timetable information had made a considerable
impression.

Janes had never heard the name Peter Verloet, nor the expression 'Pierre Le Frog'. He had no idea that daylight robbery with
violence was being planned – but then he had to say that, didn't
he? – but, more credibly, admitted that he had no inkling that it
would involve a fake film crew.

It came as no surprise to Superintendent Yeo that the abandoned film cameras left at the scene of the robbery had been rented from a company on Wardour Street which had, until recently, employed a Mrs Rachel Daubney.

At Gilpin's, the Campions were released from under the steely eye of Miss Prim and into the custody of Veronica Hatherall, who asked them to follow her upstairs to her office. As they climbed the steps she complimented Amanda on her outfit and on the way 'those new seamless stockings' really suited her. Amanda thanked her politely and said she was delighted that somebody had noticed, because her husband certainly had not. But then, she added, 'he is notoriously unobservant'; at which Veronica laughed and wagged a finger in disbelief.

Once her office door was securely closed and they were seated around her desk, the pleasantries ceased, and she became all business.

'This is all very irregular. I have not informed the directors that you are here, nor why I thought it necessary to see you, but I felt I had to tell you about Evadne's forthcoming book which we publish in November.'

'*Camera Obscuring*,' supplied Amanda.

'Why, yes,' said Miss Hatherall, her eyes widening in surprise.

'You told me that much on my last visit,' Amanda reassured her.

'Of course, of course. I couldn't tell you much about it because we were – we are – keeping it under wraps until simultaneous publication here and in America, except to say we have very high hopes for it . . . or had.'

'Until this morning's rather shocking headlines, I presume,' said Mr Campion.

'Shocking? They were awful! Goodness knows how Evadne is going to explain this to the directors.'

'I think the directors of Gilpin's may have to join the queue behind the Metropolitan Police when it comes to questioning Evadne Childe.'

Miss Hatherall was stunned into silence and appeared suddenly close to tears by the very thought. Amanda flashed her husband a warning look to remind him of the conditions under which he had been allowed to accompany her to the publishing house:

Veronica had telephoned *her* and Campion was given clear instructions not to bully or annoy the poor woman.

'Of course, in sordid commercial terms, I would think the attendant publicity will boost sales considerably, which ought to please the directors,' said Campion lightly to soften the mood.

'And there's no question, as I see it, that Gilpin's has done anything to attract the attention of the police,' soothed Amanda. 'I mean, you haven't actually published anything incriminating yet, have you?'

'Perhaps you might tell us the exact extent of your publishing . . . conundrum?'

Miss Hatherall took a deep breath, swallowed hard and placed a thick packet of paper on the desk in front of her, pushing it towards the Campions.

'These are sheet proofs fresh from the printer, which I am showing you without any authority other than my own as editor. This is Evadne's new novel, *Camera Obscuring*, which we intend – we hope – to publish in just over two months' time in November. It will be our lead title for the Christmas market and plans are already well in hand for serialization, book club and paperback editions, advertising and publicity – publicity of the right sort, I hope.

'If you agree not to show the text to anyone else, I will let you take these proofs away, but only if you give me your word that you will not divulge their contents to any third party.'

'Of course.' Amanda leaned forward in her chair and two sets of perfectly manicured and painted nails began to wriggle in anticipation. They were stopped before they reached the desktop by Mr Campion's hands, equally well manicured but only flesh coloured, gently enveloping his wife's, trapping them like angry spiders in her lap.

'I'm afraid we can make no such promise, Miss Hatherall, as the police may well be involved. Perhaps you could outline the plot to us now and, please, in our case, do not worry about spoiling the ending.'

'Very well then, I will give you a brief synopsis,' said the editor, 'which is something the author should provide with each new contract, but with an author as experienced as Evadne, we tend to overlook that formality and usually she tells me her outlines over lunch.'

'I've heard of publishers' lunches,' murmured Campion. 'I'm sorry. Please continue.'

'Evadne's very popular detective hero is an archaeologist, Rex Troughton, and in this novel he is at work in the City on a bomb site left over from the war. The Luftwaffe very kindly provided a window – or perhaps that should be a trapdoor – into what lay beneath what used to be the offices of a nineteenth-century insurance company. Excitingly, it could be the corner of a building on the forum of the Roman city established in the first century, so Rex is pretty engrossed organizing the dig. It's only when one of his diggers, a bright young girl reading archaeology and anthropology at Cambridge, who incidentally is called Veronica in the book . . .' She paused to allow herself a faint blush about the cheeks. '. . . Anyway, this girl tells Rex she has been spotted by a film director who has offered her a part in a film being shot nearby. It was only as an extra and she wouldn't have any lines, but she would have her face on the big screen and that could lead to bigger and better parts.

'Rex doesn't take much interest as he cannot think of anything more interesting than archaeology, or solving crime, and as the girl says it can all be done in a couple of hours and filming is just round the corner in Bishopsgate, Rex gives his blessing. Come the day of the shoot, which has been kept a big secret, Veronica gets changed into her best clothes and does what she is told as an extra, making sure she's never very far from one of the cameras. Basically, the extras are there to form a crowd and block the street as a mail van coming from Liverpool Street station is rammed and then robbed, but the robbers are actually the good guys and they are doing the job to prove the innocence of some post office workers who have been unjustly suspected of some other crimes.

'I admit that part of the plot is a little hazy, and of course when the robbery is pulled off, poor Veronica finds that the camera crews and the director have vanished, along with all the loot, and all the extras are arrested as accomplices. Rex Troughton has to step in and sort things out.'

'I wonder if he's free this weekend,' said Campion quietly. 'May I ask about this mysterious film director, who I assume is the mastermind behind this scenario? He's not a foreigner by any chance?'

At first, Veronica seemed puzzled by the question.

'No, he's not. He's a cashiered ex-army officer called Lawton, John Lawton. Turns out to be really clever but a very nasty piece of work, but don't worry, he comes to a sticky end.' Light dawned in her eyes. 'Oh, I see, you were hoping he might be French – or was it Belgian? – and called Peter.'

'It was a long shot,' Campion conceded, 'and far too convenient.'

'Well, I'm sorry I cannot help you there, but after what was in the papers this morning . . .'

'As you said, Evadne seems to have done it again,' said Amanda.

'Not quite,' Campion pointed out. 'In *The Bottle Party Murders* she recreated a murder she almost certainly could not have known was going to happen. At least we must assume that. With *Camera Obscuring*, she seems to have set out a plan for someone to follow. Substituting Euston for Liverpool Street, the resemblances are remarkable. Now the cynic might say she knew this robbery was going to happen and she arranged for the publication of the book to cash in on all the publicity.'

'That's ridiculous,' said Veronica sharply. 'Can you really see Evadne Childe as some sort of criminal mastermind, or gangster?'

'I'm not saying she personally directed the robbery, but she has conveniently laid out a plan which could work for someone else to follow.'

'But the book hasn't been published yet,' said Amanda.

Campion pushed his spectacles higher up his nose with a middle finger and stared across the editor's desk. 'But it has been written, and read by at least one person, probably more.'

Veronica Hatherall cleared her throat. 'Apart from myself as editor – and I assure you I am very happy with a career as an editor and have no plans to move into robbery with violence – and a copy editor whom I trust implicitly, no one has read the script outside our typesetters, who are down in Devon, and our printers in Glasgow.'

'Not even the firm's directors?'

'They rarely read anything for pleasure except balance sheets, but here at Gilpin's we have never had a leak from an unpublished manuscript, and we have published several controversial works in our time.'

'I think the police will require a comprehensive list of those who have read the manuscript and the obvious one, whom you have not mentioned.'

'I'm sorry?'

'Evadne Childe herself. No one is more familiar with the plot than she, are they?'

'Albert,' chided Amanda with relish, 'surely you can't suspect your *godsibling* of planning a robbery?'

'Of course not, but she may have told someone about the plot. A close friend, a fellow writer perhaps?'

'Evadne is rather reclusive,' said Miss Hatherall, 'most writers are, and she rarely mixes with other authors.'

'Isn't there some sort of trades union, or a Friendly Society for writers of detective stories?' Campion asked her, adding, 'Though Friendly Society is probably a misnomer given their bloodthirsty trade.'

'It's not really a trades union, but there is a thing called the Detection Club; though Evadne always thought the members were rather full of themselves, except she put it slightly more forcefully than that. She was elected to membership two years ago but turned them down. That, it appears, is something that is *never* done, and it put Evadne somewhat beyond the pale, not that she minded in the slightest. I doubt she would have told any fellow writer about a plot she was going to use in case they borrowed it before she got into print.'

Mr Campion looked suitably shocked. 'Tut-tut! Are you saying there is no honour among thieves, or rather people who write about thieves and murderers?'

'One has to make allowances when it comes to writers,' said Veronica, and Campion suspected it was a line she had been forced to use to the directors of Gilpin's in the past.

'And one must allow Evadne the benefit of the doubt,' said Campion, 'or at least wait until she returns from the Continent so we can ask her ourselves.'

'Whatever Evie admits – I mean says – is it likely to have consequences for our publication date?'

'You intend to go ahead with publication?'

'Naturally.' Miss Hatherall looked almost offended at the suggestion, but she was the first to break eye contact with Campion. 'Do you think we should take legal advice?'

'It might be a good idea,' said Campion. 'There are far too many unexplained coincidences for comfort.'

'But perhaps that's all it is,' Amanda intervened. 'It's just a horrible and quite bizarre coincidence.'

'Perhaps, perhaps not,' said Campion, determined to crush the faint glimmer of hope on Veronica's face. 'Tell me, Miss Hatherall, in *Camera Obscuring*, this villain – Lawton, was it? – fools people into being extras in a film to cover the robbery . . . would it be called *The Honest Job*, by any chance?'

'Why yes!' For a moment Miss Hatherall was the enthusiastic and proud editor, but the moment faded quickly. 'But you haven't read the book. How did you know that?'

Campion smiled at his wife.

'Perhaps I'm psychic.'

The Campions' return to the York Hotel was marked, over tea and crumpets, by a strategy meeting on domestic matters.

Lugg, who had been charged with entertaining Rupert by taking him to Hamleys, that Mecca of toy shops, reported that their afternoon had been a complete success, though only after considerable debate and discussion. Lugg had been quite prepared to allow Rupert to spend his allowance on a Dan Dare Cosmic Ray Gun – mostly, Rupert pointed out, because he wanted to play with it himself – but the young Campion had decided, rather haughtily in Lugg's opinion, that he should put aside childish things now that he was on the verge of going away to a senior school where they probably had a Cadet Corps with real rifles. Spurning the cornucopia that was Hamleys, Rupert was dragged into a Woolworths, ostensibly in search of a packet of Spangles, to which Lugg had become particularly partial, once he realized that the 'personal points' at the back of his ration book were for sweets, and emerged with an Airfix kit of the ship *Golden Hind* and a tube of glue.

With both Rupert and Lugg temporarily satisfied, the senior Campions agreed a plan of action. Amanda and Rupert would be driven home the next morning by Lugg in the Daimler, which was overstaying its welcome in the South Audley Street mews in which it was parked – if, as Lugg had remarked, the word 'parked' could be applied in the sense of an occupying army. At home Rupert could pack his trunk ready for his first term at

boarding school, to which Lugg had volunteered to chauffeur
him, and Amanda now had a book she not only wanted to read
but had to. Indeed, since they had left Gilpin's she had not let
the parcelled-up sheet proofs out of her sight and was clearly
itching to get a two-month head start on all the other fans of Rex
Troughton's adventures.

Campion would remain in London to supervise the work at
Bottle Street and would retain the new Bentley for a second foray
out into Essex when Evadne Childe returned from the Continent.
He would thus be on hand should Yeo wish to consult him.

'Are you going to tell Freddie about *Camera Obscuring*?'
Amanda had asked him.

'I would prefer to delay until I've had a chance to speak with
Evadne,' Campion had answered her carefully. 'It might be, as
you said, just a bizarre coincidence, but the similarities between
what happened in Somers Town and what Evadne predicted in
her fiction are too many to ignore. Still, I doubt very much if
we'll find a criminal mastermind called – what was it? – John
Lawton behind the robbery. I mean that sounds more like the
name of a vicar in rural Derbyshire than a gangland villain.'

The next morning Campion waved off his son, wife and a
fuming Lugg behind the wheel of the 'hatbox' with its outlandish
coachwork, then sauntered round to Bottle Street, where two
plumbers were struggling over a U-bend and an electrician rapped
the walls with his knuckles trying to find ancient wiring while
making the same sucked-in noises that garage mechanics
specialize in when asked to fix a misbehaving engine. The
consignment of tea, sugar, milk and biscuits that Campion came
equipped with, obtained with equal parts charm and bribery from
the kitchens of the York Hotel, soon won over the workforce,
and their loyalty was confirmed by Campion offering to put the
kettle on.

Campion watched the Bottle Street flat being transformed in
front of his very eyes as plasterers and painters plied their trade
with impressive speed, partly due to their employer being there in
person and partly, Campion fancied, due to their worksite being
directly above a police station, something he had always found
concentrated the mind wonderfully.

On the morning of the second day, Yeo telephoned the flat
from CID headquarters.

'Campion? Glad I caught you. Thought you might have left town by now. Sorry not to have been in touch but we've been rather busy just lately.'

'That's understandable, Freddie, given what the newspapers have been reporting from Somers Town.'

'They don't know the half of it. We've got nearly five hundred men out on this one and there's a ten-thousand-pound reward about to be offered, which will bring all the conmen and scroungers out of the woodwork with fairy stories to lead us up the garden path.'

'That is a very generous reward,' Campion admitted. 'I'm almost tempted to apply myself.'

Down the line, Campion thought he could detect a reluctant smile.

'Your services come for free, Albert, just you remember that, or I'll have words with your landlord about the lease on that flat of yours. Now listen, because I'm up to my eyes here and I haven't got much to tell.'

'All ears, Freddie, all ears.'

'We haven't got very far with Mrs Daubney's murder, I'm afraid. To be honest, we're nowhere; not an inch further forward with the actual killing. No witnesses, no evidence, and everyone she came into contact with regularly has an alibi which checks out. Only point of interest to you might be that we heard from the husband yesterday. He said he'd had a postcard from a book-shop on the Charing Cross Road, addressed to his late wife, telling her the book she'd ordered was in and ready for collection. You'll never guess what good book Rags Donovan was planning to settle down with.'

'An Evadne Childe detective story?' Campion felt a distinct chill as he suggested it.

'Dead right. Sorry; bad choice of words. Yes, it was one of hers, *The Bottle Party Murders*, which takes us back to the Tony Valetta killing and the Grafton Club, doesn't it, not to mention your favourite godmother.'

'God*sibling*, Freddie. Evadne and I share the same godmother, but that's hardly important in the scale of things. I'd like to think Rags's death was, though.'

'Oh, it is, Albert, for two reasons. One, we don't forget a murder, not on my watch; and two, Mrs Daubney has a connection with

the Somers Town investigation through the place she worked at
in Soho, renting out film gear.'

'Go on,' Campion said uneasily.

'It seems it was her who rented out the cameras used to fool
the public and confuse us, while the post office van was being
robbed. Rented them to a chap who claimed he was a film director,
a couple of days before she was topped near the Fitzroy.'

'You have a name?'

'Oh aye, plus an address, which turns out to be a seedy bed-
and-breakfast place on York Road, the other side of King's Cross;
but naturally he's done a runner and there's no one home now.'

'The name, Freddie? You're not expecting me to guess again,
are you?'

'No, we'd be here all day if you tried to guess. It was Lawton,
John Lawton.'

'And he doesn't feature in any of the Yard's copious records?'
said Campion after a full ten seconds of silence.

'We should be so lucky,' said Yeo, almost snarling. 'Since they
ditched identity cards, anyone can call themselves anything.'

'Some of us were doing that long before Herr Hitler made us
carry identity cards,' Campion quipped.

'Oh yes, of course, but that's different,' Yeo said quickly,
remembering Campion's true identity. 'There's them, like you,
who move in certain circles, who don't like using fancy monikers
or titles when they move in other circles. That might be a bit
eccentric but it's not yet illegal.'

'That's good to know. Is there anything I can do to help,
Freddie?'

'Well, you could have a word with the Childe woman. I've
just taken a call from the Customs chaps at Harwich. She was
on the overnight ferry from Antwerp. You said you wanted to be
tipped off.'

'So I did, thank you.'

'You can ask her if she has any idea what's going on,' scoffed
Yeo. 'She's the one who's supposed to be psychic, isn't she?'

TWELVE
No Good News from Ghent or Aix

'Your wife is considerably younger than you, Mr Campion. Does it ever bother you?'

It was not a question Mr Campion had been expecting, and he could not have anticipated that it would be Mrs Walker-Pyne's opening gambit.

'Not at all,' he said after a significant silence during which he suppressed an initial surge of umbrage. 'And if it bothers other people, I simply couldn't give a fig.'

'That's because you're a man.'

The new Bentley had made good time up the old Roman road into Essex, and Campion had stopped for a sandwich and a pint of Ridley's bitter in a pub called The Olde Crown in the village of Messing. He had been neither particularly hungry nor thirsty, but simply could not resist when he saw the signpost for that quaintly named place and had taken the opportunity to sit with what the advertising men would have called 'a contemplative pint' in a well-aged country pub and gather his thoughts for his forthcoming . . . well, he wasn't quite sure . . . interview? . . . interrogation? . . . cross-examination? . . . with Evadne Walker-Pyne.

He had felt guilty about telephoning Mill House when he estimated that Evadne could not have been more than an hour off the boat, perhaps had not even taken off her travelling coat yet, and was not surprised when she answered the telephone brusquely. Only the famous Campion charm at its most bewitching and Evadne's innate good manners prevented the call from being an extremely short one. The connection between Piccadilly and Eight Ash had almost been severed when Campion announced his intention of visiting Evadne that very afternoon and though, yes, he knew it was probably inconvenient and downright inconsiderate, it really was rather important. It was only when he added that he wished to speak to her about her forthcoming novel and that he had been asked by her publisher to consult on a technical matter that her tone changed from polite irritation to angry, demanding curiosity.

Having first telephoned Veronica Hatherall at Gilpin's to establish his cover story, Campion was in a position to reassure Evadne that his business was a professional matter and he was not, in any way, a deranged fan attempting to circumvent the strict embargo on *Camera Obscuring*. It was, however, business which could not be discussed over the telephone, but he could be with her by mid-afternoon.

Evadne had, with good grace considering the imposition, agreed to see Campion and added, stingingly, that she might just have time to unpack from her holiday before he arrived.

Campion's diversion off the main London-to-Colchester road into the tiny village of Messing, would – he decided magnanimously – give Evadne more time to settle herself after her travels, which was only doing the decent thing. In fact, it provided a welcome respite for his brain, which had been feverishly struggling with the problem of how he should approach Evadne face to face. Was there a diplomatic way of saying: *Hello, you haven't seen me for twelve years and our only connection is through a shared godmother, but may I come into your house and poke my nose into your business?*

The saloon bar of the Olde Crown was the perfect place for quiet contemplation, Campion being the sole customer, and the only background noise being a hum of muted conversation from the public bar on, as far as Campion could tell, the agricultural problems of the day, yet inspiration failed to arrive with his lunch. His sandwich, a thin slice of tinned ham between two slices of flabby white bread, made him almost nostalgic for the darker, grittier, wartime 'National Loaf', but at least the beer was sparkling, hoppy and refreshing, and he finished his pint in slow sips while smoking a single cigarette.

Yet neither food, nor alcohol nor nicotine brought inspiration, and his mind wandered. Evadne had just returned from Belgium and, ridiculously, Browning's poem 'How They Brought the Good News from Ghent to Aix' lodged itself in his brain. It was the sort of poem beloved of schoolboys because of its galloping meter, a rhythm which was difficult to dislodge from the brain as it carried the story of the breathless night ride by three horsemen, west-to-east from Ghent to Aix-la-Chapelle, now better known as Aachen. Quite why the poem had sprung, unbidden, from his subconscious amused him for the most foolish of reasons. He was not aware that Evadne had been anywhere near Ghent or Aix and he was certainly not galloping towards her with good news. But then, as he recalled, the exact nature of the crucial 'good news' which those night-riders bore was never revealed in the poem, or subsequently by the poet. And Browning himself disproved the theory that the poem, once heard, was impossible to forget as, late in life, the poet had attempted to recite it into a newfangled phonograph machine. He had managed only the first two lines before his voice was recorded for posterity saying, 'I'm terribly sorry but I can't remember my own verse.'

As he left the pub, he was no clearer in his mind as to the best strategy to approach Mrs Walker-Pyne. The lowliest uniformed policeman on the beat soon became skilled in handling confrontations with the parents of the most wayward, even villainous children who were, in parental eyes, absolute angels, totally innocent of any wrongdoing.

Campion had a far more delicate, even dangerous, problem on his hands; he had to tackle an author about misdeeds committed in her books and, when their writing was threatened, authors could be more protective than polar bears with a single cub.

By the time he reached Eight Ash he was no further forward in his own plan of campaign, but he had accepted that – however diplomatically he posed the problem to Evadne Walker-Pyne – Evadne Childe the author was likely to react forcefully. He had not, however, expected her to immediately go on the attack with the ferocity of a she-wolf.

She had opened the front door of Mill House and asked him into her sitting room with a frosty 'Good afternoon, Mr Campion' and a slight nod of her head. Campion had followed her lead and was removing his hat and still formulating a pleasantry or two about her recent holiday when she turned on him with that opening salvo about the age disparity between himself and his wife.

'I am fifty-two years old,' said Campion through tight lips, 'and my wife is fourteen years younger than me. That is a matter of public knowledge, but I fail to see what that has to do with anything.'

'When I married Edmund, he was twenty-two years my junior, and at the time we ignored the jibes and snide remarks, the snubs of society and the palsied attempts at sarcasm in the press because we were in love. We had less than three years together before Edmund was taken. And *that* has everything to do with it!'

'I am afraid you are going to have to explain that, Mrs Walker-Pyne. Everything to do with what?'

'The reason you are here, of course, though I cannot think what possible business it might be of yours. I may be an old, widowed, country vicar's daughter, but I am not stupid, Mr Campion.'

'Far from it, good lady. By your imagination and craft, you have managed to get away with murder many times and make a living out of doing so, but I am still at a loss as to why the respective ages of our dearly beloveds should have a bearing on my visit. If I have implied anything which has given offence, I do, of course, apologize.'

Mrs Walker-Pyne put her head on one side and examined her guest more closely, narrowing her eyes so that Campion suspected she was, or soon would be, in need of spectacles.

'I knew you would return, just not quite so soon,' she said in the voice that a teacher would use to say how disappointed she was in a pupil. 'My handyman and driver, Reuben Stopes, when he collected me from Harwich this morning, told me of your previous visit and that you had subsequently called on Miss Kitto in the village. Your snooping was quite the talk of Eight Ash while I was away, I understand.'

'Curiosity – a failing of mine, I admit, but hardly snooping.'

'When it's personal, it's snooping in my book. When my husband was taken from me in 1939, I was determined not to lose him completely. Through the Spiritualist Alliance in London and then through Miss Kitto here, Edmund and I have been able to keep in touch across the divide.' As she spoke, her head turned, almost involuntarily, to the framed black-and-white photograph hanging over the fireplace which showed a single-funnel steamship at rest in a deep-water anchorage. At the bottom of the grainy photograph was a strip of paper providing the inked caption *SS West Riding*. 'I am not ashamed of that, but I have no illusions as to how the gossip columnists would lap it up, with stories about a sad old woman still in widow's weeds yearning for her young lover. They would do their sums and realize that, were he still with us, Edmund would be forty this year, still seven years younger than I was when I married him before the war. That is not the sort of publicity I, or my publishers, want, Mr Campion.'

'I think you may be overgenerous in your assessment of the mathematical prowess of the average journalist, Mrs Walker-Pyne, but I fully understand your sensibilities. If your . . . communications . . . with your husband bring you comfort and peace of mind, then so be it, but your arrangements with the redoubtable Miss Kitto are not the real reason I needed to talk to you.'

'Then what is?'

Campion allowed his face to soften, expressing, he hoped, only genuine concern.

'I know you've been on the Continent, but have you, by any chance, seen a British newspaper lately?'

Within a minute of commencing his narrative, a precis of the press coverage and police intelligence regarding the Somers Town robbery, Evadne's eyes widened in realization and she sank into an armchair, waving a limp hand to indicate that Campion should also be seated.

She wore a blue plaid house dress with apron pockets, dark stockings and brown court shoes, a perfectly acceptable ensemble for a woman of her age at home in the country on an autumnal afternoon. Yet as she listened to Campion's narrative, she seemed to shrink and allow the armchair to envelop her. To her lecturer, it was as if she was not just dissolving, but ageing before his very eyes, touching her hair nervously and continuously. Her hair, Campion knew thanks to Amanda, was cut in the 'poodle clip' style, but he was sure there had not been so many white flecks among the brown curls when he had arrived, and the plaid house dress had begun to look more like a blanket wrapping an invalid.

'You have to admit,' said Mr Campion in summation, 'the similarities between the fictional robbery in your book and the real one which took place in Somers Town are really quite remarkable.'

Evadne stopped touching her hair, placed her hands in her

lap and, as if to control them, interlaced her fingers. After half a minute of silence she looked up at Campion, her face composed. 'Similarities, yes, but that's all they are. You cannot seriously be accusing me of coming up with a master plan for a robbery then revealing it in a book – and a book not yet published, can you?'

'You are known for your thorough research, Miss Childe. If you remember, that is how we first met twelve years ago. You were taking shooting lessons with Stanislaus Oates of Scotland Yard. May I ask how you did your research for *Camera Obscuring*?'

'Where do I get my ideas from?' she said with a loud sigh. 'Goodness, if only I had a pound for every time I have been asked that! Well, you can keep your pound notes in your wallet, Mr Campion, because that one's quite easy, I remember it well. I was in London last year and looking for a new site for my archaeologist hero Rex Troughton to ply his trade. For some reason, the Tower of London attracted me, so I took a walk down through Billingsgate and came across a film crew from Ealing Studios. There were shooting exterior scenes for the film *Pool of London*, and watching them, and how the public reacted to them, gave me the idea of using a film crew as a cover or a distraction to aid a real crime.'

'Clever,' admitted Campion, 'and it clearly worked.'

'And it was written months before the event, the real event, that is. And what I wrote could hardly have given anyone larcenous ideas as nobody has read it yet! Unless, that is, you suspect someone in the editorial department at Gilpin's.'

'Myself, I do not, but others may. What I would like to ask you is whether you divulged your plot to anyone else, however casually, either before or during the writing process.'

The author did not hesitate. 'No one, not a living soul. You clearly do not know many writers, Mr Campion. We are a superstitious bunch, and if we think we have come up with a good idea we do not jinx it by telling too many people, especially not other writers who may well steal it.'

'I have heard they are an unscrupulous bunch, but are you sure you did not discuss your plot with anyone, anyone at all?'

'My editor at Gilpin's, of course, but absolutely no one else. I talk to few people these days, and as few as possible when I am writing a novel. When a book comes out one has to do the literary rounds, naturally, but to discuss a book before it is published would not only be tempting fate but fairly pointless as no one could buy one.'

'And when you have finished writing a book, am I right in thinking you hop across to the Continent for a holiday?'

'I have got into that habit,' said Evadne after a slight pause. 'It helps me clear my mind and hopefully come up with an idea for the next book, but not only when I have finished a book. I cross the Channel two or three times a year for short breaks, but once again, I am not sure what business that is of yours.'

'Belgium is your preferred destination?' Campion persisted.

'It is the most convenient destination from Harwich, which is the most convenient port of departure for me here in Eight Ash.'

'But do you travel on, to France or Germany for instance?'

'I have, in the past, but I visit Belgium more than anywhere else and I have a sneaking suspicion you already knew that thanks to Reuben Stopes. It is true, I like Brussels and go there regularly. I can assure you that while there last week, I did not discuss or even think about the plot of *Camera Obscuring* for a single minute.'

'And you had no idea that your fictional plot was being acted out in reality while you were in Belgium?'

'No, I did not!' The first spark of anger. 'I had no desire to seek out an English newspaper while on holiday. I rarely take one when I am in England either, as Gilpin's monitor the press for any reviews and send them to me.'

At least she was an honest author, Campion thought, not one of those precious ones who, like many actors, claim never to read their own reviews; and she left him in no doubt that she was a writer of detective stories.

'But let us assume that if I were to put my fictional plot into action, then being out of the country when it happened would provide me with an excellent alibi, would it not?' Campion nodded agreement. 'So why should I return to England, knowing that I have already committed my master plan to paper, which will surely incriminate me when the book is published? Would it be to claim a reward perhaps? Is there a reward?'

'I believe £10,000 has been offered.'

'Good gracious! That far outweighs any advance Gilpin's might offer. What do I have to do and where do I apply? Writing fiction but being paid for fact seems a very lucrative way of making a very tidy living.'

'It wouldn't be the first time,' said Mr Campion.

'What do you mean by that?' Now the anger had sparked into full flame.

'Do you remember your novel *The Bottle Party Murders* from 1946?'

'Of course I do. It's regarded as one of my best and went down very well in America.'

Mr Campion found it fascinating that an author's righteous anger could be so easily assuaged by a reminder of past praise.

'Yes, I believe you went on a tour of America at the time.'

'I did indeed, a highly successful tour. How did you know?'

Campion's gaze faltered towards the carpet. 'I had intended to talk to you at the time, but circumstances intervened. You were in America and I was then . . . elsewhere.'

'Talk to me about what?'

'Your talent for predicting crime.'

'I am not sure I understand you, Mr Campion. In fact, I am sure I have no idea what you are talking about.'

'You did your research for that book in the Grafton Club, which became the Reynard Club in your novel, and it was the owner of the Reynard, whom you called Jake Muscat, who was the murder victim.'

'That's correct.'

'Do you remember the owner of the Grafton who showed you around? You gave him an autographed book.'

'Did I? I usually do when someone helps me with my research. I vaguely recall . . . he was an immigrant, or perhaps a refugee. Maltese, that was it – he was from Malta and he was named after a place there.'

'Valetta. Tony Valetta.'

'That's it. A strange little man in an unsavoury business. I was never tempted to keep in touch with him.'

'You would have found that difficult,' said Campion, thinking that with Miss Kitto's help, she might have done just that. 'I'm afraid he's dead.'

'Oh dear, should I send condolences or a wreath? I hardly

knew him, but I suppose he was helpful when I was writing *Bottle Party.'*

'Valetta died just before Christmas, 1945. He was shot and robbed in a fashion almost identical to what happened to Jake Muscat in your novel.'

Evadne's hands gripped the arms of her chair fiercely enough to whiten the knuckles.

'Believe me, I had no idea!'

'I think I do,' Campion said to himself.

'Why has this come to light only now, six novels later?'

Campion noted the professional author's habit of quantifying time in number of books written.

'Because it was only noticed some months after the event. As you had actually delivered your finished manuscript before Valetta's murder, you were not directly a suspect.'

'Well, thank heavens for small mercies.'

'It was a remarkable coincidence, though; your prediction of a crime so accurately.'

'Fiction! I write fiction, Mr Campion, and as far as I know, there is no law against that yet, however much the Revenue would like there to be one.'

Campion curbed a smile; here was the author revealed in tooth and claw.

'And now there is your latest work – of fiction – which uncannily predicts the Somers Town mail van robbery, even though, I accept, it is not yet published.'

'Coincidence, pure coincidence. My novels are about criminals. I write about crime and its consequences, so I have to think myself into the mind of criminals. It is not difficult because most criminals are of low intelligence which is why many of them get caught. If I have successfully predicted what a criminal or criminals might do, it is surely a mark of my skill that I have observed the same opportunities for crime as they have.'

Evadne had released the arms of her chair and folded her arms across a bosom which now positively swelled with professional pride, and her voice rose with certainty.

'Were I a man and my name was Berkeley or Blake or Dickson Carr, and I was one of the patricians of the Detection Club, you'd say I was ingenious and clever, but because I'm a woman, there must be something suspicious about my skill. Witchcraft, perhaps?'

Before Campion could respond, she made to rise from the armchair but then relaxed and sank back into its protective shell as a new thought occurred to her.

'Is this why you went to see Miss Kitto? It is, isn't it? You think I'm getting some sort of psychic guidance, don't you?'

'I have said that your dealings with Miss Kitto were not the prime reason I came to see you, but they do interest me.'

'I sense that you are about to patronize a foolish old woman,' said Evadne, tight-lipped.

'I do not believe I am talking to a foolish woman,' said Campion, 'and I hope I would not presume to patronize one of any age. It is clear that you missed your late husband very much and sought comfort by trying to contact him in the . . . afterlife . . .?'

'We prefer "on the other side".'

'My apologies. I am unfamiliar with the process and the terminology.'

'Don't apologize, Mr Campion, and do not worry about offending my feelings, however bizarre you think my beliefs.'

'I try not to judge other people's beliefs if they are sincerely held.'

Evadne's eyes darted to Campion's face. 'Did that include Mr Hitler's sincerely held beliefs?'

'Ah, well, there are always exceptions,' Campion conceded. 'I should have said beliefs that are sincerely held *which do not harm others*. My point was that your séances with Miss Kitto were private conversations between a wife and a husband she sorely missed and as such should be of no concern to anyone.'

In agreement Evadne nodded her head and said a gentle 'Thank you' under her breath.

'There is one thing about your sessions with Miss Kitto, however, that I must press you on, and that was the point when you asked her to put you in touch with someone who wasn't your husband.'

'You mean the Belgian boy, Peter.'

Mr Campion felt a tingle of excitement: at last, a confirmation, of a sort, of the existence of Pierre Le Frog.

'Indeed I do, Peter Verloet. I brought him here to this very house in 1940 along with another young refugee, Simon Moorgat.

They were billeted on you for several months. Clearly he must have made quite an impression on you.'

'They both did; they were charming and intelligent boys. It was a pleasure to play mother to them during the war.'

'Why did you ask Miss Kitto to contact Peter for you?'

'Because he had passed over.' Evadne looked at Campion as if he was slow in the head. 'He had been killed – on active service, I think the phrase is.'

'But how did you know?'

'Simon told me. Simon told me lots of things. We became quite close during the war.'

'You kept in touch with Simon – and Peter – during the war?'

Campion realized the question was a hostage to fortune, given that Evadne was confident that death was no barrier to staying in touch.

'I certainly did. They were charming boys, and if Edmund and I had ever been blessed with sons, I would have wanted them to be like those two.' For the first time since he had arrived, Campion saw Evadne smile. 'Everyone in Eight Ash thought they were French, of course, and the idea of a middle-aged widow living with two young, virile Frenchmen was almost too much for them to bear, especially as I was, in their eyes, still the vicar's daughter.'

'But your mother was living here when they were billeted on you.'

'Yes she was, so of course it was all perfectly respectable, but she had little to do with them. She did not like the idea of foreigners in her house, though everybody told her it could be worse; they might be Germans. She pretended she could not tell them apart and often confused their names. It became something of a joke between us.'

'I understand they were posted away from Essex in early 1941.'

'Yes, duty called, and they got their marching orders.'

'But you still managed to see them?'

'Occasionally. When they had leave, they would make their way back here for a few days – they had no family in this country – and I made them welcome.'

'My understanding is that one of them, Peter, went off for special training with a commando unit. I would have thought his military masters kept him rather busy.'

'I certainly saw less of Peter after 1942, and not for the last year of his life, sadly.'

'So it was Simon who helped you research your novel set in Soho?'

'*Dark Moon Over Soho*? Yes, it was, and he also helped me with *The Bottle Party Murders*, getting me into all those seedy clubs.'

'You are sure it was Simon Moorgat?'

'Of course I am sure, what do you take me for?' Evadne paused as if wrestling with a memory. 'Wait, you think I was with Peter in London when I was researching those books?'

'It was your editor who said someone called Peter had been showing you around Soho and the Mayfair clubs. Perhaps they got the two Belgian boys mixed up.'

'That's ridiculous; it's not as if they were twins. Peter was a quiet, well-mannered boy, blond hair and blue eyes. A bit of a baby-face. Simon was all black curls and green eyes; a touch of the gypsy about him and a bit of a scallywag. I used to call him my Heathcliff. Had I been a teenage girl, he might have made me swoon, whereas I just wanted to mother Peter.'

'I believe Peter Verloet was on active service for much of 1943 and 1944,' said Campion, 'so he couldn't really have been showing you around Soho, could he?'

'He wasn't; I've told you that. It was Simon who showed me the seedy side of London.'

'But how did Simon know so much about the black market and the Bottle Party clubs? He was, like Peter, an officer in the Belgian army, and must have had duties.'

Evadne's expression was now one of pity. 'Oh dear, you haven't done your homework properly, have you? Simon was in the Free Belgian security services and had a very hush-hush job based in London. I don't know what sort of war you had, Mr Campion, but it was common for those involved in cloak-and-dagger work to have false identities. The Belgians had a clever system of "doubles" where their agents in England adopted the identity of a real soldier away on active service.'

'Let me guess,' said Campion, hiding his irritation. 'Simon took Peter's identity while Peter was off training to be a commando.'

'Who better? If anyone asked him anything about Peter Verloet,

Simon knew his story backwards. He even had a set of identity papers in Peter's name but with his own photograph. Everyone knew him as Peter, or sometimes Pierre because they thought his accent was French, and I had to call him that. It was a bit of a private joke between us.'

'Until the real Peter was killed serving in Belgium and it was Simon who told you?'

'Yes, that's right.'

'And then you went to see Miss Kitto to try and make contact with him?'

'I did, I was very fond of Peter in the short time I knew him, but Miss Kitto wasn't able to help. It was Simon who recommended Madame Rawnie.'

'I'm sorry, Madame who?'

'Madame Rawnie. She is the best medium in Brussels and had absolutely no trouble in finding Peter. Coming from the same country probably helped.'

'That's why you often go to Belgium.'

'It is, if it is any business of yours. I'm still not clear on why you are asking all these questions, which have absolutely nothing to do with a post office van robbery, either a real one or the one in my new novel.'

'Please bear with me, I only have two more.' Campion felt the need to get to a telephone, and an uncharacteristically desperate yearning for a cigarette. 'When did you last see Simon Moorgat?'

'Nineteen forty-five,' said Evadne without hesitation. 'It would have been after VE Day but before *Bottle Party* came out.'

'For that one he introduced you to the Grafton Club.'

'Yes, he did.'

'And you've had no contact since?'

'He sends me a card at Christmas, from Belgium, but that's all.'

'And when he was helping you research the *Bottle Party* book, at the Grafton, do you remember meeting a young woman called Rags Donovan?'

Evadne gave a shrug of indifference. 'I don't think so.'

'She was the cigarette girl in the Grafton and the model, I suspect, for the character Sapphire in your book.'

'Oh, *her* – now I remember. She was a bit too tarty for my

taste and came on to Peter – I mean Simon – with eyelids fluttering and bosom heaving, but then I suppose that was normal
for a girl of that type; not that it did her any good. Still, she
provided me with one of my most popular jacket covers, among
male readers that is.'

'You have not seen her since then?'

'Good Lord, no. Why do you ask?'

'No reason,' said Mr Campion.

THIRTEEN
Police Work

'I could get used to this,' said Detective Superintendent Yeo,
surveying the extensive range of scones, cakes and fondant
fancies displayed for his delectation at high tea at the York
Hotel, 'though in other circumstances this spread could easily
qualify as a bribe.'

'A bribe would imply I was expecting something in return,'
said Mr Campion, reaching for the teapot. 'Shall I be mother?'

'Please, and don't worry about charges of bribery and corrup-
tion. I think this qualifies as an exchange of police work, and
some of us have been very busy since you rang me yesterday
and added to my overflowing in-tray.'

'Sorry about that, Freddie. Idle hands making work for already
busy hands, or something like that, but I thought it important to
let you know that the name we should be interested in is Simon
Moorgat and not Peter Verloet.'

'Which was the name you gave us, the name of a dead
man.' Yeo helped himself to the plainest, most puritan biscuit on
offer.

'Again, apologies for setting a false hare running.'

'Not your first, won't be your last.'

Yeo had spent years in the metropolis measuring his words
carefully and adopting a droning monotone when on official
business, so his native Somerset burr surfaced only occasionally,
and it almost always took Campion by surprise.

'You said you'd been busy. Dare I ask if there is progress on the Somers Town robbery?'

'You may indeed,' said Yeo, reverting to his best courtroom diction. 'Substantial progress, you might say, if you call two arrests and recovering a good chunk of the loot.'

Campion put down his teacup so that he could gently applaud the news.

'How splendid! I do hope my telephone tip-off was of some use.'

'No use at all, I'm afraid, Albert, so no sniff of the reward money for you. We did it by old-school coppering.'

'So the name Simon Moorgat was no use to you?'

'Not a bit, but John Lawton proved a useful lead.'

'The man who hired the cameras for the fake film crew? I thought you said he'd flown the coop.'

'Oh, he did, faster than slush off a shovel. He had a car in a lock-up just round the corner from his digs on York Road and, thanks to a nosey neighbour, we know the car left there within an hour of the robbery. Our boy was all set up for a quick getaway and was long gone before my lads got there to find his room and the garage clean as a whistle.'

'But you said you'd made arrests and recovered the money.'

'Two arrests so far, and *some* of the money.' Yeo's bony fingers hovered over an oblong of sponge cake then, thinking better of it, flitted over a ginger nut and pounced. 'That's where the good coppering came in. We flooded the area with plainclothes men, covering every boozer, illegal bookies' and knocking shops in Camden, Kentish Town and West Islington.'

'On the assumption that some of the gang were local,' said Campion.

'They were, and in the finest tradition of the capital's criminal population, they were local and stupid and couldn't resist splashing some of their ill-gained wealth. We picked the first one up that first night in a pub down the Caledonian Road, waving fivers around like the ink was still wet. He didn't spill the beans though, not even after he'd sobered up, but I had a back-up plan.'

'I would have expected no less, Freddie.'

Yeo acknowledged the compliment, dunked his biscuit in his tea and continued.

'When we traced this Lawton's digs, we turned the place over and found nothing, so we pulled out sharpish, but left a couple of lads there to watch for visitors. We knew Lawton had done a runner, but did the rest of the gang?'

'I'm guessing not.'

'You guessed right. A hard man called Billy Bright, plenty of muscles but not much up top, turns up looking for Lawton. He's carrying a new passport in his real name in one hand, and a suitcase containing three thousand pounds in used notes in the other. He coughed fairly quickly. He said he was going with Lawton to Croydon airport to catch a plane to Amsterdam. He'd been looking forward to it, had Billy, as he'd never been in an aeroplane before and never been abroad – and he had lots of spending money.'

'But Billy Bright's not very bright, is he?'

'You can say that again. He didn't know Croydon was winding down and all flights were going from Northolt until the new airport at Heathrow is ready. Fair disappointed, he was. In fact, he was more cut up about missing out on his holiday than he was about being arrested. He said he'd always wanted to see the windmills and the tulips and buy his mum a set of miniature clogs to hang on her Christmas tree. Like you said, Albert, Bright isn't bright, but he's bright enough to know that things might go easier on him if he turns King's evidence on the rest of the gang.'

'I think you mean Queen's evidence now, Freddie; you really should try and keep up with things.'

'Maybe it'll finally sink in next year when we have to turn out in force for the Coronation. You involved in that?' Yeo allowed himself a cheeky grin.

'You know me, Freddie. Never could resist fancy dress and the odd bit of pageantry . . . but get back to Billy Bright and his gang.'

'It wasn't his gang; he was adamant about that. All the planning and the orders came from this Lawton chap; he was the big cheese, or should I say big *fromage*?'

'He was French?'

'Billy said the gang thought he was foreign due to the way he said certain things and because he smoked those black tobacco cigarettes, but he knew his way round London, Soho in particular. He certainly knew where to recruit his crew. There were four of them and the inside man at Euston, John Janes, who was the first we picked up. Billy gave us three names; all of them are villains on our books, and we got one of them down his local pub. The two others, would you believe, took their wives and kids off to Brighton for a week at the seaside. The Sussex police are rounding them up as we speak.'

'Did they all get their cut?'

'Far as I know, the deal was ten grand each for the gang on condition they all disappeared for a few weeks. Billy didn't know where to go. You know the sort, went to Margate once for the cockles and winkles, but it rained, so never went back.'

'And the boss man suggested a trip to Amsterdam from an airport no longer operating?' said Campion, eyebrows raised. Yeo nodded. 'Shows he has a sense of humour, and it might have worked as a diversion to keep your lads busy, knowing he would be well out of the picture before Billy found out he was on a wild-goose chase. Could Billy identify him?'

'I doubt Billy Bright could pick his own mother out of a line-up, and it seems this Lawton, or whatever his name is, had a thing for meeting in shady places, always wore a hat with the brim pulled down and a scarf as a muffler; dark glasses a lot of the time. Made sure none of them got a good look at his face, and all the civilians he conned into being extras for his so-called film shoot, well, they were all so keen on being film stars, they were more concerned that their hair would look good on camera than in remembering the chap who was giving out the ten-bob notes. Not even the people who shared the digs on York Road with him could give a good description.'

Campion chose his next words carefully. 'So the only person who could have positively identified Simon Moorgat or John Lawton . . .'

'If they are the same person,' cautioned Yeo.

'. . . was Rags Donovan, the late Mrs Daubney.'

'The investigation into the murder of Mrs Daubney will take its course, Albert,' Yeo said in his dress-uniform voice, 'as we pursue the Somers Town robbery. It may well be that they are linked.'

'But they are, Freddie, they must be. Rags Donovan recognized the man who hired the film cameras used in the job.'

'Recognized him as who? Someone she saw briefly years ago

and thought was called Peter Verloet, who turned out to have been killed in the war?'

'I'm sure she recognized him, and he recognized her and was following her. She was coming to tell me . . .'

'But she never made it, did she, Albert? So we can't be sure who she saw and whether it was this Peter, who you call Simon, or the mysterious Mr Lawton who did for her.'

'Unless they are one and the same person, which I am willing to bet on.' Campion jutted out his jaw and poked himself in the chest with a forefinger. 'And you know I'm not a betting man, Freddie.'

'Well, I certainly wouldn't play cards with you,' said Yeo, 'not even Happy Families. Talking of which, shouldn't you be getting back to yours? From here on in it's policework – checking the ports, the airports, the banks, taking statements, sweating his partners in crime. Honest Injun, Albert, we've got more chance of nailing him for the mail-van job than for Mrs Daubney's murder. I don't like to admit that, but it's true.'

'Neither will be easy. You've got to find him first.'

'Fair point, and *that* won't be easy. He's got a head start, anything up to fifty thousand pounds, and he seems to know how to work several false identities.'

'Can the cash be traced?'

'Some of it, where we've got serial numbers, but you know as well as I do that hard cash is always easy to dispose of as long as you spread it wisely and don't flash it down the pub.'

'Or on Brighton seafront,' Campion observed mildly, 'but I think our Somers Town mastermind has gone way beyond Brighton.'

'Across the Channel? I think so too. He gave his crew plenty of cash so they'd be sure to get noticed and provide a suitable distraction for us. Meanwhile, he's doing the moonlight flit which he's had planned for some time – and could be anywhere.'

'My bet is Belgium.'

'But you're not a betting man, Albert.'

'*Touché*. In that case, my guess would be Belgium.'

'A good place to start, unless your detective-story writer friend has any bright ideas that might help us . . .?'

'I don't think she has.'

'Then it looks as though we'll have to call in Interpol.'

*   *   *

'So who's this Interpol when he's at home?' asked Lugg.

'Oh, my faithful dunderhead, I would have thought you of all people would have kept up with the forces of law and order. Know your enemy and all that.'

'Well, pardon me for living, I'm sure. Some of us menials don't have time to put their feet up with the *Police Gazette.*'

As if to prove his point, Lugg set to his task with grim determination and a totally superfluous display of physical exertion accompanied by loud grunting noises.

They were in the main garage, formerly the stables, of the Campions' family home, where much of the space was taken up by Amanda's remodelled – by Dr Frankenstein, as Campion had once observed quietly – Daimler landau, formerly known affectionately, if only to her and Campion's sister, as The Running Footman and now to Campion and Lugg as The Footman (Retired). Indeed, the two men were preparing the car for its retirement, or at least its over-wintering if a buyer could not be found. Lugg thought it highly unlikely one would be, while Campion knew for certain that the sale price demanded by his wife would be exorbitant, as to her the monstrous vehicle was more precious than rubies.

Lugg was stripped down to vest and braces, applying polish to any surface which would shine. Campion was taking a more supervisory role, unfolding the massive canvas tarpaulin which would encase the Daimler during its period of hibernation and topping up the anti-freeze.

'Make sure it's got enough petrol in the tank to get as far as the gatehouse and the main road,' Lugg had counselled, 'in case somebody breaks in and pinches it. You'd want to give them a decent head start.'

It was the mention of a head start for wrongdoers which had raised the topic of the Somers Town robbery and the police's lack of progress in tracing the ringleader, and Campion's subsequent dropping of the word 'Interpol'.

There was no reason why Lugg should have been familiar with the term – few members of the public were – but Campion was sure it would eventually catch on beyond its shorthand use among police professionals, diplomats and inquisitive amateurs such as himself. Perhaps, in time, even writers of detective stories would use 'Interpol' as common currency, even though its humble derivation was as the Paris telegraphic address for the International Criminal Police Organization.

Originally formed as the International Criminal Police Commission in 1923 in Vienna, with Britain joining in 1928, the commission fell into bad odour when, with the Anschluss in 1938, it was effectively taken over by Hitler's Nazi party; it had been run from Berlin during the war years, directed by presidents such as Reinhard Heydrich and Ernst Kaltenbrunner, both of whom were notorious for committing rather than preventing or detecting crimes.

With the outbreak of peace and the noble ambition that the nations of Europe should work together rather than tear each other apart, the commission was reformed and revitalized and headquartered in Paris. The prime mover in the creation of Interpol was, as Campion was well aware, the Belgian police force.

Which was why, he had explained to Lugg, he was confident that a net thrown wide across Europe, through Interpol, would bring Superintendent Yeo the catch of the day when it came to the brains behind the Somers Town robbery and, in his opinion, the murderer of Rags Donovan.

'So the long arm of the law is getting longer?' said Lugg in philosophical mood.

'I am happy to say I think you are, for once, completely right,' Campion had replied.

But he was wrong and the long arm fell short.

'I don't care how bad the smog is, we have to go up to London and get Rupert something for Christmas before term ends and he comes home.'

Amanda had made her mind up and there was, Campion knew, little point in arguing with her; certainly not where their only child, on completion of his first term at boarding school, was concerned.

'The papers say it could be a worse pea-souper than last year,' said Campion. 'The people in the balcony seats couldn't see the stage at the Royal Festival Hall and buses can only travel with a man walking in front with a red flare. The hospitals are all on full alert and there are likely to be deaths.'

'Well, thank you, Mister Season-To-Be-Jolly. Christmas will be on us before you know it and we have to risk a shopping trip.

Two nights at the most should do it and we really ought to make use of the Bottle Street flat now it's habitable.'

'I suppose I could drop in on Freddie Yeo and see if there are any developments.'

'Really, Albert? It's been over two months now. I'm sure it would have been in the papers if they'd made an arrest.'

'Obviously the press has more important things to write about. Evadne Childe's latest bestseller for instance.'

'Now don't be bitter, darling, I thought you'd be proud of your godsibling; she's done very well with *Camera Obscuring*, both here and in America.'

Campion allowed himself a cynical laugh. 'All the newspapers say it's one of her best and has a plot which "could have been ripped from the headlines". Little do they know that it pre-empted the headlines! Nobody seems to have found that suspicious.'

'That's because readers don't understand the time lag from an author writing a story to a book being published,' said Amanda patiently. 'Journalists work from one day to the next and are only too aware that their efforts will be wrapping fish and chips by the following evening. It is a good book – you really should read it.'

'I would find it too depressing, my dear, but you're the expert. How does it end?'

'Violently,' said Amanda.

PART FOUR
Luke, 1962

FOURTEEN
For God and What's Left of the Empire

No one could remember the last time a party had been held in the London offices of J.P. Gilpin & Co.; not even Miss Prim, who was said to have been there to supervise the adhesion of William Morris's new wallpapers. Publishing *events* – a word used only pejoratively by the directors of the firm – were held in suitable venues such as museums, colleges of higher learning, libraries and, if the dictates of rampant commercialism demanded it, bookshops. For the directors, the business of publishing was always best conducted in the gentlemanly atmosphere of one of the establishments in the Piccadilly corridor stretching from the Cavalry Club to White's. They tolerated the occasional presence of an author, and even a literary agent, actually on the Gilpin premises only because they employed a praetorian guard of readers, copy-editors and editors (who themselves were guarded by a fearsome secretariat of Miss Prims), to ensure that visitors did not stay long and certainly never breached the sanctity of the fourth floor.

It was to the astonishment of the staff, then, when a general invitation was extended from those Olympian heights, to join the directors in a celebration to honour the firm's most successful author. The occasion was to be marked by an extension of the usual lunch hour from forty-five to sixty minutes. That this assemblage of staff would take place in the ground-floor entrance foyer was made abundantly clear to disabuse the junior employees

of any hope that they might achieve access, however fleeting, to
the upper floors.

Several Gilpin veterans refused to believe that a 'party' would
ever materialize, thinking it might be some cruel practical joke
played by the directors, even though their track record for playing
practical jokes was as unsullied as their history of throwing sociable
gatherings. It was only when deliveries began to arrive from an
external caterer early one morning, followed by a delivery from
Berry Bros & Rudd, and the fact that this latter arrival did not go
directly upstairs, that even the most cynical of Gilpin's old
contemptibles admitted that there was a party spirit abroad.

The proceedings were graced by three of the directors, a father,
a son and an uncle, all Gilpins, and so naturally speeches, along
with mushroom vol-au-vents were on the menu. The directors'
address, given by the senior Gilpin, had been carefully scripted,
almost choreographed to within an inch of its life, by Veronica
Hatherall, which was as it should have been, for the party had
been her idea, although carefully presented through channels to
make it seem as if it had been hatched by the directors. Moreover,
the party was in honour of one of Veronica's authors: Evadne
Childe.

There was no reason why Evadne should have been nervous
on entering Gilpin's offices, for she had been there many times
before over the past thirty years. Usually, her visits to the building
had involved rapid access to Veronica's office without the need
to speak to, or acknowledge beyond basic politeness, any of its
other inhabitants. Not that the staff of Gilpin's were in any way
threatening; in fact, they were as far removed from the spectral
forms roaming Dracula's castle as it was possible to be, but they
did *stare* as she entered their sanctum. The rational part of her
brain told Evadne that the personnel of the firm had every right
to stare at her as she was one of their greatest living assets, but
her innate shyness always triumphed over the arrogance which
soon affects successful authors. She much preferred to meet
Veronica outside the office, for lunch or a trip to a theatre or a
gallery, where she could blend into a crowd and remain anonymous; it was why she insisted on being Mrs Walker-Pyne back
in Eight Ash, where few people read books, hers or anyone else's.
She long ago appreciated that while a pen-name, or an invented
character, might become common currency, most successful

writers, unlike television or film stars, could go about their daily lives unrecognized and unmolested by the general public, and that was the way she preferred it.

Yet on the day of the great party, even as she climbed out of her taxi, Evadne's stomach was a disturbed flock of butterflies, her mouth was dry and the palms of her hands distinctly moist. She had read somewhere that a cat's paws would be damp when feline insecurity struck, usually on a visit to a veterinarian, but she shook her head to clear it of such irrelevancies, pulled down the hem of her suit jacket, gripped her handbag tightly and strode up to the door of her publishing house, relieved to see that it was not decorated with bunting.

She had refused the offer of a party at Gilpin's to mark her seventieth birthday, chiding Veronica Hatherall that two things should never be given away: the ending of any of her books, and a lady's age. She had been tempted by, but finally rejected, an invitation to the New York branch of the firm to a party to celebrate an award from the Mystery Writers of America, though she had accepted the award, a small percussion cap pistol mounted on a block of mahogany, when it had been sent via airmail, and had despatched a fulsome three-page handwritten letter of thanks to all her readers on the other side of the Atlantic.

Neither was the fact that she was now celebrating her thirtieth year with Gilpin & Co. a good enough reason for a party, in her opinion, but when that anniversary coincided with the award to her of a CBE in the Queen's Birthday Honours list, the directors, lacking in royal honours themselves, insisted that a party would be held, if only to show the company's loyalty to Queen and country, and once the publicity opportunities of such an award had been pointed out to them.

If anything, Evadne felt more nervous as she stepped over the threshold of Gilpin & Co. than she had when she had attended the Palace to receive the medal which enlisted her as a Commander of the British Empire. Lacking a husband (although the wartime sacrifice of Edmund Walker-Pyne had been commented on by a thoughtful royal), or close family, Evadne had chosen Veronica Hatherall to accompany her, somewhat to the chagrin of the Gilpin board of directors. As a quid pro quo, Veronica had insisted that Evadne agree to a celebration at the publishing house, where the directors could bask in her reflected glory.

Her nerves began to subside as soon as she saw Veronica, her face almost exploding with pride, waiting to escort her along the receiving line.

'Deep breath,' Veronica whispered, taking the older woman's arm, 'keep smiling and try and ignore all the difficult questions.'

Evadne had always thought of an official receiving line as an experience akin to running a slightly less bloody gauntlet organized by an angry South Pacific tribe armed with clubs. She had long ago inoculated herself to the constant interrogation suffered by all writers as to where she got her ideas from (she had toyed with the idea, but never put it into practice, of replying that she sent a postal order to Potts' Plots of Pontefract, whence Mr Potts would supply a plot by return). Similarly, she had always wanted to reply to the question 'How do you write your books?' with the inaccurate and uninformative information, 'On a typewriter'.

But when Veronica had warned her about difficult questions, they were not of this ilk, but rather, sordidly, more commercial, and mostly asked by Gilpin's directors. They may never have seen the need to actually read any of Evadne's novels, but they were quite concerned about where the next one was coming from.

Ten years previously, with the Somers Town robbery still fresh in the public memory, *Camera Obscuring* had proved to be the most successful Rex Troughton adventure to date, with book club and paperback editions following with almost indecent haste. The novel had also done exceptionally well in America, where misgivings about the title being rather . . . well, obscure . . . had resulted in a change to *The Hollywood Hold-Up*, which had not only boosted sales but attracted the interest of a real film company. The resultant feature, now with a California setting and a young, heart-throb singer with no acting experience in the lead, was not well received by the critics, but the film rights, bought with US dollars, had been very welcome, not to mention the film 'tie-in' edition and its knock-on effect on Evadne's backlist.

The publication of *Camera Obscuring*, however, had marked the end of Evadne's regime of delivering a new novel annually, and the gap between titles had lengthened to three years, although the most recent, *Terrifying Angel*, had been accelerated so that publication could coincide with her seventieth birthday. Publicly, Evadne's reasons for the slowdown in her productivity were that she had more than earned a rest, and a lady of her age and station really should be enjoying more dignified pursuits than murder and mayhem. In one reluctantly given interview with a woman's magazine, ostensibly featuring her garden at Mill House, when the topic had come up, she had, in an unguarded moment, admitted that perhaps her muse 'had gone for good' but elaborated no further.

Now, two years on from *Terrifying Angel*, and without a whisper of a new book in the offing, Gilpin's directors had only one question to ask their star author, but being gentlemen of the 'old school' (the school in question being, invariably, Marlborough), they had agreed that Evadne's editor should be delegated to ask it.

'Once again, congratulations Evie, and thank you for taking me to the Palace as your plus one,' Veronica told her after steering her gently away from the conclave of tweed jackets surrounding a waitress holding a tray of canapés, and through a group of women from the typing pool wearing long, baggy cardigans and carefully sipping Babycham. 'As you can see from the turnout here, Gilpin & Co. are very proud of you.'

'I'm still not quite sure what I've done to deserve such an honour,' said Mrs Walker-Pyne, CBE, 'but it was a splendid day out.'

'We've also got a card for you, a rather large one, I'm afraid, from the New York office, signed by all the staff there.'

'Goodness knows what they make of our quaint honours system.'

'Oh, I've told them that being a Commander of the British Empire gives you full plenipotentiary powers to demand the return of the thirteen colonies.'

'That was very naughty of you,' said Evadne, with the deadpan smile she had perfected for her visit to Buckingham Palace. 'You know the Americans don't appreciate irony.'

'I know what they would appreciate: another book.'

'Please, Veronica, I will not allow you to badger me until you have brought me at least one very large drink.'

'Your wish is my command, Commander,' said Veronica with a slight curtsey before diving for the drinks table with the determination of a seasoned fly-half.

When both the guest of honour and her editor were armed with substantial Gin and Its, the interrogation began.

'When we meet at this time of the year, it was usually to hear your ideas for the next book.'

'It hasn't been *every* year for quite some time, my dear. And I made my position clear some time ago. I am becoming slower as I get older and am not prepared to be manacled to the treadmill of a book every year.'

'But it has been two years now since *Terrifying Angel*, and by now we would have hoped to have the next in the series locked into the schedule for 1963 and publicized in our next catalogue. Your readers are desperate to discover what happens to your characters next.'

'Well, I'm sorry, Veronica, but one rather important thing is missing from that equation.'

'Which is?'

'A single, solitary idea for a decent plot worthy of Rex Troughton's attention and my commitment. You know I have never had any time at all for the more delicate of my profession, the ones who melt like snowflakes under the weakest flame, who claim they have "writers block".'

'You've always said there's no such thing.'

'There isn't. There are writers who have written more books than they have read, then there are proper writers who won't commit anything to paper unless they are sure it's a good idea and it will work. That way they will not short-change their readers.'

'No one here at Gilpin's would want you to do that – not that I think you are capable of short-changing your readers, Evadne. And I for one simply cannot believe that an imagination as fertile as yours hasn't got at least an inkling of an idea for a plot.'

Evadne shook her head wearily. 'I could impress you with an idea but turning an inkling into ninety thousand words of care-fully researched fiction is another matter. I am old, Veronica, and I don't have to prove myself to anyone. The typewriter may be willing, but the inspiration and incentive are no longer pressing the keys, which is a stupid analogy as I cannot use a typewriter.'

'Is it a question of money? I could ask the board to sanction a larger advance if that would help.'

'Help concentrate my feeble mind, you mean? No, my dear, I am not in need of money, I have more than enough to see me to the end of my days. I am old—'

'Stop saying that!' Veronica blurted out the words and immediately lowered her voice as heads turned towards them. 'There
are lots of authors still writing who are older and still producing
fine work.'

'You don't understand, Veronica, how could you? I am on
the edge of a double-edged sword. Because I am old, the ideas
do not flow as they once did and, because they don't, I feel
even older and slower, and writing detective stories is an occupation for the young and the quick these days. Now let's drop
the topic. This is supposed to be a party – my party – so let
us mingle and enjoy it, even though I will be smiling through
clenched teeth every time someone asks me when the next book
is coming.'

'Somebody is bound to, I'm afraid,' admitted Veronica.

'Then I will tell them that I'm halfway through it and it will
be the book where Rex Troughton gets killed off!'

'Evadne! Don't even joke about things like that.'

As she said it, Veronica studied Evadne's face closely, but the
author's expression remained implacable as they began a sedate
circulation.

In the course of the party, Evadne was not called upon to make
good her threat, but there was one unexpected question which
surprised her, and it came from an unexpected source.

'I don't believe you know Lady Amanda Fitton,' Veronica started
the introductions.

'No, we've never met, but I shared a godmother with her
husband.'

'As he is very fond of saying every time he sees me reading
one of your books.' Amanda smiled. 'I am a big fan.'

'She is,' said Veronica, 'I can vouch for that. Lady Amanda
is always the first in the queue when you have a new book
out.'

Evadne flashed her editor a warning look and Veronica, fearing
her star author may release her ultimate weapon, changed the
subject immediately.

'And what a lovely suit, Lady Amanda. It's Dior, isn't it?'

'Yes, it is. Not one of the new line, I'm afraid, but thank you
for noticing – and for introducing me to Mrs Walker-Pyne.'
Amanda smiled sweetly at the older woman and prolonged their

handshake more than was seemly, almost as if she was pulling the writer closer to her in order to share a confidence.

Veronica viewed the almost intimate moment with alarm and a sense of foreboding.

'There's something I am most anxious to ask you,' said Amanda into Evadne's eyes.

Veronica's heart sank.

'I want to hold a séance. Could you recommend a good medium?'

Once Evadne had done the rounds of the party, speaking to everyone she was expected to speak to, and the directors had decided that the junior staff had enjoyed quite enough of their largesse, she was allowed to escape with Veronica, who had been charged with taking her out to dinner and then getting her safely back to her hotel. Evadne had asked if Lady Amanda might join them once it had been established that she had attended the party unaccompanied by her husband, and Veronica, knowing the directors, who had always shown a certain vulnerability when it came to a title as well as a Birthday Honour, would approve, had agreed immediately.

Emboldened by the Gilpin expense account, Veronica had insisted they take a cab – despite Evadne's mutterings about 'extravagance' – to Beoty's in St Martin's Lane, a popular eatery in the publishing world, at least for executives at Veronica's level. It was an ambition of hers to be, one day, senior enough to be able to take an author for lunch at the White Tower in Percy Street, but for the moment Beoty's was friendly enough and offered the novelty of having one half of its menu offering French dishes, and the other Greek.

'We must have something flambéed,' Veronica said enthusiastically once the three were seated. 'They bring a trolley up to the table and cook things on little stoves right in front of you and then throw in alcohol and it all goes whoosh! They call it "lamp work" and the waiters here are rather good at it.'

'As long as we are not hoist by our own petards, I will go for the steak Diane,' said Evadne.

'And I'll try the veal,' said Amanda quickly, to cover the silence while Veronica puzzled over what a 'petard' might be. 'But I really should save myself for the dessert. Have you seen the Greek pastries on offer?'

'Let us indulge ourselves,' Evadne patted Amanda's hand, 'and have whatever we want from the sweet trolley. I am far too old to worry about my figure and you have no need to, so bring on double helpings of *baklava* and we might even persuade Veronica to treat us to a nice dessert wine.'

The meal was enjoyable and unhurried, and the conversation flowed across multifarious subjects, from politics – the prime minister's 'night of the long knives', to the ludicrous suggestion by a professor at University College that there should be a referendum on Britain joining the Common Market; to the shortage of postmen in London and the prospect of colour television arriving as soon as 1964, not to mention a second BBC channel. And when Evadne produced her CBE medal in its presentation case and showed the silver-gilt cross patonce with its inscription *For God and the Empire,* it had provoked not girlish giggles but a serious evaluation as to how much of the British Empire was left, given that former colonies seemed to be achieving independence on a daily basis.

There was no 'feminine chitchat about frocks and hairdos' as the Gilpin directors had hoped there might be when they had instructed Veronica to 'keep the old dear happy, keep it light and at all costs sign up the next one', clearly not appreciating the dangers of raising the topic of Evadne's next book. In a roundabout way, it was Evadne herself who brought the subject to the table.

'What a pity your husband cannot be with us, Amanda. He was very interested in my books once.'

'He still is,' said Amanda, keeping her expression neutral, 'but I'm the one who reads them avidly and can't wait for the next.'

Veronica gripped her cutlery tightly while in the process of slicing steak, and the blade of the knife made an ugly screeching sound on her plate as if she was sounding an alarm.

'I think Veronica may be having a heart attack,' said Evadne, concentrating on her own meal, 'as I threatened her earlier that if anyone asked me about the next book tonight, I would make it Rex Troughton's swansong and kill him off in such a way that he could not possibly be revived!'

'Oh, you mustn't do that,' said Amanda, her face now a picture of innocence, 'but what you should do is write Rex's tragic end, then have your publisher lock it away somewhere safe on condition they don't publish until after your own passing. That would give you both a splendid memorial and Gilpin's cannot complain you have not given them a book.'

Evadne dropped her own knife and fork and clapped her hands.

'What a splendid idea, it would drive the directors crazy! I'm surprised no one has thought of that before.'

'I don't think the company would . . .' Veronica began.

'Just look at her face!' laughed the star author. 'And you, Amanda, ought not to tempt me with such a deliciously naughty idea. It might just get my creative juices flowing again.'

'Really?' said Veronica hopefully.

'I didn't get myself invited to your party to influence your writing, Evadne.' Amanda never knew how close she had come to having her foot kicked by Veronica under the table.

'Did your husband send you?'

'Certainly not, it was entirely my idea. I doubt that Albert would approve as he has little interest in trying to contact the . . . other side.'

'Men rarely do, though he seemed very interested in my séances with a local medium in Eight Ash when he came snooping ten years ago.'

'I'm sure he wasn't snooping,' Veronica offered as a peacemaker.

'Of course he was,' said Amanda dismissively. 'That's what he does, he snoops; but I remember him telling me about your Miss Kitto, and I thought that if an intelligent and successful woman such as yourself believes that contact can be made, then there must be something in it and that you might be able to help me.'

'That's very flattering, my dear. I'm not used to such flattery.' Evadne pointedly turned her head to stare at Veronica. 'You should try it as a tactic the next time you want me to do something.'

Veronica giggled nervously and applied her wineglass to her face like an oxygen mask.

'I can't recommend Miss Kitto to anyone,' continued Evadne, 'as she has passed over herself, and in any case her powers had been on the wane for some years. Since the war, I have had another spirit guide, or rather I should say a guide to the spirit

world. But may I ask why you consider yourself in need of a
medium?'

'I need advice,' said Amanda, 'on a . . . I suppose you could
call it a question of morals.'

'That's actually quite an unusual motive. Most people are
looking for contact to get even with somebody, or find out where
the family's hidden treasure is, or what the winning draws on
next week's pools will be.'

'Well, I'm definitely looking for guidance, but there is a sort
of family treasure involved. Not that I'm treasure-hunting. The
treasure is found and already firmly – and legally, as far as I'm
aware – in my possession. What I want to know is what I should
do with it.'

'You intrigue me, Lady Amanda.'

'Please – Amanda.'

'Very well, you intrigue me, Amanda. It's almost as if you are
dangling a plot under my nose, which will only get Veronica
here overexcited.'

Amanda recoiled as if affronted. 'I'd look an absolute fool if
you put this in a book; in fact, I'd never live it down!'

'Live what down, dear? There's no stigma in consulting a
medium,' Evadne said soothingly. 'It can be very comforting.'

'It's not that per se.' Amanda took a deep breath and made a
prayer tent of her hands. 'It's that I am a woman, often the sole
woman, in a very male industry in a man's world. I wouldn't want
it to be broadcast abroad that a rational, scientific woman who
helps design aircraft and is responsible for the safety of thousands
of travellers feels she has to contact a dead relative as to whether
she should wear a string of pearls or not.'

The silence which followed was taken as the signal for two
waiters to advance to clear the table. Evadne froze them mid-
stride with a glare and waved them back with the slightest of
movements of a single upraised forefinger.

'Now you really have intrigued me,' she told Amanda. 'Who
is the relative who has passed over, what's all this about pearls,
and are we going to need another bottle of wine?'

'To answer the last question first: almost certainly. As to my
deceased relative and the pearls, how much do you know about
the Boxer Rebellion?'

FIFTEEN
Boxers

In the year 1900 Redvers Fitton, a distant, almost forgotten, cousin of the Fittons of Pontisbright, was a young subaltern in the Royal Welch Fusiliers, suffering in equal measure from heatstroke and seasickness travelling on board HMS *Terrible* from Hong Kong to China. To take his mind off the discomforts of troop transportation, he began to keep a journal with a view to turning it into a book with a suitably dramatic title such as *The Peking Relief Expedition* or perhaps, more tantalizing, *Battling the Boxers.* Redvers' journal, written in minuscule script, remained unpublished and probably unread until it came into the possession, sixty years later, of Amanda Campion.

The preferred first title for Second Lieutenant Fitton's memoirs may have been prosaic but it was technically accurate. The Royal Welch were part of the British contingent of a truly international force which had been tasked with relieving the diplomatic legations of the foreign powers currently besieged in Peking by fanatical Chinese insurgents backed, unofficially, by the empress dowager who was known, even in the more respectable newspapers, as the 'Chinese Jezebel'.

The rebellious insurgents, mostly of peasant stock, who had taken up arms against Christian missionaries and the foreign diplomatic corps, the perfect symbols of the modern powers who were carving up China for their own economic gain, were known as 'The Fists of Righteous Harmony'. As that collective nomenclature proved too difficult for the common British soldier to appreciate philosophically, or even pronounce, though the word 'Fists' was clear enough, the enemy became known as the Boxers. One tenet of the Boxers' semi-religious credo, that they were impervious to the bullets of the hated foreigners, had quickly been disproved, thanks to the Maxim gun, and the allied expeditionary force had made sure they had plenty of ammunition, for the Boxers were many in number and Peking was at least a hundred miles from the Taku Forts on the coast, the first obstacle the relief force had to overcome on landing.

The title, *The Peking Relief Expedition*, became more problematic if the book was to be biographical, given that Redvers Fitton never actually made it to Peking to relieve the beleaguered legations (who held out for fifty-five days until the siege was lifted) and the *Battling the Boxers* alternative applied to a single solitary martial encounter which was mercifully brief, if painful.

It was upriver from the Taku Forts, in Tientsin, an important railhead and the site of a large imperial Chinese arsenal, which also had a significant besieged enclave of foreign merchants and diplomats trapped in the French and British concessions, that Redvers Fitton saw action and found a fortune and a curse.

Although overshadowed in the history books by the actual relieving of the foreign legations in Peking, the battle to take Tientsin was a ferocious engagement and an object lesson in how disciplined army units from six modern military powers, although vastly outnumbered, could defeat even the most fanatical enemy armed mostly with spears and swords.

In his journal, Redvers cheerfully admitted that he was lucky to be serving alongside a contingent of American marines, as they were brave fighters and well led, as well as speaking English, making them the only comrades-in-arms he could communicate with. On several occasions he noted that he felt 'deficient' in the fact that he could not speak a word of any other language, especially as the allied force comprised army and naval units from France, Germany, Austria, Russia and Japan, not to mention Chinese auxiliaries recruited by the British.

At Tientsin, a combined force of British, American, French and Japanese assaulted the south gates of the walled city while Russian and German contingents attacked the north. The key to victory for the allies was turned by the Japanese units, who showed even more contempt for death and danger than the Boxers. They also proved to be the most cruel and ruthless looters of the city, although members of every nationality joined in the ransacking of the finer houses once an ill-founded rumour about hidden silver ingots began to circulate among the troops.

The journal was judiciously vague as to whether Redvers Fitton was involved in house-to-house fighting or house-to-house looting when shells from a battery of imperial Chinese artillery began to explode in the street he was on, although it was unclear whether they were aimed at rebellious Boxers or invading foreigners. In a sense it was immaterial, as when the smoke and dust had cleared, the casualties were evenly spread between easterners and westerners and among them was young Redvers.

Hit by flying masonry, Redvers suffered a broken arm and a deep gash across his forehead, which allowed blood to pour down over his eyes. He must, he noted modestly, have looked quite a sight as he was helped away from the city, along the riverbank to the French concession by 'a burly Cossack type', to where a hospital of sorts had been established behind defensive barricades designed and built by an American engineer called Herbert Hoover. (And at this point, much later, a pencilled note had been added to the journal stating that this did indeed refer to the thirty-first president of the United States.)

Redvers found himself lying on a pungent straw mattress surrounded by the injured of, it seemed, every nationality under the sun. (Here the journal went into exhaustive detail about the sights and smells, particularly the smells, of the hospital – in fact a rat-infested warehouse – in which he was confined, surrounded by soldiers and civilians crying out in more languages than the Tower of Babel could cope with. The one language heard the least was Chinese, as there were no wounded Boxers in the hospital – the Japanese contingent had made sure of that – and the Christian Chinese servants and orderlies who bandaged wounds and dispensed opium tincture and pills for pain relief went about their work silently in fear of being mistaken for Boxer sympathizers.

And yet, as he lay on that filthy, crowded floor, plagued by flies and a raging thirst, Redvers did hear Chinese being spoken in a soft drone as if a prayer was being incanted. With some difficulty he turned his body, as his broken arm had been strapped up tightly and uncomfortably by his company medical orderly, in order to take stock of his surroundings and to view his neighbour for first time. He had been aware of a stretcher arriving some hours earlier, or it might have been five minutes past – the opiates had made time difficult to pin down, but now pain had returned to clear his head.

Amid the background noise of voices demanding help or water in multiple languages, the rumble of distant artillery fire and the occasional burst of a shell close enough to rattle the tiled roof of the warehouse and send showers of dust down on to the supine occupants below, only Redvers seemed to have noticed the quiet stream of words coming from the figure next to him and which, to his surprise, appeared to be addressed to him. And the lips which mouthed the words were distinctly feminine.

In the journal the words 'a half-caste girl' had been crossed out and replaced with 'a Eurasian woman' and then 'woman' had been replaced by 'lady', which perhaps indicated young Redvers's confusion at the time. But he was clear enough later to record that the woman was of a similar age to himself, had almond eyes and straight black hair, that she was dressed in tunic and trousers – but of rough silk, not cheap canvas or peasant wool – and that she wore sturdy 'western' boots. He also noted that the woman was lying, unlike the majority of patients, prone, with her face squashed into her straw mattress, due to two gaping wounds in the small of her back. Redvers Fitton had been a soldier long enough to recognize bayonet wounds when he saw them.

The woman, her face pleading at him, continued her quiet praying, if that was what it was, and Redvers, captivated by those almond eyes, hauled himself into a sitting position and tried to show her a kind pair of eyes in return.

His journal's descriptions of this no doubt tender moment extended for more than a dozen pages and proved beyond doubt that Redvers's natural calling lay not in reportage nor even romantic fiction. But Redvers was observant and noticed that the Eurasian lady was wearing a small bronze crucifix on a thin leather strap around her neck. He also realized, to his surprise, that his belt, with holster and ammunition pouch, had been left curled like a cobra at the foot of his mattress. The ammunition pouch, he knew, was empty, and his Webley-Wilkinson revolver contained only six spent cartridges, but at least the pistol was still in its holster.

He asked loudly, in English, if any of his wounded companions could speak Chinese, and for his pains received 'a cacophony of wails and rough language, all of it in the negative'. He looked around in desperation as the woman continued to speak, even though no one except Redvers could hear her, for her voice, frail to begin with, was becoming weaker. When he caught the eye of a Chinese watercarrier across the floor of bodies, he signalled with his good arm for the man to come to him and, when he was ignored, shouted, '*Coolie! Jildi, jildi!*' The words, which he had learned from an Indian army officer in Hong Kong, would have meant nothing, but the tone did, as did the fact that Redvers was pointing a revolver at him.

The water-boy hastened to Redvers's pallet and offered a tin cup of water from the large pot strapped to his chest, only to follow the muzzle of the revolver as it indicated the Eurasian girl. Nervously the cup was offered to that heart-shaped mouth, but the girl made no effort to drink. The water-boy looked at Redvers, made the sign of the cross and slowly shook his head, then he placed the cup and his water jug on the floor and took off at a fair lick towards the doors of the warehouse, leaping with some agility over the rows of mattresses.

Redvers quenched his thirst and muttered, as he put it, 'sweet nothings' to the girl, until he saw the water-boy returning with a priest, a Roman one in full hooded-crow garb; they picked their way between and over the patients, several of whom reached out a hand to touch the priest's muddied cassock as it swept by them.

The priest, who had a long, thin white beard any mandarin would have been proud of, stepped over Redvers's legs, ignoring the pistol he was still holding, and knelt beside the Eurasian girl, leaning over her so that his head was almost level with hers, listening to her then whispering to her in another language, which Redvers recognized as French.

This quiet conversation continued for perhaps a quarter of an hour until only the priest's quiet voice could be heard and Redvers realized he was delivering the last rites. The priest straightened his back and turned, still kneeling, to face Redvers.

'*Anglais?*'

'Yes, Father.'

Fortunately the priest spoke English. 'Did you know this girl?'

'No, Father. I cannot speak Chinese.'

'It was not Chinese,' the priest informed him sternly, 'it was Tahitian and her father is French, attached to the French legation in Peking. She was trying to get back there but got trapped in Tientsin.'

'Poor girl. She was so young.'

Here, in his journal, Redvers indulged himself in another passage of purple prose in honour of the beauty and brave calm in death displayed by the Eurasian girl. Fortunately for the benefit of posterity, the French priest had a much more interesting story for him to record.

The girl had been on a secret mission to collect a valuable package from one of the merchants based in Tientsin's French concession and return it to the legation in Peking. She had been sent because – with the countryside in uproar thanks to the Boxers – she could pass unhindered due to her appearance, as long as she hid her Christianity. It was an affront to God, the priest had declared, that the girl had been thrown down prostrate, raped and bayoneted by Christian soldiers, if one could call Russians Christian, supposedly coming to rescue her from bloodthirsty heathens, although they did not discover the package strapped tightly to her chest.

The package, in a leather wallet still warm from the girl's body heat (Redvers imagined), was now in the hands of the priest, who explained that it contained a necklace, a pearl necklace, of special interest to the Empress Dowager Tzu Hsi, the Chinese Jezebel herself, whom the girl had referred to as 'Yehonala', the empress's Manchu clan name. The necklace, originally a single string of pearls, had been a gift to the empress in order to secure certain trading concessions for the French. But such a lowly bribe, to an empress, would have been of little interest, had it not been for the promise that every year of successful trading would result in an extra string being added to the necklace.

The necklace now had a fourth string added, the pearls imported from French Polynesia, and had become such a favourite of the empress dowager that she was said to allow it out of her sight only on pain of a curse that any other woman who wore it would never bear children.

The Eurasian girl, realizing that she was dying, and unaware that the empress dowager had actively encouraged the Boxers to intimidate and then besiege the legations of the foreign powers in Peking, had made a dying wish. The brave Englishman with the kind eyes would surely complete her mission and carry the necklace to Peking for her once his wound had healed.

At this point, with the sleight of hand of a magician, the priest slid a flat parcel wrapped in blood-splattered leather from beneath the dead girl's body to under the corner of Redvers's straw mattress.

'She has chosen you,' said the priest.

'But Redvers Fitton never made it to Peking, then or later,' said Amanda. 'He was shipped back to Hong Kong until his broken arm mended, and then to India, where he caught malaria and was again hospitalized for several months, before returning to England.'

'Hardly the luckiest of soldiers,' observed Mrs Walker-Pyne, 'unless he hung on to the pearls, that is.'

'He did hang on to the necklace, although at first he thought it of little value as, to him, all the pearls seemed discoloured. "Dirty" was the word he used in his journal. It was only in India that a jeweller recognized them for what they were, when Redvers was in the process of pawning them: black pearls from French Polynesia. Not the most valuable pearls in the world, but rarely seen in such a configuration of graded colours in a single setting; the four strings contained two hundred and eighty-nine pearls in total.'

'They were meant to impress an empress,' said Evadne. 'One presumes she was rather annoyed at their loss.'

'We'll never know. Redvers does not seem to have made any attempt to contact the French legation and the empress dowager had other concerns when the allied relief force finally made it to Peking.'

'So Lieutenant Fitton was actually a thief – or should that be a looter?'

'Evadne, really!' Veronica Hatherall, who until then had been spellbound by Amanda's commentary, spluttered inelegantly into her wine glass.

'I don't think Redvers saw himself as a thief,' said Amanda, 'but he would not have objected to the term "looter", and towards the end of his journal he did refer to the necklace as his "unholy loot".'

'Unholy?'

'It brought him neither wealth nor happiness.'

'The curse!' squealed Veronica, obviously a fan of a good curse. 'But that was only on a woman who tried to wear it.'

'So it turned out,' said Amanda. 'Redvers married on his return
to England, where he became a clerk in the City. His wife was
six months pregnant with their child when she was killed in a
tram accident near the Aldwych in 1906. During the Great War
he was called back to the army, but in keeping with his military
track record, on his first day of a posting to the line on the
Western Front he was caught in a gas attack and spent the rest
of the war convalescing in a military hospital near Bristol, where
he met a nurse, a war widow with two young daughters, to
whom he proposed. They were married in early 1918. The nurse
and her two girls died in the Spanish flu epidemic the following
year, but Redvers survived and tried to find love a third time,
during the last war. He had joined his local Home Guard. By
then he was in his sixties and living in a village in Buckinghamshire
and had struck up a friendship with the postmistress, another
widow with two grown-up sons serving in the navy. In the week
he proposed marriage, the two sons went down with the *Prince
of Wales* when she was sunk by the Japanese.'

'How awful!' Veronica wailed.

'The wedding did not take place and Redvers never considered
marriage again.'

'Had he given her the necklace?' asked Evadne.

'If he did, she returned it, for it was still in his possession
when he died last year at the age of eighty-two, quietly and in
his own bed.'

'You must miss him very much,' soothed Veronica.

'I'm afraid I hardly knew him. No, to be accurate, I didn't
know him at all and I hardly knew *of* him. It came as a total
surprise to hear from the solicitors that he had left me his journal
and the pearl necklace in his will.'

'Why would he do that?' asked Evadne.

'I don't know. That's just one of the questions I would like to
ask him. Will you help me?'

When she returned to the Bottle Street flat later that night, Amanda
found her husband with two balloons of brandy ready and waiting.

'Did she fall for it?' asked Mr Campion.

SIXTEEN
Is There Anybody There?

Lots of famous people were said to have taken an interest in spiritualism, Shakespeare, Bacon and the Earl of Oxford among them, though it would take a very brave medium to ask that trio where they got their ideas from, as well as Mary Todd Lincoln, Arthur Conan Doyle, Oscar Wilde, Harry Houdini, Edvard Munch and Heinrich Himmler. Mr Campion did not share their curiosity in the subject, but was willing to give Mr Houdini, a long-time hero of his, the benefit of the doubt.

Miss Sally DeLuca was a believer, and came highly recommended by the Spiritualist Alliance, yet anyone less like Madame Arcati in *Blithe Spirit*, which Mr Campion had seen both on stage and screen, it was hard to imagine. He knew very well what a Teddy boy looked like; indeed, it had been difficult not to notice their curious dress sense over the past few years, and avoiding their taste in music had become impossible. He knew, thanks to the popular press and his nineteen-year-old son Rupert, that there were such things as Teddy girls, but he was unsure if they could be identified by a particular code of fashion. If they could, then perhaps Miss DeLuca epitomized it.

She wore black drainpipe trousers, a light blue wide-lapel drape jacket, a man's white shirt with a packet of Ransom double filter cigarettes in the breast pocket, a bootlace tie and thick-soled black suede shoes which reminded Campion uneasily of the plimsolls he had been forced to wear on wet afternoons on a school running track.

But however Miss DeLuca chose to dress, her most distinguishing feature as a professional medium was that she was young; still in her early twenties. That, of course, should not have mattered a jot, Campion felt, if she was good at her job.

She was not.

'Nice 'ouse this,' was her first comment on entering the four-storey corner house in Fitzroy Square, but she seemed totally unimpressed to hear that it was owned by Jonathan Eager-Wright, the famous mountaineer, who was away for six months supervising a climbing expedition to an obscure high-altitude plateau in the Andes. Perhaps it was the fact that Jonathan Eager-Wright was still alive made him less interesting to her.

As she was getting down to the business of the day, she began proceedings by asking if there was 'anyone particular on the other side?' that the assembled party wished to contact. Mr Campion supressed an urge to list Herodotus, Agrippina the Younger (just to ask if she really did poison Emperor Claudius), Charlemagne, Leonardo da Vinci and Botticelli, among others, and tried to nod enthusiastically when his wife said 'Redvers Fitton'.

He struggled valiantly to keep a straight face when Miss DeLuca said, 'And who shall I say is calling?'

The scene had been carefully set in the first-floor living room of the tall, thin house, which might have been designed by a mountaineer, such was the climb from the basement pantry/wine cellar through a ground-floor entrance hall, kitchen and staff quarters, to a living room at the front and a dining room at the rear, and then two further floors of bedrooms and the attic which was rumoured to top them all off. It was fitting that it had become the London home of the globe-trotting mountaineer, though his passport said he was a 'geographer', Jonathan Eager-Wright, who happened to be an old and distinguished friend of Albert Campion's. He had gladly loaned the Campions the use of his house on condition that none of the hundreds of paintings and framed photographs, all of jagged peaks or jungle valleys without a human in sight, were damaged or even moved slightly.

The living room had French windows, a small balcony suitable for pot plants rather than addressing a crowd, and a view down Fitzroy Street of the cranes involved in building something called a Post Office Tower. Fortunately the windows had thick curtains to hide any distractions, and Mr Campion had introduced low-wattage bulbs into the light fittings to improve the atmosphere. Furniture had been rearranged and a small, circular dining table introduced along with five plain chairs, situated under the central light, well away from any wall or hidey-hole which could conceal any unofficial equipment or artefact.

The arrangement met with the approval of Evadne Childe,

who also noticed the four-strand string of black pearls hanging from Amanda's neck over a crisp white blouse.

'Those are the pearls in question?' she asked quietly, holding a finger to her lips and nodding towards the medium, clearly indicating that the significance of the necklace should not be trumpeted in advance, so Amanda merely nodded.

Miss DeLuca seemed to approve of the setting and, refusing any refreshments or the need for introductions on arrival, handed her large shoulder bag to Mr Campion and immediately took a seat at the table, Amanda on her right and Evadne Childe, then Veronica Hatherall on her left, with Campion forming the last link in the chain with his wife.

That chain, as per Miss DeLuca's instructions, was made of hands loosely held by the attendees, though it was not clear to Campion whether this was to somehow improve the flow of psychic energy or simply make those of a nervous disposition feel more secure. It also reassured the more sceptical that the medium, safely anchored by two female hands, was unable to perform any act of legerdemain.

The dimly lit room was silent but for the faint hum of traffic outside, which at least indicated that it was a clear night. Campion recalled that Jonathan Eager-Wright was possibly the only man alive who welcomed a London pea-souper fog because he could climb out of a fan-light on to his roof and pretend he was up a mountain above the cloud line. An added advantage provided by the thick grey blanket was that it deadened the noise of the nearby Euston Road, the crossing of which during rush hour, Jonathan said, was a hazard compared to swimming across the Amazon in a rubber tyre.

Miss DeLuca repeated the name Redvers Fitton several times, her voice becoming progressively quieter until her lips moved silently, then she closed her eyes and allowed her head to slump forward on to her chest.

For a full two minutes she remained silent. Amanda and Veronica had also closed their eyes and bowed their heads, but Evadne stared openly at Miss DeLuca, studying her every facial twist and rise and fall of her breathing. Mr Campion studied Evadne Childe.

Miss DeLuca's head snapped upright but her eyes remained closed.

'Redvers? Redvers Fitton. Are you there? Can you speak to us?' she declaimed, but answer came there none.

'There is someone there, trying to get through, I can feel a presence. Is that you, Redvers? There is someone here who wishes to communicate.'

Her voice changed, becoming deeper, fuller, more masculine. 'Amanda?'

Amanda's eyes opened and she made as if to answer, but a glance from Evadne, along with a gentle squeeze from Mr Campion's hand, warned her not to.

'Yes, we have an Amanda here,' said Miss DeLuca in her normal voice, 'and she wishes to give a message to Redvers Fitton.'

Then, in the deeper, male voice: 'Was she close to that poor soul?'

Now Evadne caught Amanda's eye across the table and nodded. Amanda cleared her throat nervously and answered.

'No, I cannot say I was, I'm afraid. I hardly knew him.'

'Yet you want something from him?' Miss DeLuca was Mr DeLuca still.

'Only the answer to a question.'

'What is the question?'

'Why did he leave me something in his will?'

'Because you were his favourite?' This from the female DeLuca.

'Hardly. I had no idea he existed until I heard from his solicitor.'

Miss DeLuca shook her head, opened her eyes and broke her hands free from the circle and massaged her forehead with her fingertips.

'I'm sorry,' she said, 'there was a spirit present, but it was not Redvers Fitton. I think we should try the talking board; it's in my bag and it won't take a moment to set up.'

A 'mystic talking board', better known as a Ouija board for reason lost in the mists of time and American patent law, was a thin wooden rectangle no bigger than a fold-out board used for playing chess or draughts. The version Miss DeLuca produced from her capacious shopping bag was adorned with mystic symbols featuring the moon, stars, a compass and, oddly, a mermaid, but nothing sufficiently eye-catching enough to distract from its main purpose. Printed in bold lettering was the alphabet, A–M and then N–Z, forming semicircles one above the other, and beneath them the numbers 1–9 with an added 0 and the word GOODBYE. In opposite corners were similarly printed the words YES and NO.

Mr Campion had been warned by his wife in the strictest of terms that he must make absolutely no references such as 'baggsie the top hat', 'when do I pass Go?' or 'who wants Mayfair?' when the board was laid out. Mr Campion had protested that he knew full well there was only one piece in a game of Ouija, a pointed, heart-shaped wooden one, with a hole big enough for a fingertip, called a planchette, which Miss DeLuca placed on the curve of the printed alphabet, holding it steady with a single, manicured fingernail painted bright shellfish pink.

'If there is a spirit willing to contact us, they will guide my hand. One of you must be responsible for noting the letters indicated.'

'I can do that,' Veronica volunteered.

'Is there anybody there who wishes to communicate with this table?' Miss DeLuca declaimed.

The planchette refused to move and Miss DeLuca opted for Plan B, which was to invite everyone to place a finger lightly on the back of her hand.

'I ask again: is there anybody there?'

This time the planchette did move, sliding away from the alphabet to the single word YES in the corner of the board.

'Do you have a message for someone in this house?'

The planchette, steered delicately by five fingers, or five fingers being guided by an unseen force, moved slowly towards the layout of the alphabet then suddenly shot back up to the YES.

Miss DeLuca ignored the sharp intake of breath from Veronica. 'Are they at this table?'

The planchette slid across the board to NO.

'Then who is it you seek?'

The pointer of the planchette began to point to letters which Veronica dutifully read out.

'J–O–N–A . . .'

'Jonathan Eager-Wright,' said Mr Campion calmly. 'It's his house. Can we take a message?'

The planchette moved again.

'B-E-W-A-R-E-H-I-G-H-P-L-A-C-E-S.'

'Good advice for a mountaineer,' whispered Campion, wincing as the heel of his wife's shoe scraped down his shin.

'Our business is with Redvers Fitton,' Miss DeLuca pressed on, speaking to the ether. 'Is he there?'

The planchette moved again, the fingers on it scurrying to keep up.

NO.

'Is Redvers in the spirit world?'

NO.

'Then we are done here.' Evadne Childe spoke for the first time and Miss DeLuca put back her head and opened her eyes to see the older woman scrutinizing her face.

'I feel you may wish to contact someone, Miss Childe.'

'I will make my own arrangements, thank you very much,' said Evadne.

'Are you sure? Have you not lost someone recently?'

'Not recently, but twenty-two years ago I did. Someone who was very dear to me.'

'They may be close by. I certainly feel a restless spirit trying to get through. We could try. Shall we join hands again?'

'Only if the spirit can prove their oneness.'

'I'm sorry, what does that mean?' Miss DeLuca said exactly what three other minds were thinking.

'The only spirit I wish to talk to is familiar to me. We have a word – a phrase – which is only significant to the two of us. I call it our "oneness". By using the phrase, I know I am speaking to the right spirit.'

Evadne looked down deliberately at the Ouija board and the planchette.

'Would your restless spirit be willing to spell out our "oneness"?'

Miss DeLuca shook her head.

'I thought not.'

While Mr Campion nipped around the corner to flag down a cab for Miss DeLuca on the Euston Road, Amanda invaded the kitchen, brewed a pot of coffee and bore it upstairs on an osten-tatious silver tray, along with a jug of hot milk, both Evadne and her editor having dismissed the need for anything stronger.

'I'm sorry for you, Amanda,' said Evadne. 'That didn't get you anywhere.'

'And I can only apologize for wasting your evening. You could have taken in a show or a film.'

'Don't worry about that, I am only sorry we couldn't get through to Redvers. The problem was you were given a very poor medium. And her dress sense! If she'd arrived on the back of a motorcycle, I wouldn't have been surprised. Let me have a think about things and see how I might help.'

'In what way?' asked Amanda, remembering to try and look disappointed.

'I know a very good medium who may be able to establish contact with Redvers.'

'That would be wonderful.'

'Unfortunately she is almost as ancient as I am, and if she were to help she would have to travel some distance, at some expense, to get here.'

'Travel expenses are not a problem,' said Mr Campion, 'if she helps give my wife peace of mind. She's been fretting about those pearls since she heard from Redvers's blasted solicitor. I almost wish somebody would break in and steal them.'

'I will do what I can, and quickly,' said Evadne, 'but the lady is foreign and not used to travelling abroad.'

'We will look after her most royally,' enthused Campion. 'She could stay here and be waited on hand and foot. The butler here is first rate.'

Campion kept his eyes on Evadne, avoiding the glare his wife was giving him.

'Well, I might be able to persuade her to come to London for a few days but I don't think she has travelled much.'

'That sounds like putting you to far too much trouble,' Amanda protested. 'We couldn't possibly—'

'Nonsense, my dear. You've just been treated to a performance by the worst medium in London. I can assure you that there are genuine guides to the spirits out there and to prove it I'll get Madame Rawnie here as soon as I can persuade her to get on an aeroplane. She has never been to England and she doesn't speak much English, so perhaps it would be better if she stayed with me out in the country.'

'Oh, we couldn't allow that, could we, Albert? She must stay here and you must stay too. It's a comfortable house and we can get in a housekeeper to look after you. Treat it as a holiday and show this Madame . . . Rawnie? . . . the sights; all on us, of course.'

Evadne considered the proposition for a few seconds.

'Well, I'll write to her tomorrow and see what she says. She has modest needs and tastes, but she might be up for a bit of an adventure.'

'I would be happy to organize tickets for concerts and shows and so on,' offered Mr Campion, 'and we could even lay on a car and a driver for you.'

'If you are sure two old ladies wouldn't get under your feet.'

'Nonsense! We can stay in our flat in Bottle Street and you can have the run of this place. Eager-Wright won't be back until next year.'

Evadne raised a finger. 'Ah, yes, the mountaineer. Did you notice how that silly girl had us spell out the warning about high places on the board? Very useful advice in the house of a mountaineer, don't you think?'

'I hadn't noticed that,' Campion said innocently.

'I presume she knew whose house it was, or perhaps all those pictures on the walls gave it away. That's an old trick of the charlatans; take one small piece of information to bait a hook to dangle in front of the gullible. In a true visitation, the spirit will always give a oneness.'

'Which is what exactly?'

'A word or a phrase which only the spirit and the person trying to contact them are privy to, and which the medium cannot possibly know beforehand. Call it a sort of psychic calling card. That DeLuca girl didn't even try to guess one or give a fake one, so perhaps she wasn't a charlatan, merely a second-rate medium. Very second-rate. Leave it to me and I'll bring you an absolutely first-class one.'

After Mr Campion had exercised his long legs to chase down another taxi, and Evadne and Veronica had been packed into it, he poured himself a generous amount of Jonathan Eager-Wright's whisky and settled back in an armchair.

'To be fair,' he told Amanda, 'we did *ask* for the worst medium in London.'

'Oh, she wasn't that bad,' said his wife. 'At times I thought her quite convincing, but she must have sensed that Evadne was watching her like a hawk.'

'A hungry hawk at that. And she did get some things right. I mean she was spot on when the Ouija said there was no spirit of Redvers Fitton present.'

'It would have been a surprise if there had been,' agreed Amanda, 'considering he never existed in this world, let alone the next.'

'A pity we couldn't have planted a oneness password on her. That would have convinced Evadne.'

'We didn't know we might need such a thing, though I suppose we could have had her shout "Boxers!" at the top of her voice. But the point was not to convince Evadne that Miss DeLuca was any good.'

'I think we succeeded there,' said Campion, 'and she got a good look at your pearls. Our next move is to plant the idea that they're terribly valuable, even though they're not.'

'Well, you know who is perfect for that job.'

'I do indeed.' Campion quaffed more whisky, 'and I must say I thought Veronica played her part very well.'

'She did, didn't she?' said Amanda with a smile.

Mister no longer Master, Rupert Campion, having strayed into that twilight zone between obedient schoolboy and unruly student, did not look forward at all to the prospect of temporary employment as 'a domestic' in the service of his parents. Not, that is, until he met, and discovered he would be working with, Giulietta.

Having been taught that there was no 'j' in Latin or Italian, and the fact that she did indeed hail from fair Verona, Giulietta became Juliet whenever Rupert referred to her in speech or in idle doodles on the edges of newspaper which might, in the hands of a less sensible youth, have developed into putative poetry of the sort a young male might write to an older (albeit only by two years) female. Armed with impeccable references, Juliet quickly proved very good at her job and something of an ideal co-worker. The fact that she had an hour-glass figure, perfect skin the colour of milky coffee, and curls which cascaded down to the small of her back in a lustrous black waterfall, did not influence Rupert one jot, or so he said.

To prepare for the visit of Evadne Childe and her personal spirit adviser, the Campions had installed a temporary staff in the house on Fitzroy Square and Rupert had been volunteered to apply for the post of assistant housekeeper, a position entirely in the gift of his father.

Mr Campion had argued that it was now fashionable for young people faced with a gap of a year between school and university, as Rupert was, to broaden their horizons by learning a foreign language, or travelling abroad, or taking gainful employment. As Rupert was to study in America, a second language was barely necessary, and he would clearly be travelling abroad. That left gainful employment, which was being offered in the 'family business', so to speak, and it would take up only a limited amount of time, leaving Rupert to pursue an active social life in humming and vibrant London rather than sitting, bored and moping, out in the country.

To sweeten the deal, as some of his mother's American business contacts would say, and as a reward for passing his driving test, Mr Campion had bought his son a new Riley Elf, praising its luxurious interior, its front-wheel drive and its mighty 850-cc engine. Rupert had, rather churlishly his father thought, pointed out that many of his former schoolmates now had motorbikes with larger engines and the Elf was merely to distract him from borrowing the new Jensen CV8 which Mr Campion had bought for himself. The boy, the father thought, was not stupid.

The boy was in fact destined for a higher education in the United States at Harvard, where educations rarely come higher. His decision to apply for the famed business school there had surprised his father; not because Rupert had rejected Cambridge out of hand – he often said that his own experience as a graduate of St Ignatius College, while thoroughly enjoyable, had spectacularly failed to equip him for any decent (legal) career – but rather Rupert's choice of subject to study.

Mr Campion, who had never put much stock in practical subjects, had suggested a more esoteric and frivolous field of study: archaeology, anthropology, even Latin poetry perhaps. Rupert had considered these options and then admitted that he had always had a secret desire to study acting. Mr Campion had said, 'I wouldn't go that far', and the topic had not been raised since.

For the moment, though, Rupert Campion reflected that life was really quite sweet. He was free of the routine of school, he had independent means of transport and free accommodation in a fine town house, albeit in a square which Dickens had derided for its 'barrenness and frigidity' in *Nicholas Nickleby* – but then Dickens had certain issues with portions of his early life in the area. Rupert also had a job of sorts and could, now he was over eighteen, spend his income legally in a public house. There were films to see, long-playing records to play and live music to be experienced at the Marquee Club in Oxford Street, and best of all he intended to share these delights of the big city with his co-worker Giulietta.

The only fly in the ointment was the other member of the below-stairs staff at the Fitzroy Square house, the butler.

Lugg.

'The boy's trying to move up a division too quick where that girl's concerned. He ain't got the weight to carry it off,' was Mr Lugg's considered opinion, while polishing a canteen of cutlery, a knee-to-throat black apron protecting his clothes.

'Why all the pugilistic metaphors? I doubt very much that Rupert wants to go ten rounds with her.'

'If you asks me, that's exactly what he's set his sights on.'

Mr Campion sighed. 'Youthful fantasies of the heart, I fear.'

'Mebbe so, but he's also sulking about that car you bought him. Says he wanted a Fiat 500 like all his mates who went up to Cambridge, but I reckon that's only because it's Italian and he thought it might impress Juliet.'

'The Riley's a perfectly good little car for nipping around London, and he's only going to have it for a few months. When he goes to America, we'll sell it to some careful lady driver – or perhaps you'd like to buy it? We'd have to widen the doors to get you in and make the car bigger, of course. What's bigger than an elf? A goblin? A troll?'

Lugg fixed Campion with a scowl, took a deep breath and strained several muscles pulling in his stomach. The material of his black apron fluttered like a sail touched by a very light breeze.

'Cheek!'

'Seriously though, old fruit, is Rupert impressing young Juliet?'

'Like 'is father, he's trying – very trying. Speaking of cars, though, do I get to drive your fancy new Jensen when our visitors are here?'

'Certainly not. If they want to go sightseeing, take taxis, preferably ones not driven by any of your relations or former cellmates. That car is something of a personal indulgence I admit, but why should teenagers have all the fun these days? And anyway, it's a patriotic gesture.'

'Patriotic?'

'The man at the motor show said it would be the last one before we joined the Common Market, so we really should buy British before we're swamped by Continental models.'

Lugg grinned his most lascivious grin. 'I saw some of them motor show models on the Pathé News at the flicks. Thought you might have gone for another Bentley, though, something big and stylish.'

'I was tempted, by the cars not the models, but only briefly. The Bentley Continental looks like something in which the lord mayor would arrive at a ribbon-cutting, and in the new Humber Hawk I would look like a chief constable. Neither were suitable for the rakish image I wish to project.'

'Rakish? You mean flash – an' at your age!'

'I knew you'd lower the tone. It's a beautiful machine.'

'Does Her Ladyship approve?'

'Of course not, but she'll tolerate my whims, at least until we get this Evadne business sorted. Is the house ready to receive visitors from this world and the next?'

'All shipshape, larder and kitchen fully stocked, beds aired; but strewth, I've never known a house with so many stairs. I'd have shed pounds going up and down, down and up, if it hadn't been for the sweets and savouries which Juliet brings with her. She's top notch as a cook.'

'She should be,' said Mr Campion. 'Her family is opening one of those new trattorias in Soho. They're all the rage, very fashionable, and they serve spaghetti which doesn't come out of a tin. We only have her on loan because her father owes me a favour, so I don't want anything to upset her. Just make sure Rupert lets her concentrate on her cooking.'

'I'll do me best to keep them both busy.'

'Good. Did Rupert bring over his tape recorder?'

'He did; even showed me how to use it.'

'And the microphone?'

'Well hidden. I doubt you could spot it and you know we've bugged the room. Funny way to treat people you've invited to stay, though.'

'It's more to record the visitors we didn't invite.'

Veronica Hatherall experienced that butterflies-in-the-tummy feeling she always felt when summoned up to the directors' office at Gilpin's, even though on this occasion she had been expecting an invitation she could not refuse.

Two Gilpins, one younger than the other, were lying in wait for her, seated behind a leather-topped oak desk. There was no chair on her side of the desk but a circular Persian rug on which she was allowed to stand.

'Sorry to pull you away from your desk, Veronica,' said Gilpin the Younger, 'but Miss Prim has drawn to our attention your recent request to Accounts.'

'For a limousine and a chauffeur,' snarled the Older.

'A car and a driver, actually,' said Veronica, digging her heels, physically and metaphorically, into the Persian pile, 'and not for personal use, but to meet and transport our leading author from Gatwick.'

'Gatwick?' asked Older Gilpin, not in a snarl but in a tone which would have been the same had she said El Dorado or Timbuktu.

'The new Gatwick Airport. BEA are diverting some of their European flights there from Heathrow to help develop it. Mrs Walker-Pyne is flying in from Brussels with a friend and I thought it would be a nice gesture to meet them off the plane.'

'It would be nice, and very generous of the company,' Young Gilpin observed over the top of a pair of half-moon spectacles, which made him look as if he was in a competition to appear older than the Older, 'and we have been known to treat our most favoured authors with such largesse in the past.'

'As Evadne Childe, Mrs Walker-Pyne has been the top-selling author on our fiction lists for five out of the last seven years.'

'But not this year, as she has no new book out. I'm not sure we should be pushing the boat – or in this case the hire car – out for an author who is, shall we say, resting.'

The Prosecution seemed to rest, sliding back in his chair. But the Defence was prepared and ready.

'Not resting, researching. She's started work on a new book and it sounds jolly exciting. It could be her best yet.'

'Has she signed a contract for it?' asked Older Gilpin sharply.

'Not yet, but I'm sure she will,' answered Veronica with confidence, 'if we treat her right.'

'Very well, you can have your car and driver, but make sure you get that contract signed.'

'Of course. I doubt that Evadne would be looking to move to another publisher at this stage in her career. She seems to like the close working relationship we have.'

Veronica left no doubt that the relationship she referred to was with her as editor and not Gilpin's the publisher.

'Is it another Rex Troughton?' asked Young Gilpin. 'We have to keep the fans happy.'

'It is, and the fans will be very happy with it, I think, although I've only seen a few early pages so far.'

'So what's it about?'

'Evadne hasn't given too much away yet, but the plot revolves around a valuable pearl necklace which comes with an ancient Chinese curse.'

'And is there a murder? There has to be a murder.'

'Oh yes, there are at least two murders. So far, that is.'

SEVENTEEN
Madame Rawnie

Mr Campion could remember another age, between the two wars, when guests invited to a country house weekend party or a shoot had to run the gauntlet of a receiving line of domestic staff who would pamper them and care for their every need during their stay. The butler would do the honours, introducing the housekeeper first and then an exhausting line of under-butlers, footmen, cooks, ladies' maids, scullery maids, chambermaids, gardeners, gamekeepers and perhaps even stable boys, though only in England, or stalkers and ghillies when in Scotland.

It was a spectacle which had not been seen for many a year and, in the sum of all things, was one which would not be missed. There was certainly no need for such formality in an end-of-terrace town house in foggy, fume-filled modern London, but Mr Campion thought some formal introductions should be made and so had the entire staff, all three of them, assemble in the entrance hall to greet their houseguests.

The Campions, with Amanda taking the lead, had done their duty on the pavement, having been tipped off by Lugg from his observation post at the basement window, of the arrival of the hire car containing Veronica Hatherall, her prize author Evadne Childe, and her special guest, Madame Rawnie.

'Delighted to meet you, Madame Rawnie, and may I say how grateful we are that you agreed to visit us. I hope your journey was not too exhausting,' said Amanda in passable French.

Madame Rawnie replied in the same language, but with an accent that reminded Amanda of metal chiming on metal, somehow harsh and yet slightly melodic.

'I could not refuse my old friend Evadne, and I have never been in an aeroplane until today; plus, I have never seen London. I have been given a chance to do both and, at my age, I may not get another.'

Amanda found it impossible to guess how old Madame Rawnie was. From the way Evadne took her by the arm, helping the tiny woman – who smelled rather cloyingly of lavender – ascend the steps to the front door, the obvious assumption was that she was helping an older friend. Amanda knew that Evadne was ten years older than her husband, which would make her seventy-two this year; so could Madame Rawnie be near to eighty? It was difficult to tell as so little of her was showing.

She wore a thick woollen coat, which covered her from the neck down to Victorian ankle boots, a wide-brimmed soft felt black hat with a black ribbon down the back and a half-veil at the front, along with suede gloves. Thus the key strategic areas where one female could best judge the age of another – under the eyes, the neck, the upper arm, the back of the hands, the ankles – were all hidden from the inquisitive viewer; though Amanda admitted to herself that she was using criteria she had only read about in detective novels – and, what is more, written by Evadne Childe's greatest rivals.

'I do hope you will be comfortable here. We thought you would feel more at home than in a hotel.'

As she shook Amanda's proffered hand, Madame Rawnie applied a suede-lined pressure which told her hostess that whatever her age, she was firm in body and mind also when she said: 'My dear Lady Amanda, this house even from the outside is far more grand than any hotel I have ever stayed in. I look forward to being treated like a queen, or a duchess at least. May I ask if this is your house?'

'It is not. We live in the country and keep only a small flat in London. The house belongs to a family friend who is abroad for the rest of the year. For the time you are in London, the house is yours and Evadne's, but let me introduce you to the staff and allow you to explore.'

As they mounted the steps, Evadne on one side of her, Amanda on the other, Madame Rawnie's gaze went to her left to the narrow steps leading down to the basement door and window in a square concrete well protected by a new generation of spiked iron railings, the originals having been turned into Spitfires in 1940.

'I'm afraid there are a lot of stairs in this house,' said Amanda. 'It's very tall and thin but quite spacious inside.'

'Stairs do not trouble me as long as no one in a hurry is waiting for me.'

'We will manage perfectly well,' said Evadne in English. 'We have survived a bumpy aeroplane flight and an even more hair-raising drive from Gatwick, thanks to a driver who thought he was Stirling Moss at Brands Hatch.'

'We will manage very well indeed,' Madame Rawnie said quietly in French, while betraying the fact that she understood the language of her hosts, 'if this handsome young man is to look after us.'

Rupert, looking unusually smart in a crisp new blue striped shirt from Hornes in the Tottenham Court Road – his father had insisted and even loaned him a matching tie – was holding the front door open for the three women on the steps and, a yard behind them, Veronica and Mr Campion, who was carrying two suitcases.

'Welcome to London and to Fitzroy Square,' he announced as he had secretly practised in front of the bathroom mirror.

'This is my son, Rupert,' said Amanda. 'We've given him something to do before he goes off to the United States to university.'

'A pleasure,' said Madame Rawnie, offering a hand and not at all intimidated by the young man's looming height as Rupert returned the gesture. She twisted Rupert's hand until it was palm upwards and peered at it intently. 'It will go well for you in America.'

Rupert blushed and smiled weakly. He might not have fully deciphered the old lady's accent, but he understood the sentiment, and was saved the embarrassment of parading his schoolboy French by a deep cough from behind his right ear as Mr Lugg stepped into, and blocked, the frame.

Unperturbed by this mountainous apparition, Madame Rawnie released Rupert's hand and offered hers to the megalith in grey-striped trousers, white shirt and a straining grey waistcoat that gave off a distinct whiff of mothballs.

'And this is Mr Lugg, our butler,' said Amanda, thinking that the French *majordome* so much more impressive than mere 'butler', a term she knew Lugg rankled at.

'*Bon-jooer, mes dames,*' said Lugg, with a nod to both Madame Rawnie and Evadne; then he glanced down suspiciously as his paw was turned upwards so his palm could be read.

After a full minute's silence as she studied a hand more than twice the size of hers, Madame Rawnie simply shook her head then released it without comment, moving on to the dark-haired girl who had been hidden behind Lugg's bulk. With her the same routine produced an approving chuckle and the conclusion: 'You will do well, my pretty one.'

'Please follow me upstairs to the living room,' said Amanda, leading the way. 'More stairs, I'm afraid.'

Veronica and Mr Campion followed on, Campion bringing up the rear with the suitcases, which he handed to Lugg.

'As you appear to have no future, old chum, you'd better make yourself useful while you can,' he whispered, and received only a curled lip in reply. 'But for you, Giulietta, it sounds as if it's all going to be rosy.'

The young Italian girl raised her eyebrows and, judging that the arrival party was sufficiently out of earshot, said, '*Zingara.*'

'Very probably,' said Mr Campion.

Once the guests were settled in their rooms, and Lugg had grunted his way up three flights of stairs with a tea-tray, Veronica took her leave to return to the Gilpin offices, while Giulietta retreated to the kitchen to begin preparations for dinner, aided enthusiastically but ineffectually by Rupert, who had up to that point in his life shown not the slightest interest in culinary matters.

The Campions opted for a late afternoon stroll around Queen Mary's Gardens in Regent's Park; not that they expected to see much in bloom on a damp, misty October afternoon, against which they had wrapped up well – Mr Campion in a tweed Jaeger overcoat and Amanda in a long suede coat in truffle brown – but it gave them a chance to plan their campaign.

'So what do you make of the mysterious Madame Rawnie?' asked Amanda, her arm linked through her husband's as they walked.

'Small, but powerful.'

'Don't say like a racing car! You've got cars on the brain at the moment.'

'I was thinking more of a pit pony, and please don't refer to the Jensen as a racing car, it's a very stylish tourer.'

'It's flashy, far too flashy for a man of your age.'

'But not for the age I *think* I am. I have never pretended to act my age, that's why you love me.'

'Tolerate might be a better word, but why "pit pony"?'

'Because she looks small and frail, but if she planted her feet firmly, not even Lugg could shove her over.'

'She didn't give him much succour with her impromptu palm-reading, did she?'

'Put it this way, a reaction like that from a qualified palmist would not inspire confidence in a life-insurance salesman.'

'Rupert got a good bill of health from her. She was very quick to pick up on the fact that he was going to America.'

'Well, you had just mentioned it,' said Campion, 'and I think the main trick of the medium, or fortune teller or clairvoyant, whatever you call them, is the ability to listen and remember small, personal facts.'

'And as we hadn't said anything at all about Giulietta, she kept it fairly vague and all-purpose.'

'Exactly, though the girl's reaction was interesting. She called her *"zingara"*, which is Italian for gypsy.'

'And is she?'

'She could very well be. "Rawnie" is a Romany word for lady, so that may be a little bit too obvious, but I have made a few enquiries and I understand that she comes from a village near Charleroi called Liberchies, which had a substantial Romany population and has produced some quite well-known gypsy musicians.'

'So the palmistry is all part of a "cross my palm with silver and I'll look in the crystal ball for you" act? The sort of thing you see at church fetes – or fetes worse than death, as we used to call them when we were young?'

'Younger,' Campion corrected her with a smile, 'but Mrs Walker-Pyne does not for a minute strike me as someone who would be fooled by a gypsy headscarf sewn with coins and a cut and shuffle of the old Tarot cards in a tent on the vicarage lawn. She's been popping across to Belgium to see Madame Rawnie since the war, so perhaps she really is a genuine medium who can connect us to the other side.'

'But if she's so good a medium, what if she discovers that there is no spirit of a dead Redvers Fitton trying to get through to us?'

'As he was never alive, that shouldn't be terribly surprising. Let's just stick to the plan and see how she plays it tomorrow evening. Have you left the pearls hidden in plain sight?'

'Oh yes, she couldn't possibly miss them.'

Evadne Childe, as a writer of detective stories, had naturally spotted them first and had questioned the wisdom of leaving them on a living room side-table in a box which had once held Cuban cigars and was secured only by a small gold swivel hook and eye.

'I thought it might be useful to have them in the room,' Amanda had explained, 'to help Madame Rawnie make contact, but I really don't like wearing them until I know more about why I was left them by cousin Redvers. In fact, I think I'll leave them here as I really don't want them in our home or at the flat.'

Evadne had quite understood Amanda's trepidation but had pressed her on the absence of security arrangements.

'Jonathan leaves the house empty for months at a time, there are simply not enough mountains for him in Westminster, but when he's away a local beat bobby always checks the place on his rounds during the night. So even if we are not on the premises, someone keeps an eye on the place.'

'You could always sell them,' Evadne observed.

'And pass the curse on to some unsuspecting soul? I couldn't do that.'

Amanda wondered if she had overplayed her dramatic hand, but Evadne had nodded sagely, as if to indicate that she quite understood and that Amanda's position was the morally correct one.

Madame Rawnie, however, had no qualms about making the odd dramatic gesture.

When everyone due to attend the séance had been assembled in the first-floor living room, she made her entrance in a long, diaphanous black silk dress with a high neck and ruffed hem and sleeves. High heels had added a couple of inches to her height, but she still, apart from the absence of jet jewellery, looked like an actress impersonating, with uncanny accuracy, Queen Victoria in her mourning period.

She glided silently around the room, ignoring those present but examining the pictures on the wall and allowing the fingertips of her right hand to drift over every free-standing surface, including the backs of chairs, the mantlepiece and the small round occasional table on which sat a wooden box advertising a brand of Cuban cigars. Her hand hovered over the box and then she tapped the lid with a forefinger, just once, and then swept on by.

'Shall we begin, Madame Rawnie?' said Evadne, pulling out a chair for her.

'First of all,' she answered slowly in English, 'I must ask if there is anyone else in the house?'

'Only the five of us,' said Amanda. 'The staff have been given the night off.'

And they had taken up the offer with alacrity. Lugg had been perfectly happy to establish his headquarters in the basement, but the constant need to climb stairs to perform the simplest of tasks, due to the layout of the house, had put him in a foul mood, which could only be assuaged by an evening round the Albany in Great Portland Street. Rupert had magnanimously agreed to take Giulietta to the cinema for the evening, and Giulietta had, to his delight and slight surprise, agreed, knowing that had she opted to spend her night off with her parents in their Soho trattoria, she would have immediately been pressed into service.

'That is useful, but I was asking about those who have gone . . .'

'Madame Rawnie wishes to know if anyone has died in this house,' Evadne intervened.

Amanda just knew that her husband was restraining himself from making a cute rejoinder such as 'Not yet!' and so quickly took command.

'We are not aware of any deaths here but, given the age of the house and its occupation over one and a half centuries, it is highly likely there have been some along the way, but no one we were familiar with.'

Madame Rawnie spoke in rapid French to Evadne while pointing to the centre of the table, and Evadne assumed the role of translator.

'Does this house have any connection with the late Redvers Fitton?'

'None at all,' said Amanda. 'He died in a nursing home in Dorset. Is it important?'

'A physical link to those who have passed over always helps; a place or an artefact. The necklace he left you would be something we know he had in his possession, something he touched and held. It might serve as a oneness to help make contact as you did not know him personally. Could the pearls be placed in the centre of the table, please?'

'Certainly.'

Amanda transported the cigar box with a mixture of reverence and trepidation and placed it in the centre of the round table, opening the lid fully so that the four strands of dullish black pearls were exposed.

The participants took their seats, Evadne taking Madame Rawnie's right hand and Amanda her left, Mr Campion next to his wife and Veronica linking him with Evadne. There was no Ouija board this time, indeed no props at all. The curtains were drawn, the lights were low, or at least low-wattage, the room quiet and calm.

'We should now concentrate with an open mind,' said Madame Rawnie rather enigmatically, if Mr Campion's raised eyebrows were to be believed.

The ensuing silence, apart from the sound of breathing and the odd squeak of a chair leg, was complete.

Campion became aware first of the dampness of Veronica's palm in his, and then an increased pressure in her grip, before he realized that she was reacting to the changing expression on Madame Rawnie's face.

The movements were minute but telling. Her eyes were closed and she never spoke, but the corners of her mouth twitched, her brow furrowed and her cheek muscles undulated as her body pressed back and down on the chair as if she was making herself shrink and was straining from the effort.

'Is there anyone there wishing to visit with this table?'

Madame Rawnie had spoken in high-pitched, rapid French, which Evadne translated in a low, calm voice, though neither seemed to receive an answer.

'*Redverrrs Feeton!*' Despite the pronunciation, it was clear that Madame Rawnie was issuing a summons, not asking a question. But answer came there none.

'There is someone there,' said the medium softly, her face contorted with concentration. Then, louder: 'Do you wish to speak to someone here? Are you *Redverrs*?'

Madame Rawnie shuddered, as if a pitcher of cold water had been poured over her.

'Have you a message for the *Laydee* Amanda?'

The ten hands clasped around the table stiffened their grips, forearms left the table's surface and elbows dug in harder as Madame Rawnie's eyes suddenly opened and became fixed on Amanda.

'There is a spirit prepared to visit with us,' she said in a voice which had suddenly deepened to be almost masculine, 'but it is not the spirit you seek.'

Evadne came to the rescue of a confused Amanda.

'Will this spirit help us find Redvers Fitton, Madame Rawnie?'

'I think that spirit cannot be found; perhaps it is at rest. But, if you wish, you may ask.'

The medium turned her head slowly to face Evadne and all at the table noted the way their joined hands seemed to shake as they tightened their hold on each other.

'You may ask, not Lady Amanda,' said Madame Rawnie firmly and in English.

'Me?' said Evadne.

Madame Rawnie said two words which took three people at the table by complete and utter surprise.

'West Riding.'

Mr Campion was later to remark that if it was possible for a woman to faint dead away while sitting down and being supported by two other females, but then to snap back to full consciousness before her head had reached her chest, then Evadne Childe had just demonstrated the skill.

'Edmund!' she breathed, her head upright, her eyes flashing. 'It's my husband. My husband is here.'

Madame Rawnie did not undergo any physical transformation, nor did her voice alter, but somehow she *became* Edmund Walker-Pyne, at least in the eyes of Evadne Walker-Pyne, whose expression as she concentrated on the Belgian woman's face was nothing short of beatific rapture. There was no shaking of the table, no hint of ectoplasm and no exhibition of *glossolalia*, which Mr Campion knew meant 'speaking in tongues'; he had been waiting for many years for it to appear as the answer to a crossword clue.

The connection between the two elderly women was clear and it was a bond which would not easily be broken, effectively demoting Campion, Amanda and Veronica to mere bystanders at the proceedings.

'Is Edmund able to help us tonight?' Evadne asked.

'Edmund is willing,' relayed Madame Rawnie in English without a trace of an accent.

'Can he help Lady Amanda?'

'How?'

'She needs to speak with the spirit of Redvers Fitton.'

'Edmund says that spirit refuses to visit here tonight.'

'Does he know why?'

'No, he says that you will know, not now, but eventually.'

'How will I know?'

'By working hard and following . . .' Madame Rawnie

hesitated and for the first time seemed confused and lost for words, '. . . by following . . . it is difficult but I think he is saying *Yehonala*.'

Mr Campion felt his left hand being squeezed tightly by Veronica and he risked a fleeting glance, only to find her staring intently at the two older women.

'Edmund says you have not been taking your work seriously of late. He does not want you to waste your talent or for it to fade away. He is proud of your work and you must continue.'

'I will not disappoint him.'

'He knows that, just as he knows you still love him. That is why he still comes to you after all these years.'

'But can he not help Lady Amanda? She has questions for the spirit of Redvers Fitton.'

'Edmund cannot conjure a spirit who does not want to appear, or who cannot.'

'It is important.'

'Edmund knows that, and he knows it has to do with those pearls. He says Lady Amanda should leave them where they are and must not wear them in public.'

Now Mr Campion found his right hand being mangled by his wife's left, but the circle held tight, even when Madame Rawnie's body suddenly jerked forward in her chair and she gasped out loud as if suddenly struck.

'Edmund has gone,' said Evadne. 'Would someone please get Madam Rawnie a glass of water?'

Campion pushed back his chair and stood, his first action being to link his fingers and flex them without cracking his knuckles – something he had always regarded as vulgar – but almost immediately felt his sleeve being tugged by the very hand which had just released its vice-like grip.

'And get me something much stronger,' whispered Amanda.

With Lugg still setting the world to rights to anyone who would listen in the public bar of the Albany, and Rupert positively glowing in the dark of a cinema with Giulietta somewhere, Mr Campion found himself on housekeeping duty. Having transported a glass of water to Madame Rawnie and an unobtrusive gin and tonic to his wife, he then returned to the kitchen to heat milk in a saucepan for the cocoa requested by Evadne and

Veronica. By the time he delivered it, he was fully in agreement with Lugg's view that there were far too many *blank-blank* stairs in this house.

The séance circle had broken and those present had adjourned to more comfortable seats. The cigar box containing the black pearls, still open, lay in the middle of the table, and it was as if those present had chosen to relax as far away from it as possible, studiously ignoring its presence in the room.

'I must thank you for your efforts, Madame Rawnie,' said Amanda in her best French.

'I am sorry I was not successful, but the spirits can only be contacted, not controlled.'

'I understand.'

'But what you probably don't appreciate, Lady Amanda,' Evadne interjected, 'is that contact with the spirit world drains the energy of the medium. Madame Rawnie must be quite exhausted, though she hides it well.'

Amanda thought she did hide it well, but perhaps the subject of remuneration might revive her.

'You are both welcome to stay on here for a few days, should you wish to see something of London or perhaps take in a show. We would be happy to cover your expenses and, if you would name your fee, my husband will be able to arrange cash, either in sterling or Belgian francs.'

Madame Rawnie shook her head slowly but allowed Evadne to answer for her.

'No fee is necessary, Lady Amanda. We will certainly avail ourselves of your generous hospitality for a few days more, but Madame Rawnie does not charge for a consultation if the right result is not achieved.'

'Well, if you are sure you won't be too bored here . . .'

'Not at all,' said Evadne cheerfully. 'If your charming son is here, he can help me show Madame Rawnie the sights; your Italian girl will make sure we are fed and watered, and your butler . . . well, I am sure some of the stories he tells will find their way into some of my novels.'

'I sincerely hope he has told you the clean versions,' said Mr Campion.

'Clean, but colourful.' Evadne laughed. 'He's quite a fund of material for a novelist.'

'So you are writing a new book?' Amanda asked innocently.
'Yes, I am. Didn't you hear me promise Edmund I would?'

Lugg returned from the Albany a good twenty minutes before closing time, which was unusual but not suspicious, as it was fairly common for him to run out of fellow imbibers to talk to, especially when the topic of the day was who might be a good bet for the pending FA Cup competition and the hope that next year's final would be less boring than this year's victory by Tottenham over Burnley, even if this latter conviction did result in an exchange of harsh words with two Spurs fans.

The two elderly guests having retired to their rooms in the heights of the Fitzroy Square house, and Lugg volunteering to wait up for Rupert, once he had dropped '*Joo-lee-et*' off at her parents' home, the Campions and Veronica went out into the night and claimed a taxi, Mr Campion paying the driver in advance to call first at Bottle Street and then take Veronica home to Cricklewood.

'Well, that was enlightening,' said Mr Campion from the drop-down seat behind the driver, 'but was it genuine?'

'Evadne certainly thought so,' said Veronica. 'She was convinced Edmund was there talking through Madame Rawnie.'

'What was that "West Riding" reference? Evadne seemed to understand but it baffled me.'

'It was her "oneness",' said Campion, 'the codeword to prove it really was Edmund; something only she and he would know.'

'Did they go on honeymoon there or something? The West Riding – of *Yorkshire*? Surely not.'

'Now, now, darling,' Campion chided his wife, 'don't be snobby. That was the name of the ship on which Edmund Walker-Pyne died very early on in the war. I remember that Evadne has a framed photograph of it on her mantlepiece in her house in Essex. Probably still does.'

'So her "oneness", her password, was genuine? Only she and Edmund knew the relevance.'

'It certainly begs the question as to how an elderly Belgian gypsy woman would know such a thing without genuine psychic powers.'

'And she was right about there being no spirit of Redvers Fitton,' Amanda said quickly. 'If she had contacted Redvers, we would have known she was a fraud.'

'She did try and tempt you, darling.'

'She did?'

'When she offered a "oneness" which only you would recognize and latch on to, but you resisted with magnificent stoicism.'

'I did?'

'When she said *Yehonala*. Isn't that the tribal name of the Empress of China in the story you concocted about the pearls?'

'Well, yes,' said Amanda, suddenly feeling guilty but not quite sure why, 'but how did Madame Rawnie know that?'

'You mentioned it to Evadne when we had dinner at Beoty's,' said Veronica, 'when you told her the story of Redvers Fitton. It's what got her creative juices flowing and she started writing again.'

'So there really is a new book on the way?' Amanda said, hoping she did not sound too much like an awestruck fan.

'Oh yes,' said an enthusiastic Veronica, now on her home ground, 'she's throwing herself into it with gusto and is making good headway. The working title is *The Yehonala Curse*, but we'll probably change that before publication. It sounds a little too crude for a Rex Troughton mystery, don't you think?

EIGHTEEN
The Man from Interpol

'**A** London Particular means only one thing: a rosy time for thieves and thieving.'

Detective Superintendent Charles Luke blew into the Bottle Street flat, hands deep in the pockets of his raincoat, its wings flapping as though his arms had been determined to disperse the fog in the name of the law.

'Good evening, Charlie,' said Campion, closing the door to keep outside the floating shards of grey smog which had infiltrated with his visitor. 'I thought the Clean Air Act was supposed to have put a lid on these pea-soupers.'

'People still burning coal, Albert, and if they've seen the weather forecast, they'll be stocking up. They reckon there's a cold snap coming, but this is the worst smog since '52 when there were more than four thousand deaths. The medical boffins estimate we could get away with hundreds rather than thousands this time.'

'That's cold comfort for those suffering, Charlie, and it can only be another burden for you above and beyond your usual load. It's a good thing your shoulders are broad.'

Luke's shoulders certainly were broad, physically and mentally. The youngest son of William Luke, a London copper who had shared a beat with a young Stanislaus Oates, Charles's rise up the police hierarchy had outstripped his father's, though his father had delayed his retirement in order to be the first to salute him on his promotion to divisional detective inspector in 1948, at the age of thirty-four. Over the following decade, he established a reputation as an efficient thief-taker and a commander who would not ask his men to do anything that he would not. He was equally respected, without exception, by his colleagues in the Metropolitan Police and by the leading lights of the Metropolitan underworld.

At forty-eight, when many a man might have decelerated into middle-aged spread or deflation, Luke's muscular frame still spoiled the cut of the finest made-to-measure suit, and his short, wiry black hair showed no tinge of white. His energy was boundless and as Lugg, that veteran observer of the human condition, had once noted, Luke was a man who had no truck with a five-day working week, and had apoplexy waiting for Monday mornings to come round.

Yet life for the perfect policeman had been far from perfect. In the space of two years Luke had married, become a father and almost immediately a widower. A star-crossed marriage, which the Campions had thought ill-advised from the outset (though both now regretted their misgivings), had resulted in a death in childbirth for the mother, but a healthy daughter by the name of Hattie, who now lived with Luke and his formidable mother, and who would want for nothing.

The way Luke had come to terms with life's malevolence had been to throw himself into his work, which came as no surprise at all to anyone who knew him. His energy was as forceful as ever, his smile just as ferocious, his frown just as fearsome, and when he was laying down the law as he saw it, his words were punctuated by stabbing hand movements, almost karate chops, to emphasize the sense of what he was saying.

There had been plenty of work to keep Luke's rarely idle hands busy that year. Thefts from cars were running at 30 per cent up on 1961, with robberies in general by twenty-five per cent, and the smog which now suffocated London would only give the thieves and malcontents a further advantage. Rosy times indeed.

Luke peeled off his raincoat and flexed those broad, load-carrying shoulders.

'You know I'm not one to moan, Albert . . .'

'When someone says that, it's a sure thing that a full-scale moan is coming over the horizon, but you are not one to mewl and puke like an infant, Charles. If anyone's allowed a moan, or even the occasional whine, it's you. I'd say you were long overdue for a good moan, so moan away, old chap, and let me share your burden – or at least take your coat and hat.'

Luke's diamond-shaped eyes glinted cold, but only for a second before warming to his friend, with whom he could never be really angry.

'I did come here to tear you off a strip for dropping me in it as you usually do, but halfway up those blasted stairs I thought: what's the point? You'd only put on your butter-wouldn't-melt expression, the one Lugg calls your standing-by-the-font fizzog, and give me the old "owl eyes", and then it'd be me apologizing to you for interrupting your busy day to deliver a message.'

'As you can see,' said Campion with a broad grin, sweeping an arm wide to indicate the flat's living room, 'I am up to my old owl eyes in things to do. I have books to read, newspapers to iron, cushions to plump and the dust is simply mountainous. You wouldn't know how to work a Hoover, would you? Or know where it is?'

'Ho-ho-ho, highly comical, and just for that, I'll get it off my chest.' Luke drew in breath and raised a fist, from which fingers sprang to count off his concerns. 'It's been a hell of a year all round. We've got a new spy scandal every week according to the newspapers; I'm still chasing 750 cases of whisky hijacked from a lorry in Bethnal Green in July – not that there'll be much left undrunk by now; we've got Teddy boys attacking West Indians; and we've had, though it's hard to credit, a riot in Trafalgar Square sparked off by a rally of the National Socialist

Movement calling for Britain to awake. National Socialists! Can you believe it?'

Luke now had three fingers and a thumb on display, then he closed his fist and showed just a forefinger aimed at the ceiling.

'And what else do I have to cope with? A phone call from dear old Stanislaus asking for a favour. Now that's not really something I could ignore or refuse, is it?'

'Absolutely not,' said Campion, who knew that Luke venerated the former head of the CID. 'How is the old boy?'

'Raging against retirement and keeping his brain ticking over with some cold cases.'

'Let me guess, one of the cold cases involves yours truly.'

'It does.'

'How cold, would you say?'

'Freezing, in my opinion, but I'm not going to tell Mr Oates that, especially not when he was prodded into taking it up by Freddie Yeo. When those two get their false teeth into something, they don't let go.'

'You'll have to be clearer, Charlie. I'm not as young as you. I don't think I ever was.' Campion was well aware that Luke was almost exactly the same age as his wife. 'So explain slowly, and in small words, what is going on.'

'Mr Oates turned up an unsolved murder from 1946, a Maltese club owner called Tony Valetta, and when he mentioned it to Mr Yeo at one of their regular sessions down the Platelayers' Arms, he said you'd had a theory that the killer was also responsible for the death of a woman, six years later in 1952, who had worked in Valetta's club. And that it was connected to a post office robbery and the bloke in question seemed to be getting his ideas from some detective stories written by a relative of yours. Ring any bells?'

'A full Kent Treble Bob Major.'

'A *what?*'

'It's a whole peal of bells, or so I believe, but don't take my word for it; I really have no idea what I'm talking about when it comes to bells, but the murders of Tony Valetta and Rags Donovan, for whom no one was ever called to account – yes, I certainly do remember them. If this raddled old brain of mine had a filing cabinet fitted, they'd be filed in the Could-Have-Done-Should-Have-Done-More drawer.'

Luke leaned back on his heels and strained his neck to give himself extra height from which to look down on his host.

'Mr Oates said you were probably still beating yourself up over it, even now. Has this writer relative of yours given any more tips to the villains?'

'Evadne Childe? She's not actually a relative and we're not exactly pen pals, but Amanda is a big fan of her novels and reads them as they come out. She hasn't mentioned reading of any plans to steal the Crown Jewels, or Goya's portrait of the Duke of Wellington from the National Gallery last year.'

'Oh, we know where the Goya is,' said Luke with a huge grin.

'You do?'

'It's in the secret lair of Dr No on his Caribbean island. Haven't you seen the new film? It's a hoot.'

'I think Rupert has,' said Campion. 'I'm more of a *Mutiny on the Bounty* man, though I understand that doesn't exactly end happily. Anyway, enough of this Film Fun stuff; something must have got Stanislaus and Freddie excited. What was it?'

'A *development*!' said Luke, with dramatic exaggeration.

'After ten years? Has somebody confessed?'

'I don't think so, but that's for you to find out. I haven't the time or the men, especially with this smog providing cover for all sorts of recidivism, so you'll have to meet the chap who has got the old boys all excited.'

'What chap?'

'The man from Interpol, of course.'

As their lives had intertwined, Mr Campion had surprised Charlie Luke on more occasions than he cared to remember, and he should have known not to be taken in by his friend's perfect act of bewildered innocence. But Luke now felt – on that dank November evening, as one of the brand-new Ford Zephyrs reserved for the police, its headlights turning the fog yellow, conveyed them to his headquarters – that he had the chance to spring a genuine surprise and catch Campion on the back foot, even if only for a moment.

Yet when he came to open the door to Room 49, he was himself surprised, or rather his nostrils were, as they detected the pungent aroma of black French tobacco.

'Strewth,' muttered Luke, as he ushered Campion into the

office, 'that'll stick to the curtains. Better open a window and let the fog in to clear the air.'

Sitting on one of the pair of oxblood leather Chesterfield 'Captain's' chairs in front of Luke's desk, under an impressive cloud of blue smoke, was a white-haired man in a smart three-piece suit that was far too lightweight for the London weather. Judging by the overcrowded ashtray on the edge of the desk and the crumpled blue packet next to it, he had been chain-smoking Gauloises. On the other chair was a pile of *Evening Standard* newspapers, which Luke's visitor was clearly working his way through, and so intent was he on the issue he was reading that he did not look up as the door to the office was opened, nor as Luke steamed past him to get to the sash windows.

'Albert,' Luke said as he spanned the office in three extended strides, 'allow me to introduce—'

'Alex, you old bloodhound!' Campion exclaimed, and Luke's spirits sank. 'Never thought we'd get you to foggy old London town.'

The white-haired man put down his newspaper open on the desk, transferred his current cigarette to his left hand and stood up. He was at least a foot shorter than Campion and a good quarter of a century younger, even though his shock of wildly unkempt white hair belied that fact.

'Albert,' he said, pronouncing it the French way, 'it is good to see you again.'

Luke pushed up the window like a weight-lifter, but only used his fingertips. Had he exerted his full strength, there was little doubt that the whole sash would have come loose, frame and all.

'I take it you two know each other,' he said without turning round, knowing that the two of them would be in a clinch, kissing each other on both cheeks, a very un-English habit which Campion seemed quite relaxed about.

'Of course. Alex Gérardy is my absolute favourite Interpol officer,' said Campion. 'I didn't know you'd invited him over from Paris.'

'I didn't.'

'Officially,' said the man called Alex Gérardy with a mischievous grin, 'I am here on a goodwill visit with some of your famous detectives, and I thought I might as well see you as well.'

Campion acknowledged the dig with a broad grin. 'Don't let Alex's white hair fool you, Charlic, even though it makes him a dead ringer for Einstein looking for a comb. He's a mere chicken compared to old boilers like us. Whereas mine has blanched naturally and gracefully, something made his hair turn white at a very young age. He says it was the war; I think it may well have been a female of the species.'

'You know very well that it was the shock of meeting you,' said Gérardy, 'and your flowing white locks make you look even more distinguished. Also much older.'

'Your English is as annoyingly good as it always was.' Campion pointed to the pile of *Evening Standard* newspapers on the chair and leaned over to peruse the one open on the desk. 'Is that your secret? A close reading of the juicy stories in London's evening papers?'

'Superintendent Luke kindly gave me yesterday's issue to read while I was waiting and I discovered this wonderful serial, a new spy story called *The Ipcress File*. I simply had to know what had gone before and one of the constables found me copies of last week's papers. It is really very good; you should read it.'

'Are you sure it's fiction? Our newspapers seem to be uncovering spy stories every week these days.'

'This story reads like it is true, but it is fiction. The paper says there will be a book soon.'

'Then I will put it on my reading list,' said Campion, 'but we have other books to discuss first, don't we?'

It was the most unlikely reading group ever assembled, and it was meeting in the most unlikely venue, for books were rarely seen, let alone read, in the snug of the Platelayers' Arms. The tabletop around which the five men sat had great patches of its varnish removed through years of mistreatment, multiple rings of staining, and had probably never had a work of fiction rested upon it, but it served its purpose by supporting three pint glasses of bitter, and smaller glasses of lemonade and barley wine. The lemonade was understandable as Charles Luke was, technically, still on duty, but the barley wine raised a concern in the mind of the oldest man present.

'You know that's not wine like the sort you Frenchies drink, don't you?' said Stanislaus Oates, now in his seventies and looking every inch of it.

'I am Belgian, not French,' said Alex Gérardy, 'and therefore well aware that wine comes from grapes and not barley.'

'They are big beer drinkers in Belgium, Stanis,' said Mr Campion, 'and there are monks there who brew stuff that would blow your socks off.'

'Sorry to have trodden on anyone's toes, I'm sure,' muttered Oates, 'but when Albert told us to invite you over from Paris, I just assumed . . .'

'Interpol is based in Paris,' said Campion, raising his glass to the assembled company, 'but not all Interpol officers are Parisian. Cheers.'

'Hang on a minute,' said Luke, pointing an accusing finger at Mr Campion. 'You got Stanis and Fred to invite him?'

'Well, I thought the names of two senior, very senior, former CID officers would carry more clout among international crime-fighters than mine as a private citizen now devoted to a life of leisure and, as it happens, literature. Which is why we're all here: to discuss books. Specifically those of Mrs Walker-Pyne, better known as Evadne Childe.'

'Pah!' Luke's frame shook, as did the table, as he expressed his disgruntlement. 'I ain't got time for fairy stories, I'm up to my eyes in real crimes.'

'Now, now, Charlie,' Fred Yeo soothed the big man, 'you know Albert's not a time-waster and we wouldn't have dragged Alex over the Channel in November if there wasn't something in it.'

Yeo spoke as if anyone following the example of M. Blériot, even fifty years on, was to be admired for their pluck and daring.

'We need to brief you, Charles,' said Campion, 'and if you'll listen, we'll do that as quickly and painlessly as possible. We all have a part in the story. Stanislaus started it, Freddie got caught in the middle of it and Alex here is going to help write the last chapters. But before we start, just let me check something. Did you listen to the recording I sent over, Alex?'

Before the man from Interpol could respond with other than a brief nod, Luke intervened. 'Recording? What recording?'

'A tape-recording of a séance, Charles. Don't worry, it would almost certainly not be admissible as evidence in a trial. Not even the dottiest of our High Court judges accept testimony from the spirit world, at least not until after a very good lunch.'

'There were one or two things I did not understand,' said Gérardy, 'but it seems to fit the pattern.'

'Hold on,' complained Luke, 'draw it mild. Recordings? Trials? What is going on?'

'We are being unfair, Charles. I apologize. Let us start to fill you in. Stanislaus can go first as he made the first connection.'

'Now don't go blaming me, Albert, that's not fair. She's your relative, after all.'

The former assistant commissioner buried his face in his pint glass.

'We happen to share a godmother, that's all,' said Campion, 'but let's start with you back in 1946 and let's do it before Charles blows a gasket.'

Mr Oates did not relish leading the discussion, but if he had to 'kick things off' then he wanted it known that 'back then' it had all seemed like just a daft coincidence and the odds were that if he hadn't known Mr Campion, things might not have gone any further. But it was because he was acquainted with Campion and his penchant for anything served with a sauce of the bizarre or a whiff of the unusual, that he had raised the topic. Had he put in a formal report to the Home Office that there was a definite link between a murder-robbery in a seedy drinking club in the wrong half of Mayfair, and a work of fiction by one of the nation's favourite female authors – an author known to be read and enjoyed by the current Queen Mother – then he would have found himself back on traffic duty.

Yet there was no denying it was odd that the murder of Tony Valetta, owner of the Grafton Club, seemed to be following a script written by Evadne Childe when she described the murder of a character called Jake Muscat, owner of the Reynard Club in one of her books. That, to Oates, had seemed something likely to be right up Albert's street, and it didn't come as a surprise to anyone to find out that he was related to this blasted writer woman.

'We only share a godmother!' Mr Campion wailed despairingly.

Anyways, Oates continued, nothing came of that as Albert was called away on official government business to Germany, not that he had ever heard the full story there.

'Nor will you,' said Campion firmly.

'Germany in 1946?' said Alex Gérardy. 'I could hazard a guess.'

'Please don't,' said Mr Campion.

The police had no leads in the case or physical evidence, the only person of interest being a cigarette girl called Rags Donovan, who was never a viable suspect. The detective-story lady seemed to be in the clear, and certainly didn't make a habit of predicting real crimes in her books.

'Until 1952, that is,' said Freddie Yeo, 'when she laid out a blueprint for a mail-van robbery at Euston in another of her damned fairy stories.'

Yeo outlined the daring daylight robbery and was able to report some success in that the police had made several arrests and recovered a large chunk of the stolen loot. They had run into a dead end, however, tracking the mysterious 'John Lawton', the gang leader, who had disappeared without trace though not, it was thought, before he had killed Rags Donovan, the one person who could have linked him to the murder of Tony Valetta six years earlier.

Like Stanislaus Oates, Yeo still held a grievance. Neither case could be properly closed if there was still a double murderer out there somewhere. That sort of thing did not lead to a good night's sleep.

'I can vouch for that,' said Campion. 'My dreams are troubled too.'

'You did what you could, Albert, nobody's blaming you,' said Oates.

'I am,' said Mr Campion. 'You see, it was I who introduced Evadne Childe to a young Belgian officer back in 1940. I thought he had come over here to carry on the fight against the Nazis. His companion, another lad who escaped with him certainly had, and went on to prove himself a useful addition to the war effort. The pair were called Simon and Peter. Peter was the good soldier who ultimately paid the good soldier's price; Simon Moorgat, however, was anything but the good soldier, and certainly not the good citizen.

'I have not seen him since 1940, and I believe Evadne Childe when she says she has not seen him since 1945, but I think he spent the war in London as a deserter from the Free Belgian Forces, re-emerging in 1952 under the alias John Lawton to mastermind the Euston mail-van robbery. Unfortunately, the only people able to identify Moorgat, or Moorgat-as-Lawton post-war are both dead: Tony Valetta and Rags Donovan.'

'Hold on,' said Luke, 'let this simple wooden-headed copper get this straight. You, Albert, have somehow arranged this Brains' Trust to consider two old cases which are linked by an old lady who writes detective stories and a villain who hasn't been heard from in ten years?'

'That is where I can help, if I may,' offered Gérardy.

Mr Campion patted the man from Interpol on the shoulder and raised his glass to him. Somewhat nervously, with the unblinking stares of three senior policemen firmly targeting his face, he began by addressing Campion personally.

'I once asked you if you knew Brussels. Can you recall how you answered?'

'I think I said something to the effect that I knew enough not to get myself invited to the Amigo for breakfast,' said Campion, 'but that was back when the Amigo was a prison used by the Gestapo. I understand it is a very respectable hotel these days.'

'I remembered that reply when you asked me to find Simon Moorgat, and it made me think: where was the best place for a man with a criminal past to disappear? Why, a prison of course. I found him serving an eight-year sentence in Saint-Gilles in Brussels.'

'Eight years? For murder?' gasped Oates, shaking his head.

'And robbery,' said Yeo equally disparagingly.

'Neither.' Gérardy seemed almost apologetic. 'He was not charged with any of your crimes, nor even with being a deserter from the army, but a crime committed in Brussels in connection with his gambling.'

'So he was a sore loser, as the Yanks would say,' observed Luke.

'He was a very angry loser, and had been thrown out of casinos in Brussels, Spa and Antwerp for being violent and abusive whenever he lost – and he did lose. He lost a lot of money.'

'Where did he get it from?' asked Oates.

'I can guess,' said Oates, before the Belgian could answer, 'the Grafton Club.'

'No one knows for sure. Simon Moorgat returned to Belgium in 1946 with enough documentation to suggest he had been working on unspecified duties for the Belgian government in exile in London and considerable funds. The first thing he did was to pay for a memorial to his friend Peter Verloet in his local church.'

'Good public relations,' said Mr Campion.

'Exactly so. No one asked enough questions about how he had earned his wealth and how he managed to live a life of fast cars, women and visits to casinos, but he never committed a crime, at least not in Belgium. And then, it would have been 1951, he disappeared.'

'To London,' said Yeo, 'where he became John Lawton and robbed a mail van.'

Gérardy shrugged his shoulders. 'Whoever he was and what-ever he did, when he returned to Brussels it was as a rich man – at least for a while. Though he soon fell into his old bad habit of visiting the casinos.'

'It's only a bad habit if you lose,' said Campion, who was immediately glared at by the three policemen for his flippancy. 'Which, of course, one always does,' he added weakly. 'Pray continue, Alex.'

'Moorgat lost a lot of money very quickly, and then, stupidly, opened up a line of credit with some dangerous gangsters – yes, we do have them in quiet little Belgium. When he could not pay back what he owed, he visited one of the gangsters in a nightclub in a bad area around the old Brussels Fish Market. The police thought he may have gone there to liberate some funds to ease his debts.'

'Nice way of putting it,' said Oates. 'Sounds like a repeat of the Grafton Club job.'

'Except this time he was caught, where he should not be, by the owners of the club. There was gunfire. Moorgat was shot in the arm and was taken to hospital under police guard. When he was fit enough to stand trial, that's when he was sentenced to eight years.'

'Go back a bit,' said Yeo, making a circling motion with a finger. 'If this Moorgat was the John Lawton behind the Euston robbery, then he got away with a fair chunk of money. We recov-ered a lot, but not all. He would have had enough to live comfortably.'

'Moorgat was never accused of the robbery in Belgium, so there was no reason to investigate where his wealth came from, but it was around that time, 1952, that his mother was suddenly able to buy a small farm in her home village and an apartment in Brussels. Moorgat himself enjoyed living in hotels, fast women and even faster cars – the "high life", I think you call it – and gambling. The money soon ran out and he found himself in debt to some dangerous people.'

'Well, there's one thing that story proves,' said Oates with great deliberation. 'This Moorgat chappie was no stranger to carrying a gun and using it if he needed to.'

'I think Alex has more to tell us about Simon Moorgat's propensity for violence,' said Mr Campion, sipping his beer.

'It has to do with the death of the woman Rags Donovan,' said Gérardy, fixing his eyes on Yeo.

'Mrs Rachel Daubney,' said the old policeman with some dignity, 'was strangled, not shot.'

'Forgive me, said Gérardy, not terribly sure why he was apologizing. 'But Albert mentioned that the wom— The lady . . . had been strangled with a length of rope.'

'Aye, that's right enough,' said Yeo, 'a length of clothes line, like the commandos used during the war.'

'Exactly.'

'But this Simon Moorgat wasn't a commando.'

'No, but his close friend Peter Verloet was,' said the Belgian, 'who went on to serve in an elite unit called the SAS. He would certainly have been taught that technique, and there is evidence from Peter Verloet's diaries, which were given to his mother after his death, that he and Simon met several times during the war in London. They could have talked about such things; soldiers do talk about such things.'

'But this chap Moorgat was a deserter!' Luke was indignant.

'Did Peter know that?' asked Campion. 'Simon fooled a lot of people during the war, and after. I say, if we all join hands, we could hold a séance and try and contact Peter to ask him direct. Oh sorry, was that in bad taste? I only thought of it because Evadne Childe firmly believes in the power of séances when it comes to asking the dead for advice.'

'So we're back to the detective-story writer, are we?' said Luke. 'I knew we'd get there in the end. What's the connection, then, Albert? There is one; there must be, judging by that smug look on your face.'

'There is indeed, Charlie. You see, the spiritualist medium whom Evadne Childe began to consult as soon as the war was over, and to whom she confided her deepest secrets as well as the plots of her books, was recommended to her by Simon Moorgat.' Campion showed the table his best non-simpering smile. 'Which is not surprising really, as Madame Rawnie is Simon Moorgat's mother.'

'So your favourite author lady, she believes in all that séance stuff?' Oates radiated dismissiveness.

'I'm afraid she does, but I must say that Madame Rawnie is a very convincing gateway to the spirit world. I arranged a séance here in London at which she officiated.'

'I presume you laid a trap for her?' said Luke.

'We did and she did not fall into it; rather, she very cleverly turned the tables on us.'

'She did?' said Luke in mock surprise. 'Why wasn't I given a ringside seat for that?'

'You don't have the patience to sit still that long, Charlie.'

'Nor the gullibility,' added Oates, 'but do tell, Albert. How did this Madame Scrawny best you?'

'Rawnie,' Campion corrected.

Oates furrowed his brow. 'That's gypsy, a Romany name, innit?'

'It is indeed, and it means "Lady", so "Madame Lady" is clearly a disguise, or a stage name. I am not even sure that Evadne Childe, who has consulted her for many years, knew that her real name was Moorgat.'

'So how did this gypsy fortune teller put the evil eye on you?' Luke demanded.

'We created a fiction, and by "we" I mean Amanda, myself and Evadne's editor, which involved contacting the spirit of someone deceased but who, in fact, did not exist.'

'So if your medium says "Is anybody there?" and the table rattles and thumps and she says it's your wandering spirit, you know she's a fraud.'

'Exactly, Charlie, except she didn't fall for it, and instead she plucked at Evadne's heartstrings by channelling her late husband Edmund.'

Gérardy raised a forearm, almost as if he were back behind a schoolroom desk.

'There was something I did not understand on the tape-recording, Albert. The words "west" and "riding".'

'That was what Evadne called her "oneness"; it's a sort of password to prove that the spirit is genuine. It is a word or a phrase, or a place or a name, which only the spirit and the person trying to contact them would recognize. For Evadne it was the name of the ship on which Edmund Walker-Pyne died in 1939.'

'Something which a Belgian clairvoyant could not possibly know?' asked Luke, the detective without an off switch.

'Unless she'd been told by somebody who had seen the picture of the ship above Evadne's mantlepiece in her house in Essex, which Simon Moorgat certainly would have as he was billeted on Evadne shortly after Dunkirk. I know that for a fact as I was there to introduce him, something I regret to this day.'

'Don't play the blame game, Albert,' said Oates, 'it's not worth it. I blamed myself for not following up on the Grafton case as well as I should have, and I know Freddie here regrets the same with the murder of the Donovan girl.'

Yeo nodded morosely in agreement. 'I got too distracted by the Euston robbery,' he said quietly. 'Recovering the money seemed more of a priority than the murder of a young woman. That wasn't right then; it isn't right now.'

A melancholic air descended on the table; in such circumstances, Mr Campion would usually insert a burst of frippery or flippancy to lighten the mood, but Luke pre-empted him with a blunt, pull-yourself-together injunction.

'What a bunch of moping Minnies! Albert hasn't got us here together to cry into our beer, he's got something in mind, unless I'm very much mistaken. Interpol haven't sent a man over here to watch two old coppers reminiscing about past oversights, and I don't think I'm here just to make up the numbers.'

'You're quite right on both counts, Charlie,' said Mr Campion. 'Alex here brings news hotfoot from Brussels.'

Gérardy finished the last dregs of his barley wine and looked at the glass with appreciation before placing it on the table.

'Simon Moorgat will be released from prison this week,' he said, clearly expecting a more dramatic reaction from his audience.

'Stands to reason,' said Luke. 'You said he'd been given eight years. I'm guessing Albert thinks he's coming back to London – it seems to be a happy hunting ground for him – and I'll be expected to arrest him.'

'I knew I could rely on you, Charlie, my most solid policeman.'

'On what charge, Albert?' asked Oates. 'There's no concrete evidence to connect him to the murder of Tony Valletta.'

'Or Rags Donovan,' added Yeo gloomily.

'So, if he does come to London,' said Luke, 'what reasonable grounds for arrest do I have? What crime can we prove he's committed?'

'Oh, he hasn't committed a *provable* crime – well, not yet.'

Silence descended on the group, and for a moment the only sound was the hiss of beer pumps and clink of glasses from the public bar on the other side of the wooden partition wall.

It was Luke who asked the question.

'What sort of game are you playing, Albert?'

'A long one,' said Mr Campion.

NINETEEN

Pearls Before Swine

'It's going absolutely splendidly. I've never known Evadne write so quickly. I think she must be making up for lost time as she hasn't had a book out for two years. It's jolly exciting too, though of course I can't tell you anything about it; it's all top, top secret.'

'I think you can tell me, Veronica,' Amanda said down the telephone in her best headmistress voice, 'after all, it was my idea.'

'Oh yes, I suppose it was.'

Amanda had the distinct impression that Veronica Hatherall had placed a hand over her telephone and lowered her voice before she was willing to part with a top, top secret.

'We had four new chapters this morning in the post, and Miss Prim is typing them up as we speak. She's an insufferable woman but a lightning typist, and she's got her eye in when it comes to

Evadne's handwriting. I'm expecting her drafts on my desk before
the day is out.'

'So, what's the story so far?'

'Very much as we hoped. She followed the trail of crumbs
that we dropped: the story of the Boxers, the mystery of the
black pearls, the curse, even the house on Fitzroy Square. She's
left out the séances element, as Rex Troughton does not need
any help from psychic detectives, apparently, but the layout of
the house and the pearls are described in great detail.'

'Did she notice the flimsy sash window by the basement
entrance?'

Amanda certainly hoped she had, as she had broken two
fingernails loosening the catches.

'Naturally she picked up on that. She has, after all, a criminal
mind – fictionally speaking, of course. She's even noted that the
best time to approach the property would be between nine and
ten in the evening, before the policeman starts his patrol
and when the butler has a night off and has gone to the pub.'

'She's put Lugg in the book?' Amanda held back a fit of
giggles.

'Well, he's not called Lugg, of course, he's called Hogg, but
he is unmistakeably Lugg. He is constantly moaning about young
tearaways zipping around London on Vespas, which he calls their
"buzz-buzz wasps" and there's a passage where she describes
him in a grey morning suit walking by the Serpentine and being
mistaken for a Dreadnought by some boys playing with pond
yachts on the far bank. I hope he won't mind.'

'Oh, don't worry about Lugg, he only reads the Greek philoso-
phers and the *Racing Post*. I think he might be rather flattered
to be included and I'm sure he won't sue. I hope Albert's not
in it.'

'Certainly not,' said Veronica firmly, protecting her employer's
most valuable asset. 'No other detective is allowed to upstage
Rex Troughton.'

'I'll be sure to tell Albert that. Just how is the great detective
progressing with his investigation?'

'I'll have a better idea when I've read the latest chapters. Miss
Prim will leave them on my desk tonight before she goes home.'

'So you'll be working overtime? In your case, reading is work,
isn't it?'

'You know that, I know that, but the directors don't always think so. But I don't care about them. With our accountants positively salivating at the thought of a new Evadne Childe book, I can, to coin a phrase, get away with murder. As I will be burning the midnight oil, I am therefore taking the afternoon off and going to see *How the West Was Won*. It's got Richard Widmark and George Peppard in it, and both of them are dreamy. Our New York office say it's very good. Which reminds me, the American end doesn't like the title *The Yehonala Curse* and they've suggested an alternative.'

'Which is what? I'm curious as I am a sort of stepmother to this book.'

'They suggest *Pearls Before Swine*, which isn't bad, I suppose. I voted for *Pearls Are a Nuisance* but New York said that had been taken by some American writer and seemed rather cross that I hadn't heard of it.'

Mr Campion was on edge. Not nervous, but definitely anticipating action, if not this day, then soon. His physical movements, even when supposedly relaxing, were a mass of microscopic twitches and flutters which would have gone undetected by all but his wife. He seemed unable to sit still for more than a minute and could not concentrate on a newspaper, or a conversation, for more than two. He was smoking more than usual and had taken to pacing the Bottle Street flat as if preparing an estimate for new carpets. He reminded Amanda, who had some experience thanks to her work in aircraft design for a military contract, of a well-trained paratrooper who knows that his parachute will open perfectly on command but still dreads the moment he has to step up to the open door of the aeroplane.

It was not, she decided, the moment to tackle the subject – now it was December – of Christmas, and the domestic arrangements which had to be planned with the precision of the D-Day landings. She had thought of raising the topic light-heartedly by announcing she had bought Rupert that latest thing in gadgetry, an electric toothbrush, which she knew would amuse her husband greatly. Alternatively, she considered a tangential approach by quoting one of the stories in the newspaper Campion was restlessly reading, which declared that no trains would run on Christmas Eve.

Eventually Amanda chose to broach the subject of lunch, as breakfast had been a silent, sulky affair at which, judging by his facial expressions, Mr Campion might as well have been eating cardboard. She had taken a deep breath and was about to suggest that Simpson's in the Strand might prove both a distraction and a treat, when she was saved by the telephone bell.

It was the telephone call for which Mr Campion had been anxiously waiting for the better part of two weeks, and it came from Charles Luke. By the time Amanda had said, 'Hello, Charlie' and, 'Yes, he's here', Campion had materialized at his wife's side, all traces of agitation and nervous tics completely gone. He took the receiver from Amanda and spoke for no more than a minute, but listened in silence for over two.

'Alex Gérardy has been in touch with Charlie,' he said after terminating the call. 'Our Belgian friend is on the move. He visited his mother in the village where he was born, a place called Liberchies, stayed for a few days then relocated to Brussels, where he skulked around with some known minor hoodlums and bought himself a scooter, one of those stylish Italian ones which swarm around Lugg whenever he tries to cross Shaftesbury Avenue.'

'They probably mistake him for a new traffic island,' said Amanda, delighted to see the first genuine smile in days light up her husband's face, if only briefly.

'Moorgat then visited a well-known – well-known to the police, that is – jeweller in Antwerp.'

'To get a valuation, I presume.'

'That's what I would do. You were deliciously vague about the potential value of the pearls, though Lugg had instructions to talk them up whenever he got the chance.'

'But did you see Madame Rawnie's eyes light up when she saw them, and when she saw I kept them in a cigar box! She was tempted, I could tell, plus I knew I could rely on Evadne's novelist flair to exaggerate their value. The crime has to be worthy of the talents of a Rex Troughton.'

'Well, the bait seems to have been taken,' said Campion, 'because Simon Moorgat turned up in Ostend, booking himself and his scooter on the MV *Artevelde*, the Ostend-Dover ferry.'

'So he is coming back to England,' Amanda said with some satisfaction.

'He's already here,' said Campion. 'His ferry docked this morning and Luke's man down at Dover says he got off using a Belgium passport in his own name.'

'Wasn't that a risk?'

Campion shrugged his shoulders. 'There is no warrant out here for Simon Moorgat and Charlie gave orders that he was not to be picked up at the port, so at the moment I suspect he and his Vespa are putt-putting their way through Kent to foggy old London town.'

'If we are sticking to the plan, we'd better get the Fitzroy Square house up and running again, or at least cleaned up. Goodness knows what state Lugg and Rupert have left it in. I think they've been having too much fun using it as a bachelor pad. Do we need to recall Giulietta?'

'I don't think so, Lugg can dig out his chef's hat. Giulietta had her fill of him when she sent him out for olive oil and he came back from the chemist's with a medicine bottle and a teaspoon. Tell Rupert he can live here while we move there. I'd feel happier if he was safely out of the way.'

'You are sure Moorgat will come?'

'We know he's a gambler and he's almost certainly in need of cash or something he thinks he can turn into cash. He will have been well briefed by Mum on how careless the stupid English are when it comes to protecting their valuables, and he knows his way round London, even though it's been ten years. He'll come, or my name's not Tootles Ash.'

'Well, not recently, darling. Before we actually get to action stations, can I slip in a little piece of domestic admin?'

'Of course.'

'Is there anything you would especially like for Christmas?'

'A clear conscience,' said Mr Campion.

Veronica Hatherall had long regarded going to the cinema alone as a guilty pleasure, but it was not one she was really ashamed of, or tried to hide from anyone curious about her private life; not that many people were. True, she never mentioned that one attraction for her was that she could, in the darkness, smoke cigarettes with impunity, a habit among females which the directors of Gilpin's frowned upon; nor would she ever have admitted her passion for expensive ice creams on sticks during the intervals.

Being perfectly honest, her weakness for a Lyons Maid toff 'n
choc sundae, or a peach sundae, was something she did feel
slightly guilty about, as they cost one shilling and tuppence, so
she always delayed her dash to the ice-cream lady with her tray
of delights until the lights were about to dip, so she could enjoy
her treat without disapproving looks from other patrons.

If she could indulge her cinema-going habit 'on the firm's
time', as it were, her pleasure was doubled, and when she emerged
into the early evening London fog from a matinee showing of
an epic western, her nicotine and ice-cream habits satiated, she
thought nothing of navigating her way back to the office on foot.

It was true what they were saying on the television, this could
be London's worst pea-souper since 1952, but Veronica was used
to them by now and carried a bicycle lamp in her capacious
handbag, not to illuminate a path for her, as the beam was far
too weak to cut through the fog, but rather to signal her presence
to other pedestrians and wayward motor vehicles. The going,
however, was very slow, and crossing the Tottenham Court Road
especially hazardous, despite the presence of uniformed policemen
armed with red flares at numerous junctions.

She used the bicycle lamp to check the time on her wristwatch
when she reached the steps of the Gilpin & Co. building, its dark
outline looming above her. To her surprise, she found it was
almost eight o'clock so, naturally, the offices would be empty
and locked, but if Miss Prim had been her usual efficient self,
there would be a neat pile of typed pages on Veronica's desk,
along with a handwritten memo claiming at least one hour's
overtime.

Using her lamp, she located the set of office keys she had
been entrusted with in her handbag and let herself in, a shadow
of fog entering with her. Thanks to years of familiarity, she
located the main board of light switches and flicked three in rapid
succession, illuminating the entrance hall and the staircase, the
clumping of her heels on the stairs echoing through the empty
building as she climbed up to her office.

It had been her intention to collate the typed pages, pack them
in a large envelope and pick her way through the gloom to
Baker Street and the underground to Willesden Green and
then home, where she could devour them at her leisure, but as
soon as she saw the thickness of the pile of paper, her heart

leapt into her throat – a cliché which, as an editor she would never allow. Evadne had been busy and Miss Prim worth her overtime bonus.

Without taking her coat off, Veronica sat down at her desk, and from a lower drawer removed the sheaf of pages bound with a rubber band which carried a title page with *The Yehonala Curse* crossed out and *Pearls Before Swine* handwritten under it in red ink.

She consulted the last two pages of script to remind herself where Evadne had got to in the story, then turned to the fresh pages and began to read.

So entranced was she that she totally forgot the fact that she had closed, but not locked, the front door.

'Yes, this is Lady Amanda Fitton, but I prefer Mrs Campion for day-to-day use.'

'Forgive me, Lady Amanda, but I really thought you ought to know.'

'Know what? And just who is speaking?'

'Oh, I'm sorry, how stupid of me, but I've had something of a shock. It's Miss Prim, Catherine Prim, from Gilpin's, the publishing house.'

'I remember you, Miss Prim. You are, I understand, doing some important typing work for Veronica Hatherall on Evadne Childe's new novel.'

'I am, and that's why I am ringing you, even though the police have told me not to talk to anyone.'

'The police?'

As she spoke the words aloud, Amanda realized that her husband was gliding across the floor towards her.

'Has something happened to the manuscript?' Amanda said into the receiver, turning her head towards her husband.

'Yes, it has,' wailed Miss Prim. 'It's gone, been stolen. At least the top copy I left on Veronica's desk. I put the carbon copies in the office safe before I went home last night, but that's not the worst of it.'

Amanda kept her voice steady and clear. 'Tell me the worst of it, Miss Prim. I'm sure the police won't mind you talking to me or my husband.'

'It's Miss Hatherall. She must have disturbed whoever stole

the Evadne Childe manuscript. She must have been in her office all night.'

'Miss Prim, is she all right?'

'No, she's not, she's dead.'

Amanda cleared the breakfast things from the table and began to do the washing up slowly and methodically, concentrating intently on each action of soaping, rinsing and then drying while her husband commandeered the telephone. Her careful, deliberate actions in a mundane task helped to calm her raging thoughts.

When Campion took her gently by the shoulders and looked into that heart-shaped face, he could see moist eyes, but the tears were being held in check. Amanda pushed two fists glistening with suds from the washing-up bowl into her husband's chest.

With what his mother would have called 'delicate quietude', he repeated in soft, undramatic words what Luke had told him on the telephone, suitably censored for more delicate ears.

'Veronica did go to the cinema yesterday; the police found a ticket stub in her purse. Then she must have gone to her office at Gilpin's and was almost certainly reading the typescript of Evadne's new book when she was disturbed by an intruder. She was strangled with a length of red rope which one of Luke's boys has identified as just the sort of rope which secures lifebelts to the railings of ships – ships such as cross-Channel ferries. It happened about nine o'clock last night, they think. The killer left the rope in situ but took the typescript.'

Two delicate, soapy fists beat a short tattoo on Mr Campion's shirt.

'How can you stay so calm?'

'I am not, my dear; I am furious with myself but, as we are now on a war footing, there is no point in going into a panic.'

'You can't blame yourself, Albert.'

'Yes, I can, and yes, I do. What a fool I've been! I have been working on the assumption that the only people who could identify Simon Moorgat from his London escapades were dead, but I'd overlooked poor Veronica. She met him during the war, if only briefly, but she might have recognized him. More importantly, he might have recognized *her* and thought it prudent to eliminate her.'

Mr Campion's Séance 229

'Prudent? I'd say callous, and don't forget the other person who knew Moorgat in the war.'

'Me?' said Campion, pointing a finger at his chest. 'It's been twenty, no, twenty-two, years since I saw him, and he was very young and in uniform at a time when all young men were in uniform. Age, and prison, will have changed him and my eyesight's not what it was. I am not completely sure I could honestly pick him out of a line-up.'

'I was thinking of Evadne and how she called him her "Heathcliff". I bet she will recognize him.'

'You are absolutely right, and that's why we have to bring Evadne into the fold before the wolf descends upon it.'

'You mean we should bring her into our little scheme? She might not like it. We have, after all, involved her without her knowledge. You'll have to brief her very carefully, or would you like me to do it?'

'No, I'll go, because I'm not just going to brief her, I'm going to kidnap her. Moorgat knows where she lives, remember, and she'll be much safer here with us.'

'Will she see it that way?'

'I doubt it.'

Mr Campion steered the Jensen grim-faced out of London on the Mile End Road towards Stratford and then the Colchester road, taking no pleasure in the performance and comfort offered by his new car. He did feel some satisfaction at being able to put his foot down once beyond Romford and turn a blinkered eye to the speed limit, musing on the coincidence that the last time he had driven out to Essex to see Evadne Childe, ten years before, he had also been running-in a new car.

He had driven into East Anglia many times in his life; it was the road trip he had made more than any other, yet he was once again struck by the scenery. Flat, certainly, but by no means boring, and after fog-smothered London, fantastically clear and clean. This really was a place where the sky came right down to the ground.

The Jensen performed well and he made good time, despite the obligatory delay in negotiating the road through Chelmsford, which may have been the county town of Essex, but most agreed it sorely needed bypassing.

The village of Eight Ash had already been bypassed, not by
tarmac and concrete, but rather by time. Campion was hard
pushed to spot anything which had changed since his previous
visit in 1952, or indeed his first in 1940, apart from the television
aerials which had sprouted if not from every, then certainly every
third roof. The remains of a pillbox still guarded the lane down
to Mill House, a very solid reminder of the war years, which
conjured a memory of him driving down the lane in a borrowed
staff car with two motorcycles and their young foreign riders in
pursuit.

He had asked Amanda to wait an hour after his departure
before telephoning Evadne to warn her of his arrival, without
telling her the reason; not because he did not trust his wife to
impart the bad news in a sympathetic way, but because he felt
duty-bound to undertake that task himself.

'Albert! Welcome, I was forewarned.'

'Amanda got through to you, then,' said Mr Campion as Evadne
took his coat.

'Yes, she did, but she didn't say much of substance, just that
you needed to see me about something important.'

'I'm afraid I do, and it is important. If I am disturbing your
writing, I apologize.'

'You are. I am in what you might call "full flow" but I will
permit a disturbance and put it down to a coffee break. The kettle
is on, so please come through.'

If nothing much had changed in her village, Evadne Childe's
living room had certainly come crashing into the 1960s, its bare
walls painted in pastel shades. The shabby, overstuffed furniture
that Campion remembered had been replaced with a pair of
pointy, pine-framed modern armchairs and a red leather sofa of,
he guessed, Danish design. In the right setting, Campion would
have approved of the Viking influence, but in this house it seemed
more of an invasion, especially as all the seating positions were
angled towards one of the largest television sets he had ever seen.

Evadne followed his train of thought. 'I don't use this room
very much,' said his hostess, 'but some of the elderly ladies of
the village come round to watch our favourite programmes, such
as *Dixon of Dock Green*, *Laramie* and *The Avengers*, and we've
been promised BBC2 the year after next and even colour!'

Mr Campion raised an eyebrow and scanned the room, noticing

that one thing still present was the photograph of the *West Riding* above the fireplace, which now housed an ugly three-bar electric fire.

'I can see you don't approve, Albert, but the place was in need of an update, or so the estate agents said.'

'You are putting it on the market?'

'I will be soon. I have started to rattle around in here. I am seventy-two years old and no longer have a driver I can call on. This house can be very lonely in the winter, so I will sell up and retire somewhere hot. Jamaica, perhaps, or Sicily.'

'Won't you be lonely there too?'

'Possibly, but then' – she glanced involuntarily at the framed photograph on the mantlepiece – 'I'm never *completely* alone. But before I can think of moving, I have a book to finish, and I can tell you now, it will be dedicated to Lady Amanda because she sowed the seeds of the plot in my fuzzy old brain.'

'I'm afraid she did more than that, Evadne. You'd better sit down.'

They chose the two modern armchairs and sat facing each other, Campion instinctively controlling his long legs so that their knees were a respectful distance apart.

Mr Campion launched into the monologue he had mentally rehearsed on the drive from London, on how the original desire by Veronica Hatherall to prod and provoke Evadne into writing a new novel had encouraged Amanda to come up with a storyline which would appeal to both Evadne and her hero Rex Troughton. From there, it had escalated into a deliberate plan to finally bring to heel a double murderer who had avoided justice for far too long, and that had involved – and there was no other way of putting it – the duping and manipulation of Evadne, for which he could only apologize.

'Am I to assume, Mr Campion,' said Evadne, deliberately shunning the use of a Christian name, 'that the whole story of Redvers Fitton and the necklace of black pearls was a sham? A falsehood?'

'It was a fiction, certainly.'

'And it had to involve Madame Rawnie and an intrusion into my very personal beliefs and feelings?'

'I'm afraid it did,' said Campion, holding her gaze.

'Am I allowed to know why?'

'Because of Simon Moorgat.'

'Simon? The Simon and Peter I knew in the war? The boys *you* brought here back in 1940? Have we not gone through all this before? Why are you obsessed with Simon?'

'Because I believe Simon Moorgat, who was your guide to the sleazy side of Soho and Mayfair in 1944, realizing that the plot you were researching for *The Bottle Party Murders* was a very workable one, actually put it into action, robbing the Grafton Club and killing its owner in the process.'

'That's ridiculous, or at best pure coincidence . . .' Evadne began to protest but Mr Campion held up a hand to silence her.

'Once may be a fluke, but then he saw a perfect blueprint for a robbery in *Camera Obscuring* and successfully hijacked a mail van. The only fly in the ointment in the execution of that crime was that he was recognized by someone from the Grafton Club. That was the unfortunate coincidence which got Rachel Daubney, or Rags Donovan as she was, murdered.'

'But that's insane!' the woman protested. 'We've been over this. My book didn't come out until *after* the Euston mail-van incident. How could it have been a blueprint? Nobody had read it.'

'But you had described the plot to someone, hadn't you?'

'I might have given my editor a brief outline, but it would have been no more than an outline, something which would fit "on the back of a fag packet", as the vulgar expression goes. But certainly not to anyone else.'

'What about Madame Rawnie?'

'How dare you even suggest that? My dealings with Madame Rawnie are personal and very, very private!'

'So they should be in normal circumstances, but crimes are being committed, including by me.'

'By you? Is deceiving an old lady a crime now? I thought it might be no more than a pastime for men like you.'

'I had more serious crimes in mind, but you are perfectly right; I am guilty of deception and worse. You see, I know you have discussed the plot of your current novel with Madame Rawnie and am confident that you did the same with the plot of *Camera Obscuring*. In fact, you probably told her all your plots, because you were trying them out on Edmund through her. When I asked you before, you told me that you had not divulged a plot "to a living soul" – but what about a dead one?'

It was a combination of his implied criticism of her plotting skills as a writer of detective stories and his invocation of the name of her late husband which jolted Evadne out of her chair and on to her feet so that she loomed over Campion, who suddenly and uncomfortably felt he was within striking range. Fortunately, Evadne's violence was verbal rather than physical.

'How dare you say such a thing? How could you possibly *know* such a thing, you arrogant little pipsqueak?'

Mr Campion removed his spectacles and, fluffing a paisley handkerchief from the breast pocket of his jacket, began to polish the lenses. It was almost as if he was trying to remember the last time anyone had called him a 'pipsqueak', confident that someone, at some time, must have.

'I know such a thing because I have a tape recording of a conversation between you and Madame Rawnie at the house in Fitzroy Square last month.'

'A private conversation,' scolded Miss Childe.

'I'm afraid so. I had intended to record the séance, but the microphone picked up much more interesting things when Amanda and I were out of the room.'

The lines on Evadne's face rearranged themselves as a thought struck her.

'Veronica was with us at the séance. Did she know about this?'

'She did, and she helped Amanda cook up the whole Redvers Fitton and the cursed pearls story.'

'But why? To trick me into writing another book?'

'Not primarily, though they were both excited at such a side-benefit, but if anyone was to be tricked it was Madame Rawnie.'

'Why?' Evadne's voice had become a shriek. 'Did you feel the need to torment two old women rather than just one? What has Madame Rawnie ever done to you?'

'To me, nothing, but she has betrayed your trust. She did it ten years ago and I am certain that she is doing it now, by passing on what you tell her to Simon Moorgat.'

'Simon again! You are mad, Campion, you must be. Why would she do that?

'Because he's her son! Was it not Simon who recommended Madame Rawnie to you as a medium to help you contact Peter Verloet?'

'This is insane! Now I am going to ask you to leave and then I will telephone Veronica and give her a piece of my mind.'

'You should sit down, Mrs Walker-Pyne,' Campion said in earnest.

'Don't tell me what to do in my own house! I want you to leave.'

'You cannot talk to Veronica,' Campion snapped. 'She's dead. She was murdered last night, almost certainly by Simon Moorgat.'

He caught her as she fell.

It took an hour for Evadne to recover her composure, pack a small suitcase with clothes, stuff a slim briefcase with notebooks and a sheaf of lined paper covered in neat handwriting and insist on making a pot of tea and some ham sandwiches as a makeshift lunch. She then insisted on telephoning a neighbouring farmer to inform him that Mill House would be unoccupied for a few days. The farmer, whose wife had long cast an envious eye on Mill House, would be a far more efficient watchdog than the overweight and congenitally lazy village policeman. Only then was she prepared to lock up the house and join Campion in the Jensen.

They were halfway to London when, having answered a multitude of Evadne's questions, Campion asked one himself.

'When you knew Moorgat in London during the war, when he showed you around Soho and the clubs, what story did he give you?'

'It rather seems I gave *him* a story,' said Evadne grimly. 'After he took me to the Grafton Club, I explained in great detail how the manager's office could be robbed. You see, I'd worked it all out for my book. I never thought he would turn my fiction into fact.'

'I appreciate you have a criminal mind,' said Campion, 'and I mean that in the best possible way, but I was curious to know how Simon explained his presence in London during the war. He and Peter were in the Free Belgian army and Peter was off doing commando training, but what was Simon supposed to be doing?'

'He insisted it was all hush-hush, secret work for the Belgian government in exile,' said Evadne, her eyes fixed firmly on the road ahead, 'but I suppose you're going to tell me that was all hogwash.'

'I'm afraid it was; he was a deserter, but the fact he survived and indeed prospered in those years, showed he had most of the attributes of a good spy, or criminal, which is more or less the same thing.'

'And you say he is back in London?'

'He is.'

'So why are you so insistent that I go there with you?'

Campion exhaled slowly. 'Because you are the one person who can positively identify him and because he knows where you live. You'll be far safer in London.'

'Was Veronica?'

Mr Campion said nothing.

TWENTY
The Long Game

Lugg was furious and displayed his displeasure by stomping up and down the stairs from basement to bedroom in the Fitzroy Square house as noisily and as heavily as he could. Being naturally equipped to do this most effectively, the resulting deep rumble sounded like, when ascending, the approach of a slow-moving freight train and, when descending, a stampede of cartoon elephants in a race for the last packet of peanuts.

'It's 'arm's way he's puttin' you in. 'Arm's way,' he grumbled as he buffeted around the house.

'Albert knows what he's doing,' said Amanda repeatedly, mostly to the extensive surface area of Lugg's back.

'I ain't too sure about 'is nibs. I was there when we found that Rags Donovan dead in the gutter opposite the Fitzroy. I don't think he's stopped thinking about that ever since. Doesn't do to fret like that for so long over something a jury wouldn't convict you over.'

'Well, we have common ground there, Magers, but the wheels are in motion now, so we'd best get on with things. Do you need any help in the kitchen?'

Lugg snorted in derision. 'As if I ever needed help doin' a

fish pie! Got me a nice piece of cod off the bone, some smoked haddock and a few shrimps because we've got company. Spuds mashed with milk and half-a-pound of butter and vintage Red Leicester grated on the top for decoration. A work of art, though I says it myself, and the beauty is only one pot to wash up afterwards.'

'Sounds delicious,' said Amanda sincerely. 'We'll eat early at the small table, away from the windows. You're au fait with the rest of the plan?'

'If *ho fay* is French for happy as sandboy, then no, I ain't. I should be hiding behind the arras, wherever that is, like you lot will be. I should be there to protect you if there's a rough house. 'Is nibs isn't getting any younger, you know.'

'Neither are you.'

'Mebbe not, but I've always fought dirty. Get your retaliation in first, that's my motto. Plus, I'm several weight divisions higher. On a good day your old man looks like nothing more than a well-dressed shadow. I don't like leaving you scared and defenceless.'

'I am not scared and we won't be defenceless, you soppy old ape. Charles Luke has promised to have plain-clothes men in the area as well as the regular beat patrols.'

'He could have men on horseback outside the front door but if the smog sets in again like it's predicted, Ali Baba and 'is forty thieves could waltz by wiv impunity.'

Amanda gave a mocking sigh. 'I never thought we would have trouble giving you a night off to go round the pub. This is the world turned upside down.'

'I go, but under protest,' Lugg declaimed, as if summing up for a jury. 'I've left the number of The Albany on a billet-doux by the telephone. I will be' – he sniffed the air imperiously – 'in the Four Ale bar should my services be required.'

'They should put that on your tombstone,' Amanda said quietly to the fat man's retreating figure.

'I 'eard that,' said Lugg without turning his head, 'an' I like it. Got a bit of a ring to it; quite dignified really.'

Although she had put on a brave face in front of Lugg, Amanda was very nervous about one approaching confrontation, that with Mrs Walker-Pyne. Campion had delivered her to Fitzroy Square and immediately driven off to garage the Jensen, before night and fog joined forces to restrict mobility to a snail's pace throughout the city.

Amanda had not counted on Mrs Evadne Walker-Pyne, CBE being equally apprehensive about their meeting.

'You must think I am a terribly stupid old woman.'

'Goodness me, no! Why would I think such a thing of someone who writes such clever books?'

Evadne seemed impervious to blatant flattery. 'Not clever enough to spot when I am being manipulated into writing a book to someone else's scenario.'

Amanda, who often had to play the headmistress, found herself in the role of recalcitrant schoolgirl.

'We can only apologize if you feel used, but Albert thought he saw a way of exposing how Madame Rawnie was using you. For myself, I was just immensely proud that you saw merit in my story of Redvers Fitton and chose to use it; as for poor Veronica, she thought you needed snapping out of your writer's block.'

Whatever anger Evadne was trying to marshal, it suddenly seemed to dissipate at the mention of Veronica. Indeed, the older woman seemed to shrink into the fur collar of her coat, which a casual observer would have said was suddenly two sizes too large for her.

'When Albert explained the way things were to me this morning,' she said, her voice wavering, 'my first thought was to ring Gilpin's and tell Veronica she could burn what she had of the manuscript of *Pearls Before Swine* and that I had no intention of completing the final chapters. But then your husband told me what had happened to her. Has anyone told her poor mother? They lived together in Cricklewood, you know, and I always envied their close relationship.'

'I understand the police broke the news to her and are taking care of her,' said Amanda softly. 'I have offered to help if there is any way I might.'

'I will write to her tonight and try and get to see her.'

'Perhaps we could call on her together,' Amanda suggested tentatively.

'Perhaps. Let's see what happens here. If your theory proves valid, then we should be expecting a visit from Simon Moorgat, shouldn't we?'

'It may not be tonight, but Albert thinks he will have to make his move quickly now the police are looking for him after—'

'There is no doubt that he killed Veronica?'

'Not in my mind. The only thing taken from Gilpin's was the manuscript of your book.'

'Which does not yet have an ending; perhaps Simon will provide one.'

Amanda showed Evadne upstairs to the bedroom she had occupied when they had held the séance, carrying her small suitcase and the briefcase she had brought with her. Evadne held on to a capacious brown leather handbag, which she had clutched to her chest since climbing out of Campion's car. She maintained her grip on it up the staircase and into the bedroom.

'If you wouldn't mind sticking to rooms like this at the back of the house, it would help, as we're trying not to show too many lights,' said Amanda as she placed Evadne's cases at the foot of the bed.

'I know,' the older woman said sternly, 'I used that in my book. The burglars watch the house – this house – from a little tent on the corner of the square where they are pretending to do something with the telephone wires, and they note which lights go off and on. It's called "casing the joint" in America.' She paused and fixed Amanda with an unforgiving eye. 'But you knew that, didn't you, because Veronica let you read it.'

Once more Amanda was in the headmistress's study, if not the dock. 'Only the very early chapters, and I know I shouldn't have but I couldn't resist finding out if you had used my plot.'

'Your idea, *my* plot,' said Evadne, settling ownership once and for all, 'in *my* book, which Veronica should not have shown to you.'

'I know that and so did she, but she was so excited that you were writing again. She loved your books, really loved them.'

'Yes, she did, she was a stout supporter of Rex Troughton throughout his career and possibly she was a little bit in love with him, as I was.' Evadne placed her handbag on the dressing table on the other side of the bed from Amanda and began to unbutton her coat. 'She was a great comfort to me after I lost Edmund, although she did not approve of my attempts to contact his spirit. She thought I was being foolish, but never criticized because she realized it brought me the sense of peace and calm I needed to carry on.'

Evadne slipped off her coat and moved to hang it in the dark oak wardrobe which Lugg had twice, with much swearing under his breath, cleared of 'half a hundredweight' of boots, pitons, ropes and other assorted climbing equipment belonging to Jonathan Eager-Wright.

'In a way, that's what has brought us to this,' she said as she wrestled with a wooden coat-hanger.

'I'm sorry?'

'My refusal to let Edmund go, my need to contact him, and then, of course, poor, sweet, Peter. I enjoyed the company of both my Belgian boys during the war and I was actually grateful to Albert, back then, for bringing them to me.'

She hung up her coat and closed the wardrobe door then walked back to the dressing table and collected her handbag, which she clutched to the front of her cardigan. 'I knew Simon was a bit of a Jack-the-Lad, and he knew I consulted mediums to contact Edmund. That's why, when Peter went missing in action, he suggested I should try to reach him, but my usual medium, Miss Kitto, could not manage it. Simon suggested Madame Rawnie, who had gypsy blood and the gift of psychic attraction, as he called it. As soon as the war was over, I began to visit her in Brussels.'

'And did she?' asked Amanda. 'Have the gift?'

'I certainly thought so. She channelled Peter's spirit convincingly enough, and that of Edmund, but now I know that she was Simon's mother, I can guess where she got much of her background information. She's been taking my money and making a fool of me for more than fifteen years.'

'But did it bring you comfort at the time?'

'Yes, I admit, it did. You have no idea how much I missed Edmund – and Peter, too. He was such an angelic boy.'

'The son you never had?'

'Oh no, Edmund and I never considered having children. I married rather too late, but if I had felt a twinge of motherhood, it would have been for a daughter; a bright girl like Veronica.'

Evadne fell silent and held her bag even closer to her heart if that were possible. Amanda, embarrassed at raising the topic of motherhood, was relieved to hear the front doorbell chiming from below.

'Don't panic,' she said, 'that will be Albert.'

'I'm not worried, my dear. Burglars rarely ring the front doorbell. Not even in my stories.'

They ate in the small alcove extension to the first-floor dining
room, isolated by an archway and sliding pinewood doors, well
away from the French windows and the tiny balcony overlooking
the square, over which the fog was gently pressing down a dank,
grey pillow. Lugg puffed up the stairs with his signature fish pie
and served it before he peeled off a slightly charred apron the
size of a bell tent and sat down to eat. Mr Campion had skipped
lightly down the stairs to the refrigerator and returned with a
bottle of Chablis and a corkscrew.

Evadne declared it to be a superb fish pie and Lugg glowed
like a wakening volcano as he cleared the plates, muttering that
a bit of appreciation was always a nice surprise.

When he had begun his clumping descent down to the kitchen,
Campion produced from his top pocket a Metropolitan Police whistle.

'Our secret weapon,' he said with an idiotic grin. 'I've always
wanted one of these.'

'Never mind secret, that's our only weapon,' said Amanda.

'I am assured by young Charlie Luke that there will be half-
a-dozen policemen within earshot when the time comes.'

'Which will be sometime after eight and before ten thirty,'
said Evadne, casually ignoring the stares of the two Campions.

'Why do you say that, Evadne?'

'Because, Albert, around eight o'clock your man Lugg will
exit the house as noisily as possible after making a show of
turning off all the lights. He will then proceed to a local public
house until closing time, or ten thirty to be on the safe side.'

'Very good,' said Campion. 'That is more or less the plan.
Did Amanda let you in on it?'

Campion was aware that his wife was shaking her head, but
he was concentrating on the older woman.

'That's the way I did it in my book,' said Evadne. 'I do hope
you've remembered to leave the sash window in the basement
unlocked.'

That was Lugg's allocated task; one of many thankless ones, as
he repeatedly pointed out. Having cleared and pushed back the

dinner table, he brought in three more comfortable chairs and placed a rubber-encased torch on each one.

'In case you've got reading material while you're waiting,' he said in explanation, 'unless you fancy playing footsie in the dark, that is.'

Then he turned off the lights in the annexe, marched into the main dining room and, fully illuminated, pulled back the curtains on the French windows. With his arms outstretched, and with the light behind him, he must have looked like Samson straining at the pillars of Dagon's temple in Gaza, even though his hair had not grown back.

'It's thickening up like good gravy out there,' he said as he turned away and walked towards the doorway and the light switch for the room, 'couldn't see yer 'and in front of yer face unless you was holding a cigar to lead the way. I'll be leaving you now.'

With that, he snapped the Bakelite wall switch and the first floor of the house was plunged into darkness.

The three seated figures held their collective breath as Lugg's footsteps faded down the stairs. They heard the kitchen door open and faint clatterings and thuds as crockery was piled into a sink and cupboards opened and closed. Campion knew that Lugg would be making a show, for the benefit of any outside observer, of his skill in the scullery and would even make a trip to the basement, to deposit the empty Chablis bottle (and several bottles of stout which had mysteriously emptied themselves during the cooking of dinner), turning lights on and off as he went. Finally, he would hang a damp tea towel over the eye-level grill, pull on his jacket and then an overcoat and his favourite bowler hat, and leave by the front door.

'Now we wait,' said Campion. 'By all means read by torchlight but keep the beams pointed downwards. Perhaps I should have taken up knitting.'

'Or we could just talk,' said Amanda, hoping desperately that her husband would not suggest holding a séance.

'I have something to say,' said Evadne, from the gloom. 'Whatever happens tonight – or doesn't happen – I wish to go to Gilpin's tomorrow and, if possible, to Cricklewood to visit Veronica's mother.'

'I am sure that can be arranged. Superintendent Luke might

insist you go with a police escort, but otherwise I will drive you myself.'

'Do you really think I am in danger?'

'It's a risk I would rather not run. You are the one person who can positively identify Moorgat and connect him with the Grafton Club robbery and the murders of Rags and Veronica.'

'I have been thinking about that.' In the dark, Evadne's voice was both ethereal and commanding. 'You saw Simon during the war; you introduced him to me. Surely you are just as likely to be able to identify him as I am, so why am I here?'

There was a silence before Campion answered. 'Because he may be in the business of tying up loose ends and it is easier to protect you here in London.'

'Yet you have brought me to this house, the one place we are leading him directly to with our trail of breadcrumbs, tempting him to come for those black pearls, which I notice have conveniently been left in that cigar box on the dining-room table. If Simon comes, I will be in the front line here, surely?'

'You are perfectly safe, Evadne,' said Amanda. 'Albert would not endanger you, or me, if he thought either of us faced a real threat.'

'My point is that I do not think I was in any real danger at my home in Essex. I think Albert suggested I come here not for my benefit, but for his.'

'You are very perceptive, Mrs Walker-Pyne.' Campion's voice was little more than a whisper. 'There have been three deaths for which I believe I bear some responsibility and I will not allow any more. It may be inconvenient and uncomfortable for you to be here with us tonight, but it puts my mind at ease to be able to keep a watchful eye over you.'

'So I am here to salve your conscience? I thought perhaps I might be here as bait.'

'No, no,' Amanda protested, 'the black pearls are the bait. You were never part of the plan until . . .'

'Until Veronica.'

'Yes,' said Mr Campion, 'I admit I never saw that coming. It rather frightened me and I felt I had to do something and do it immediately. You see, I was distracted by other events at the time of the Grafton case, or the case of the Bottle Party Murder, if I may appropriate that phrase. And then everyone was distracted from Rags Donovan's murder by the Euston mail-van robbery. I do not want to take my eye off the ball this time.'

'Neither do I,' said Evadne and, in the dark, felt for her handbag which she had placed under her chair. Once her fingers had located it, she pulled it up on to her lap and leaned forward, so that her arms could surround and hold it tight.

At one minute to nine o'clock, by the luminous hands on Amanda's wristwatch, they heard the first sound of forced entry.

'That will be the basement window being forced,' whispered Evadne. 'It's the way they do it in my book.'

Amanda shivered involuntarily, more because of Evadne's confident assessment of the situation than the situation itself. Mr Campion got silently to his feet and moved to his left, taking a position behind the sliding door leading to the main dining room and the door to the staircase. Lugg had deliberately left the sliding panels about a foot apart so that, without the over light on, the entrance to the alcove could have been mistaken for an open armoire.

There were more sounds from below, the tall, empty house acting almost as an echo chamber and the fog outside insulating it from any traffic noise. A door definitely creaked open and then there came a soft thud as if a shoe or a shoulder had suddenly connected with an unseen obstacle.

Campion held his breath and strained his ears, waiting for the inevitable footfall on the stairs. It came in tandem with a loud *click* as a torch was turned on and a narrow, irregular rectangle of light played off the far wall of the staircase and inched its way upwards. His own torch was a hefty, rubber-cased one, and though his thumb was over the rubber 'On' button, he held it at shoulder height so it could be used as a club.

There were clearly audible footsteps now, confident ones, the intruder seemingly convinced that the house was uninhabited, and undeterred by the creaking of stair treads long past their prime. And then the first finger of torchlight entered the room and Campion instinctively recoiled behind the alcove door, pressing his shoulder blades against the wall.

He had told the two women to remain seated and absolutely quiet until he reached the main light switch, no matter what they heard or thought they saw, and through the gap in the alcove doors they could see the alien torch illuminating the dining room in a sweeping motion which reminded Amanda of a camp search-light in one of the prisoner-of-war films so popular in the Fifties, at least among British audiences.

The beam swept on and pointed downwards as the carrier of the torch reached the door from the stairs and stepped into the room. Campion realized that the lens of the torch must be partially 'blacked out' with tape or paint, as had been the practice during the war, so that its beam was restricted and would be less likely to be noticed from outside. It was still powerful enough to light up the key features of the room and Campion felt an odd sense of satisfaction when it came to rest on the small round table prominently supporting a cigar box.

Amanda, however, felt far from satisfied. As there was now some ambient light, she could see Evadne's face; it shocked her, for it showed not fear or apprehension but pure, undiluted anger as the intruder entered the dining room fully and walked directly over to the cigar box.

As he flipped the lid and shone his torch down into the box, he exhaled loudly in surprise and, at that precise moment, Mr Campion clicked on his torch and aimed it fully at the interloper's face.

'Hello, Simon; it's been a long time.'

The face Campion's torch picked out had an open mouth and the eyes were wide and wild, framed by a dark stubble of closely cropped hair, the complexion deathly white; prison white. Yet the most fascinating thing about the figure, or the portion of him that could be clearly seen, as his black clothing melted his outline, was that despite being disturbed, startled and possibly frightened, his face transfixed by Campion's torch, his own torch remained firmly aimed at the cigar box and, with his free hand, almost as if on autopilot, he was reaching in and removing the chinking, clinking mass of the necklace, which he held as a child might hold a frond of seaweed found on a beach.

Mr Campion reached out an arm and flipped the light switch and the spell was broken.

'You. I know you.' The intruder spoke as if the words hurt his mouth; he blinked and screwed up his eyes, behind which a brain was racing furiously.

'My name is Campion and we met twenty-two years ago. It

is to my eternal regret that our paths did not cross earlier, even twenty-four hours earlier, when I might have stopped you murdering Veronica Hatherall.'

'That was her name?'

The callousness in Moorgat's voice chilled Campion and, for the first time that evening, he experienced a tingle of fear. He was several inches taller than the man he faced, but more than twenty years older and therefore slower. Moorgat was as trim as Campion, as far as he could tell through the black pullover and corduroy trousers, but a prison regime had probably encouraged more muscle than fat. If it came to a rough house, Campion had no doubt that Lugg would bet against him, and yet there he was, facing a triple murderer armed only with a rubber torch and a police whistle.

Moorgat sensed the doubt in the older man. It was a skill quickly learned in prison. 'You will forgive me if I do not stay to renew whatever acquaintance we may have had,' Moorgat said calmly, his eyes flicking to the door to the stairs which Campion was attempting to block with his slender frame.

'You cannot get away this time,' said Campion firmly.

'I think I can,' said Moorgat confidently, switching his torch off and hefting it slightly in his grip while stuffing the necklace into a trouser pocket.

Campion knew what would happen next: the coiling of his body, a slight crouch, and then the head-down charge to take him in the chest and either bulldoze him out of the way or project him down the stairs. And all before he could remove his spectacles or reach for that ridiculous tin whistle.

Throughout their encounter, Campion had kept his torch on and shining into Moorgat's face, though it did not appear to disturb him in the slightest. Campion concentrated on making sure his hand did not shake and the beam did not waver for, however small an advantage it might be, it was worth having.

There was a sudden sound from behind his head and it took Campion a second to register that the doors to the alcove were being slid open. His first thought was that now he had two doorways to defend.

'That's enough, Simon.'

The authority in the voice alone should have dissuaded Moorgat from any sudden physical movement.

The fact that Evadne Childe was advancing steadily towards him holding a revolver should have made certain.

TWENTY-ONE
Cozenage

It was a gun Campion had seen before, the short-barrelled Webley dating from the First World War and inherited from Evadne's father, with which she had bested his score in the ad-hoc shooting gallery beneath Bottle Street in 1940. It explained why Evadne had insisted Campion remained downstairs at Mill House while she packed her bags that morning, and why she had been so protective of her handbag throughout the day.

The revolver looked clean, oiled and evidently in full working order, and the hand which held it was steady as a rock, which pleased Campion immensely. So much, in fact, that he lowered his torch and switched it off and finally remembered to breathe normally.

Moorgat, still holding his torch, raised both his hands in a gesture of surrender. 'Evie . . .'

'Don't call me that! Don't call me anything. You have been nothing but deceitful.'

Campion took a half-step towards Evadne and offered a hand, palm upwards, suggesting that she pass him the pistol. Behind Evadne, in the alcove, Amanda shook her head vigorously in a warning to her husband, and Campion was forced to withdraw his hand limply and ignominiously as the revolver was waved briefly but firmly in his direction, leaving him in no doubt that she was unwilling to relinquish it. From his rather pained expression, it appeared that Mr Campion was more concerned about the weapon than Moorgat was. In fact, Moorgat was smiling.

'Mrs Walker-Pyne,' he said formally but not quite politely, 'was I not your handsome gypsy boy who showed you around London during the war days? Did I not look after you, keep you safe in the clubs and the black markets?'

'Don't you dare!'

'Did I not guide you to your precious Edmund through Madame Rawnie?'

'You mean your mother? Another deception.'

Evadne took a pace forward and Moorgat immediately took one backwards into the centre of the room, as if they were automaton figures locked in a clockwork tango.

'One you took pleasure in, or you would have stopped coming to Brussels. Rawnie helped you talk to your beloved Edmund, did she not? Was that not a comfort to you?'

'It was a lie!' Evadne's voice began to crack for the first time. 'It was a way to steal the plots of my books.'

'I only wish you had given me more that I could use. You should not have been so anxious to boast to Edmund.'

'Say his name again and I will shoot you!'

The woman took another step forward and the man another one back, until he was positioned directly under the central room light hanging from the ceiling, which reflected the sheen of sweat on his forehead, the first sign of nervousness Campion had been able to spot.

He edged himself closer to Evadne. 'This isn't one of your novels, Evadne. At the very minimum, this man is a burglar, caught in the act red-handed. Let the police deal with him.'

'He's not just a thief,' said Evadne, sparing Campion a brief glance, 'he's a murderer.'

'And he will be dealt with.'

'Albert's right,' said Amanda, who had silently stepped up behind her and to her right, positioning herself, Campion feared, to make a grab for her gun arm. 'Don't ruin your life for the sake of that stinking bit of work.'

'Stay back, Lady Amanda. I am not doing this for myself, but for Veronica.'

It was as if some sort of critical mass had been achieved, or the air had suddenly been sucked out of the room. Whatever was going to happen was going to happen now.

The metallic click of Evadne's thumb cocking the hammer of the pistol set things in motion.

Both Campion and Amanda lunged at Evadne, attempting to envelop her with their arms and confine or deflect the hand holding the gun.

As they moved, so did Moorgat, jumping upwards from a

standing start, extending his arm and the hand that still held his torch, aiming for the hanging overhead light and connecting with a bang and a tinkle of glass.

If Moorgat had expected the room to be plunged into darkness, he was disappointed, for the second ceiling light on the same circuit, in the alcove, remained on. But it was enough to distract Campion, who slackened his embrace of Evadne and prepared for an assault from Moorgat, hoping that Amanda could control the older woman.

She could not. The second she felt Campion's grip relax, Evadne, with a dexterity and a strength that a man half her age might have envied, freed her right arm and shoulder and barged Amanda away, immediately raising the pistol back to its target.

Simon Moorgat had not waited to see the failure of the Campions to contain the vengeful Evadne. He had turned on his heel and in two long strides was at the French windows, grappling with the double handles and wrenching the doors open.

He was faced with a thick wall of fog and the thought ripped through Campion's brain that if he jumped, he could not possibly see where he was going to land. Straight down to the basement level would almost certainly be an ankle-breaking landing. To try and clear the basement level, over the spiked railings, and land on the Fitzroy Square pavement, could result in at least a broken leg, if not worse, even if one could see a safe landing spot.

Moorgat paused, his hands still on the window handles, then took a tentative step on to the tiny balcony and coiled his body as if to spring out into that smothering grey blanket.

Evadne Childe straightened her arm and fired and Simon Moorgat plunged into the fog.

'You all quartered safe up there?'

Mr Campion peered out and down but could not tell where Lugg's gruff voice was coming from.

'Albert?' another voice from the fog but unmistakeably Luke's. 'Is everyone accounted for? We came when we heard the shot. I've got men here.'

'Get as many torches as you can on the steps down to the basement door by the front steps,' Campion yelled down. 'The man we're after should be down there somewhere.'

'Well, he ain't got by me, that's for sure.'

'Very little can, old fruit. I thought you were supposed to be in the pub.'

'I wus. Virtually had the place to meself due to the fog, so no decent company. Gave it a couple of hours and wandered back here, tripping over Charlie's men at every turn. Thought they might need an 'elping 'and.'

'We could use one up here, chum. Let yourself in the front door and find a light bulb for us from somewhere,' Campion shouted. 'And Charlie, you'd better get up here too.'

Below him, Campion could make out the muted beams of half-a-dozen torches converging through the fog towards the railings guarding the basement steps and door. The reflected orange glow they gave off wavered over, then concentrated on a distorted dark mass which seemed, bizarrely, to be suspended in mid-air.

'I think I'm going to be rather busy down here for a while, Albert.' Luke's voice left no doubt that he was facing a situation that needed his calm authority and he was employing it.

'Is that what I think it is?' asked Mr Campion, peering down.

'You can bet your pension it is,' said Lugg, his boots pounding up the steps to the front door, 'but I wouldn't look too closely if I was you, and I'd keep the ladies back if you've got any sense.'

Campion could now make out Lugg's gargantuan silhouette as he fumbled a key into the door lock.

'I'll turn on the cellar lights so Charlie's men have some light to work by,' he said cheerfully, 'but if I was you, I'd go back inside 'til they've made things decent. This is the bloke we were after, ain't it?'

'Yes, that's Simon Moorgat,' said Campion. 'I take it he won't be giving you any trouble, Charlie.'

'That doesn't look likely,' Luke answered from the swirling opaqueness.

'Proper skewered, 'e is,' Lugg added with ghoulish relish. 'Landed plumb over the railing spikes, like that saying: hoist wiv 'is own assegai.'

'Your man is prone to curious turns of phrase,' remarked Evadne Childe dryly. 'I think he means "hoist with his own petard", though that is equally inaccurate in this case. I take it Simon is dead.'

'I think we can assume that,' said Campion, leaving the windows open to the fog and striding across the room.

'Good,' said Evadne firmly, the word echoed by Amanda's loud gasp of shock.

'I will pretend I did not hear that, Mrs Walker-Pyne. From here on, this is a police matter, so please hand over that revolver.'

Evadne held out the Webley without protest. Campion took it and dropped it into his jacket pocket, surprised at its weight and the way it distorted the fabric of the pocket. How had he not noticed it in Evadne's handbag? Yet it explained why she had rarely let the bag out of her sight, nursing it on her knee in the car and at dinner.

The stairwell light came on and they heard the first rumblings of Lugg ascending.

As if finally remembering that Amanda was there, Evadne turned to her. 'My dear, I am so sorry if I lashed out at you. I hope I didn't hurt you.'

She had, but as Amanda, to quote Lugg at his most lugubrious, was 'the perfect gent', she could only reply, 'It was nothing. Heat of the moment and all that. We were all a bit too frantic for our own good.'

'Yes, it was all rather frenzied, wasn't it? Things are far more straightforward in my books.'

Mr Campion, who never claimed proficiency in reading his wife's mind, thought for a moment that she was going to ask how the writer would play out the scene in her next book. He realized that the thought was as uncouth as the un-posed question, just as Lugg arrived clutching a light bulb in a cardboard cover displaying the brand name Mazda.

'Here am I,' Lugg announced, 'the bringer of light. Guaranteed to burn brighter longer.'

'Spare us the commercial break, you oaf,' said Campion, 'and get up on a chair and plug it in. Oh, and watch out for broken glass.' And then as an afterthought, he added, 'And electricity.'

'Could you also close the French windows, Magers?' asked Amanda, chafing her upper arms with her hands. 'It's getting rather chilly in here.'

'Best wait until Charlie Luke gets here to see . . .' Campion hesitated, but Evadne finished his thought.

'The scene of the crime. That's what you meant to say, Albert, wasn't it? And of course you are perfectly correct. We must await the superintendent.'

'Better get your stories straight then,' said Lugg.

He was balanced precariously on a dining-table chair, reminding Amanda of a circus elephant on its tub about to perform a trick, bulb in one hand, the lighting socket on its wire in the other, his tongue between his lips in concentration.

'It looks like somebody owes Mr Eager-Wright a new lamp-shade but – *voilà!* – let there be light!'

The bulb clicked home and the room lit up. From his perch, Lugg surveyed his audience with a distinct air of superiority.

'So who was the dead-eyed Dick who shot the light out?'

'The light wasn't shot; Moorgat did that.' Mr Campion pulled the Webley from his pocket, transferred it to his left hand and then back to his right. 'And I shot him.'

'As he was throwing himself out that window and on to them railings? What, just to make sure?'

'Magers, don't be so rude – or vulgar,' snapped Amanda.

'I didn't know 'is nibs was expecting gunplay,' wheezed Lugg as he carefully dismounted from the chair in as dignified a manner as possible given his bulk. 'If he'd said, I would have got him a Tommy gun. He was never much good with a pistol and his eyesight's not what it was.'

'It is actually Mrs Walker-Pyne's gun,' said Mr Campion, replacing the revolver in his pocket, 'but Charles Luke will find my fingerprints all over it. It will be a fair cop, as you might say. It was I who shot Simon Moorgat.'

'No, Albert, you did not,' said Evadne firmly.

'Please, Mrs Walker-Pyne, do not say anything until Luke gets here, and then let me speak first.'

Evadne ignored Campion and Lugg and turned to face Amanda with a faint smile on her lips. She said something, very quietly, which Amanda later swore sounded like 'Watch this', and then strode beyond Lugg to the French windows, which were still open and allowing tendrils of grey vapour into the room.

It never occurred to Campion that Evadne might rush for the open window and throw herself out, as she walked with purpose, head up as if looking for something above eye-level. She stopped in front of the open window and turned slightly to the right-hand side of the frame.

'You didn't shoot anyone, Albert,' she said without turning, running her fingertips up the wooden frame, 'and if Superintendent Luke has a penknife, I think he will find the bullet fired from my gun is still here in the plasterwork and not in the body of Simon Moorgat.'

'I knew it!' chuckled Lugg, who almost slapped a thigh in pleasure. 'Told you he couldn't hit a barn door these days.'

'Please, Lugg, a little decorum – and once you've looked that up in the dictionary, make yourself useful and find us something to drink. I know I need one. I think we all do.'

Both Campions approached Evadne, who pointed up at a splinter of wood missing from the frame and a dark hole about half an inch in diameter in the wallpaper and plaster behind it.

'It was noble of you to offer to take the blame, Albert,' she said, 'but it is really not necessary.'

'Nonsense,' Campion replied, 'I need to retain my reputation as a gunslinging man of action.'

At his side, Amanda snorted a laugh, which he pointedly ignored.

'I was defending my friend's house from a violent burglar in the commission of a crime and fired a shot to warn him off. He went into a panic and jumped out of the window before we could stop him. Luke will find the stolen pearls on the body. Case closed.'

'Very neat, but how do you explain the fact that you had my revolver?'

'I had admired it from afar as something of a collector's piece and you owned it perfectly legally. In fact, I remember telling you how much I admired it when we met back in the war on a shooting range supervised by a high-ranking police officer.'

'I remember no such thing. Stop trying to take the blame.'

'But he does it so well . . .' said Amanda innocently.

'In this case, he does not have to.'

'Think about it, Evadne,' said Campion. 'My reputation could not be damaged any further; even my family gave up on me years ago and only mention my name in exasperated sighs and long, mournful pauses these days. Evadne Walker-Pyne is a respectable personage, a Commander of the British Empire, no less, with an unsullied reputation and undeserving of such publicity.'

'Publicity is good for sales, say my publishers.'

'I have never subscribed to the theory that there's no such thing as bad publicity. *You* would be the object of press interest rather than your books, and once the newshounds sniff a story, they don't stop. Your private life would be theirs. The intrusion would be intolerable, particularly your interest in spiritualism.'

Evadne nodded her head in reluctant agreement and murmured the single word 'Edmund' before lifting her face to Campion.

'You are correct, Albert. I would not wish to suffer that and therefore I accept your version of events. Whatever you tell the police, I will go along with.'

Campion relaxed and gestured to the bullet hole in the wall.

'I think you might be able to tell the police quite a lot, Evadne. That was first-class police work spotting where the bullet went.'

Evadne shrugged her shoulders. 'It's what I do for a living.'

'I suppose,' said Charles Luke, pushing the brim of his brown check tweed trilby back above his hairline with a stout forefinger, 'this is where you expect me to enter stage right and say "Hello, hello, what's all this then?" Well, you can forget that. I've got a very messy body out there on the street, thought to be a foreign national, and thank heaven for this fog which is keeping the neighbours indoors and the gawking passers-by at bay. Unfortunately, it's also delaying the ambulance, which means I've got half the Marylebone night shift holding hands playing ring-o'-roses round the corpse. And far be it from me to point out that the weather clamping down like this is giving the green light to burglars and scallywags all over the city, so I'd be very grateful if someone could clear up what happened here as quickly as possible, keeping to the facts rather than the fiction.'

'I don't believe you've met Mrs Walker-Pyne, Charles,' Campion offered with gallantry, 'better known as Evadne Childe, the novelist.'

Luke nodded a stern acknowledgement.

'I know who you are, Mrs Walker-Pyne, and it is Mrs Walker-Pyne I wish to hear from, not Evadne Childe. Do I make myself clear?'

'Completely, Superintendent.'

'Evadne can confirm that Simon Moorgat broke into this house and attempted to steal a string of black pearls,' said Mr Campion, as if reading from a policeman's notebook. 'In the commission of that crime, he was disturbed and attempted to flee via the first-floor French windows. I fired a shot to deter him. I'm afraid it startled him and he must have lost his balance, hence his rather rapid, and fatal, exit into the square.'

'You had a gun?'

Campion took out the Webley and offered it to Luke, who produced a fountain pen from his top pocket and threaded it through the trigger guard.

'Careful, Charles, there's no safety catch on these antique models.'

'I didn't know you had a permit for this.'

'I do, Mr Luke,' said Evadne. 'It belonged to my father, but is now registered to me out in Essex.'

'What's it doing here then?'

Evadne and Campion exchanged glances.

'Albert wanted to see it, so I brought it with me.'

'Evadne – Mrs Walker-Pyne – and I had a shooting match years ago,' Campion said quickly. 'Stanislaus Oates refereed it, as a matter of fact. I just rather fancied seeing the gun she bested me with.'

Luke was suspicious. 'That's a bit thin, Albert, even for a thin man like you, but you have the God-given advantage of looking like butter wouldn't melt in front of a jury.'

'Albert's telling you how it happened, Charles,' Amanda joined in. 'The bullet's still in the window frame, he never shot Moorgat.'

'Did I say he did?' Luke spoke with hooded eyes. It was a look which had terrified many a professional crook.

'C'mon Charlie,' growled Lugg, 'cut some slack. You know old Four-Eyes here couldn't hit a barn door if it was waving a white flag.'

'You weren't even here, so for the moment, keep the lip buttoned,' snapped Luke, then immediately softened. 'Old Four-Eyes, eh? I'll remember that one.'

'At school I was called Gig-Lamps,' Campion said cheerfully.

'Gig-Lamps?'

'Carriage lamps or coach lanterns,' said Evadne, 'because of those large round glasses he favours. It dates from our generation, Superintendent, you are far too young.'

'Flattery rarely works on the Metropolitan Police, Evadne,' said Campion.

'Very little does,' said Lugg gruffly.

'I won't tell you again,' Luke shot back at him. 'Now, where were we?'

'You had just decided that you had three respectable eyewitnesses all willing to make voluntary statements at your convenience,' Amanda said politely. 'You know where Albert and I live, and Mrs Walker-Pyne is our guest. We will report to you whenever and wherever you command.'

'And you'll all be singing from the same hymn sheet, I suppose?'

'As if in church,' said Amanda sweetly.

'Ambulance is 'ere,' observed Lugg, and there was indeed a faint blue flashing light bouncing off the fog outside the French windows.

'I'd better go meet the doc,' said Luke, and Campion offered to accompany him down the stairs.

When they reached the front door, Luke put a hand to Campion's chest. He did it gently, but Campion knew that to press against it would be like trying to walk through a wall.

'It didn't go quite to plan, did it?'

'No,' Campion agreed, 'not exactly. Moorgat did come and he did steal the pearls; you'll find them in his trouser pocket. I wanted to take him in one piece and get a confession out of him. He did sort of confess to killing Veronica Hatherall, though.'

'Sort of?'

'I'm not sure it would stand up in court, but that is no longer an issue.'

'No, it's not.' Luke reached for the door handle and had to release Campion to do so as in his left hand he still held the Webley balanced on his fountain pen. 'I know you're not good with blood, Albert,' he said, 'so don't come out until we've got him off the railings.'

'No,' said Campion, 'I'll see it through. I am responsible for all this.'

'If you're sure . . .' Luke hesitated. 'Any regrets?'

Campion reached into the top pocket of his jacket. 'I never got to blow my police whistle.'

PART FIVE
Albert Campion, 1965

TWENTY-TWO
Honour Bound

The coroner's inquest on Simon Moorgat recorded a verdict of accidental death during the commission of a crime. Only one very junior newspaper reporter was present, one who did not read detective stories and therefore did not recognize the name Evadne Walker-Pyne, though Lady Amanda Fitton received a mention because she was a Lady, as did, as an afterthought, her husband. The thrust of the brief story as reported was that the death had occurred at the home of famous mountaineer Jonathan Eager-Wright, who was currently on an expedition to the Andes.

Another, longer but even more sanitized version of the events at Fitzroy Square, although the location and personnel were heavily disguised, appeared in *Pearls Before Swine*, the bestselling detective story by Evadne Childe, which was published by Gilpin & Co. in the summer of 1963. The novel was dedicated to 'dear friend and editor' Veronica Hatherall, and was the first Rex Troughton book since 1937 not dedicated to Edmund Walker-Pyne. All royalties from sales worldwide were assigned to Veronica's mother in Cricklewood.

It was to be the last Rex Troughton story published in her lifetime. Her publisher had asked for more of the same, as publishers always do, but Evadne had refused to sign a contract for a new title and had been infuriatingly vague about her plans for any future fiction.

Only a select few knew that she was writing, though not for

publication during her lifetime. No one knew that her lifetime had not much longer to run.

She died, peacefully in her sleep, in mid-July 1965, and was buried – in accordance with her wishes – in the church at Eight Ash where her father had once had the living. At her funeral in the third week of August, one of the directors of J. Gilpin & Co. – Mr Campion was unsure which – gave an oration which contained two minor bombshells.

The first was that she had, with great sorrow, returned her CBE to the Palace, as she did not feel herself worthy of the honour. Given that the Beatles, a mop-haired musical group idolized by young females to the point of hysteria, had been named, rather controversially, in the Queen's Birthday Honours List in June as recipients of the MBE, this tenuous link was thought worthy of coverage by the more populist newspapers and even respectable obituary writers.

The second surprise announcement was that the very last, positively final, Rex Troughton adventure had been completed by Evadne before her death and would be published posthumously.

Apart from local villagers, representatives of Gilpin's, and two local journalists stringing for the London papers, the only mourners of note were the Campions and Superintendent Charles Luke.

The traditional funeral meats, or at least the modern equivalent of tea and cakes, were offered at the vicarage courtesy of the present incumbent and his wife, both of whom felt guilty for not being readers of detective fiction.

Mr Campion professed sympathy and politely shook hands where necessary and, after a decent amount of time had passed, he began to say his farewells. He lingered with only one of the guests, Miss Prim, the guard dog of Gilpin's and Evadne Childe's loyal typist. With one of her hands clutched in both of his, and his tall, lean frame bent over her, they spoke for several minutes so quietly and intently that their words could not be overheard. Eventually Campion nodded seriously and lifted her hand to his lips in a clear gesture of thanks. It was a gesture which went unnoticed by all gathered there except for Charles Luke.

The Campions had given Luke a lift from London to Eight Ash for the funeral on the understanding that Campion and Luke would return by train, as Amanda intended to commandeer the

Jensen in order to drive to the Midlands where she had an important date with a manufacturer of jet-engine parts first thing the
next morning.

She drove the two old friends into Colchester and deposited them
at the station, where they discovered they had twenty-five minutes
to kill before the express from Norwich. They used the time in
exercise, striding purposefully up and down platform three which,
as Campion pointed out, was a component part of the longest station
platform in England and perfect for a good stretch of the legs, even
though Campion's naturally long stride had trouble keeping pace
with Luke's piston gait, which had more than one juvenile trains-
potter scurrying out of his unswerving path.

'Pity the old dear didn't live to see her last book in the shops,'
said Luke, staring down the long line of railway track which
would take them to London.

'Oh, she always intended it to be published after her death,'
said Mr Campion, buttoning his jacket against the unseasonably
chilly early evening air, having forgotten that platform three was
not only long but also terribly exposed to the east winds.

'A posthumous bestseller? What's the good of that?'

'Don't be so cynical, Charlie. If it makes money, which I'm
sure it will, several charities will benefit, as will Mrs Hatherall
again – Veronica's mother, who is now in a very nice nursing
home down in Brighton, so I'm told.'

'So it's not a gambit by the publishers, then? They're not going
to go on finding Rex Troughton stories in bottom drawers or
safe-deposit boxes for years to come, are they?'

'Absolutely not, Evadne made sure of that. In the book to
come, she actually kills off Rex Troughton, and in such a way
that an encore would be impossible.'

'How do you know?' said Luke, quickly reverting to policeman
mode.

'Because I've read the manuscript.'

'That explains your tête-a-tête with Miss Prim back at the
vicarage.'

'Well deduced, Charlie. Dear old Miss Prim, who isn't half
the dragon she pretends to be, slipped me a copy of the manuscript last year on condition I didn't tell anyone, not even Amanda.
Not that I dared, having discovered that her hero detective meets
a very sticky end.'

'You could get her a copy for Christmas if it's out by then.'

'I think the publisher will certainly want to cash in on the Christmas market, but I have to say it's a rather curious book. She called it *Cozenage*, though they'll probably change the title.'

'Not surprised,' said Luke grumpily, 'sounds like a brand of throat sweet. What the Dickens is "Cozenage" anyway?'

'It means deception, deceit, duplicity, trickery, falseness and particularly self-deception, and I personally found it an uncomfortable read.'

'Because you're in it?'

'Crikey no, I'm not, but Evadne herself appears as a character, a genteel elderly lady who is deceived and robbed by an unscrupulous psychic medium playing on her lost love for a dead husband. It's all rather sad, self-absorbed and apologetic, and quite shocking at the end when Rex Troughton tries to sort things out.'

Luke thrust his hands into his overcoat pockets, put his head down and lengthened his stride. Campion made to match him, but Luke stopped suddenly near one of the cold iron benches distributed along the platform. He pushed out a foot, indicating with his shoe the bundle of newspapers tied up in twine nestling under the bench.

'There's a coincidence,' he said, as Campion leaned over the bench and peered through the metal slats to read the masthead of the newspaper on top of the pile.

'Well, blow me!' laughed Campion. '*Psychic News*, of all things. I'd totally forgotten that it's printed in Colchester. Must be waiting for the mail van. It's tomorrow's edition. Do you think we should liberate one just to check it doesn't carry a story about a gruesome accident involving the Norwich-to-London express?'

'Best not to know the future, Albert, and I'd have to arrest you for petty theft.'

'Quite right, Charles. Let tomorrow bring whatever it brings, but if you do have to drag my mangled body from a train wreck somewhere near Hatfield Peverel later today, I'll never forgive you.'

'I know, you'll come back to haunt me.'

'Unlikely. You would be a long way down the queue of people I could usefully haunt, but that is not, today of all days, a matter for ribaldry.'

'Fair enough, we should behave ourselves out of respect to Mrs Walker-Pyne. She believed in all that psychic stuff though, didn't she?'

'Yes, she did, and she thought that her beliefs had caused a lot of trouble, so her last book was something of an atonement, though of course she was not to blame for anything other than being fooled by a criminal chancer, and we've all had the wool pulled over our eyes at some time or another.'

'You blamed yourself more than anyone in this business. Stanislaus Oates and Freddie Yeo both say you couldn't have done more than you did.'

'Perhaps I could have done it sooner,' said Campion wistfully, 'and perhaps Evadne was telling me that in her swansong.'

'I thought you said you weren't in it.'

'I'm not, but the dedication is simply *To My Godsibling*, so I think it was aimed at me. It makes me sad, because I think she was, for a long time, a very sad, lonely lady.'

They walked on in silence, reached the end of the platform, turned smartly and began the return march.

'The other thing that was a bit odd,' started Luke, 'was her sending back her CBE. What was that all about? Guilt? Feeling not worthy? Did she think she was responsible for those murders? Or was it the fact that the Beatles are getting a gong from the Palace? A lot of people are threatening to return their medals because of that.'

Mr Campion, for he had talked to her on the telephone, knew that Evadne's decision was taken long before the Birthday Honours had been announced or even decided, and that it had been taken under the crushing weight of an unjustified guilty conscience. Her motives were misguided, but they were hers and hers alone and deserved to be buried with her.

'Yes, Charles,' he said, spotting their train coming round the long bend in the track from Manningtree, 'it was because of the Beatles, that's all it was.'

SOURCES

For the historical background to this story, I am indebted to the following sources: *1940 The World In Flames* by Richard Collier (Penguin, 1980), *An Underworld At War* by Donald Thomas (John Murray, 2004), *Wartime Britain 1939–1945* by Juliet Gardiner (Headline Review, 2005), *Remember When* by Robert Opie (Bounty Books, 2006), Bartholomew's London Pocket Atlas (1946), *The Fifties Mystique* by Jessica Mann (2012).

And, of course, the novels of Margery Allingham. Placing *Mr Campion's Séance* in the Allingham 'timeline', Part 1 takes place just after *Traitor's Purse*; Part 2 just before the adventure described in *More Work for the Undertaker*; Part 3 in the aftermath of *The Tiger in the Smoke*; and Part 4 in a moment of calm before the case of *The Mind Readers*.

My account of 'The Great Somers Town Hold-Up' was inspired by the Eastcastle Street robbery in May 1952, where thieves got away with £236,748 and 10/- (!), roughly £9 million in current values, from a post office van. Despite a £20,000 reward and thousands of police hours devoted to the crime, no convictions resulted. The exchange of vehicles in my fictional robbery takes place on the site of what is now the British Library, and the number plate LKL 238 appears on the bank security van robbed in the film *The Lavender Hill Mob*.